Sadie's Mountain

Shelby Rebecca

Songs
"You Are My Flower" by A.P. Carter. Used by permission of Peer International Corporation.
"Greensleeves," poss. Henry VIII of England, 1500's.
"Amazing Grace" Lyrics by John Newton (1725-1807).
"Down By the Salley Gardens" is a poem by William Butler Yeats published in The Wanderings of Oisin and Other Poems in 1889.
"What Are They Doing in Heaven Today" by Charles Albert Tindley published in 1901.
"Talking to the Moon" by Bruno Mars.
By Adele:
"Make You Feel My Love"
"Don't you Remember?"
"One and Only"

Scriptures and quoted material
All Solomon's Song of Songs Scripture quotations, in this publication are from the HOLY BIBLE, NEW INTERNATIONAL VERSION ® NIV ® Copyright © 1973, 1978, 1984, 2011 by Biblica, Inc.®. All rights reserved worldwide. The "NIV" and "New International Version" are trademarks registered in the United States Patent and Trademark Office by Biblica, Inc.®. Use of either trademark requires the permission of Biblica, Inc.®.

All other scripture quotations in this publication are from the NEW INTERATIONAL VERSION website, the KING JAMES version of THE BIBLE.

Five word excerpt from the Ann Landers column, "Love or Infatuation" in the epilogue of this work reprinted by permission of Esther P. Lederer Trust and Creators Syndicate, Inc.

Edited by Stephanie Lott of Bibliophile Services
Proof Read by Marlene Engel of Book Mama Blog
Cover Art by Kari Ayasha at Cover to Cover Designs

ISBN-13: 978-0615846088 (Superb Publishing, Elk Grove, CA)
ISBN-10: 0615846084
Print Edition

DEDICATION

This book is for victims of sexual abuse or violent crimes. You're not alone. It's not your fault. Reach out for help. Healing is possible.

RAINN
Rape, Abuse, Incest National Network
800.656.HOPE
www.rainn.org

Childhelp
800.4 A CHILD
800 422 4453
www.childhelp.org

National Domestic Violence Hotline
800.799.SAFE (7233)
www.thehotline.org

Trigger warning: For those of you concerned with reading a particularly dark and violent scene, you may wish to skip chapter two entirely. It will be clear what will happen and has happened when you end chapter one and resume the rest of the story at chapter three. The chapter is included so that readers will understand the emotional changes in Sadie because of this scene. It lets the reader into her mind and shows that she is a survivor, not a victim. Thank you.

Chapter One

That Day

I do my best not to think about West Virginia. But, the past—it owns me. It pulls, and I'm forced to go backward in my mind—always to that day, that moment when my pain and fear linked me to *him* with a rope as thick as steel.

There are triggers everywhere.

Sometimes all it takes is the feel of the wind as it passes over my skin or the way it churns my hair around in circles and I'm there again in my mind. The wind always blew in our part of the Appalachians. It couldn't help itself. It was so happy to be there, near the top of the world.

Sitting next to the open window, the wind jerks my concentration away from the red laptop propped on the table and over to the grass in the field lying in wait. What I see pulls on a string attached to *the* memory in my brain. My hands shake as I fidget with the buttons on my white shirt. I run the tips of my fingers along the annealed scars on my neck and a rumble of adrenaline pushes through my blood stream.

Look away, I tell myself, but I know I can't. The pull is too strong. The past will never change and it is always with me.

I've completely focused on the flicks of sunlight out there on the grass—part real, part memory, like two photos that got developed one on top of the other. I shudder and grasp the edge of the table so hard my knuckles turn alabaster white.

I can't even blink. I know it's coming. And just like that day, I fight for a little while. But, eventually, I always succumb. Just like then, like now.

I start to shiver. There is nothing I can do. My mind, it tortures me. Reminds me like a demon breathing down the back of my neck. Numbness takes me swiftly, like a merciful enemy—making me feel nothing. Cold. Distant.

You see, it was the way the sun came down and shone on the tall wispy grass back home that has never left me. The horses hadn't gotten to it yet so it was windblown and long, just like my hair. Mosquitoes were swarming all throughout the chilly air as I stood in the dirt on the edge of the property. I was near the stable curtailed by the square horse fence waiting for him—waiting for Dillon, my neighbor who had been my best friend since, well, I couldn't really remember a time before Dillon—he'd known me all my life.

Between my fingers I can still feel the grit of the West Virginia dust as it curved over Monty's black fur. I loved being with him. Brushing him like I was that day, back when life had grace and dignity. Momma had told me to pray for a horse and I had, every night—for years. Momma always said to keep my faith strong, to be good, and God's will would be done.

I already had Frosty; she was a white, mountain horse. But Frosty wasn't too capable of being friendly. She had been bitten too many times by other horses and had to fight too much for food at the boys' ranch my daddy had gotten her from. Poor Frosty was stuck in a perpetual state of fright—sort of like me, now.

Everything scared her: the grass if it moved too fast in the wrong direction, a mud puddle that was bigger or smaller than yesterday, a dragonfly with its bull-dog face roaming too close to her tail. All or any of these things could produce a strong guttural reaction in her.

She might buck around or run, neither of which, in my opinion, would be good while on her back. That's why I loved Monty so much. He was safe.

Pulling on the hem of my pretty, little-flower-dotted dress Daddy told me I couldn't wear anymore since it was too short, I walked back to the stable crunching dirt with my brown faded boots that used to be my sister Missy's when she was my age. Then I buttoned up the old denim jacket that was daddy's when he was a rebel teenager.

Since it was Friday, Daddy was, no doubt, pacing the front of the church, his fist pounding into the cover of his Bible, in preparation for next Sunday's sermon—he wouldn't know what I was wearing anyway, I surmised.

Standing by the stables, I watched as Dillon's brown boots stroked the ground on his way up to me. His slow, shy smile was contagious. He always looked at me as if he was seeing me for the first time. I know I was mirroring his look as he motioned for me to come over to where he was.

"Look, Sadie," he said, pointing to a spider web that had been engineered in between two bushes near where he stood.

"That's neat," I said, patiently, as I opened the gate and trotted over to him. I knew he would explain it to me as he pulled my arm down and squatted with me. He always loved to teach me things. He appreciated nature. He knew a lot about all the little creatures most of us would swat with a broom or a hand because he was always reading science-type books.

As he talked about the spider, I gazed up at him, putting his face to my memory. I didn't want to forget the way he looked. It was a strange compulsion; as if I'd intercepted an odd feeling about how that day would end from the moment I'd opened my eyes that morning.

He was a fine sight with his crooked just-for-me smile. My eyes moved up those faded, long jeans that hung on his hips just so to the dark blue button-up shirt over his broad shoulders. His messy hair, the color of the hay in Monty's stable, was catching the fading daylight, shimmering like stars at night.

"This is a Micrathena gracilis," he said, as he took his ocean blue eyes off the spider and placed them somewhere on my face. I was looking at his mouth, still thinking about the way his tongue caressed the two long words *Micra-thena grac-i-l-is*. I smiled at him with my eyes.

Just then, I caught him as he glanced down at my upper thigh that was peeking out from my short summer dress—although it was one month from summer and I was cold, I wore it for him. He blushed slightly and pursed his full lips. "Haven't seen that dress for a long while," he said.

"It's still pretty, ain't it?" I pulled the hem of my dress down to no avail. It was just too short, but I didn't care. And besides, we were going to get married. This dress could be for his eyes only.

"Yeah, it is," he said, through a little nervous chuckle.

The first time he said he was going to marry me I was five years old and he was eight—almost nine. It wasn't like he asked me to marry him. He just said, *"I'm gonna marry you someday and buy us a big white house with lots a' rooms for all our babies."* I didn't say anything. Being so young, I thought marriage to Dillon was either gross, or super perfect. I remember I smiled trying to hide my feelings. But, he knew.

"You'll see," he said.

I ran my finger over the little cloth ring I always wore. He made it by braiding green and white strings together. He said it was a promise ring. I still have it to this day. It's one of the only things I brought with me when I left Appalachia.

I'll never forget him telling my parents for the second time, on my birthday six months before, when I'd turned fourteen, that he was going to marry me someday.

"Not now, Sir, but when she's older—I'll be 'a waiting for her to be my wife. I'll wait as long as I have to—'till she's ready." I can still hear his earnest voice in that West Virginia accent when I close my eyes, even now. The words still make me swoon inside, like women do in the old black and white movies.

As Daddy answered in his stern pastor voice, I distinctly remember watching Dillon's older, huskier brother Donnie make a sour face like he ate a bad blueberry.

Donnie got up and murmured something I couldn't hear and walked off. His black hair bounced with each step he took. I never knew he liked me—that was what stood out in that moment. It was clear that he was upset about Dillon's announcement, but I felt like I was missing something.

Donnie was always shy around me, too quiet, broodingly so. I don't think he'd ever stuck more than a few words together toward me in all my life. He was a lot older than me so we never really spent time together. But the times we did, I knew I didn't like the way he looked at me, like I was a dead butterfly pinned into one of those glass boxes. And, I didn't like his scent. I always bristled when he was near.

"It's a spider that's okay with being out during the day," Dillon said matter-of-factly. *I mean, who would know a thing like this?* He always amazed me with his smarts.

"See its back end?" He pointed at the odd shape of the spider's body. "It looks like a pokey rock attached to its body, don't it?" he snorted.

"Yes, it does," I said with a giggle as he turned to look at me again. In his eyes I saw an emotion I didn't understand quite yet, being as young as I was, but it made my mouth dry and my eyelashes flutter. Now, as I think back I realize it was *real* love I saw in his eyes all those years ago. The I-would-do-anything-for-you kind of love. The kind of love that happens when two people know each other so well and for so long that they become a part of one another.

"Come with me?" he said, intently, standing up. He wasn't telling me, he was asking.

How could I say no? I wanted to be alone with him.

Things were changing between Dillon and me. We'd always been best friends, but for a while now, deep down in my body I felt a warmness that I'd never experienced before—like I was blushing from the inside out when he looked at me. Sometimes I tingled where he touched my skin in passing, or I'd find myself watching the intricacies of his mouth when he said things in a certain way. I started noticing new things about him that I'd never noticed before, like the color of his eyes when he looked into mine, or the ropey bend of his muscles when he worked, or the way he smiled different smiles for different feelings.

I glanced up at my house and the two little ones were looking at me from the front porch. I turned back to him and excitedly nodded my head yes.

He grabbed my hand and we ran into the woods and down the hill toward Rich Creek behind my family's place. He stopped me abruptly when we made it to the giant rock some said bore the image of a woman's face embedded into its façade.

Many times I had stopped on my way to fish for red tinged trout in those waters and gazed at that rock until I went cross-eyed and couldn't tell my right from my left. I'd get so lost.

He held my hand so tightly now that it throbbed. It was getting darker out, but the crimson and lavender sky behind his head made me think I had insight into his mood. At that moment I would have done anything for him if he'd asked—I knew it. So did he. Not because I was reckless. No, not at all. I knew that he wouldn't take me too far, that he would take care of me. I trusted him implicitly.

"Sadie, I know we're not ready for marriage," he said, clasping both of my hands up to his chest, "but, you know I'm going to college after this summer and I don't wanna lose you. I need to know if you're my girl?"

His girl! I didn't even have to think about it "Yes!" I exclaimed.

There was relief in his eyes. He smiled at me with a new smile. One that meant I was his and he was mine. His face got serious again. "Well, then, I'd like to ask you if," he cleared his throat, "if you'll do me the honor of being able to give you your first real kiss." It was a practiced speech and he was anxious when he said the words; his eyes were darting back and forth searching mine for consent. His lips were pursed together, his eyebrows arched in anticipation.

I felt shy all of a sudden, although I'd already imagined this moment so many times. He had kissed me before but they were chaste kisses with our eyes wide open. The first time he'd done that I was only twelve years old and he was almost sixteen. We giggled after, each time. Sometimes he tickled me, or he'd hold my hand once in a while. I'd wrapped my arms around his waist and pressed the side of my face into his back when I rode on the back of his bike or went tandem on the horse. But those were the only kinds of touches before that day.

I said nothing as I thought. *A real kiss. Can I do this? What would Momma say?* I'm sure I looked wide-eyed and innocent as he pulled me into his chest. My heart was beating like the sound of the train near the railway.

We are going to get married. It's just a kiss.

His face looked long with worry. His muscles under my shaky fingers were taut, his body charged with emotions. His eyes never left mine. They seemed to be staring through me into my private thoughts. It seemed like we stood there for ages like that on a precipice.

Yes!

I nodded so slightly that if he'd blinked he would have missed me giving him my consent. His lids closed and when they opened again I saw something like devotion in his ocean blue eyes. It made my stomach flip.

With one arm wrapped around my back he tilted my chin up with his other hand. "Close your eyes," he said, evenly but resolute and I did as he asked.

When his lips met mine I found them to be so, so soft and his breath to be as warm as a blanket on the line in the hot sun.

He started with a few of those meandering, slow kisses that shot electricity through my mouth, into my tummy, and out my limbs. Then he tilted his head to the side and pulled me toward him until I felt his heart beating against me. We fit together perfectly. I remember that. It was as if our bodies were made by the Creator just to be together.

He opened his mouth and tenderly took my top lip between his causing my mouth to open too. Then he did the same to my bottom lip and I to his top one. Again, he was teaching me. His tongue found mine and we began to deepen the kiss. I whimpered, and it surprised me.

I didn't think I would know what to do, but I just let go and felt everything about this cherishable moment. In my mind I saw a tiny rose with its petals growing pink and steady deep in my belly. It felt like I was on my way to becoming a woman in that moment. I almost didn't even notice that there were mosquitoes biting into my sweet-scented legs.

He moved away from me and swatted at one with his hand. I closed my eyes again as he cradled my face in both hands and gently placed soft, wet kisses first on my eyelids, then my cheeks, my chin, down to my neck and then over to my ear. "Is this okay?" he asked.

I was lost in him. I nodded my head yes. I could feel his grin just there on my neck before he took my earlobe into his mouth and nipped it gently with his lips. I felt that in a part of my body Momma told me was off-limits. It stunned me but I didn't pull away. I was stuck to him and to the ground.

He pulled back as my body responded to his touch. My eyes opened and it was like he could see right through me into my core. I felt so exposed, so raw. My lips twitched because I wanted to laugh with joy and cry at the same time. He grabbed me tightly around my waist and kissed me again. This time he wasn't as tender as he moved his hands up into my hair getting tangled in it. We were just sensation, just experience.

His enthusiasm was unyielding, but I didn't want to stop. I was keeping up with him. He turned me and pressed my back into the rock, pinning me to it with his hips. Still, I wasn't scared. I was emotional, giddy.

Suddenly, he let go of me and pushed away swiftly as if he was moving heaven and earth to part from me. Confused, I left my arms wrapped around his waist. His eyes were hooded, his wet lips in a relaxed, shy grin. Both of our breaths were ragged like we'd been chopping wood or carrying water up a steep hill. His eyes never left mine.

He put his arms on the rock on either side of my face and smiled that new smile—the one where I'm his and he's mine. His face just inches from mine. His proximity was heady, his body radiating warmth as the air seemed to chill all around us. He smelled so good, like his momma's homemade soap and freshly laundered clothes—distinctly like him.

"I love you, Sadie," he whispered.

I smiled back, mirroring his admiration. "And I love you, Dillon," I responded.

He looked like he'd conquered the world. He was so amorous. So young. So perfect. The picture of him right then will never leave me. It's as if I've painted it there in my mind with soft wet brushes.

I must have been wiggling during our first real kiss because it was then that I noticed the hem of my dress was hitched up above my hips still up against the rock. He looked down at my pale pink panties. I blushed but left the hem up—for him to look.

"You're getting bit," he said, as he innocently reached down to my back side to swat the offending pests assaulting my hips and thighs. His hand there, those long deft fingers traipsing in the forbidden zone sent a shiver up my spine. I knew right then that we'd gone too far.

Like Daddy said, *"God writes your sins on the cross… He clothes you in His righteousness…Writes your name in His blessed book of life…you must keep yourself pure for God's will to be done…"* I know the look on my face changed. I was no longer smiling or giddy. I bit my thumbnail and I flinched away from him.

"I'm sorry," he pleaded. His eyes were pained with remorse. He pulled my dress down and lifted his left arm to cover his guilty eyes. I wish I hadn't, believe me I do—but right then I ducked away from him and ran from the safety of his hold.

I was so angry with him for making me feel all of this. *That was…WOW! But what we did is wrong. It's against God's will. We have to be married before he can touch me, especially touch me there. But his hands felt so right, so perfect I can still feel him; everywhere he touched is tingling.* I ran and he followed calling my name but I was faster or just too far away from him already.

I ducked under a low tree, and ran between two bushes. As I did so, I bumped into the shed at the edge of his property. I knew they didn't lock it so I opened the door and ran inside shutting the door behind me. The last bit of evening sun was shining through the cracks between the wood slabs making slivers of dust particles in the air.

In that moment I was so glad I was alone. I leaned up against the bags of chicken feed stacked against the back wall to catch my breath. How did I feel? Was I really angry with Dillon? No. I wasn't. I wasn't angry at all. I was only scared because I'd felt emotions I didn't know existed. Deep down I knew I wanted to kiss him like that. A smile beamed across my face making my cheeks hurt. I bit my thumbnail. I liked it—a lot.

I don't think either of us expected to get so carried away. After all, when he'd touched my behind he was just swatting the mosquito, that's all. He had already stopped himself from going too far. He'd pushed away from me by that point. Of course, I knew I could still trust him.

In the distance I could hear him calling me. "Sadie! Sadie! I'm sorry. Please. Come on, darlin'!"

His voice wasn't so far away. If I'd walked out of the shed right then he might have even been within eyesight. I pushed away from the chicken feed and was within inches of grabbing the door handle when it creaked opened on its own. It was dim outside the shed but the silhouette standing in the doorway was not that of my beloved. This man was bigger, more threatening in his stance.

It was Donnie.

I could tell by his scent wafting through the gap between us it was him.

I bristled.

"Well, now, Sadie," he said, his voice husky and determined.

He speaks.

He stepped forward and because there was nothing I could do to protect myself, it felt like years passed in the time it took for him to close the door behind him. He pulled a board across the door locking it and turned to face me, his eyes like a wild dog before a planned attack.

Chapter Two

The Shed

"**D**onnie, what are you doing?" I said in a thin, wobbly voice.

"I wanna talk," he said, his voice a hoarse whisper, his eyes twitchy, his mouth in a thin line. "I need to...," he said, almost confused.

"Well, let's just go outside and talk," I tried.

"You're just gonna run back ta' him."

"What do you want?" My voice became tougher than normal, like a little dog trying to bark deep.

"You...you're," he said, stumbling over his words, "supposed ta be with me," he said, his voice cracking as he slapped his chest and started to walk toward me. "I don't wanna hurt you. But I will if you don't let me," he said, in a soothing voice as if he was trying coax me.

"Let you what?" I said. But I knew what.

"You'll be mine. You won't never want him no more once I been with you like this," he said, as he reached out to grab my arm.

"No," I screamed as I jumped back. "Please, don't do this...," but before I could finish my plea for mercy, he leapt forward, his hand was covering my mouth and he had twisted my right arm around my back. He smelled like the fish he'd just been cleaning down by the river, so I held my breath.

I tried to push him away but it was like trying to move a boulder with a feather. It was then that I realized he had moved a sharp blade up to my neck. He pushed it in but not enough to cut me—just to scare me.

It worked.

"You ain't gonna make me use this," he cautioned.

I put my left arm down to my side and shook my head no so that he knew I'd be quiet. I felt like I was going to throw up but my fear kept everything down. I was so still.

He pushed me, slowly, until my back was against the bags of feed stacked near the wall.

"I saw you," he said through gritted teeth. "My little brother prolly cain't get it up. That why you ran, you little tease? What'chou need is a real man," he said, as he stabbed my stomach with the sick arousal he had growing between his hips.

I shook my head no, violently, mindful to keep my neck still. My eyes were so wide, shocked tears sprang from them like drops of wax. Smiling, he grabbed my face with his hand, held it stationary.

"Shhhhh," he whispered before he assaulted my mouth with his hard tongue. At the same time, his hand moved from where he was squeezing my face, over my right breast, and down the front of my stomach.

I tried to move my mouth away from him as I whimpered in disgust and squirmed so he stopped and pushed the blade in more. It pinched, I halted, and something trickled down my throat.

Is it sweat? Please, just be sweat!

"Look what you made me do," he chastised before kissing me again even harder. This time I let him.

"Sadie! Darlin', please come out!" I heard Dillon yell right next to me on the other side of the shed's wood slabs. Donnie stopped his tongue assault by biting my bottom lip in warning, putting his fishy hand over my mouth. He pushed the knife. "I'll do it," he promised in a portentous whisper with his mouth right up to my ear.

We both listened. I wanted to cry out but there was no hope.

How would Dillon get to me with the wood across the door? Donnie would probably kill me first and then, as the bigger of the two and the only one armed, he would kill Dillon, too.

In half a second, the handle of the shed shook. I tensed and Donnie pushed the knife in even harder, my neck warm with *my own blood.*

"I'll kill him *too*, I swear to God." His mouth came up to my ear, his voice still a low whisper. I held my breath.

"Sadie, darlin', are you in there?" I closed my eyes and my lips trembled. We both heard as Dillon's footsteps moved away from the shed.

Donnie relaxed the knife a bit. "I've been a' waitin' for my chance. You think you can run around teasin' me wearin' clothes like this." He yanked the bottom hem of my summer dress and then hastily pushed it up above my hips.

I was like a statue. I couldn't move. Slowly, so agonizingly slow, he pushed his huge bear-like paw into my panties and down toward my forbidden zone.

I tried to move away as my stomach turned upside down. He started to gnaw greedily on my neck under my left ear. I tried to squeeze my thighs together but his fingers pushed their way in. He sucked his teeth and hissed. My hands curled up in cringing fists as I burned in a way I'd never imagined.

This can't be real! was all I could think as I looked around for a way out.

"Oh, yessssss," he whispered. "See, yer wet for me. I know you want it. It'll feel good, I promise."

Wet? What? I shook my head no and the blade pinched again. It was as if he was trying to seduce me.

And then he switched, "I'm gonna fuck you so hard you never gonna want that little pussy brother a' mine agin."

My heart fell into my stomach like someone dropping a hammer on the floor.

"Sadie, please, baby. Come on. I'm sorry. It's gettin' dark. Let me take you home!" Dillon yelled, in a panicked voice, but he was much farther away now—almost an echo of a memory.

If I could only get out of here my Dillon could save me. He loves me. Then it hit me.

He's not going to want me after what his brother's going to do to me.

My fear over this, over the thought that Dillon wouldn't want me anymore, filled me with a rumble of adrenaline. I shoved Donnie's heavy frame away, pushed back against the bags of feed with my back, and kicked him in his stomach as hard as I could. The knife scraped across my neck for just a brief second and I almost screamed but before I could, Donnie punched me in the gut causing the air to leave my whole body.

I was doubled over, mouth opening like a fish needing water. I couldn't breathe. Before I could do or say anything, he turned me around and slammed my face into the bags of feed. Then he kicked my feet apart one at a time with his dirty boots.

I heard the sound of his zipper, and then he pulled my panties with his knife, tearing them off me, and viciously ripped into me robbing me, in that moment, of my choices, of my virtue, of my future, of the girl I once was and never would be again. That girl died right then.

I caught my breath and cried out, "No!"

"Shut the fuck up!" he whispered through gritted teeth as he grabbed my face and pinched my mouth shut.

I tried to straighten my back. But with his knife-hand he pulled me up by my stomach, my feet left the ground with my legs dangling, and he pushed me back onto himself as I gasped and clawed at the bags in front of me.

His fist and the handle of the knife pushed into my belly. I was pinned in place as my cringing fists pressed against the bags of feed. He covered my mouth with his other hand, jabbing his fingernails into my face as he set my feet back on the ground.

He moaned deep in his throat and thrashed into me again, piercing me with pain, but I couldn't make a sound. Screams were stuck in my throat. "Yer so tight," he hissed in my ear, twisting his pelvis around and around.

I screwed my eyes shut to take my thoughts upward on my body. A tearing, slicing pain shot through me. It was more than I could take. But I was powerless to stop it. Helpless.

"So. Sweet. Just. Like. I. Knew. You'd. Be," he mumbled into my ear while he slowly sunk farther into me—relishing me. "This is mine," he claimed, as I felt something warm trickle down my right leg.

I hurt so badly. I thought he was ripping me in two—in a way he was. *There was her, and now there is only me.*

Tears were forcing themselves down my face onto his hand and I had a lump in my throat from the screams that were stuck there. I felt his feet slide farther apart pushing mine with his, forcing them wider. He tilted his pelvis and pushed my chest into the bags of feed. "Stay still or I'll cut you agin," he admonished, his voice strained.

I didn't move. I couldn't have anyway. I was like a dead butterfly pinned into one of those glass boxes. My legs were restrained with his feet, he held my stomach with his knife hand, the blade of the knife engraved my pale flesh before he let go.

He grabbed my hair, pulling my head back and slammed into me over and over. A deep, pummeling rhythm ensued with his crass grunts and my pained breaths as a static background.

I remember the strangest things from this moment. The smell of the bags of feed, as he pushed my chin into them, they smelled sweet and nourishing and reminded me of my horses. Then I looked up at the dust in the shed as it was being highlighted by what was left of the sunlight shining in through the slabs of wood in a strand of air right above my head. The dust sparkled and performed until it disappeared.

Then in the dark, my thoughts turned to Dillon not wanting me anymore. I could actually see Dillon's image, his ocean blue eyes gleaming at me as if he was standing near a clear lake and then it rippled and he disappeared—I was alone.

He's never going to love me now.

Then I thought about momma saying babies come from sex. I had an image of myself with a pooched out tummy over my Daddy's knee getting whipped with his belt for being with child—a hussy.

I pinched my eyes shut and pretended my body was not my own. *Please, dear God. Just take me now. Forgive me of my sins.* If I wasn't in this body anymore he couldn't hurt me. I wished I was dead. But I couldn't scream so he'd make it that way.

Thankfully, numbness took over then. I became just a husk as if a bucket of Novocain was poured over me. He was just mounting this shell of my body. It wasn't me anymore. I was thankful for my answered prayer.

Vaguely, I remember him slamming into me one more time, stilling, tensing, and then quivering as he pulled my hair back tilting my chin to the ceiling. His whole body went lax and he leaned his full weight on my back—heavy, like a burden that never goes away.

He was still inside me. I could feel *it* throbbing and twitching like a rattlesnake's tail between my stretched thighs. His breath was sporadic—foul on my cheek. My neck was warm with blood. The front of my chest felt cold as he stepped out letting my legs go. I winced as we separated, tucking my behind under me like a whipped dog.

I moved quickly over to the wall and leaned my left side against the shed wishing I'd disappear. I was watching him out of one eye as he touched his now limp weapon as if he was proud of what it had done for him. He shoved it into his underwear, pulled his pants up and zipped the crotch closed.

He squatted down to fetch my ripped panties, put them up to his nose and sniffed them like a dog imprinting a scent before he put them in his pocket.

As soon as he straightened up, he pushed me, pressing my face hard against the wall and put his mouth to my ear. "If you tell anybody, I'll cut yer stupid head off and bury it in my god-damned yard. That'd be better than seeing you with *him* anyways."

I just closed my eyes. *Bide my time.*

"Say it!"

"I won't tell." My voice sounded fast and shaky like a salt and pepper shaker in his hand. He laughed and if I could have been anymore shocked—I was. I waited as he breathed me in.

"I'm the first. Ain't I?"

I couldn't speak.

"Ain't I?" he pressed.

I nodded my head yes.

"And the last," he stated.

I just stood there, shivering.

Please, just go away.

What he'd done to me combined with his words attached themselves inside my brain like a virus that impregnates its host with its diseased atoms and molecules. Deep in there where nothing could remove it and it has room to grow and multiply.

He leaned into my side with his now tamed hips and moved my hair away from my face. "I didn't wanna hurt you. It's always a little rough the first time, baby. I'll be gentler next time." Bile rose in my throat so I held my breath.

"You 'member this. I ain't sharin'you with *him*. This is mine now," he said, his face a shadow or a demon as he cupped me between my thighs and flicked at me with his finger, growled, and then stuck his finger in his mouth and sucked.

"You taste like me," he said. I stood there silently, hating him with the tiny pieces left in me that weren't broken.

I felt his fingers move up to my mouth as he rubbed something wet all over my face. I heard his words. They just didn't make sense to me. It rattled around in my brain not making contact with reason. He scowled in the shadows of the moon, and shook me with both arms. "Say it. Whose is this?" His voice sounded like a hail storm on a tin roof.

"Yours," I said, defeated.

"You better not do nothin' like that with my brother agin. I swear to god. I'll kill him, too."

"I won't. I promise." I sounded like a robot.

He smacked me hard on my behind and grabbed it. "Good girl," he said, while he squeezed.

I can still hear those words sometimes when I close my eyes at night. Sometimes I hear it when I'm grown up and some poor soul tries to make love to me. *"Good girl."*

Then he kissed me on my neck just under my ear—softly this time, as if he was my lover and not my rapist.

"I love you, always have," he whispered into my ear. It took everything in me that was strong not to scratch at his face with my nails. I closed my eyes and waited. I heard him pull the piece of wood from the door, it creaked open and all was silent.

My legs were shaking. I wiped my bloody mouth on my daddy's denim jacket and watched the door with my uncovered eye. My knees were touching and my ankles were pointed out.

Go! I told myself, and darted out of that shed as fast as I could. *What if he comes back for round two?*

I ran and ran for seconds, minutes, hours, I have no idea. I ran until my legs gave out and I fell into a moss patch under nothing but the starry sky. And then I started throwing up. I threw up until there was nothing left inside of me and I was heaving emptiness—kind of like my spirit.

It was so dark and cold. I'd never felt so alone in all my life until then. *What just happened to me?* I touched my neck. It felt jagged and warm. I felt so odd, as if everything around me was in slow motion but it wasn't. My heartbeat was fast but so weak that it hurt and suddenly I was so very tired, and for a brief moment I wondered where I was and why I was there.

I started crying, deep, and guttural. My skin was damp and clammy; my limbs were tingling. I was breathing fast, but the breaths were shallow and I felt like I was suffocating. There was a strange sensation as if I had to go to the bathroom, something came out of me and I wiped my behind. It was slimy and smelled like cut grass and shards of metal. I wiped my hand on the spongy moss and decided I had to get up and make my way toward the sounds of Rich Creek.

This is where my memory becomes unclear. I remember parts but not all: I followed the sound of the creek, falling at times when my legs and arms got too heavy. I'd reach up to branches and pull myself up as if the water would be a panacea—a cure all. I could think of nothing else as I stumbled into the freezing creek and stung my neck and between my legs with water. I couldn't keep my eyes open—my eyelids felt like steel weights.

I was spitting up water and I was so thirsty for air that I gasped.

"Oh, God. Sadie," Dillon said. I was on the shore with rocks poking into my back. I couldn't see his face but he was breathing fast and he was shaking as he leaned over me. He picked me up in his arms and hugged me so tight he felt like a vice. "Sadie, Sadie," he cried into my ear.

"Dillon?" I rasped.

"Hold on, Sadie. I've got you," he whispered, through hitched breaths as he effortlessly stood up and started walking with me draped over his arms like a wet towel. He was so warm against my cold body. *I'm safe.* I put my arms around his neck and tried not to slip away again.

"You won't want me no more," I said, tearfully.

"Hush, baby. I've loved you all your life. That won't stop for nothing."

"I died. He killed her," I said, breathy. I was so exhausted.

I was in my house in Dillon's arms and Daddy was yelling and pounding his fist into the living room wall. "Look at the dress she's a' wearin'," he yelled. "It's no wonder she got tooken advantage of!"

I fell or was pulled down and I was sitting on the floor. Momma was trying to pull me up but she was pushing Dillon away.

"Go home, Dillon!" Momma yelled. When I looked down there was blood streaked down the inside of my legs and all down the front of my too-short dress. I tried to rub the blood away from my legs but more came to replace it.

"Oh, God!" I screamed at my blood covered hands. Momma was trying to cover me with the blanket from the back of the couch.

"Get out of here!" Momma was yelling at Dillon. "You'd better not be here when he comes down them stairs!"

I was half covered by the blanket and screaming now in short, frantic squeals as I saw Daddy stomp down the stairs wielding his belt—the skinny one that hurt the worst. There was blood everywhere. It was my blood. "Am I dying?" I managed to say through the screams.

"Please, sir, don't hit her," Dillon said, frantically as he stood in the doorframe with his right arm reached out to me.

"This ain't none'a yer concern," Daddy said, "Go on home, Dillon," he ordered as he came at me with the belt held above his shoulder ready to strike.

"Daddy, no!" I yelped as he slapped the belt into my back. I slipped on the blood on the floor. He whipped me again as I pulled myself up. The belt stung me over and over as I crawled on my hands and knees into the corner of the room. Momma was trying to grab his arm. She pulled like a slight wind on a steel frame.

"Stop!" Momma yelled.

"Don't hit her," Dillon said, his voice rough like a callous.

"Sinner!" Daddy yelled as he flogged me over and over. I curled into a fetal ball. "Please, God almighty! Forgive this child of her sins! Rebuke the demon enemy that makes her weak and wanton!"

"Dillon!" I screamed, as if my life depended on it. Through the hair covering my face I saw Dillon's boots running toward us and he grasped Daddy's now tired arm.

"Please, sir. That's enough, ain't it?" He sounded like he was crying.

I was so worn-out. My shallow breaths weren't enough.

Momma was holding me. I don't know where I was—maybe still in the corner of the living room. She wiped my feverish forehead with a warm cloth. She looked scared. She kissed me with small, newborn kisses all over my cheeks.

"You're okay now, my baby," she kept saying over and over.

I was on my bed. It was dark but I felt a bandage on my neck. I reached down and felt that my clothes were off and a nightgown was buttoned up over my chest and down my tummy. Missy wasn't there. I was shaking so badly that the bed felt like an earthquake. "I'm s-s-s-so cold," I said, to no one but myself. The chill was coming from the inside of me. Nothing would make me warm.

I was curled up on my bed. *Alone. Alone.*

Chapter Three

Come Home

I *can do this!* I think, waking up on the airplane with a jolt as the little speakers are telling me to put my seatbelt on. Looking at my phone on airplane mode it's 10:30 a.m. I've been traveling all night. I left last night from the Sacramento Metropolitan Airport at 10:20 p.m. There was the one layover in Charlotte, which I trudged through sitting anxiously in the first class lounge drinking a too-sweet cocktail with a plump fresh cherry slinking around on the bottom of the glass.

My mantra has been: *It's just for a few days. Momma needs me. She's so sick and all she wants is to see me again one more time.* This is what got my bag packed. What got my feet to actually propel me forward as I walked down the ramp to the airplane in the first place.

I haven't been back there since, it's been how long? Well, it was just before my fifteenth birthday when I left, so yes, it's been ten years. I don't have to stay long if I don't want to. I can just rent a car at the airport, drive over to her house, hug her, talk to her, say our goodbyes and come back home the next evening. A quick trip won't hurt me. If I don't let it, that is.

The jet is making its descent, pulling my stomach down with it. But I know that's not the only thing wrong with my stomach. Nerves are bouncing around in there like a boomerang in a cage of foil. I realize just then, as I have to concentrate to keep my horrible airplane salad down, that I'm nauseated. I can't run to the restroom now with the little seatbelt light shining up above my head.

I hastily grab that little bag so nicely provided for people who are sick and push it up to my face in preparation for the impending projectile vomiting that feels imminent.

The wheels touch down and hop, pushing me into the back of my first class seat. I hold my breath and put my head back. The brakes do their job and slow the human-filled-missile to a stop. The pilot is talking now about arriving at the Roanoke Airport and having a good trip.

Oh shut up, I think as I frown at the chipper flight attendant. I've never liked them. Their smiles always seem to be masking other feelings just under the surface. It's unsettling and makes me realize that's probably what I look like, too.

"Ms. Sparks," she chirps. "I'm so sorry to bother you, but I was wondering if you'd be so kind as to sign my book?" she asks as she takes one of the books from the *Fire Bound* series out from behind her back.

"Of, course," I say, and smear my name all over the inside flap. "Thank you for reading."

"Thank you so much," she beams.

I get my luggage—just one small suitcase—and rent a car. It's a decent one. A black, four-door Buick La Sabre, since that is the nicest one they have. It smells new and sanitary. At least I have that. Who knows what the house will be like when I get there in almost three hours.

Momma was a good housekeeper but with four kids to pick up after, sanitary wouldn't be the word I'd use to describe my growing up. My two little brothers, who I don't even know anymore, are teenagers now. And Missy lives so close. She probably cleans the place since Momma is so sick. That eases my mind a bit.

As I pull into a fast food place to order a fruit and yogurt concoction and coffee, it dawns on me that I could rent a hotel room or a little cabin somewhere. That is an option. One night in my old room wouldn't kill me, though. It would be the last time I see my mom, her illness being terminal and all. Her type of cancer most certainly is—I'm told. It would be wrong to leave her and drive into town for the night.

As I settle into the steady hum of the car cruising up the VA-311 North, I start to let my mind ease into the thoughts behind the thoughts. I can face this. I'm not some little victim anymore. I'm a successful author with sixteen books in print. Twelve of them are best sellers. I write paranormal new adult, and women's fiction with strong female characters so different from me. Some of my characters have powers I wish I had like the ability to become invisible. Some can fly. All of them can kill demons. My platform usually includes an eco-theme with Biblical allusions and women who are anything but victims.

I've also written a trilogy, middle grade, about bugs on an organic farm. It was just optioned to be made into a computer generated movie in the coming year. They're already auditioning celebrities for the voiceovers. I'm rooting for Ashley Judd for the voice of Polly— my praying mantis protagonist.

My point is that I've got everything I need: A custom home in the dreamlike hills of Newcastle, California, acquaintances, money, success. But do I have safety? That's something I haven't been able to buy.

Maybe I should hire a bodyguard?

My thoughts are blaring at me now. The person I'm really anxious about is not Donnie. Donnie almost seems like a figment of my imagination—a nightmare so bad that it couldn't be real. It's Dillon I'm really worried about. He still lives there, or rather he's moved back there to work on some government grant. Missy had told me about that about three years ago. His job was rather a mystery to her, it seemed.

I'm sure I can avoid him. I'd done it for months before Daddy gave up on me and Momma finally took pity and sent me to live with my Aunt Lotty in Sacramento. Well, the difference then was that I hadn't left the house for months. Maybe I won't have to go anywhere. *I'll only be there just the one night.*

That whole summer, Dillon never gave up hope that I'd talk to him. He'd come to the door but I wouldn't come out of my room. He brought me flowers he'd picked himself and leave them on my window sill. Sometimes he'd bring us some fresh fish from the creek for Momma to cook for dinner, or he'd write me letters and ask Missy or Momma to give them to me.

Dillon had gone off to college right after I left. I knew he'd move on if I gave him time. Right before he went to college, he got some huge scholarship because of his grades and an experiment that created some new type of fuel. He was in the local paper and on the news holding his medal. I wasn't in the frame of mind to listen to him speaking on the TV back then.

I'm not sure what college he went to but I know he must be some type of scientist now.

My GPS just told me to merge onto the I-64 West in Quinwood, West Virginia. Someone left a CD in the car. Bruno Mars has been my background noise this whole trip. I like him. He's singing about *Talking to the Moon* and it seems so fitting considering I was just thinking about Dillon.

His final letter to me talked about the moon and how it could bind us no matter where we were—no matter how far apart we drifted we would both be looking up at the same moon each night. I actually think about that every time happenstance causes me to look at the moon. I'm going to have to find that letter when I get to Momma's house. I know exactly where I hid it.

The thing is, I knew then and I know now that I can't talk to Dillon because he wants to know what happened to me. I have always worried about what would happen if Dillon found out. I'm sure he'd try and fight Donnie. He'd be no match for his dark-haired, tank of a brother.

Besides, Donnie promised death if anything happened between Dillon and me. That's the crux of our relationship. Talking to him means danger—for both of us. I did talk to Dillon again. Just once.

I was walking into the kitchen in the morning to get some water when I heard a conversation taking place out on the porch. It was just two days after…after…I was raped. Yes, I can say the word rape. It's taken me a long time to realize that's what it was. I pay a fortune to Dr. Amy to deal with this mess. At least I can admit the truth to myself. It had been so confusing for so many reasons.

"Reverend Sparks," Dillon spoke in his coaxing voice, "We really should talk to the Sheriff so they can find the dirt bag that hurt Sadie." There was venom in his voice when he said those last few words.

"Absolutely not!" my daddy snapped, abruptly cutting him off.

"But, sir…"

"I'll not hear of it. The sin is a heavy burden in that one. Always has been—Just too strong-willed. I just need to pray harder, lay my hands on her and pray, whip it out a' her agin if I have to. To bear witness to Jesus Christ, who is 'the Way, the Truth, and the Life'."

"She was attacked. There was blood runnin' down her neck, sir. She was cut, bleedin' everywhere, in shock when I found her. She didn't ask for this."

"She was dressed immorally. She weren't raised that way. And, it ain't right ta blame a man fer havin' needs, son. Whoever it is, I'm sure he's repentin' as we speak, layin' his sins at the Cross. It's in God's hands now to deal with him. I have ta think of that girl's soul, not punishin' the man she tempted."

"Tempted?" he repeated as if to make that word fit in the scenario he saw. I heard Dillon's heavy boots pace back and forth across the porch. I peeked out through the front window and he was pinching his forehead between his thumb and index finger. Daddy was sitting in his porch chair smoking his pipe.

"Can I take her, sir?" he begged, his voice shaking with fear, or need. "I'll take care of her. If she needs time, ya know, before she's ready to be man and wife in the Biblical sense, I'll wait. I'll marry her right now. I'm almost eighteen. It won't cause no shame on ya since we'll be married. If she's in the family way, no one will know the difference."

"A youngin'!" Daddy screamed. It was a guttural response.

"I don't…Well, sir, it's possible," Dillon stated matter of factly.

"She's stayin' right here! If she's with child then the Lord will have to deal with her, with her shame. Her consequence might be just that! Go, son. She ain't goin with ya. She ain't no good anyhow."

"Please, sir, I love her. I need to see her. It's killing me."

"Go!" Daddy stated with the authority that comes from preaching to those even in the back pews.

I watched Dillon's tall frame as he hunched his broad shoulders, turned on his heels and stomped down the front steps. He turned around again. I saw his face and he saw mine in the window. There were tears moving down over his cheeks. He looked relieved to see me. I closed the curtain and bit my thumbnail. That choking lump in my throat was still there. I rubbed it but felt the scabs on my neck instead and closed my eyes.

I'd never seen him like that, other than the time he broke his arm trying to catch me when my ankle got stuck in his bike chain and we wrecked his bike. I was almost unharmed, his arm took all the weight for both of us as we fell together. But, he cried then, too—a brave cry. The kind that comes even though you don't want it to. That's the only other time before then, and well, last night.

He came to me that same night. I wasn't sleeping as he tapped on the window in my room. I got up slowly, trying not to wake up Missy in the bed next to mine, but also because of how sore I was.

All my muscles felt like deep bruises reminding me of how they were abused. My neck was just newly scabbed over. It was rough and itchy. I had crescent shaped fingernail marks on my face where Donnie's hand had been when he was trying to keep me quiet. There were small cuts in little x patterns on my stomach from Donnie's knife when he'd held me in place. Bothersome mosquito bites burned on my bottom and thighs. The stinging belt marks were swollen on my back, arms and legs, and it ached, like ripping paper, at the apex of my thighs.

I opened the window letting in a healthy breeze that pushed my hair away from my face. The air sounded of crickets and frogs.

He looked so relieved to see me as he stood slightly below the edge of the window. It took him a moment to remember to breathe. I knew I was standing there but I felt like an empty vessel. He smiled at me but I didn't smile back. He looked worried again and swallowed.

"You look better," he said as if I was a wounded animal about to bolt. I didn't respond. "Will you come outside and talk to me, Sadie?"

"What for?" I said, my voice drone-like.

"I just want to help you, darlin'," he said, softly, but his face looked pained.

"You can't help now." My voiced sounded foreign like it belonged to another person I didn't know.

"I can take you away from here. When I go to college you'll come, too. Or I'll get a job right now and buy us a little house."

"That can't happen."

"You're angry at me," he said. It wasn't a question.

"No." I shook my head.

"This is all my fault," he said, putting his hand over his stomach in physical pain.

"No," was all I could say in protest. "Mine," I said under my breath. I don't think he heard.

"I'm sorry I touched you, baby." He put both his hands on the windowsill. "I hadn't even realized what I did. It was just so natural."

I know.

"I'm not mad about that, now," I said. He reached toward me through the window as if he was going to soothe me somehow. I flinched and he stopped.

"I'm sorry," he apologized again, his eyes wider than I'd ever seen them. I didn't like to see him that way so I just looked down at the dirt instead.

"Nothin's changed about how I feel for you. You know that. You're still my girl, right?" He sounded like he was begging.

"I'm no one's," I said. Maybe I meant to say *I'm no one.*

"Who did this to you?" His voice was hot lava.

"You should go," I said as I rubbed the lump in my throat and felt the scabs on my neck again. He looked wounded and I felt sad for him through my numbness. This wasn't his fault. All I kept thinking of were Donnie's words, *"I'll kill him too."* I needed to let him go, to free him of this obligation he had to the girl I used to be two days before.

"I'm not the girl you loved anymore, not the same at all. She's gone now." I looked away from him as if I was looking for where that girl might have gone.

"I'll wait. Forever if I have to. You'll get better. I can help."

"I don't want you to." He deserved better was all I could think. He was so perfect and I was so dirty now. I disgusted myself. "Look, I won't see you again, Dillon. Just go and live a happy life."

"I won't force you, Sadie." His voice sounded louder now, his fists clenched, with the pain right at the surface. "You're my best friend. I'll never love anyone but you!"

His volume caused me to turn and check on Missy. She wiggled from her back onto her side but was still asleep.

I looked back out the window and just shook my head at him. "You shouldn't say that." He would move on someday. He would be okay. This was protecting him, too, like throwing rocks at a dog so it wouldn't come with you and get hurt. He had no idea.

"I have to go," I said, as I started to close the window. He put his hand out to me but stopped at an imaginary line between us.

"Please, don't shut me out." He was panicked now, his voice like red silk waving in a wind storm. I couldn't look at him anymore. I had to let him go.

"Goodbye, Dillon," I said and I slowly shut the window on him. He stood there for a long while, stunned. I was behind the curtain but it was see-through enough so I could watch him illuminated by the moonlight. I wondered if it went both ways if the lights were on in here and it was dark out there.

Suddenly, his knees buckled under him and I heard him cry out as he punched the ground with his fist. The sound made its way through my cloud of emptiness and echoed around like a lone wolf howling in a low holler. That sound will never leave me.

I watched his hunched-over shape silently writhing in pain. His dream of me, of the girl I was and the wife I could have been to him, must have died right then. He was mourning that girl, the one who went into that shed, not the one who came out twenty minutes later.

He could never love her. No one could. No man ever has.

Chapter Four

Goldenseal Roots

Before I take the slight turn at Kanawha Avenue, I stop at the little corner store with a name entirely made of initials and the word grocery. I know I'm just stalling but I go in anyway. The clerk behind the counter speaks with a heavy accent that summons mine whenever I hear it. I ask for the restroom with a native twang and she obliges.

In the mirror, I stare at the woman before me. She's not much different than the girl who lived in Ansted, West Virginia. I'm still about 5'5", my hair, still long but a darker reddish blonde, more managed, more sleek. I smooth my fitted denim pants tucked into suede boots, and straighten my white linen blouse, cinched with a belt around my slim waist. I have my grey scarf on today—the vintage Schiaparelli silk in three shades of grey. It covers my scars nicely.

I look like an author—a person who has it together. There's a glow coming from my skin that comes from good makeup and the reality of financial security. But the eyes—my eyes are dull. I've stood in front of the mirror I don't know how many times and tried to make my moss-green eyes look alive again.

To compensate, I practice smiling by taking my natural grim expression and forcing the corners of my mouth up making my cheeks look like little apples. It's amazing how a smile fools every-one—even me. I wash my hands, smile at the clerk, and make my way back to the car.

I know I'm close to home as Gauley Mountain comes into view. The road tilts dramatically upward. My ears pop, and I feel my back press into the seat. I drive right by the Mystical Gravity Tunnel, a new spooky attraction made of rusty shards of metal with a plastic wolf guarding the entrance. This place 'defies the laws of gravity,' it says. Then the road abruptly straightens and I'm here. I'm in Ansted, my town with my people. I unexpectedly feel delight glowing from my pores.

The town looks different, foreign. It's as if it's dressed for an occasion. The buildings have new paint and there are new stores. It's a tourist town now. Missy told me, but I hadn't imagined it right.

There's a new auto dealership, and Tudor's Biscuit World Res-taurant looks spiffy and dignified. From the light posts hang green signs with little red birds on them that welcome one and all.

I hold my breath out of habit as I make my way over New River Gorge Bridge. I'm nearly home.

A left at the bent tree. A right up the rocky hill. I don't need the GPS voice that I've set on British mode to tell me how to get here. My tires crumble the rocks as they climb up my childhood driveway.

That's it. The house looks nice. But smaller, I think. *Wait, it's brown. I thought it was beige. Maybe it just wanted to be brighter in my mind.*

Before I can think too much about it, I kill the engine and open the car door. The familiar scent of the trees, the dirt, and the clean mountain air fills my lungs. The long grass gets pulled to the side by the wind. It stirs something in me. An emotion I can't deal with is right on the edge of my perception. I push it away like swallowing a big hard pill stuck in my throat as I walk slowly, timidly up the steps to the porch.

I realize that it has felt like this place really didn't exist until right this moment. Maybe as a coping mechanism, I'd turned my house into a figment of my imagination. But, here it is. It's real, just like all the rest of the things in my head I wish weren't.

Before I can knock, Missy opens the door and squeals. She pulls me into her long, slender arms and hugs me like nobody's business.

"You look great!" she croons. "So fancy!"

"You, too!" She's wearing a pretty, loose dress over her thin frame. Her light hair is shorter now. It's cute on her. As she smiles, there are fine lines around her eyes that didn't used to be there.

She stands back and looks at me. "You're too skinny," she decides. "I'm gonna have to fatten you up while you're here."

"Well, I'm only going to be here just today and tomorrow. I don't know how much fattening you can do in that amount of time," I say dryly.

Her mouth goes into a thin line. "Sadie Jane! You are not tellin' me you are a' leavin' tomorrow. Your momma's been waiting on you. She's dying, Sadie. You have to stay 'til she does and that's that."

"I can't possibly…"

"Why not?"

"I can't just drop my life."

"What? You too busy to be here when your only momma dies!"

I stand here like an errant child as I kick the back of my left boot with my right toe. She's right. I can't let my fears over Dillon or his devil-spawn brother disturb me so. She's my momma, after all.

"No. You're right, Missy," I say with my head down. "I'll stay, until the end."

"All right, then. Let me fix you some lunch."

"Well, I'd like to see momma," I try.

"Oh, Lord Jesus! I nearly forgot. You got me all flustered. Come on." She grabs my arm and pulls me through the front room and promptly up the creaky stairs. Momma and Daddy's room was upstairs with the room the babies shared. Downstairs was Missy's and my room.

"The house looks exactly the same as I remember. Except smaller. Maybe I'm just bigger now."

"Well, you're probably used to that fancy place you got over there in Cal-i-forn-ia." She says the last word almost mockingly.

Outside the door to momma's room, she stops. "Now, I want to warn you, Sadie. Momma looks different. She don't talk much no more, neither. She's sleepin' now but I'm gonna wake her up for you. She'd be devastated if I didn't."

I realize my mouth feels like a dry cotton ball. I nod yes.

As I walk in the room, it smells like a medicine I don't know. It must be evaporating out of momma's skin and being released into the air.

Missy walks over to the old metal bed and taps momma's shoulder. She leans down and announces me in a loud voice. Momma opens her eyes and they dart around the room until they settle on mine. She motions for me to come closer, so I do.

"My baby," she croons and softly grabs a hold of my right hand. Her hand feels light and fragile like a broken bird wing in mine.

I sit in the chair next to her. That's all it takes for the tears to force their way out of my eyes. I have different types of cries: the ugly cry, the loud cry, the surprise cry, the whiny cry, the knot in the throat cry. This one is the stinging cry. My eyes will sting without the knot in my throat and they won't stop stinging until I'm over it. Usually the stinging cry comes when I'm particularly saddened— usually reserved for things and people I love a lot. Sometimes it takes all day to go away—I just tell people I have allergies.

Momma looks so old, so weak, as if her body is being sucked up from the inside and her skin couldn't keep up.

"Sadie," she says, breathlessly.

"Yes, Momma."

"I want ya to go up the mountain and get me some yella root for my skin and fer these sores in my mouth. It. Soothes. Me," she says, painfully.

"Of course." I look at Missy who shrugs her shoulders.

"Go, please," she begs, dismissing me.

I'm so confused as I get up from the chair. But then again, I can't really expect momma to be rational. She wants me to go up to Gauley Mountain and dig goldenseal roots. She might be perfectly lucid. Okay. Fine. I guess I have to go out after all. What harm can come of that?

Chapter Five

Jerky Jake

"**E**at this," Missy says, as I come out of the bedroom we shared as children. I'm wearing the clothes Missy threw at me out of a box in our old closet. It feels like I'm wearing my old skin in this well-worn black t-shirt, some washed out jeans, and my old, faded brown boots. The ones that were hers and she'd given me when my feet grew big enough for them. The ones I was wearing when...*No. I can't go there right now.* But, as I wiggle my toes inside them, I wonder if I can find traces of my blood embedded in the old leather like they do on CSI. *Stop!* I tell myself. *This is sick.*

She's made me a plate: fried chicken, greens, and potato salad.

"I'm a vegetarian," I explain as I slide into the heavily waxed chair around the old, knotted wooden table.

"Of course you are," she decides.

I run my hand along the arm of the chair. It's just as I remember except there may be a few more layers of wax now. I smile at the familiarity.

This table reminds me of all the ways I used to hide meat so I didn't have to eat it. Sometimes I pulled the meat off into strips and hid it under the rim of the plate, or I'd drink all my juice and hide it in the plastic cup. Sometimes I fed it to my dog, Nancy, under the table.

That reminds me, she died on the side of the road after being hit by a car when I was thirteen. She was so funny. She'd get mad at momma when, come summertime, momma buzzed away her thick mane of peach-colored fur. She'd hide under the house for days, and walk around with her nose in the air after that for another week or so. She used to sleep in the bed with me and Missy. She'd press her little body against my side, reminding me she loved me with little pink-tongued kisses on my arm. She was a love.

I close my eyes and let these things come back to me. It reminds me that not everything about being here is bad. It's just one bad thing happened, and somehow that painted all of the past with a darker hue. Like a line got drawn in my memories that wouldn't let me through to all the good that rests on the other side of fourteen and a half. You know what; I'd love to get another dog someday. But, what if it makes a mess, or pees on the floor? I need things clean, orderly. I need things to be in control.

As I think about the pros and cons, I eat the greens Missy gave me even though I suspect there may be some bacon fat in them or something, and the potato salad. I leave my chicken-friend remains on the plate as Missy glares at me. I gulp down the sweet tea. I shrug my shoulders and she stares at the chicken, back at me, and then she frowns as she picks up my plate in defeat.

"You guys shouldn't have let me hold 'em when they were hatched, let me name 'em and then cut their heads off in front of me."

"That's just the way life is, Sadie," she explains. "How were we supposed ta know you'd be so…sensitive?"

I shrug my shoulders.

"Are you goin' to drive over and walk a little ways or take the walkin' trail over yonder?"

"Drive, but couldn't I just go buy some goldenseal in a jar? She won't even know."

"Momma wants you to get it for her, from the ground," she says, her mouth in a grim line. She rummages around in the pantry behind me as I stare at the kitchen walls, the pictures, the knick-knacks. Memories are just being held back by my purposeful blankness.

"Here," she says, as she hands me a thin sack made from the leg of some old britches.

I look inside and find a root digger and some cheesecloth.

As I hold the digger, it tugs on a little string tied onto a memory in my brain. The wooden end feels so familiar. I run my hand up and down the soft edge and realize this is the very same one Momma had taught me with. She said she'd found it in a ginseng patch when she was a little girl, obviously discarded accidentally by a veteran digger. It had been sharpened into a perfect claw. Slowly, I put it back into the old britches.

I bet they were daddy's, I think as I run my fingers over the soft fabric. I hadn't come back when daddy died three years ago—he'd had a heart attack. I just sent a really ornate, probably gaudy, flower arrangement from Ansted Floral & Gift. I couldn't come. I can't tell anyone this but I'd never wanted to see daddy again—not even dead. I know Missy doesn't want to talk about him right now. Her memories of him are different than mine.

"Where are the babies?" I ask before I turn to leave.

"Elise is at school, Sadie. And little Joe's takin' a long nap. You'll meet 'em later," she says, proudly.

"What about Dale?"

"He's on a run 'cross country," she explains. "He'll be back in four days."

"The life of a trucker's wife, huh," I joke.

"Yep. We put up with a lot. You'd better go, Sadie, or you'll miss dinner."

"Okay, bye," I say. She waves me out. She seems a bit busy.

When I step on the front porch, I remember—*I think my horse Monty is still in his stable.* He's, what? He's got to be about twelve years old. Missy never said anything about him dying like Frosty did; and I know the boys like to ride the horses so they didn't sell him—I don't think.

I walk slowly down the trodden path toward Monty's stable. The familiar scents in the air tug on memory after memory. I try to swallow them down but they feel like they're choking me. My throat swells with that hard lump again. I hate this feeling. That lump in my throat had stayed for almost a year after…I was raped.

Why is it so hard to say the word rape in my head? I wince. I wonder if the lump will just stick itself in my throat the whole time I'm here. It doesn't hurt but it's annoying. It feels like I'm going to cry but even if I pinch myself until I do, the lump stays put.

I'm distracted from my throat when I catch sight of my horse. He's standing behind the fence in the pen. His back leg is bent and his tail is swatting a fly buzzing around his hind end. He whinnies when he sees me like he's looking for something. Slowly, in a trance, I walk up to the fence separating us.

"Monty Montana," I croon, a huge, *real* smile planted on my face. He nickers and his back shakes while he stays still, his black eye assessing me—his other one is covered by his thick mane. I reach down and pick some grass and hold it out. He walks gracefully over to me, grazing his lips over my palm to retrieve his treat.

"The grass is always greener where you can't stick your muzzle, huh, boy," I whisper to him and pat his forehead and his long face. He makes the blow-sound as he exhales with his mouth shut as if to say, "Hello, friend!" His scent is intoxicating. There's nothing like the scent of a horse to get rid of a lump in the throat.

His front hoof scratches the West Virginia dirt. Then he neighs, his voice sounding every bit as beautiful as when he was a youngster.

It's then that I notice he has grey fur mixed in with the black. He hops once and then goes into a full gallop around his pen. He rears up on his hind legs, neighs in his throaty way looking at me with his one uncovered eye.

"Haven't seen him do that in a long while," says a voice from inside the stable. It's dark in there so I can't see who it is.

"Hello?" I say with my hands steepled over my forehead to block the light. That's when a teenage boy walks out from the shadow.

"Seth?" I say, surprised.

"Na, I'm Jake. The younger one," he says, to clarify.

"Oh, Jake!" I reply, unsure of how to greet my little brother. He was only two when I left.

"So, what are you doing home? I thought you'd be at school."

"I ditched," he says, matter of factly.

I don't say anything. I just nod and stick out my bottom lip in contemplation while I pretend to kick something that's not there on the ground. I wonder if he does this a lot.

"So, you're thirteen?" I say.

"Yep."

I feel like crap. I don't even know my own flesh and blood. He's tall for his age, with feet he's still growing into. Skinny, too, with long legs like daddy had. He has my nose but dark hair like momma's sticking out under his ball cap. His face is impassive as he leans against the wooden beam at the front entrance of the stable watching Monty gallop around his pen. I wish I knew what he's thinking. Monty neighs again long and loud, hooves scraping the ground.

"Ya want me to saddle him for ya?" Jake says.

"Really?" I say because that's all I can think to say. I haven't ridden a horse since I left.

"Really," he says.

"Yes, please. I can take him up the trail that leads up the mountain to find some yellow root for momma. She asked me to go," I explain.

"Okay," he says. He winks at me and walks over to Monty. "Whoa boy," he says, making himself big until Monty succumbs and lets him grab his halter.

He walks him into the stable as I follow. It smells like wood, hay, saddle leather, horses, and fresh mountain air. I feel giddy.

"Can I brush him?" I say, through my huge grin.

"Yep, brush is right there," Jake says, pointing at the wooden box on the floor by the door.

I watch as little particles of dust float into the air while I brush him. His muscles flex under the brush and he clears his horsey throat over and over. I've missed this. I think I have a real honest to goodness smile on my face. This is a rare thing.

"Yeah, you should be glad it's me here and not Seth," Jake explains.

"Why's that?"

"He's pissed at you. He still remembers you from when he was four. He don't like to say it but it hurt his feelings when you just left like that. He remembers you pretty good from before."

"Oh," is all I can say. I guess I'm going to have to deal with an angry fifteen year old tonight at dinner.

"Is he at school?"

"Yep," he says, as he slides the saddle on top of the saddle blanket. The saddle says, 'Sadie' on the part that runs down the side of the horse's belly.

"I forgot about my saddle," I squeal.

"We didn't want to throw it out. Nobody'd buy it with your name on it like that. 'Cept Dillon maybe," he says, with a chuckle.

"What do you mean?"

"Oh, everybody knows!" he laughs.

"Knows what?" I press.

"He's crazy about you. Crazy being the right word. Got your name tattooed on his arm with some Bible verse," he laughs again. "We all see it every summer whenever he wears a wife beater."

My head is spinning. "A wife beater?"

"Oh, yeah, it's a white T-shirt without the sleeves. You know," he explains.

"I guess."

"Miss Robbins is so jealous. She tried to make him get the thing burnt off or somethin' but he got mad. They were screaming 'bout it last year at the Country Roads Festival. It was kinda funny."

"Miss Robbins?" I ask as I slip the bridle's bit past Monty's front teeth.

"His girlfriend, oh, and my English teacher too," he says, plainly.

I clear my throat as I close the strap over the cheek piece and pat Monty's forehead. I don't know a woman named Robbins. There was Mike Robbins. He was older than us, though. He joined the Army and left his new wife behind when he went to basic training. I don't really remember her, though. She was a lot older than me. I wonder?

Dillon.

Here I am fresh off the highway and I'm already hearing about him. Part of me is pleased that Dillon never forgot me; the other part, the part that wants him to be happy, not fighting with his girlfriend about me, is displeased and I frown. Jake elbows me.

"Hey, earth to Sadie," he mocks.

I elbow him back, "Okay, Jerky Jake," I christen him. That will be his new nickname. It seems like I've known him forever.

"Well, over to you," he says, handing me the reins. I look at Monty and back at him. I purse my lips in a thin line. "Oh, no you don't," he scolds. "That's rule number one. Can't be nervous on a horse."

I blink rapidly and push my foot into the stirrup, pull up with my leg and swing the other one over. Monty shifts under me and jolts forward.

"See, he knows you're nervous," Jake shouts as Monty gallops around the pen. My legs tense around his belly on both sides as my nerves turn to excitement. There's a freedom I forgot about when I'm on a horse—this horse in particular.

I laugh out loud and Monty slows down, pulls against the reins, yawns on his bridle bit and walks toward the swinging gate in his pen.

"Just follow that path. It's the same one," Jake explains as he opens the gate, hands me my thin sack and points toward the trail leading up the hill toward Gauley Mountain. "Up yonder you ought to run into a patch or two of yella' root."

"See ya," I call to him. As long as I don't run into anything else.

Chapter Six

His Flower

Monty and I have been trotting up the path for probably thirty minutes. I'm starting to grasp just how much I've missed my homeland. I feel fantastic! This is better than writing. Better than signing autographs on my books. Better than shopping for antiques or silk scarves, better than anything I can remember.

The dense trees are a canopy above my strawberry blonde hair shielding me from any fear I'd felt as I left the safety of momma's house. I'm whistling a tune I remember Dillon playing me on his courting dulcimer when we were teenagers.

He'd been teaching me the song right up until the end. Once we got older, daddy insisted we play together on Dillon's granddaddy's courting dulcimer if he was going to sit with me on the porch. It had a place for two people to play as it sat on both our laps while we faced each other. Obviously, Dillon was teaching me as I hadn't a clue how to do it. But it made daddy feel better. As he used to say, *"Idle hands are the devil's playthings."*

The song was called *'You Are My Flower'*. He said it reminded him of me. He'd learned it from listening to the Carter Family's CD. He loved Johnny Cash and the Carters. He knew so many of their songs.

He played the dulcimer and the harmonica both equally well. I didn't know a lot about music, though.

I keep on humming the instrumental to You Are My Flower, remembering the way his long fingers moved over the strings as he sat the dulcimer on his lap—such a graceful touch he had when his hand grazed mine here and there. With his other hand he strummed, or he'd grasp my hand and help me strum so I'd get the pacing. He'd always say, *"You're not goin' to get everything I do 'cause I'm just havin' too much fun, but if you can get the basics of it down you'll be playin' in no time."*

I'm humming loudly when I just break out into the chorus. It comes out of nowhere as if I'd just been singing it yesterday.

"You are my flower
that's blooming in the mountain for me
You are my flower
that's blooming there for me
Hmmm…hmmmm…hmmmm
The air is just as pure
The sunlight just as free
And nature seems to say
It's all for you and me
Hmmm…hmmmm…hmmmm
You are my flower
that's blooming in the mountain for me
You are my flower
that's blooming there for me
Hmmmm…Hmmmm….Hmmmm…"

I yelp as a bicyclist turns the corner coming down the hill toward us. Monty is spooked and starts to gallop full speed up the hill and off the trail into the woods as the bicyclist skids and falls on his side behind me.

I yank the reins, yelling, "Whoa, boy!" but he doesn't seem to realize I'm on his back anymore. I duck my head as branches scratch my arms and narrowly miss my head. Monty neighs louder, runs over the path again, and tries to jump down the side of the hill into a steep ravine.

I'm not a great rider anymore, so the only thing I can think to do is jump off him so he doesn't take me down the side of the hill and break my neck. I grab a branch and hold on. Monty keeps going and the branch breaks with my full weight, crashing me into the soft ground below. It knocks the wind out of me and I'm exasperated and wide-eyed.

"What the hell!" I scream up to whoever is on the path above me.

"I'm so sorry," apologizes the voice, oddly familiar to me.

As I lay on my back, a bicycle-gloved hand reaches out to help. "I'm fine. Just be on your way," I snap.

A face comes into view, albeit upside down. He's smiling He's wearing a black bicycle helmet and black spandex shorts with a matching yellow shirt.

It's Dillon.

"Crap!" I squeak. He steps back like I'm a wolverine about to pounce as I sit up and slide around to face him. "I really hadn't planned on seeing anyone up here," I exclaim, loudly as I stand up and brush off the leaves and dirt now attached to me.

Dillon looks like he's just been bitten by a mute-causing spider. His mouth is open, his arms dangling by his sides, his legs planted to the ground. I actually feel sorry for him. He looks like he's going to faint or go into convulsions. He has to remind himself to breathe. When he does, "Sadie," pops out of his stunned mouth.

He walks forward. I take a step back, so he stops. "What are you doing here?"

"I'm visiting my mom," I state, dryly.

"Visiting your mom," he says, as if he's trying to remember what those words mean in that sequence.

"Dillon, are you alright?"

"Alright," he says, as if he doesn't remember what that means either.

"Here," I say, grabbing his arm and putting it over my shoulder. Electricity runs down my arm from the contact. "Sit down on this log, okay? I have to get my horse and I'll be right back."

"No! Don't go!" he pleads, his arm still over my shoulder as he sits down. I hear Monty pacing back and forth down in the ravine. He's stuck.

"I've got to get my horse," I explain.

He shakes his head looking so confused. "I'll get him," he states, seeming in control now.

Before I can say no, he's jumping into the ravine and grabbing Monty's reins. He finds a place up the hill and leads Monty down the path toward the trail I'm waiting on. As he brings Monty back to me, I watch his biking shoes caress the dirt under him.

He's in amazing shape and I blush all over and my scalp prickles looking at his fit body masked in spandex, leaving nothing to the imagination. He looks like a Greek sculpture standing there as he takes his helmet off releasing his hay colored messy hair. He looks much the same as ten years ago, but his face is thinner, more angular, and mature. He's stronger—leaner. It's my turn to be dazed.

We just stand here looking at each other, taking stock of each other's presence. We're saying nothing. I reach forward to take Monty's reins and he steps forward getting closer than I'd expected him to.

"You look beautiful," he blurts out. "Even with all those leaves in your hair." He smiles the long-missed I'm-yours-and-you're-mine smile. *I don't know how to feel about that.* Rather than focus on me, I realize his voice is different, deeper. His accent isn't as pronounced anymore either.

He reaches up and takes a dried leaf out of my hair. Just that small gesture makes me blush from the inside out. My breath hitches in my throat. I shake the leaves out of my hair so he can't keep doing that.

I say nothing but my lip starts to quiver. I don't know what to do so I step back and look down. His proximity is intimidating, his scent familiar and invigorating. I peek up at him through my lashes.

When I finally straighten my gaze, his eyes take mine hostage. I feel as though I cannot look away. Then it hits me. I know what color his eyes are. The summer after my eighteenth birthday, Aunt Lotty took me to Nevada to lounge at a beach on Lake Tahoe. As we drove toward the beach, I saw a small patch of white sand under shallow water.

In that spot the dark blue of the deep lake changed to a stunning aqua blue. That is the color of his eyes as I stand here. I had struggled to rationalize the melancholy that came over me that day. This must be why. I'd missed the color of Dillon's eyes.

"I'm looking for some goldenseal for my momma. That's what I'm doing on the trail."

He shakes his head to acknowledge he's listening but his eyes never leave mine, "Yellow root? That's my specialty. Let me help," he says enthusiastically as he rubs his palms together.

I say nothing, but start to walk and he follows. "Don't you want to grab your bike?"

"Oh, yeah," he chuckles and I wait as he picks up his bike and wheels it next to Monty and me on the trail. He hooks his helmet to the handlebars.

"I almost gave up hope I'd see you, Sadie," he blurts again.

"Me too, Dillon." Saying his name pains me for some reason.

"Since you didn't come back for your dad's, I just assumed, when your momma got sick…" he struggles to make his point. He still doesn't want to hurt me or offend me.

"I had to see her one last time," I explain. He nods approvingly.

"I've read your books," he says, smiling at me.

"Really!"

"Yes, some a couple of times, now. And your blog. Anything you write or anything written about you," he says. He's so forthcoming. I realize I have a huge grin on my face that matches his.

"There you go," he says, pointing to a patch of green, leafy plants with bright red, bulbous flowers in the middle.

"Goldenseal!" I say, relieved to find such a gold mine. I grab the thin sack from my 'Sadie' saddle and immerse myself in the act of scraping the dead leaves with Momma's root digger claw. Dillon is beside me like a memory, moving leaves and grabbing hold of a nice sized plant so that I can dig under it. It's like old times, me and Dillon working together as if no time has passed. With him near, I suddenly feel home.

As if by magic, the golden yellow roots are in my hand. "How many should I dig?" I ask him.

"Well, it looks like you've got three plants old enough. That's all I'd take," he explains. "Goldenseal is getting rare up in the Appalachians because of the mountaintop coal mining. We have to conserve what we can."

"Oh, I've heard of mountaintop coal mining but it just never really hit home, I guess."

"Well, right now, our own Gauley Mountain is the point of a bitter feud. The coal company wants to blow the top off it and, you know, some of the people here are for it. They know they'll get hired to help for a time. Mostly everybody else wants to preserve the mountain. We're a tourist town now and it'll hurt business and mess up the water supply."

"I had no idea," I say, shocked.

"Most people don't. Hey, there's an EDA meeting tomorrow evening if you want to come and find out more. Having a famous eco-author there couldn't hurt," he winks at me.

"Oh, yeah, maybe. Where at?" I ask as I dig up the third root from the larger plant.

"The middle school. Six o'clock." I get a flash of the old brick building with the too large 'AMS' on the front. I had so many good times there. Back in a life that seems like a figment of my imagination.

"So, how do you know so much about this?" I ask, remembering that Missy was unsure of what Dillon's job was here in town.

"I'm working here on a Federal Government grant. It'd be easier to show you, really. I'm not sure if I can explain it right," he says, as he leans back on his heels. "You could come by anytime. See what I do," he flashes his full I'm-yours smile sure to get me weak in the knees.

It works, even though I'm not actually standing up. My nervous system is going into fight or flight mode. All these feeling and thoughts confuse my body.

"I don't think that's a good idea," I say, as I wrap the roots up in the cheesecloth.

"Why not?" he asks, stubbornly.

"I'm going to be so busy here helping Missy with momma. Then, I'll be going back right after the wake." I don't want him to get his hopes up.

"But, you can't," he declares. "You've just gotten here." He reminds me of when he was younger and didn't get something he wanted. He didn't often throw a fit—unless it really meant a lot to him.

I'm just going to cut to the chase.

"Do you really have a tattoo of my name on your arm, Dillon?" I ask, coldly.

He looks baffled and tilts his head to the side in thought.

"Yes," he coughs, and rubs his left bicep and then over his heart. *Does he have two?*

"I just don't think that's fair to your girlfriend," I say, wincing.

"Of course, you think you know everything, don't you?" he scowls.

"I know that she doesn't like it and what's the point of putting her through that when..." I can't finish my sentence.

What should I say? *I'm never going to be yours again.* I guess that would work since I'm not her anymore. *You should cherish what you have instead of waiting for this idea of what you thought you could have—in another parallel life that never came to fruition.*

He stands up in one swift move and walks away from me, runs his hand through his messy hair and pinches that little V that forms between his eyes with his thumb and forefinger. I stand up, too, and decide to stand my ground.

"I mean, what do you *want* from me, Dillon?"

"What do I want!" he shouts. *He never shouts!* I hold my hands out and put my mouth in a crooked line like I'm saying 'bring it on.'

"I want you, Sadie. I've always wanted you."

"Dillon," I interrupt.

"No, you should know, Sadie, I told you the truth the last time we spoke." He clenches his teeth and his square jaw becomes more angular. "I've never stopped loving you, ever." His fists tighten until his arms look like they're about to pop.

"And I *WANT* you to be my wife. I *want* to make babies with you and see them running around the house I bought for us. I *want* to make love to you every morning and every night on every possible surface of said house. I *want* to laugh with you, cry with you, hold you in my arms, protect you, and whisper sweet nothings in your ear.

I *want* to sit on the porch and play music together so I can hear your soft voice when you sing for the rest of my life."

I just stand here. *Whoa!*

"I *want* to know the feel of your skin reacting under my fingers and to know the scent of your hair under my nose. I *want* to kiss you every day a hundred million times. I *want* to fall asleep to the sounds of your breathing. I want to lay my head on your breast every night so I can hear your heartbeat until I grow old with you. I *want* to watch our grandbabies from the porch when we can no longer get up and chase 'em around. I *want* all of that and more. I *want* the life that was stolen from us. That's what I *WANT,* what I've *wanted* ever since we were kids," he says, his hand reaching out to me as if there's a barrier he cannot cross. His breath is ragged and he begins to pace back and forth along the trail.

There's a hole in my chest that I could easily fill with the life he's just proposed to me. But, I can't. "I'm just not capable of that kind of life, Dillon," I say, honestly.

He won't look at me. He's still pacing.

"Look. You've taken this too far. This was just a crush you had a long time ago with an innocent girl who no longer even exists, Dillon."

"Doesn't exist? You're freakin' standing right in front of me. Of course you exist."

"What I'm trying to say is, you have an idea of the person I am. But I'm not her. I'm a totally different person than the girl you knew all those years ago. The girl you loved went into that shed and never came out," I explain.

"Shed? What shed, Sadie?" There's a panicked sound in his voice as he looks like he's remembering something he can't place.

I let it slip. "What I'm trying to say is I'm not *her* anymore," I clarify, and look down.

"No, you're not. You're a grown woman now. What, do you think you were prefect back then?" I peek up at him again. "Do you think I'm delusional? I know your faults. I know everything there is to know. All that does is make me love you more."

"I just think you're in love with a memory, and you should let go of that so you can have *all of that* with Miss Robbins," I say, not knowing what her first name is.

"Look," he says, eyes piercing into mine so deep it makes that hole in my chest feel rough and new—like ten years ago new. "I am in love with you, Sadie," he states, his voice as clear as a blue sky. "That will never change, ever. I'm in love with my best friend and there's nothing that will ever change that. We grew up together. We shared everything. You know me better than anyone ever has or ever will. Miss Robbins, Claire, is a friend I spend time with. She's not my girlfriend, not really. To be honest, we both just pretend, I mean, how do I say this?" he says, bewildered. "She lost her husband three years ago. You remember Mike Robbins, right?"

"Yeah."

"He was killed in combat in Iraq four years ago and I take his place a little for her. She takes your place for me. It eases the loneliness, that's all. It's entirely different than what I feel for you. It's not even on the same planet as the feelings I have for you," he explains.

"But it could be if you'd just let go of this asinine idea that you have of who I am to you. She obviously cares for you or that tattoo wouldn't matter. You're not even giving her a chance."

"I know who you are to me. That will never change," he says, solid in his conviction.

"Well, I don't. I can't," I try to explain, looking down. *Ugg!* This hurts. The lump in my throat is back and all I want to do is go back home and take a bath and sleep forever.

He looks exhausted, too. Fighting will do that to you.

"I have to go," I say, blandly. The numbness starts taking over while I'm grabbing Monty's reins from the tree he's tied to.

"Can I walk you home?"

"No!" I say, and then he winces.

"Ummm. I can get myself home, I mean." I have to look away. "No need to go out of your way."

"Please," he says, earnestly.

I turn and walk down the trail and he follows, saying nothing. We walk in silence, kicking rocks down the trail for, I'd bet, about fifteen minutes.

"I'm sorry," he says, finally.

"For what?"

"For yelling at you. That was wrong."

His arm brushes mine and I tense. He notices and gives me more room.

"Hey, why don't you get up in the saddle? I can ride my bike up ahead. I can see you're really tired. When did you get here?"

"Just today," I say drone-like again.

"Here, let me help you up," he says, holding my elbow. Electricity shoots through my arm where he's touching me. It's like two *live wires* if they were to meet and make sparks. My body feels tensed. "Up you go," he says, as I swing my leg over. As he has hold of my arm, he pauses as he notices the scratches I got from riding my scared horse into the trees. "These look bad. Let me get my first aid kit." I don't say anything as he gets it from his bike. I have to pull Monty's reins so he doesn't leave Dillon behind.

He pulls out an astringent already imbedded in a little cloth and stings me with it. I wince but say nothing. What's weird is it does feel nice to have someone take care of me for a minute. His long fingers rub ointment on all my little scrapes, taking his time. I study his face, his hands. I watch the muscles in his arm as he touches me. "There you go," he says, smiling.

I look down. "Thank you," I say, ever so softly.

He moves his bike ahead of us and I watch him ride all the way down the trail and up to the border of Momma's place. He's a skilled mountain bike rider—a very fast one, and that's why I'm in this mess in the first place.

He helps me, as much as I'll let him, to get down off Monty's tired back. I watch as he un-straps the 'Sadie' saddle, sliding it onto the wooden horse it's stored on near the wall. He hands me the thin sack that holds the yellow roots wrapped in cheesecloth and the tools. I just stand here as he pulls the blanket off and shakes it. I'm a tired, mute statue who's biting her thumbnail.

"Come," he says, taking my hand and it's all *live wires* again but I pretend not to notice. "I bet dinner's ready by the smell a' things up at the house," he chuckles. I don't even want to fight him about coming in. I'm too tired. I open the front door and he slips in at my side holding my elbow again, so I pull it out of his grasp as nicely as I can.

"Personal bubble," I say, making my arms wide around my person to show him how I like my space. He steps away to give me what I want—his face impassive.

"Missy," he says, standing near the door with me in tow. "Look who I found wandering around."

"Dillon. Hi, there. You want some dinner?" Missy says with an inward wave.

"I'd love some." He's looking at me as he says it. I just lift my shoulders like 'I don't care.'

Jake and another teen who I'm guessing is Seth are sitting at the table holding their forks and knives waiting for food. I thought people only did that in cartoons.

There's two little kids, too. Missy's kids. They look like the ones in the pictures she puts on Facebook. One is a girl and she's probably about five. The other is a boy, about two, and he's sitting in a highchair looking like he's too big for it but it keeps him still so she keeps him in it anyway.

"Long time no see, Dillon." She gives me a silent nod and a wink. I don't do anything back, so her eyebrows furrow. She always liked Dillon for me. She used to tease me about being up a tree kissing him and rocking cradles.

"Yeah. Too long. Seth. Jake," Dillon nods and smiles.

"Hey," they both say in unison. I think Jake kicks Seth under the table because I hear a thump, Seth jumps and then scowls.

"Hi, Sadie," Seth says, with his teeth clenched.

I nod at him. I don't want to try to win over angry fifteen-year-olds right now.

"I'm going to have a bath," I declare.

"Not until you eat," Missy says, glaring at me. "You're too skinny as it is."

I hand her the thin sack. "You got some roots!" she says, excitedly.

"Three good ones," Dillon explains. He looks at me and then knits his brow. I can feel it. It's Numb Girl. She takes over when I'm weighed down—to protect me sometimes, Dr. Amy says. Not like I have a personality disorder or anything. It's just a numb thing I do when I'm overwhelmed—diseased molecules that run as deep as a scar.

"I didn't know what you'd eat so I made you a Cobb salad with some boiled egg and green tomatoes. There's blue cheese and carrots, beets. Green onions too. Oh, and some cucumbers. All of us are eating pork chops, and mashed taters though if you change your mind."

I shrug as she hands me a salad filled plate.

"'S fine," I mumble.

"You okay?" Missy asks, a worried look on her face.

"Just tired," I say.

I mope because I'm too tired to pretend-smile as the rest of them talk about randomness. To be honest, most of the time, their voices sound like Charlie Brown's teacher as I crunch lettuce and other veggies. Then Missy asks Dillon how he'd come to see me and how he ended up sitting here for dinner. He explains the whole thing, but leaves out the part where he almost fainted when he saw me and the part where we were yelling at each other at the top of our lungs.

The little girl, Elise I think her name is, grabs Missy's shirt sleeve and says, "What's wrong with her?" as she looks at me like I'm an alien from Planet Weird. I stare at my plate like it's my saving grace.

"That's your Aunt Sadie. She's had a long, long day, honey. She's just real tired." I try to smile at her but she's not convinced. I look back down, uncomfortable.

When I look up, Dillon is staring at me, concern written all over the lines in his forehead. He moves his hand toward me so slightly no one else even notices, but I tense and he stops.

I crunch the last bit of salad and get up before I'm done chewing.

"Goodnight," I say to the room.

The room answers back, "Goodnight, Sadie."

Chapter Seven

The Rules

L ast night I sat in the old fashioned claw foot tub up to my nose in water trying to un-numb myself like one defrosts a chicken. The numbness is a reaction to anything being too much to handle. It started that night in the shed and comes back once in a while.

Seeing Dillon would have been enough but then add to that the nine hour flight, the three hours of driving, the nerves all day, the memories being just right at the surface, seeing momma so sick, riding my horse, meeting my little brother, finding out Dillon has a girlfriend, Monty getting spooked, and getting thrown off him. Arguing with Dillon was just the last straw.

He's really infuriating. I'd forgotten how stubborn he used to be—still is apparently. But patient is another adjective I'd use to describe him.

He's just not going to stop until he gets what he wants—but what he wants I can't give him. Let's take Donnie out of the picture for a minute, wherever he is here in town. I'm just not capable of having a loving relationship with a man. So even if both of our lives weren't on the line here, I couldn't be the girl he thinks I am. Let's say he moved to California with me, I'd never quite fulfill this ideal he's created in his mind. He'd get tired of my anxiety, of the fact that he has to handle me and my moods. I'd fall in love with him and then…he'd leave. That's the order, I do believe.

It's not like I haven't tried—Californians aren't much on waiting 'til you're married—but the crying is always a turn off. At some point, the guy will do something, say something, make a noise, or move a certain way and I'm there again in that shed. No one has been able to get past the crying—especially me.

Well, there was the one guy, Longhaired Seth from the Berkley Library, who I made out with after we ate lukewarm pizza together out of soggy boxes. I started crying when he kissed my neck—I have neck issues. He asked me to tell him everything as he looked at me like he really cared.

I explained the story in short form enough to let him know I was a girl with a past. He said maybe I just needed to cry through it one time. He was willing to try, no doubt more for his own pleasure than mine. But after the crying came Numb Girl. I just got stiff and unresponsive and he decided he liked his criers a bit more sentient. *"It feels like I'm trying to rape you,"* he said, before he scooted out the door.

I'd better get up and do something with those goldenseal roots for Momma. It's still dark outside. My internal clock is all wrong. I would still be sleeping at two a.m. if I were still in California. Here it's five a.m., but I can't force my eyes shut. Sleep likes to play hide and seek when I'm nervous. Right now it's hiding and I'm not seeking.

I put on some faded jean shorts from my old closet and a fitted white t-shirt that smells like my least used sheets in the linen closet in my new house. I give up on my hair. I shouldn't have slept with it wet, so I just pull it back in a ponytail. At this hour, I don't even worry about a scarf for my scars. No one will be up for ages.

I pad along the wooden floor and find the roots in the refrigerator. It's still the same old refrigerator I remember being here when I was a kid. I run my fingers over the dent from when I accidentally slammed daddy's hammer into it. That was a bad whooping I got for that one.

I busy myself with taking some of the root and boiling it in a sauce pan to make a tea with it. This will be perfect for Momma to use as a mouthwash for her sores—I guess cancer gives people mouth sores.

The other root I put in the spice bowl and with the masher I smash it to smithereens until my upper lip is sweaty from exertion. In the pantry I find some coconut oil and in the yellow mixing bowl of my youth, I combine the coconut oil and the mashed up yellow root to create a nice smooth paste. I put that in a large mason jar and seal it up with the lid.

The last root I wrap in cheesecloth and tie it with string. I hang it from a nail in the pantry to dry it so I can make a powder out of it in a week or so. Doing this for Momma reminds me of her teaching me how. I try to reconcile the sickly woman up there in her room with the dark-haired strong woman of my youth. It feels like a loss I can't fathom. I realize that I'd put Momma a certain way in my mind kind of like filing her away in a mental cabinet of memories. I just don't want to add this to the file.

It's almost light outside; the sun is just a little haze over the hills. I'm sure everyone will be up soon—probably another hour or so. I think about making coffee but I don't know how to use the percolator on the stove. I decide to go sit with Momma while she sleeps. I'll take the goldenseal paste and rub it on her skin.

As I'm creaking up the steps, someone taps lightly on the front door. For a moment I consider ignoring it, but they tap again.

Resolved to get rid of them, I pad my way over to the door and open it. It's not just the breeze that knocks my hair back.

Dillon stands there looking sophisticated in the door frame. He's wearing dark fitted jeans, a brown linen button up shirt, and some grey canvas high-top TOMS Botas. My heartbeat accelerates. My eyelashes flutter. *Stop that*, I tell myself. *What? Do I think I'm immune?*

He swallows hard. "Can I talk to you, Sadie?"

"On one condition." I decide on the fly, my voice raspy and deep from no sleep.

"Anything," he says, curiously.

"I want coffee and I don't know how to use that contraption on the stove top." He peeks over to the stove and smiles at the percolator.

"I think I can figure it out," he says, as he walks in and moves effortlessly toward the kitchen. Suddenly, the contraption is in four pieces and he's rummaging through the drawers. "Filter?" He looks at me questioningly.

"I'm not sure." But I help him look.

"Ah, here we go," he says, holding the filters up like a prize, obviously proud of himself for having found them in the drawer, neighbors with the tin foil and the plastic baggies.

"I'm glad you're up," he says, as he unfolds the filter and then pops it over the center stem inside the basket part of the percolator. "Coffee grounds?" he says, pointing at the empty basket and scanning the counter top.

I hand him the tin that has always held coffee grounds since the beginning of time. As he spoons the grounds in he says, "I couldn't sleep."

"Me neither," I agree.

"Maybe I'm sleeping right now. It's like I'm dreaming seeing you here," he says, as he stops and looks at me as if I might just evaporate into thin air.

"I feel that way, too." It's true. Seeing him here, like a warm memory in Momma's kitchen folding the filter over the dry coffee grounds with his long thin fingers, reminds me that for the past ten years I've tucked Dillon away in my mind in that filing cabinet, too. At first he was real-like in my memories but lately he'd kind of blurred and become really small like a driver's license picture. Not anymore—he looks *very* real now.

"What are you thinking about?" he asks, his voice sweet and smooth like red velvet cake.

"Caffeine," I reply dryly as I rest my elbows on the counter top and stare at him impassively from under my eyelashes.

"I see," he says, smirking. "Well, it seems this is the one thing I can do for you then." There was a bit of sullenness in his tone there at the end.

"What did you want to talk about?" I ask politely. *Let's get this over with.*

"Hey, um, can you fill the percolator with water?"

"Sure, I guess I can handle that," I say as I turn on the faucet.

Well water tastes like childhood, I think as I pour myself a small glass before putting the percolator under the stream.

He pushes the long stem into the coffee basket causing some of the grounds to pop out where the stem just poked through. "Oh, I hadn't accounted for that," he explains and places a lid on top of the filter.

"Here you go," I say, placing the big blue pot next to where he's working and start wiping the spilled coffee grounds into my cupped hand. He puts the whole basket that he's assembled into the percolator and places the blue lid over top of everything before setting it on the stove. It ticks a few times before the flame catches the gas and he walks back over to me by the sink.

"Well, if I may be so bold, I'd like to talk about us," he says, earnestly, overly formal, his accent almost gone.

"Us?"

"If you like," he says, with a gleam in his Tahoe beach blue eyes.

"Knock it off," I say and fake punch him in his arm. He smiles but he's still serious. "Okay, I'm ready," I state, making my face look stern.

"Well, first of all, I wanted to apologize for yesterday."

"Uh," I start to blurt but he cuts me off.

"The thing is, I heard you singing. I was riding down the mountain just like I do every day at that time and I heard a woman singing *our* song."

"Oh!" I blurt again. Embarrassed, my cheeks feel fiery.

"I started rushing down the mountain faster than I thought I was when I came around that corner and spooked Monty. I was so bewildered that you were really there and not some phantom or something. I don't even know how we started arguing but then I just said all those things. Everything I've been hoping for and suppressing just came out of me. It was unfair and I'm sorry I did that to you."

"It's okay. I know we have history together," I try.

"I want you to know that I'm here for you in whatever way I can get you. If that means we're just friends, then that's what we'll be," he says, swallowing hard. "I don't want to drive you away now that I finally have a chance to see you in person."

"Oh," is all I can manage.

"What I'm trying to say is that I just want to enjoy whatever time I get to spend with you in whatever way works for you."

"Will being friends be enough for you or will you keep trying to make me be…more?"

"It will be hard for me because I want…more, but for you, to make you happy. To see you comfortable like you were when we were kids. I'd do anything to see you like that again."

The percolator starts to boil so he turns down the heat.

"I don't want to scorch the grounds. It'll make the coffee bitter," he explains, but it seems like he's talking about something else. Like maybe he's talking about me.

"Well, I think there should be some rules then. If I'm considering being friends, that is."

"Rules?"

"Mmm hmm," I reply with a few nods of my chin up and down.

"Okay, what are the rules?" he asks, serious.

"You can't touch me. It makes me uncomfortable," I say and he looks at me like he's nervous or hurt. He's all wide-eyed like that night under the window's edge.

I square my shoulders and continue, "You can't tell me how you feel about me. Just let me be ignorant about it. That's not what I want, the kind of relationship I want. I don't want to lead you on. I did want it a long time ago, but I can't anymore. It just hurts me when you bring up that old stuff, okay?" He looks down. I've hurt his feelings.

"Okay. Anything. For you, I'd do anything." He means it, too. I can tell from the thoughtful look on his face.

"Okay," I say. "I accept your offer. Friends," I announce and stick out my pinky.

"Friends," he repeats and he wraps his pinky around mine and we 'shake' on it. Live wires.

"I just have one rule, too," he says, cautiously.

"What?"

"You'll keep in touch with me now. Friend me on Facebook, or write me emails, or invite me to a book signing now and then. Put me on your Christmas list. Call me on the phone. Maybe you come visit me, or I get to come visit you. Let me be in your life again. Just, please, don't shut me out. I can't take it," he says, his voice shaky.

"Okay, I can handle that," I say with a slight smile—*as long as Donnie doesn't know.* Then I frown. His relief is suddenly gone. He notices my change in mood. I can't hide anything from him.

"I brought you something," he says. "It's on the porch."

"Do you want some coffee first?" I ask as I take out two cups from the cupboard. "How do you take it?"

"Black is fine."

"Oh, no. Not for me. I like a little cream and a half teaspoon of sugar in mine," I say, as I pour the dark black tincture into the faded china. "Thanks by the way," I say.

"It was my pleasure," he says, looking at me like he's smoldering inside. I have to look away or I'll liquefy for sure. I think he's breaking a rule, but I don't know which one.

Sipping from our cups, we walk out to the front porch. It's surprisingly warm out already. Right outside the front door leaning against the house is Dillon's granddaddy's courting dulcimer.

"Oh my gosh! I was just thinking about this when I was going up the trail!"

"You were?" he says, as he puts his coffee down on the little table in between the two porch chairs. "Do you want to play?"

"I don't think I remember," I say, in a nervous tone, sitting down.

"Seems like you were doing a great job remembering how to sing it yesterday on the horse," he says, shooting me a huge grin.

"Let me watch you a bit first. Is that okay?"

"Of course," he says, as he sits down and sets the gorgeous wooden instrument lying flat on his lap. It looks like two skinny guitars stuck together with little hearts in the corners. He crosses his legs resting his ankle on his knee and begins to play *Amazing Grace*.

I curl up on the chair, bringing my legs up to my chin and my coffee cup up to my nose before taking a much needed sip.

His nimble fingers tap the cords and then stretch in and out of a V formation, all the while strumming with his other hand. I hum the tune with him. It makes me feel so peaceful. Brings me to a time when things were simple—when life had grace and dignity. "Can I ask you something?" he says.

"Sure, I think."

"Are you seeing someone?"

"No." Before I can say anything else he's playing another song. "What's this one?" I ask.

"Green sleeves," he replies, caught up in the song. It's a sad song as if it's yearning for something or someone. I'm going to have to look up the lyrics. As he strums the ending, that hole in my chest starts to throb. It makes me uncomfortable. I'm glad that one is over.

"You'll probably remember this one. It's your momma's favorite," he explains as he starts to play a happy Irish tune. But just as soon as I think it's going to be happy, this one, too, starts to feel poignant and sad.

"Is it that you don't have relationships at all, or just with me?" he asks, looking up from his instrument.

"At all," I reply.

"Never?" he asks to clarify.

I look down, shake my head no. I look back up as he opens his mouth and begins to sing. I'd nearly forgotten his singing voice. It's a deep and light baritone and it does things to me—always has.

"Down by the Salley Gardens,
My love and I did meet.
She crossed the Salley Gardens
With little snow-white feet.
She bid me take love easy,
As the leaves grow on the tree,

But I was young and foolish,
And with her did not agree."

This song reminds me of a feeling—a memory that I can't place. His voice is soothing but powerful—tender in the right places too. He makes this old song sound almost contemporary and brand new.

Now that hole in my chest is throbbing, aching and unbearable. To top it off, my throat feels like it's closing up. I put my coffee down and stare at him from behind my knees. He doesn't see how distressing this is to me as his eyes are shut and he's strumming so attentively.

"In a field down by the river,
My love and I did stand
And on my leaning shoulder,
She placed her snow-white hand.
She bid me take life easy,
As the grass grows on the weirs
But I was young and foolish,
And now am full of tears."

As he strums the ending he looks so content, his eyes are closed and an easy smile is bringing up the corners of his mouth. Me, I'm a mess. The hole in my chest is aching and I'm shaking a little bit like when I'm cold on the inside. He opens his eyes and then gapes at me.

"Oh, no, Sadie," he says, and reaches over to me. "Are you okay?"

"It reminds me of the last time I saw you," I say from behind my knees, my voice quivering. He looks at me, lips pursed, blue eyes aching, as if to acknowledge that it means the same to him.

"I can't breathe." I shudder.

"Come here," he coaxes, putting the dulcimer down on the wooden porch.

I don't know what just happened but I want to curl up on his lap and let him soothe me. As I realize that's what I want, I'm already doing it. I put my arms around his neck and bury my face into his neck. My knees are pulled up to my chin again. "Just breathe, baby," he says, in a gentle tone as he gently rubs my back, my arm, my hair. *What the hell am I doing? The rules!*

It's as if I'm experiencing saying goodbye to him with all my senses since I was numb back when it really happened. It hurts and my scalp prickles. I feel hot but I'm shaking. I miss him but he's right here in my arms. It doesn't feel like it in my heart because it's throbbing.

After a time, my breathing starts to calm, no doubt by pacing mine to his, and I can put my legs down again. I keep the side of my face on his shoulder and take in his scent. I've missed this. It's like a scent created by God just for me and me alone.

He's still rubbing his hand up and down my back, his nose is in my hair. *Live wires* stroking my back is how it feels. We fit together like the two halves of one of those thin, cliché, half-heart pendants—still do. Everything feels right for the first time in, well, a very long time—a lifetime ago. But I'm embarrassed at the position I've put myself in. That's the only reason I want to get up.

Slowly, I move away from him, looking down so as not to catch his eyes. As I stand up he grasps my hands lightly, like he doesn't want to break contact with me.

"Do friends hug like that?" I ask, jokingly.

"These two do," he answers. He looks so serious as he sits there in the chair. "I guess my song had the opposite effect on you than what I'd predicted," he says, assessing my face to see if I'm okay. He speaks so differently now—so grown up.

"What was that called?"

"*Down by the Sally Gardens.* It's actually an old poem written by William Butler Yeats."

"Oh, it was life altering," I should have said it was *nice* but the words just tumble out of my mouth.

"Sadie!" Missy calls from inside the house.

"Yes! We're outside," I call.

Missy appears in the doorway. "Oh! Dillon. Back again so soon," she teases.

"I'm having a hard time staying away," he admits, looking up at me and letting go of my hands, which actually makes me sad. I need to make contact again. It hurts not to, so I rub the top of his hand with the edge of my pinky and he turns his hand over letting just the tips of our fingers touch. I don't look at him. I just feel.

"I smelled the coffee," Missy says, her voice jerking me into the now. I open my eyes, "Figured someone had to help this one here with making it." She looks lovingly at me.

"I think I could'a done it," I pout, and take my hand away from his.

"How about some breakfast," Missy says, slapping her knee. "I'll make us some flap jacks, sausage, eggs, you name it."

"Yes, please, minus the sausage for me," I say, looking at Dillon to see if he wants to stay.

"I'd love to," he answers my unstated question.

Chapter Eight

Sadie's Mountain

While Missy works in the kitchen and Dillon sits at the table with my two brothers and the babies, I fetch the tea and the paste I've made and creak up the stairs to momma's room. Her room smells like that medicine again. She's laying there so still, her breaths light like she's holding onto life from a thin thread.

Missy must have just been in here tending to her because the bags hanging from the metal pole look full and the ones on the bed look empty. I guess I should learn how to help with that.

I pull up the chair that is nestled in the corner of the room and open the Mason jar with the mixture I created this morning. Seeing Momma like this pricks a nice-sized scratch in my soul.

I just want to remember her young and feisty. She almost transforms back to her beautiful self as my stinging eyes fill with tears again. I wish she never had to get sick. Her skin looks very thin, almost see through. Her closed eyes remind me of delicate prunes covered in wet paper. I scoop out some goldenseal, pick up her weightless limb and begin to rub her hand and arm with it. Her skin wrinkles and slides around over her hollow bones. That's what wakes her.

"Sadie," she says, like there are marbles in her throat.

"Yes, Momma."

"You got me some yella root?"

"I found three good ones," I say, and smile a painful smile. One that cracks my façade.

"It feels better already, honey," she says, as she smiles dimly. Then she reaches her broken bird arm and points to the oil painting that hangs above her high boy dresser. "See that, Sadie. I painted that. Bet'cha didn't know that all these years."

"No, I didn't. I remember it though—from when I was little."

I get up and walk over to take a better look. My memory hadn't done this justice. It is Gauley Mountain. That's easy to tell. It's an impressionist painting kind of like one you would see from Degas' protégé, Mary Cassatt, if she'd found her way to our homestead. Women painters always seem to capture life in a different perspective, don't they? It's as if women see it for what it really is rather than what it should be.

The colors are vivacious—greens and reds, yellows too. And the strokes, carefree—like they don't care if anyone understands what they're supposed to mean when they're all together.

"It's beautiful, Momma," I say, in earnest.

"That's Sadie Mountain," she says, breathy.

"That's what you call the painting?" I ask.

"Yes, I painted that," her pause is long between breathes, "when I was carrying you," she says, as she strokes her stomach, her eyes far off like she's reliving the feeling of me being in there.

"Where were you when you painted it?"

"I'd lean up 'gainst the rock. The one that looks like a woman's face," she says, trying to catch her breath. "My momma would come take care'a Missy so I could paint."

"You don't have to talk Momma," I say, trying to get her comfortable again.

"No, I want ta tell ya."

"Okay."

"Doc Morris said I needed ta take it easy. All the miscarriages I done had, painting kept me calm. Helped me keep you with me," she says, as a wide smile takes over her sunken face. I had no idea why there was such a big age gap between me and Missy, and then me and the boys. This makes perfect sense. Momma had miscarriages and now she has uterine cancer.

"We can't let 'em do it, Sadie."

"Do what, Momma?"

"Blow up our mountain."

"Oh, yes, Momma. Dillon told me about that. I'm going to the meeting tonight at the school."

"You have to stop 'em."

"Of course. Of course, Don't worry about that. I'll do everything I can. Rest now, Momma."

"My mouth hurts," she says, after she takes a big, raspy breath.

"I brought you the tea," I say as I bring the cup to her lips. She takes some into her mouth and swishes. I give her another cup to spit in.

"I love you, little bean," she says. "Thank you for comin' back here. I know it's hard fer ya." A little tear wells up in her eye. I want to look away as it falls down her cheek.

"I love you, Momma. Nothing can keep me away from you now," I reassure her, as I stroke her hand.

"I wish things were diff'rent," she tries.

"It's fine. I'm glad I came. Rest now, Momma." She nods and closes her eyes in one swoop, and I rub her face gently in the same way she used to rub mine. I start at her forehead and sweep lightly across, down over her nose, over each cheek, and back around the same way several more times. She sighs peacefully in her sleep.

"Sadie," a voice says from the door. It's Seth when I turn around.

"Hi, Seth," I say, trying to sound like a nice person.

"Missy says it's breakfast time."

"Okay, thank you."

"What 'er you doing there?"

"I was just trying to soothe her. Help her sleep. I gave her some yellow root." He looks at me like I'm an alien from Planet Mean. I smile again and he frowns. *Ugg.* This kid really hates me.

"I had to go, Seth," I say before I realize I'm thinking it.

"I didn't care."

"I'm sorry I left you behind. I've been a crappy sister."

"Yeah, you have," he says, shocked that I'm being honest. He steps into the room and lightly starts tapping the footboard of the old metal bed with his sock-covered toe.

"I used to chase cars 'cause that's the way I remember you leaving. I thought you would be in one of 'em."

"How old were you?"

"'Bout four. Nobody could take me no where or I'd run off." The image of him, so little, just barely a child, chasing after cars because he thought he could find me. It hurts.

"I'm so sorry," I say as I reach out to rub his shoulder. "I had to get away. I was going crazy here," I explain.

"I know what happened," he says. "Missy told me." *Oh, that's a bit embarrassing.*

"If it's all the same to you, I'd rather not talk about it. It's real hard for me to…"

"Naw, it's cool," he says.

I look him in the eye and he does look like a big version of the little boy who stole my thunder when he was a baby. I was so used to getting all the attention. For ten years I was the baby and then he came home from the hospital. It's one of my most vivid memories. The key feeling that always comes to me is that of envy. It's the first time I'd ever felt really and truly jealous.

"Yours was the first diaper I ever changed," I say, as I pretend to elbow him in the rib. "Believe me. I wished it was my last." He pretends to be wounded and winces.

"Pretty good right elbow you got there, Sparks," he says, a grin finally pulling up the corners of his mouth, making his eyes sparkle.

"Let's eat," I say and we creak down the stairs and make our way to the breakfast table. Dillon is watching me the whole time. I start to feel like I'm growing a horn out of my head or something.

"How's your momma?" he asks. There's sadness in his tone. I just put my head down. *How is my momma?* Well, she just told me things about her I never knew. She told me about the vibrant oil painting being called Sadie's Mountain, that she painted it at our *real* kiss rock, about miscarriages, and she asked me to save the mountain.

"She wants me to help save Gauley Mountain," I reply. All the mouths open at the breakfast table at the same time. They look at me like I've got fire coming out of my ears.

"Oh, no she didn't!" Missy says.

"Yes, she did," I say, hurt.

"You can't be comin' over here buttin' into this, Sadie! This is a big huge fight you just shouldn't be getting' in the middle of."

I say nothing as I fork a pancake on my plate and slather real butter all over it. I look at Dillon. He, wisely, keeps quiet.

"These sure do look tasty," I say, trying to change the subject.

"Get some eggs, too, Sadie. You're too skinny as it is. Get another flapjack, too."

"I can't eat that much," I whine. Some things never change. No matter that we've been apart, we easily fall right back into the roles we played. I was the baby and she was the wanna-be mother. Being five years older than me, she always thought I was her baby. But I'm going to that meeting tonight. There's probably nothing I can do about it but I'll go and try. That's all anyone can do.

Dillon watches me during the whole meal. Our eyes meet now and then and we exchange smiles. He doesn't say much except to correct a sport statistic he claims Jake got wrong and to compliment the chef for her superb meal. I say next to nothing but I notice that Seth isn't looking at me like he hates me anymore. That's something—to say the least.

I help Missy clear the table and walk Dillon to the door.

"Are you kicking me out?" he asks with a big grin on his face.

"You're the one who walked over to the door after looking around like you had to go," I say.

"Can I take you somewhere today, Sadie?"

"Where?"

"It's a surprise."

I lean in and whisper, "To the town hall meeting about Gauley Mountain?"

"Yes," he says. "But before that, I had another idea."

"I'm game," I say, feeling every bit as feisty as I sound. *This is not like me at all.*

"I've got to go to work for a bit. But I can come get you in about two hours," he says, enthusiastically.

"What should I wear? Wait, this isn't a date, is it?"

"Not if you don't want it to be." *I guess he's not going to tell me.* "Wear what you've got on," he says, looking down at my faded jean shorts for a bit longer than is really needed to assess my attire. I feel like covering up behind a screen. I realize I don't have a scarf on over my scars. But he hasn't looked at me weird even once. No one here has, actually. I rub my throat and look at him with a new outlook.

"Two hours then," I say.

"Two hours," he says, as he walks down the porch steps. Two hours suddenly seems like a hundred years. This is just not normal to want to be with him every second of every minute. I yawn. *Maybe I should take a nap.*

Down the driveway, he's parked a white Toyota Prius Hybrid. I grin at him behind his back. So, he's an eco-guy; The TOMS and the Prius. I admit to myself right then that I want to get to know him again. We could be friends—like old times. Yeah, he scares me, but all guys do.

Maybe his brother won't even find out we're talking. I should find out if he'll be at that meeting for some reason. He's probably some coal-loving enthusiast just waiting to blow up the mountain— violate a beautiful, innocent, life force to take what he needs from it and leave it broken and empty. This feels very personal all of a sudden. Sudden wrath powers through my bloodstream at a rapid pace. *Not the mountain, too.*

Chapter Nine

Chemical Affinity

"**Y**ou didn't have to change," Dillon says, as I greet him at the front door.

"Well, I didn't want to go on a 'friendly-outing'," I say putting quotation marks in the air, "wearing those ancient jeans."

"You look…perfect," he says. I blush under his gaze.

"Thank you," I say, as I smooth my hands over my beige silk summer dress just above the knee and straighten my teal silk scarf. I push up the sleeves of the beige cardigan and watch his gaze move down to the teal espadrilles on my feet. I've got a beaded purse over one shoulder to hold my iPhone and some lip-gloss.

Instead of taking a nap, I'd brushed and curled my hair so I could wear it down. I purse my lip-glossed lips and bat my eyelashes. The way I'm feeling, I don't think I needed that pink blush.

"Thank you. So where are we going?" I ask.

"It's a mysterious place," he says, making his ghost story voice. I know it well. He used to love to tell me ghost stories or Moth Man stories when we were kids.

"So you're not going to tell me?" I ask as we stride down the steps and toward his Prius.

"Nope." He looks amused.

He opens the passenger door for me and I slide into the car. He goes around the back side and eases into his seat, turning the key.

"Is it on?" I ask. It feels like the engine isn't on, but I guess it's not. Not the gas part anyway.

"Yes, smart-mouth. It's on," he says, smugly.

He smells so good. Not like cologne. It's just his distinctive scent, the same since he was a kid. It does things to me. Brings back memories. His scent is the essence of kindness. But there's more now. I look at his hand resting on the gear shift and wonder what his hands would feel like on mine, running along my jaw line, scooping up my breast, running up the inside of my thigh...*Stop this!* I shake my head.

We drive for a bit in silence. Once in a while I peek up at him. I want to paint his image in my mind so well that it never becomes a driver's license photo in my mental file cabinet ever again. His straw colored hair glistening in the sun. His tan skin—the way it glows. The perfect arch of his thick eyebrows. The freckle on his right temple. I want to kiss that freckle. I shake my head again. *What is going on with me?*

He reaches over and with his long finger turns on the stereo, taps the iPod screen a few times to make his choice. Suddenly there's a soft piano that begins to enrapture me. Then a unique raspy, soulful woman's voice fills the car. She sounds familiar but I can't place her voice.

"Who is this?" I ask after a bit.

"Adele," he replies.

"Oh, yeah! I like her, *Rolling in the Deep,* right?"

"The very same," he says, as if he wants me to listen to the song instead of talk. It's about holding someone. It says *Make You Feel My Love,* on his iPod plugged into the dashboard. I listen closely as she sings. I look up at him through my lashes. He stares at the road, his expression impassive—maybe hopeful.

I sink into the seat and listen to Dillon's love song to me. I take in the aching sound of the violin as it cries to me, almost like a lone wolf howling in a low holler. He'll do anything for me. I know that now. Even if it hurts him and I don't want to hurt him. I want to give in—feel everything he has to offer. Let him make my dreams come true, as Adele says. But I can't.

A stinging tear falls down my cheek before I even knew I was going to cry. My lips twitch under the feelings so I hide behind my hair. He takes my hand carefully, silently.

He knows I understand him but he says nothing. I clutch his hand tightly as I let his song tell me all he wants to say. This isn't breaking the friend rules, really, since he isn't saying it's for me. I just know it is, that's all.

I think he knows music has always been the way to reach me. All the way back to when he let me put on that little musical on his front porch when I was six and he was nine. I wrote a script and everything. I made kids audition. No one really tried hard. I think they were just bored enough to let me have my way.

Out of habit, I hold my breath as we drive over New River Gorge Bridge.

"You still do that?" he says, when he notices I'm not breathing. I nod yes and wipe my cheeks. "Okay, I'll do it, too," he says, as he takes a deep breath and his cheeks turn into a balloon.

Before the oxygen is cut off from our brains we're over the hurdle and I want to curl up in his lap again. The lump has shown up in my throat. The lump makes me mad because it reminds me of Donnie.

"How's your family?" I ask nonchalantly as if I'm trying to make small talk so I'll stop crying.

"Mom's good. She's still at the house down a bit from you all. Donnie..." I wince and my hand twitches in his hand. He stops for a second and looks at me, confused, "...He's married. I have two nephews. One's eight and the other's just a two year old. The kids, they're great. The best reason to go over there is to see my momma and the grand youngins as she calls 'em."

"They live with her?" I say, astonished. *He's that close.* I realize my whole body is stiff. Dillon looks at me puzzled. My body is talking to him. Whispering my secrets. I open my hand and he lets go.

"Donnie moved back. Momma needed help with the house. She didn't want to sell or rent it out. Might end up with one of the Whites moving in or something." I laugh. The Whites of West Virginia must still be pretty famous around these parts.

"They still raising hell?" I say, my façade coming into place.

"As far as I can tell. Rumors are that they're still shooting each other, drinking, snorting pills, just like always."

"Who's your source?" I ask with a playful wink.

"Donnie's in charge of the Ansted Police Department now. Runs the place and his two officers like they're in the military. He's heard some stuff about 'em."

I look up at him, shaken. "Yeah, hard to believe, huh. He came back from his tour in Iraq and took over when old Roemer retired about two years ago."

Adele is singing another song about always loving me. As the guitar croons I'm oscillating in a complete stupor.

I have no thoughts.

I'm blank for quite a while.

I can't even think about the situational irony here. My rapist is the Chief of Police. The Chief of Police! I almost can't stay in my seat. I grasp the door handle as if—what? Am I going to jump to my death? I just feel like I can't breathe again. The hole in my chest feels like it's growing to monumental proportions. Like everything on the inside of me is scratching to get out.

In the background I hear Dillon talking about his nephews and his sister in law. Nothing he says really registers in the thought processing part of my brain since my body is a shaking mess. I just make "Uh-huh," noises so he doesn't think I'm ignoring him.

"Sadie, what's wrong?" he says, concern etched into his forehead. *Oh, it's okay. I'm good at this.* I just turn my voice up to that sweet spot.

"I'm fine," I say, blinking at him. That look says he doesn't believe me. "We're here," he says, pulling up to the famous Mystical Gravity Tunnel I saw when I drove up yesterday.

"Oh! We're going in there?"

"Unless you don't want to," he says, concerned again.

Oh, good. No, this will be a good change of pace. I can't sit here realizing a rapist is in charge of the police department anymore. It makes me, what? It makes me MAD! That's what this is. I'm freaking furious. I get out of the car and slam the little light door way harder than is needed to close it. I stomp in the direction of the metallic wolf guarding the metal building.

"If I tell you the secret will you calm down?"

"What secret?" I say, breathless as I pace back and forth like a ravenous animal in a cage. Where's Numb Girl? She'd come in handy right about now. I don't know this feeling I'm having right now. I don't know what to do with all of these raging thoughts. I want to kill Donnie, rip him to shreds with my bare hands, boil his bones in hot water and watch him scream. Tell him *'Good boy'* when I'm done with him.

When I look up Dillon seems absolutely helpless. "About how the Gravity Tunnel works," he offers, uncertainly.

There's just too many emotions battling in me right now. The only thing I can do is throw my head back and laugh. It's a hard belly laugh—a stress reliever. I think I'm going to pee my pants if I don't stop laughing. I try holding the laugh in and that makes me just keep giggling. I think I'm doing the pee-pee dance.

Dillon is on the fence. He's part amused with that grin but then he's also confused, hence the body language, hands up as if to show he's no threat to me.

"No, I'd rather it stay mystical," I say as I suppress the rest of my giggles by biting my thumbnail. "I need a restroom."

"I thought you might," he says dryly but then that grin comes back. *My faults make him love me more.*

"This doesn't make any sense," I say as I stand at an odd angle, my ankles tilted to the right, and watch Dillon climb the wall on the other end of the room as if he's Spiderman. He was always good at climbing things—especially our favorite tree down by Rich Creek, the one that looked like a magic tree. The limbs were low enough that even I could climb it.

"I told you I'd tell you the secret," he says, and turns around to face me, just his heels holding onto the edge of the wall bracket.

I shake my head no.

"Do you want to try the chair?" he asks.

"Okay," I say, cautiously.

"Have a seat," he says, and motions to the chair near the corner of the room. I sit down and he walks in front of me, so I cross my ankles. "Put your arms on my shoulders," he says, as he bends down and grips his hands under the bottom of the seat.

"Haven't we broken enough rules?" I ask.

"It's just so you don't fall," his breath warm in my face. I close my eyes and experience his fragrance, feel the warmth of his body, imagine his scent and mine mingling in the air between us as if our auras were tangible things ready to coexist.

I place my arms on his shoulders and wrap my hands around his neck. Live wires again. He doesn't move and I don't open my eyes. "Do you feel it?" he says.

When I open my eyes he's smoldering again. I say nothing but I let my eyes say yes for me. He smiles and picks up my chair with me in it. "The Laws of Attraction," he says, as he effortlessly sticks me to the Spidey wall and I feel like I have to lean into the back of the chair. In this moment, we are not talking but it seems like our bodies are—like they are speaking on their own frequency.

"It's called Chemical Affinity," he says, his voice deep and controlled. "Attraction is something studied in science but completely unpredictable. You see, there is no real reason why one atom is drawn to another other than one is positively charged and the other negatively charged."

"Yes," I acknowledge. He doesn't step back and I leave my hands entwined around his neck. My knees are pressing against his chest with my feet dangling.

"Sometimes an atom will come in proximity to another atom and there is just this huge explosion as they fly into one another. Marriages happen in the world of atoms for no other reason than certain molecules are attracted to others."

My body gets warm and I start to tremble all over like there's something unseen between us completely intangible but very real, very powerful, and as old as the beginning of time. My breathing increases its tempo, so does his. My heart is pounding to a new rhythm.

It's been ten years since I've wanted this, but I want to kiss him so badly I begin to ache for him. That little rosebud deep in my stomach, deadened by years of neglect, is slowly rising causing growing pains.

I lean forward because I can't help it—because we are two atoms drawn together, one positively charged and one negatively. He moves the chair to the peg below so that I'm forced to open my knees and reach up to his mouth. When we come together it's like a force of fervor ignites between us as our teeth clash together momentarily.

I kiss him like I need him, because right now I do. He kisses me like he wants to crawl inside me, to be one with me. We're all hands and mouths and tongues moving together in unison, making up for all the years of kisses that haven't happened. I forgot what this felt like for real.

"Hmm—hmmm!" someone clears their throat loudly. I gasp, pulling away from him and then remember where we are. We are both out of breath.

"This kind of thing is not allowed here!" says the man who owns the place in an irritated tone. "Please, put the lady down and be on your way, Dillon."

Dillon is staring into my eyes. Tahoe blues. "Just give us a moment, please," he says, as he pulls my chair from the wall, never taking his eyes off mine, and sets me to the tilty floor.

He helps me up and it's not just the gravity defying floor that has me unable to get my footing. I start to blush and hide myself under his arm. I can hear his heartbeat through his shirt.

"I'm so sorry," Dillon says to the owner, looking away from me for the first time. I take a breath. I can't look at the man. I feel like I just got sent to the Principal's office.

"Please, just don't come back," he says, disgustedly.

Embarrassment starts to really settle in as we're outside and Dillon's proximity isn't such a drug anymore. I walk with my head down and start twisting my fingers together in knots like how my stomach feels.

"Please, don't do this, Sadie," Dillon says, with pain visible on his beautiful face.

"Do what?"

"Turn this into something bad or wrong," he says, as I shrug my shoulders, lean against his car and put my head down. He walks toward me until I see his TOMS right in front of my teal espadrilles. He puts his fingers under my chin and eases me up to his gaze. "That was beautiful, Sadie. It wasn't wrong. Not for us. Don't feel guilty, please."

I wiggle free from his hand under my chin and he steps back to give me space.

"I can't do this," I say.

Dillon's knees buckle under him and he puts his hands to his head.

"Don't, don't say this. Please. It won't happen again. I'll, I'll stay ten feet away from you at all times. I'll do anything. Please. Don't shut me out!"

"I have no control over myself right now, Dillon. This is just exactly the type of erratic behavior I try to avoid. My life is normally very controlled. I plan everything, every decision, every action. For the past two days I've been on some other planet being controlled by the moon or something."

"I'm sorry," he says.

"We had rules this morning and I'm the one breaking them. I'm not used to this. I'm all over the place emotionally. Happy one moment, crying the next, angry, hysterical with laughing fits, and then this, kissing you. If we'd been alone who knows," I say, looking around bewildered.

"Would that be so wrong? It's not like we're strangers. This is what happens between two people who have feelings for one another, who have history like we do. It was nice, right?" His voice is sweet like candied yams.

"I don't know what to say."

"I know you're scared, confused. I don't want to cause you pain. We don't have to decide anything right now, Sadie. Look, let me just get you some dinner and then we can head over to the meeting. I promise no more fireworks. I'll stay clear. Give you space." He makes the little bubble around himself like I did last night.

"Okay," I say, opening the car door for myself so he can't get too close. This isn't going like I planned. Well, I'd planned on none of this—so no surprise I guess.

"Where are we going?" I ask as he slides into the seat next to me.

"It's a cool place in Fayetteville called the Cathedral Café."

"Cathedral?"

"Yeah, it used to be an old Methodist church. It's beautiful. Stained glass windows, original old floor and everything."

He must know about my antique collections.

"They don't have dinner every night but the owner is a friend of mine. She's going to make something special for you."

"Am I missing something?"

"Vegetarians are a bit hard to feed around here." He utilizes that knee-weakening smile.

"What's my meal to be then?"

"Can I surprise you?" I feign a pout and smirk at him. He smiles again. He can really keep up with my mood. And I've been wretched today.

Chapter Ten

Beautiful Flaws

We pull up to the Cathedral Café and it really is an old church. "It's beautiful with its flaws, isn't it," I say as I get out of the car and look up at the brown stone building, very old with a stone column branded with two white crosses leading up to a steepled tower. That's why I like antiques. They have a past. They aren't perfect. But I love them because of their flaws, because of the history of the piece, or maybe because of a funny story about how I found it. This building feels full—not empty and unimportant like most contemporary buildings.

One whole side of the church is a living wall covered in ivy. The sign that hangs near the door looks like the band Sublime's album with the sun on it—kind of hippyish. *That's it. Dillon is a new hippie.* The kind that eats at old Methodist churches, wears TOMS, and drives a Prius.

"What are you smiling about?" he asks me.

"You." He raises an eyebrow at me.

"You're a hippie!" I say, trying to keep a straight face.

"Well, I hadn't thought about myself that way. But I guess you're right," he says, and smiles his crooked shy smile. As he gets to the steps he motions with his left arm and lets me go first. It's obvious he's being overly mindful of my personal bubble.

On the landing he comes up behind me; his warmth and his scent linger for a moment as he reaches the door, opening it for me. A perfect gentleman. This place smells amazing, like onions and garlic, hearty soup, or pizza baking. I'm suddenly famished and I lick my lips. There's soft instrumental music playing over some hidden speakers. It's very calm in here.

Behind the long counter a young woman wearing an apron waves at Dillon. She's pretty, with dark curly hair piled on her head, delicate features. She looks at me and stretches her arm out to shake hands.

"Sadie, this is my friend, Liz. Liz, Sadie," he says.

"So nice to finally meet you," she says, with a little gleam in her eye.

I wonder what she means about 'finally.'

"I've made you something special. Dillon says you're a vegetarian and I love a challenge." She motions to take a table. There is no one else here so Dillon picks the one in between the two huge stained glass windows.

"Great! What did you make me?" I ask as Dillon pulls my chair out for me.

"Roasted veggie raviolis with garlicky Alfredo and grilled shrimp—minus the shrimp for you, of course," she says, as I sit and Dillon pushes in my chair.

"That sounds sinfully good." *Fattening, but sinfully good.*

"Good thing you're in a church so you can repent in advance," she says, with a chuckle. "Wine?" she asks.

I look at Dillon. "White wine for me," he says as he sits down. "Sulfite free if you have any."

"I'll have the same," I say. *Sulfite free?* I giggle again.

Liz comes back with some bread and raw veggies, hummus, and olive oil with vinegar. "Thanks," Dillon says as he watches my expression. *This looks good! Definitely my kind of spread.*

As I pick up a long zucchini stick and dip it in the hummus I take a look around. It's lit with several hanging chandeliers, but it's actually dim inside making the blue slatted walls look darker than I think they really are. The ceiling is high and steep, covered in old white tin tiles. The floor is old and imperfect, making it perfect in my opinion. There are walls of books and local art, almost like a library or an art gallery got mixed together.

I saw them when we first walked in but, the two stained glass windows are as tall as the wall, like long rectangles with slightly pointy tops enhanced with beige wood. In the middle, the dominant colors of yellow and a deep red diamond pattern are absolutely dazzling to the eye. It's both calming and exciting at the same time—kind of like Dillon.

"It's beautiful in here," I say. "For a church," I qualify as I feign an eye roll.

"For a church?" he asks, his voice deeper than normal.

"I'm an agnostic. I haven't been to church since I was fifteen." He nods, slightly surprised it seems with the way he's pursing his lips.

He was there. He knows what my dad said about me that night. How he blamed me for getting raped. Said it was my fault. That I'd tempted the dirt bag. That it was my sinful thoughts that lead to it. The sickest part is that I believed him for so long.

"You don't have to explain, but, please, Sadie, don't be so sad. This is a nice place and I want you to be able to enjoy it."

"I kind of want to explain," I say, looking at him to see if he can take it. If I can be honest with him. I'd always told him everything when we were kids. He was the best friend I've ever had.

"If that will make you feel better," he says and motions toward me to say it's my turn. I look at the window before I start to talk again.

"I guess you could say religion got tied up with *my attack* on a very deep, unconscious level," I explain. "So, I started hating myself. Blaming myself. I went into such a deep depression thinking that God punished me, that he let that happen to me on purpose to teach me not to have certain thoughts about you." I look up at him.

He fidgets in his chair. His mouth is in a thin line and then he puts his fisted hand up to his mouth. His chest is tight like he's holding something in. His eyes look like someone's set fire to his feet.

Liz pours the wine. It startles him. But he recovers and takes a sip. "It's great. Thank you," he says with a tight smile. She trots back to the kitchen. He looks back to me, pained.

"I never left my house at all—but I'm sure you know that. What you don't know is that Daddy would come in and preach, sometimes. A lot of times, he whipped me." Dillon winces and looks away from me. I start playing with a knot mark on the table top.

"I couldn't really hear his voice when he preached at me, pounding his fist in his Bible. Momma'd try and talk me into going to school or ask me to go ride Monty. But I'd just lie there on my bed looking out the window. Or sometimes I'd sit in the chair and look out the window. I didn't really eat or sleep. I just laid there until summer turned to fall." Dillon's face is surely proof that he's imagining me in that state. He looks miserable.

"One day, Daddy came bursting in the room with his belt. He was screaming about the devil of silence. How it was a demon keeping me from talking. He started whipping me again—my arms, my stomach, the tops of my thighs." Dillon's other hand moves to the side of the table like he's holding on during a scary ride.

"It'd seemed like the whip marks had just healed up from the last time he'd done it. It didn't even hurt, though. It felt like it was just a husk he was hitting, not me. Momma came in the room and she pushed him away from me. I wasn't even fighting back. I was just lying there. I must have looked so pathetic to her—maybe she thought I was dead. In a way I was." Dillon fidgets in his chair again. He squeezes the table so hard I think he could crack the wood.

"So, she packed my bag. Daddy was screaming about my soul and the demons in me. She told him that he needed to let me go. She said Aunt Lotty could help me more. If it was a demon it probably wouldn't follow me all the way to California. That seemed to make sense to him so he agreed. It wasn't until I got there that she helped me see that it wasn't my fault. That I didn't deserve it. That took years, actually. She even took me to church but I just felt like I was being judged in there. But never with Aunt Lotty. In her house I flourished. I started writing then. She brought me back. She's a wonderful woman. Really, truly is. I think she saved my life."

"I'm glad you went then," he says. His voice is shaky and he's still holding onto the side of the table. His chest is still tight. He can't look at me. "I'm thankful that she helped you, even though I lost you because of it." I look down.

"I have to tell you," he says, "sometimes I hate your daddy for what he did to you." He's watching my hand as I rub my finger over the knot in the wood. "When I found you in the creek I should have brought you to my house or took you somewhere."

Taking me to his house would have been worse—deadly.

"I have a lot of guilt for touching you, and then for not finding you when you needed me. I was running around looking for you when you were getting..." his voice hitches and can't finish. He squeezes the table even harder.

"You have nothing to be guilty for," I explain. He looks at me and then looks away.

"The images in my head from that night," he stops to swallow the emotions stuck in his throat, "they've haunted me all these years." I wince thinking of what he saw.

"Tell me," I whisper. He looks at me for a moment as if to see if I'm serious. I square my shoulders and look him in the eye like I'm on a job interview. "It's just that there are pieces missing and it might help me to put it all together. It helps me feel in control, like I'm not some victim anymore." He nods his head yes as if he's building up the courage to speak the memory. Liz pops out of the kitchen to bring our plates.

"Everything okay with the hummus and veggies?" she asks.

"Oh, sorry. We've just been catching up. It's been a long time since we've seen each other," Dillon explains. That makes her feel better. "Can I box it up for you?"

"Oh, yes, please!" I say. "I love hummus." She smiles.

"It's fresh. I made it about an hour ago." I smile at her.

When she leaves, Dillon says, "I'll tell you, Sadie, but under one condition—actually two."

"Okay?"

"First, you have to eat while I'm talking. I don't want you starving when you go to this meeting tonight and second, I want you to promise me that you will stop me if anything I say is too much for you."

"Okay."

"Like, maybe you can think of a safe word. When you say it I'll stop."

"How 'bout 'stop'?"

"I'm serious. I don't want you to be sitting here enduring it if it's not helping you in some way like you said it will."

"Is it that bad?" I ask.

He bites his lip, his chest even tighter, puts his hand into a fist on top of the table. "Yes," he says, his voice deep and indignant.

"Okay, I'll tell you to stop." He waits. I'm waiting. He looks at my plate. *Oh, he wants me to follow rule one.* So I cut one of the raviolis with my fork and put it in my mouth. It tastes of cream, artichokes, spinach, carrots, oregano, fresh basil, sundried tomatoes. It's like a foodgasm. I groan, and with my mouth full I say, "It's so good."

He smiles fervently and his eyes squint and sparkle. He relaxes his chest and his fist turns back into a hand. That pleases him— seeing me happy, I think.

"Can we do this later?" he asks, suddenly buoyant. "I'd love nothing more than to just enjoy our meal together."

"Of course," I agree.

We sip wine and smile once in a while between bites. We don't talk. We just enjoy our food and the music. I think that's the beauty of a friendship like ours. We aren't afraid to be quiet sometimes.

We used to do this when we were kids. I'd be at his house or he at mine and we'd be doing completely different things—like I'd be working on some math homework and he'd be playing his harmonica or reading those science-type books. We just liked being in the same room together. No one had to impress or entertain the other. We could just be.

I like this—I like him. Not just the him from before, this him, now. I start to feel warm all over as I look at him. He's so beautiful. I love how he shakes his fork up and down twice each time before he puts food in his mouth to make sure nothing drops. It's so cute, and endearing. Some things never change. I wonder why he looks so far away in thought. And that grin?

"What are you thinking about?"

"You really want to know?"

"I think so."

"I'm thinking about that kiss," he says, and my tummy clenches. I blush at his mischievous smile.

"Well, I was thinking about how we used to just hang out sometimes not talking. How we could always be ourselves with each other." He nods his head yes as he takes a bite of bread.

"Both of us are thinking about the same thing, really."

"What do you mean?"

"'Bout all the reasons we are so good together."

"I think you're breaking a rule," I admonish, but I grin and he relaxes.

Before I know it, my plate is nearly licked clean. I look at his and his looks the mirror image of mine. "Excuse me," he says and scoots back and takes the ticket to the counter.

While he's paying the bill and chatting with Liz at the register, I actually take the bread and swipe it across the plate so I can enjoy the last little drop of that delectable sauce.

"Thank you," I say when he comes back.

"The pleasure was mine, Miss Sparks." The truth is, I think he really means it—selfless as he is with me.

"We'd better go. I don't want to be late. I have a small part to play as one of the presenters. Are you ready?"

"One of the presenters?" I ask as he pulls my chair out for me.

"Yep."

"Just what do you do, Mr. Dillon Mcgraw?"

"To put it simply, I'm an algae scientist," he says, as he opens the door for me.

An algae scientist? What the hell is that? And what does algae have to do with mountaintop coal mining?

I ponder that all the way to the car.

"Can I ask you something?" Dillon asks once we're back on the road.

"Depends," I say, looking up at his clenched jaw.

"Okay. It can wait."

Oh, it was one of those personal questions he's been asking all day.

He turns on the stereo and I wonder if he's planning on asking me the question with a song since that's not forbidden in my friend rules.

A lovely, slow guitar begins to echo within the car. It's Adele again. His iPod says *Don't you remember*. I look up at him. His eyes never leave the road. His expression is impassive—slightly distressed, maybe.

"Don't you like any other musicians?" I tease.

"She shares my angst—in this album, especially." He looks at me briefly, so sad, so confused.

Adele sings about being left abruptly. I find myself having a conversation with the song—with Dillon. *I'm sorry I didn't say goodbye. I'm so sorry I made you sad. Of course, I remember. I've never forgotten you.* It's building and building.

You did nothing wrong. I remember—everything. I do. I do love you. The missing piece, why we cannot be together cannot bring me back to you. Her voice gets louder, and he starts to sing along. *Yes, of course I remember why I loved, love you.* That's what the song is asking. I'm pinned to the seat. This hurts. The hole in my chest pinches from the inside out. Knowing how confused he is about why we can't be together the way he wants, especially after today.

I've given him so many mixed signals. I've climbed onto his lap. I've kissed him. My body has betrayed me so many times. After that kiss today there's no doubt that we have a chemistry I've never experienced—not since I was fourteen.

We're drawn together like perfectly matched atoms. For that brief moment, his lips made me forget all of my fears, my hang ups. This is the first time in my adult life that I've had a glimmer of hope for a full, and yes, fulfilling life with a man. This is what they call cohesion. The Law of Attraction in full swing.

With him life would have been perfect—in a perfect world, not the world we live in. It would have been untainted and real. I wouldn't even have to think. It would be as easy as breathing pure, clean air into my lungs on a warm evening.

But there's more—always more. How do I explain the aspect of danger to him? How do I show him that I'm protecting him, too, without telling him and getting him hurt? This is such a shadow over my life—a heavy burden. These are my thoughts as I listen to his feelings played out through another's soulful—mournful voice. This is what I need to say as I watch the trees until they become blurs…

I'm not sure how long we've been driving. I must have dozed off in the car. He's holding my hand. I haven't opened my eyes yet, but his warm hand in mine feels just right. The car is filled with his scent. It's warm in here. Perfect. I don't want to move.

"Wine always makes me sleepy," I say, as I open my creaky eyes. He chuckles.

"What?" I ask.

"You talk in your sleep."

"Huh?"

"I didn't know that. Last time we slept together I think you were five and I was eight," he says.

"What'd I say?"

"You mumbled, mostly," he says, but smiles too wide to be telling me everything.

"What else did I say?" I demand, my tone impatient.

"Ah, we're here," he says, as he looks for a parking space. The dimly lit parking lot is packed. He's not going to tell me what I said. What was I thinking about when I fell asleep? I'll worry about that later. I'm looking for a police car. Scanning for a demon behind the wheel.

"Who are you expecting to be here?" I ask, obviously nervous.

"Well, everyone who cares about Gauley Mountain is probably going to be here and everyone that wants to blow the top off the mountain, too."

As I get out of the car I feel unsafe like I want to hide under something so I grab Dillon's arm as I look around like deer-meat in an open field. He stops and tucks my hand into his arm like men and women used to do in times gone by. "Don't be nervous," he says. "I'll be right here."

Who will? He's going to be here. My own private boogie-man. I've had nightmares about him for almost half my life and it feels like I'm about to walk into one right now.

Chapter Eleven

The Hell Mouth

Walking up to the door of the auditorium tucked under Dillon's arm like a baby bird, I think about a guest professor who gave a lecture in Dr. Sander's Women's Lit course my third year at Berkley. He was talking about the Hell Mouth—an image that became popular in old Europe during the Anglo-Saxon time.

From a sinner's point of view, the hell mouth was a monster that would devour one's body as they entered. *"Christians believe that their bodies will rise again during the coming of Christ. Only then will they be granted entrance to heaven."* I'd heard this many times. But, as the guest professor explained, if the person went into the hell mouth there would be no body to rise when Christ came back for them.

It was an excellent fear tactic. If you aren't good and do as you're told, your body will be devoured and you will never reach eternity. The idea of the lack of anything in the afterlife is almost worse than the idea of burning in hell for all eternity, which is what I'd been taught.

Something comparable to the hell mouth was promised to me, I realize. I'm not allowed to have a relationship with Dillon or my body, in pieces—no less, is promised to be buried in Donnie's yard. All these years, the image of me in pieces, in a location unknown to anyone, always made me feel vacant, desolate, and embittered, just as, I'm sure, the Christians in old Europe felt when they were threatened similarly.

Showing up with him means I'm breaking that rule and there's nothing I can do about it now.

I shudder as I cross the threshold of this brick building with the too large AMS on the façade. The auditorium smells of bouncy balls, old rubber shoes, and cheap coffee. It's like being in a dream standing here inside the busy room. Dillon looks down at me as if he's unsure of what I'm thinking. I know he feels me trembling next to him.

"Are you okay?" I nod yes, but I'm not really breathing.

"I'm just nervous."

"Why, baby?" He tips up my chin to examine my eyes. It's always been his way of trying to read me. I purse my lips so they won't tremble.

"I'm not good with crowds," I lie. He doesn't believe me. I can see his disbelief as he scans the crowd inside the room with us. He's seen my blogs; fans, readers, or parents and children boxing me in behind a table during a signing, or surrounding me during a book reading. "Is there someone here you don't want to see?"

"No," I say, unconvincingly. I know what he's asking me is: *"Is your rapist here?"*

I'm afraid to look around but when I do, that's when I see him. The embodiment of all my ills is standing near the podium ready to make an announcement. He looks different—thinner, cleaner, more authoritative in his uniform. His dark hair, no longer messy and untamed, is combed backward like a black slide. His face is more rugged, but if he wasn't a monster underneath, I would say he's bad-boy attractive—*like Ted Bundy was.* His arms are stout, muscular and his stomach is now flat and narrow in comparison to his heavy broad shoulders. He hasn't seen me yet. He's looking down at something on the podium.

"Sadie, do you want to go say hi?" Dillon says, as I stare at his brother.

"No," I say, almost a whisper. "Don't you have to go get ready?" I ask, because I just want to be away from him before Donnie sees us and realizes we're together.

"They already have my PowerPoint. That's what I was doing today when I left." He looks confounded. I'm looking around, eyes darting all over the place for somewhere to hide.

Okay. He's not going to let me hide somewhere in the back row.

I move a bit to position him between Donnie and me thinking that he can block me from view. "I don't want anyone to see me." I lean over and put my hands on my knees. "I'm having a panic attack." That's true. I am.

"Do you need me to take you home?" he says, leaning down and taking me under his arm again.

"Yeah, I think this was a mistake." Just as I say that, I bristle. I feel him before I see him. Donnie stands next to Dillon leering over me as if I've just broken the law—his law.

"Dillon, what'cha got here?" Donnie says—his voice like poison wrapped in a sugar coating. I have no idea what is holding me together at this moment. I guess it's fear. I know that if I'm not calm, Dillon will notice my reaction and he might piece it together.

"Donnie, you surely recognize our old neighbor, Sadie," Dillon says, proudly letting go of me to shake his brother's hand. I'm dizzy and put my arms out slightly to gain my equilibrium.

"Of course. How could I ever forget Sadie?" Donnie says, mockingly. I'm so conscious of how I look right now, trying to keep a straight face, i.e. not looking like I'm being raped all over again. "Come 'ere, girl, and give your old friend a hug," he says, reaching his bear paws toward me. He smells of too strong, almost sour, cologne. I gasp and nearly trip over myself to get to Dillon.

Protect me, please.

"Donnie," Dillon says, putting his arm in front of me protectively, "Sadie doesn't really like to be touched."

"Sure does look like yur touchin' her to me," he says, his tone stern—jealous.

"I think the difference is, she was my best friend all our lives. She's a little more comfortable with me. Just back off," Dillon says. He looks shocked.

"You know, 'Ol Len over at the Gravity Tunnel gave me a call today," he says, widening his stance and wrapping his chest in a fist clenched, crossed-arm sweater. "Said you had some woman pushed against the wall in a compromising position—if he hadn't come in when he did, he said, you two would a' been naked in a minute or so. Sound familiar?"

"Look, that's none of your business," Dillon says, his voice like steel.

"Everything that happens in this town is my business." He looks at me like I'm a delinquent child. "Everything you do comes back on me, Dillon, and I got a reputation to uphold." Oh, so he's making this about Dillon doing something wrong to hide the fact that he's jealous. He's good at this turning tables crap.

"If you'll excuse me," I say, and walk on wobbly legs to the restroom sign. When I turn back, the two of them look like they're in a standoff. Donnie, obviously the bigger of the two, isn't being too smart right now. Dillon is in his face. Donnie's pointing a finger like a weapon. His temper is getting him in trouble. If he doesn't want his secret out, he needs to get a hold of himself, quickly.

I push the bathroom door open and turn on the sink. I splash my face with water, and rub it on my steaming neck when the door opens. A pretty blonde is standing for a bit too long in the mirror behind me. It's like she's trying to place who I am. I don't recognize her.

"Sadie Sparks?" she says, in a too sweet voice.

"Yes," I say, as I turn around and pump out a paper towel to dab my face with. She's a tall, leggy blonde in beige pants, a pink striped top, and pink high heeled shoes. Very pretty. Older than me—probably around Missy's age. "Can I help you?" I ask, unsure if I'm supposed to remember her on my own.

"I'm Claire. Claire Robbins," she says, stretching out her arm tipped with pink polished nails on the end of slender fingers.

Oh, god! Dillon's girlfriend.

I try to feign a smile, but I'm sure it looks faker than usual. "It's so nice to meet you. I've heard so much about you," I say, grasping her soft hand before dropping it quickly. I don't look her in the eyes. That's a mistake. It makes me look guilty.

"Have you?" she says. "From who?" Her voice is sharp, like a teacher catching me in a lie.

"Oh, uh, Dillon and I ran into each other on the mountain yesterday. And my brother Jake told me you're his English teacher," I say, obviously nervous. *Why am I so nervous? I don't owe her an explanation.*

"Yes, Jake's a good kid…when he comes to class."

I shake my head. What do you say to your whatever-Dillon-is-to-me's girlfriend?

"How long are you in town?" she asks, as she moves her weight from one foot to the other making her hip stick out like girls did back in my California high school before a bitch-slap.

"Just until…well, my mom's sick. Cancer. She has cancer. It won't be long now," I say looking around the bathroom. "I'm leaving after the wake."

"I'm sorry to hear that," she says. I'm unsure what she's sorry about. My mom being sick or me being here that long.

"Well, it was nice to meet you." *I want out of here.* Is there no escape route for jealousy around here?

"So, Dillon. He knows you're here?" she asks before I take my second step.

"Yes, he brought me to the meeting," I say, turning back around. Let's just get that out on the table. I'm sick of hiding. Secrets have been my life. It's like I've been hauling someone else's crime around with me in a crusty duffle bag for ten and half years.

She burns holes through me with her eyes. "Do you think it's fair," she fumes, "leading him on like this?"

"I'm not leading anyone on. Dillon and I are just friends. He knows that."

"Does he?" she challenges.

"We talked about it yesterday, and this morning. That's all we've ever been is friends, Claire."

"Not to him! To him, you are *his* ideal woman. No one will ever compare." Her hand is on that hip now and she's leaning forward, getting in my face.

"I know you're upset, but this isn't about me. This is about the fact that you've fallen for him and he doesn't feel the same way about you. That's between you and him. So if you'll excuse me," I say as I turn around. Before I take another step, she grabs my arm. I try to yank it away but she holds tight, her pink nails dig into my flesh.

"Did he tell you that?" She's yelling now. Her face is bright pink like her nails.

"Not in so many words but he's explained your…arrangement. I think he's been honest with you about his feelings—or at least that's the way he explained it to me. This is a conversation you two need to have together. Now let go of my fucking arm!" *Wow! Where did that come from?* I don't like to be held captive. Old wounds like that just never heal.

There's a knock on the door. "Sadie?"

It's Dillon.

"Are you okay in there?"

I yank my arm away and walk toward the door, but Pink Girl grabs the door first and opens it so fast the corner of the door smacks me in the face. I see Dillon, mouth gaping open, surrounded by little white sparks as I grasp my head in my hands.

"What are you doing, Claire?" Dillon yells, as he takes me into his arms, tilts my chin up and checks my forehead for a cut with the tip of his gentle thumb.

"I'm getting the hell out of here," she screams at him.

"Yes, I think you should. You're making a fool of yourself," he says, as he hugs me consolingly, protectively.

"Ouch," I whine.

"I'm not going to sit here and watch her lead you on."

"She's not leading me on. She's been very honest with me about what kind of relationship she can handle."

"I'm the one who's going to have to pick up the pieces when she leaves." She's pointing at me with that pointy pink nail.

She's right. I'm going to go home and Dillon will be devastated. What if I don't leave?

"No, you won't. I think you're confusing me with someone else," he says, his eyes stinging into hers.

"That's a low blow," she whispers, tears now streaming down her face. "Bringing up my dead husband…" She's shaking her head.

I do not want to be here. They should talk in private. Dillon is holding me up. I feel too dizzy to walk.

"No, you're right. I shouldn't have said that. But I think you've read more into our arrangement than was actually there."

"So, you're making your choice?" she fumes, tapping the tip of her pink shoe on the floor.

"There's never been a choice to make. It's her. It's always been her. I'm sorry if you ever thought otherwise." His voice is clear, concise.

She turns to me, "Little girl. You'll never be able to do the things to him in bed that I do."

She's right. They are probably great together. She's tall like him. Passionate. His equal in every way.

I look up at Dillon. He's not looking at her anymore. He's just staring at me with concern written in the creases on his forehead.

"He was with me three nights ago," she says, like poison. He winces and his eyes shut. "So remember that the next time you kiss him—you're probably tasting a little bit of me on his lips," she says as she's walking backwards down the hall and then turns and clicks her heels, presumably, all the way out the auditorium door. Her words stick to me like goo. I want to shake them off but they're all clingy and heavy.

I'm not shaking anymore. I'm Numb Girl. Sometimes I'm thankful for her. Now's one of those times. Dillon grasps me around my hips. "Sadie," he says. He sounds like an echo. "Do you need a doctor?"

I don't speak. *This it too much. I. Can't. Take. It.* I close my eyes and my knees feel weak.

"Can you walk?" he asks. I can do that. I put one foot in front of the other. He escorts me, like a protective soon-to-be father would do, through the crowd and past a metal screen that must be blocking off the lunch counter into the kitchen.

"I need some ice, please," he says to the lady who's putting little cookies on a large metal tray.

"In the freezer," she says, pointing to it with her chin.

"And a towel, please," he requests as he lifts me, effortlessly, and sets me on the counter. I cross my ankles. The lady huffs, walks over to a drawer and brings him a towel, walks slowly over to the freezer and pops a tray of ice next to me on the counter. He's inspecting my forehead and checking my eyes for dilation.

"She shouldn't be up there, Dillon." *Oh my gosh, it's the grumpy, already-old-back-then lunch lady.*

"I'm sorry Mrs. Parks but she's had a little accident. I need to take a look or she might need to go to the hospital." She huffs and slowly walks the cookie tray out the door.

"Can you speak, darlin'?" he asks me sympathetically while he's inspecting my head.

"Yes," I say, finally.

"You've got a big red bump right here," he says, and kisses my forehead. The tenderness in his voice and his lips snaps me out of my numbness. I shudder, and my breathing takes on a more frenetic tempo.

I watch as he uses those long fingers to retrieve ice cubes from the tray and place them on the towel. He stings my forehead with it. "Sheesh," I say.

"That was really unacceptable," he says. "My brother and then Claire. They're acting like idiots." I shake my head yes but don't look at him. I don't want him to see how scared I am. He reads me so well.

"I really shouldn't have come."

"That's nonsense," he says, holding the ice to my forehead. "You have every right to be here. Donnie's just mad because I embarrassed him. He hates that, and Claire, I think I messed up with her when I didn't catch the signs that she felt more strongly for me than I did for her."

"Or maybe you really like her and you didn't want to admit your feelings for her."

"No, Sadie, it's not like that. It was just a physical relationship. I was lonely. That's all."

"You really should go talk to her."

"She left."

"No, I mean after you take me home."

"I might give her a call in a few days, after she's calmed down." I nod my head in agreement.

"She's probably a nice lady when she's not around me," I say, with a little smile.

"She's nice. She is. She's still mourning her husband. Sometimes, she calls me Mike by accident. I don't say anything."

"But three nights ago, how? How do you just sleep with her and have no feelings for her. I'm so confused. That's not like you at all."

"I only have room in here for you," he says, grasping my hand and placing it over his fast beating heart like he's plugging me into an outlet. *Live wires*. I wince from the contact. I wanted to grill him about sleeping with her, but that's all wiped away now.

"That's a lot of responsibility you're giving me," I offer, looking up at him through my lashes.

"I give it freely," he says, taking the ice off my forehead and running his finger along my jaw line. "I want nothing in return. Nothing you do will change how full my heart is of you." He looks at me like I'm his most prized possession. "All I want is to know you're happy, to be in your life in some small way."

Again, our bodies are speaking on their own frequency. I feel pulled to him and right now I don't care that his malevolent brother, with his promise of death, is somewhere right outside that door. I've let him take enough from me. He can't have this. Not anymore.

My hand on Dillon's heart pulls on my memories like a bobbin on the end of a line. All the good comes up to the surface. And it's about time because it's been held down for so many years by the weight of my attack.

Suddenly, I can hear us giggling under the low branches of our tree that he'd tied a rope to so we could fling ourselves into Rich Creek. Before that, I can hear his soft voice as he coaxed me into holding my breath underwater for the first time. *"See, it's easy! I told you you could do it."*

I remember the way his tongue stuck out when he put the pink, plump fish egg on the bent hook for me so I could catch fish with him. I can hear him telling me stories in his young ghost-story voice and can feel the way he'd hold me when he'd done too good of a job scaring me. I remember how he was always teaching me. Always there when I needed to talk.

I remember when he promised me he'd buy me a big white house. He said it'd have a big kitchen and lots of rooms for all our babies.

I remember the cave he showed me that held the remains of some kind of animal. We used to go in there and play rock-paper-scissors. Mostly, he let me win.

I remember the scent of his skin when we'd been playing hide-and-seek in the grass—his perspiration mixed with the West Virginia dust, and his momma's soap.

I remember riding on the back of his bike, his scent mingling with mine in the mountain air. I remember making snow angels together and then him helping me make the biggest snowman I'd ever seen—he even ripped two buttons off his coat to make the eyes. I can see the determined look on his face when I'd helped him rescue a dragon fly out of the mud behind my house. *'Look at its face. It looks like a bulldog, don't it?"*

These memories sting—but I want to remember. Just like the song asked me to in his car. I do remember—everything.

I've made my decision.

I love Dillon. I want him in every way he wants me. We'll work it all out. We have to.

"How are you feeling?" he asks, holding my face in his hand, my other hand pressed up to his heart. He's looking deep in my eyes with those Tahoe blues.

"I think I'm cured," I say, peeking into his core, trying to see if he understands the double meaning. If he understands that I've made up my mind about him, about us. Even if it is only for this brief moment before the real world comes roaring back to me in a moment of lucidity. I trace his cheek with my index finger and he nuzzles me back.

"I love you," I say, before I can become a coward. *Is that clear enough? I never stopped and I don't want to push you away anymore—I can't.* His eyes widen and he shudders as if a chill goes through his body that he holds in. I place both my hands on his face and pull him toward me. There is only him. There is only me. It's as if we're alone on this planet and we're creating all the meaning that exists in it.

"Is this really happening?" he breathes as he leans down and easily slides me by my waist toward the edge of the counter closer to him. My legs move to either side of his hips. I take a sharp breath as my tummy clenches up. He tenderly rubs the tip of his nose the full length of mine before he grasps my chin, gently tilting it up. His chest strokes against mine.

"And I love you, Sadie," he whispers into my mouth and takes my lips between his, so delicately. *Live wires.* I move my hands up to his hair as our kiss deepens.

"Dillon!" We are forced out of our reverie; the stern voice is coming out of Donnie's mouth as he stands in the doorway. "God dammit, boy. You're out in public. Ain't nobody allowed to do this even if it is with someone like that."

I gasp and cover my face with my hands.

"Someone like what?" Dillon challenges, turning away from me, blocking me from Donnie's stare. I pull my legs up to my chin, pull my skirt over my legs, and cross my ankles.

"Someone who lets men grope her in public," he says, like it's hot and he needs to drop it on someone.

"We aren't doing anything wrong, Donnie."

"From my perspective you are, and I'm the law."

"Shut up," Dillon says, just like a brother would.

I peek out from my hands. Donnie's mouth says, "It's your turn in about five minutes," but what he's really saying is: *"I'm going to kill you both."* That's exactly the look on his face. Pure evil. I've started trembling so badly now, like I'm cold on the inside.

"Sadie, why are you shaking?" Dillon says, so concerned. I can't help it when I start to make the ugly cry face.

He's breathing harder than normal. "What's the matter, baby?" He looks at Donnie and back at me with my head hanging low. It's like something clicks. "Give us a minute, man," he says, curtly and waits until Donnie walks away.

"Does he scare you?" he asks, leaning into my legs pulled up to my chin, wrapping his long arms around me. I can't lie. He knows. I shake my head yes. "Why?"

"It's just that we keep getting caught kissing and it's really embarrassing." *Did that work?*

"Is that all, Sadie?"

"Yes," I lie again. This sucks.

"Don't be embarrassed. Who cares what he thinks?" *Well, you might if he tries to kill you with his fishy knife.*

"What just happened, Sadie, was one of the most beautiful moments of my life." I shake my head and try to calm my breathing and straighten my ugly-cry face. "When you said you loved me," he puts his hands on his head, "I don't care if this means anything for me right now, like if you're ready to be with me or if you want what I want. Just to know how you feel." His voice hitches in his throat.

I guess that depends on what Donnie's going to do now. Maybe it would be better to just tell Dillon so I would have someone to help me through this. I would, too, if I thought that Dillon could stay calm and strategize rather than turn medieval and challenge his brother to a duel. He would be no match for an ex-Army soldier. It would be like tagging him with a big red stripe and sending him to the slaughter house.

At this point it's too late to hide what's going on between us. We've kissed, like that, right in front of Donnie. There's no going back. I'm staying here to see my mother until her last day. And I'm going to help protect this mountain—for her. There has to be a way to get one step ahead of Donnie. A way to keep him away.

"All I know right now is that I love you, Dillon. I always have and I want what you want. I do. But there's so much that you don't know." He helps me put my legs down and pulls me into his strong, safe arms. *This is where I want to be—need to be.*

"There's nothing you need to say right now," he says into my ear. "You owe me nothing. I'm just happy with whatever this is right now."

"Thank you, Dillon," I whisper into his chest.

He pulls back and looks down at me thoughtfully. The iPhone in my purse strung crossways over my shoulder buzzes. I must have a new email. That's when divine providence strikes. I can get Donnie to talk. He's so angry he's bound to threaten me again and someone will hear. No, I need a way to prove what he did in a way that I can control. I look at my purse again. *That thing has to have some kind of a recording device.*

"Are you ready to go out there now? Can you walk okay?"

"Yes, I'm ready." *Yes, I am.* For the first time in my life I want to talk to Donnie. And I'm going to find out what's going through his Machiavellian mind—right now.

I bet my eyes look like a wild dog before a planned attack.

Chapter Twelve

Good Boy

We walk out of the kitchen together. Dillon holds my hand and I won't let go. I refuse to look for Donnie as we take our seats near the back wall just as an old woman stand up, leans on her cane and yells, "That's what killed my pa!"

"Now, ma'am," the woman standing at the podium tries to interrupt.

"No! I will be heard. You people come in here with this document showin' all this proof of wrong doin'. You admit you know that mountaintop coal mining will release toxins into our soil, air, and water. You even admit that the last round of coal taken out a' here back in the fifties left our whole town exposed to toxins," she says in a wobbly voice. "But you're ready, right now, to give 'em the permit to blow the top off one of the oldest mountains in the history of the world. Gauley's on the coin for goodness sake!"

She turns around on bowed legs and looks at the audience, "Ain't y'all learnt nothin' from the Hawk's Nest Tunnel?"

I'm scratching my head. I remember Daddy talking about that when I was a kid. Men died building a tunnel back in the thirties. They breathed some bad stuff when they blew up the mountain to make room for the water that was going to create power.

"Don't turn yur lights on then," yells a man wearing an 'Ansted Coal' jacket.

"Now, that's just not appropriate, son," says a man wearing a light beige sweater over a collared shirt and brown slacks. His thin glasses and calm demeanor make him look like a preacher. "We don't need to be disrespectful to the lady."

"Thank you, Sir. Ma'am, I'd love to hear more from you when we open the floor to the public. Right now I have a presentation for you all by Dr. Dillon McGraw. As you may know, Dr. McGraw…"

Doctor, holy cow!!! I look at Dillon who is holding my hand and looking even more dignified by the minute.

"…is knowledgeable about the water shed and also wanted to present material about the algae he and his team have been success-fully producing in their laboratory. Dr. McGraw…" The room claps as he squeezes my hand.

"Are you okay if I leave you alone?" he whispers to me.

"Of course, go," I shush him. He squeezes my hand and walks effortlessly up to the podium. I take out my phone and search the apps for one that records voices.

"Thank you so much for welcoming me this evening. I want to cover the water ways as well as discuss the government project my colleagues and I have been working on, which is an algae based fuel, an obvious alternative to coal, and bitumen based fuels…"

Dillon makes alternative fuel? He really is a new hippie. I'm in absolute awe of him right now. Like, I want to walk into the aisle and bow to him, the King of Environmentalism. He's perfectly remarkable and is doing so much more for the cause I feel so passionate about. That's why I wrote my children's novel. I really wanted to help change the world one page at a time.

Oh, yeah, Donnie. I scowl.

I look at the results on my phone and there's an iTalk Recorder By Griffin Technology to record with. I download it as fast as I can.

It looks easy. There's one big red button to record. Then to stop I just press the same big button again.

"With mountaintop coal mining," Dillon explains, "they'll push the overburden from the mining on down the holler that fills in the valleys and shuts off our water supply. This toxic soup, if you will, will drain into the Gauley River, which meets with the New River, forms the Kanawha which goes to the Ohio River, and empties into the Mississippi. This will cut about half the water supply as well as dirtying the remainder to half of the United States." The people in the audience grumble with this news.

I look around the room. Donnie is leering behind the table that holds the coffee pot and the many trays of cookies.

"As far as our water ways, when we first heard of this permit, Park Service reported fourteen to sixteen possible violations."

"And you're going to let 'em have that permit?" yells the old lady in the front row from before.

I check the app on my phone and slide it into the little pocket on my beige cardigan.

"Ma'am, I'm not involved in the process for allowing permits. I was asked by the Christians Against Mountaintop Removal to come out and present the facts," he says.

Someone else asks Dillon a question and he's answering her as I get up and walk toward the big metal and black coffee pot. It feels like I have to force myself toward Donnie as if we're two negatively charged atoms that are opposed to each other on an elemental level.

My body says, *Danger! Danger!*

I look back at Dillon and he's showing the room a detailed map of the waterways in relation to the mountain. I drain some coffee into a small paper cup and find a bowl that's holding little sugar cubes. I'd forgotten about sugar cubes. I grab two with the little tongs and stir it with the tiny red straw. I turn slightly and check that the app is still ready on my phone. It's not, so I swipe across and the app pops up.

Just as I predicted, Donnie steps forward, standing just on the other side of the table. I look up at him and he's staring, arms crossed like he's trying to hide his anger toward me. I reach into my pocket and press the screen. The button is so huge that I know I can't miss it. Amazingly, my coffee doesn't even shake in my hand.

"It's been a long while, huh?" he says, through clenched teeth.

"Not long enough," I retort.

"Strange enough," he responds, "I thought I'd made myself pretty clear about what kind a' consequences you could expect doing the things you been doin' today with him," he says, nodding at Dillon who's looking at us but still moving through the PowerPoint in detail.

"Why, whatever do you mean, Officer McGraw?" I stab back. "Do you mean that when you *raped* me you threatened to cut my head off and bury it in your front yard?" I'm hoping beyond hope that this app can pick up the whole conversation. Our voices are so low that no one can hear us even if they leaned in to listen on purpose.

"You know, I could arrest you right now for indecent exposure. You done it two times—one was even called in. Ain't nobody gonna be able to stand in front of ya in there and keep me from takin' what's mine," he fumes. His eyes are shaking he's so mad, but his body is completely still. I move my hand into my pocket and push the mouth piece out slightly to make sure I'm getting all of this.

"You're delusional. I'm never going to be yours. You're just a rapist pig who had to have a knife to my throat to get within ten inches of me."

"Don't lie to yourself. You wanted me. Look at you. You're so turned on right now. Your breathing changes around me. Your blood rushes to the skin and makes you all pink."

"That's because I'm scared of you, Donnie. But let me make myself clear. You will never touch me again. What you took from me, I'll never get back. But you won't take it again."

He looks impassive, all except for the eyes. "You know, we all make mistakes," he says, his voice unnerving as he runs his thick fingers through the black slide on his head, takes a toothpick out from behind his ear and puts it in his mouth. I look at him confused. "I made one mistake, that's true, but it ain't what you think." He sucks on the toothpick and moves it from one side of his mouth to the other. "I'll never regret what I took from you, as you say, 'cause I think it was owed to me," he says, defiantly.

I look up at Dillon and smile. He shouldn't have to worry right now as he's giving his presentation. I swallow the coffee in my mouth so hard it hurts.

"After I left you in the shed I watched you run off. I followed you all the way to the creek. I was pretty sure you was gonna die—as bloody as you were. I'd made up my mind that even though I was in love with you, it wasn't worth you tellin' on me. It woulda' been hard for me, cause of my feelins for you, and cause you were good. *Real good*, better than I'd thought."

You sick bastard. Go ahead. Keep talking!

"I just couldn't be sure you'd keep your promise. But then, you fell in the creek all on your own. Made it real easy fer me, I thought. Don't get me wrong. It hurt a bit to think you was dead. But it was better than havin' to watch you with *him* some more. I didn't know 'til the next mornin' when *he* came home covered in blood that my brother'd found you."

"You were following me?" is all I can say. *Where was Dillon all night?*

"I'd always followed you. Always knew where you were. I'd a' done anything fer you." He swallows hard. "Then my brother beats me to talking to your Daddy about marrying you."

I just shake my head. He's delusional. All this time, I had no idea he had been stalking me. It makes me feel like that dream when you're standing in front of the classroom and then you look down and you're completely naked—but it's like I'd been naked a million times and then raped because of it. I feel like I'm going to throw up.

"Just stay away from me, Donnie. I'm not going to tell Dillon it was you unless you don't leave me alone. I'm just here to see my mom before she passes away."

"Dillon can't stop me, Sadie. Besides, that wadn't the deal," he says, softly to mask the fury behind the words. "I ain't sharin' you with him. I *won't*, ever again. Do you have any idea the things I done to men during this war? I could take care of it so he's in extreme pain for the last moments a' his life and nobody's gonna ever find his body. Places nobody goes to up on the mountain. Perfect place to put somebody you don't want around—somebody who'd be gettin' in the way."

"So you'd kill your own brother?"

"In a heartbeat. I told you, I ain't sharin' you."

"Why are you doing this? Just leave me alone."

"I know you ain't been with no one else. It had to be that way so I could be with you all these years, in yer mind. You just didn't know it was me yer supposed ta' be with. I been waitin' fer my chance again. Always knew where you was. I kept track 'a ya. Looks like you're back in my territory. I'll be comin' to take what's mine."

"Over my dead body."

"Why you always fightin'? That's why you got hurt. But if that's the way it has ta be. I can take care a' that fer you," he says, softly but completely clear. "I'd rather you was dead than with him."

I take the last bit of coffee hovering at the bottom of my cup into my mouth. It's sour and sweet at the same time—kind of like right now.

I'm not scared of him for the first time since he took my old life away from me in that shed. I can almost picture the rope he's just tied around his neck with his own tongue.

I casually toss the cup into the trash. Run my fingers through my hair, turn to him, and with fervent charm, I deliver the line I've let take refuge in my brain for ten and a half years.

"Good boy," I say, and walk away.

Chapter Thirteen

Hawk's Nest

As my feet propel me forward, I feel a rush of fear, then a wave of astonishment, then a rumbling of adrenaline. It's as if I can feel his eyes stabbing into my back like hot lasers. I find my seat and plop down clumsily and then try to straighten myself without making a scene. I feel hot all over. I feel dizzy and euphoric.

I want to check my phone so I can make sure I got all of what he said. It feels hot pressed up against my stomach as if it's begging to be dealt with right away. I need to give it a minute or he'll know what I did and try to take my phone away from me, or worse.

I don't want to go to the bathroom to check because it's not safe in there. He could follow me. My eyes dart over to him and he's looking at Dillon. *Oh! Dillon is talking.* I forgot.

"Thank you, folks, for inviting me to come out and talk to you. Does anyone have any questions?"

"So, how long 'til we can use this algae you've been makin' for fuel?" asks a man sporting a long beard whose sitting up near the front row.

"Well, facilities are capable, it doesn't require we change any of our vehicles, as algae runs through engines just like petroleum based fuels. Gas stations won't have any trouble offering it as an option.

What's holding us back is just the fact that we don't have enough algae production plants as of yet," Dillon explains.

"Well, I wanna try it!" yells a woman with obvious false teeth who sits two seats over from me. "Is it cheaper?"

"I think it will be, since we'll be making it ourselves and won't have to drill for it," explains Dillon.

"That's nice an' all, but what I'm worried about," says a middle aged man near the middle row wearing a deep blue sweater, "is flash flooding if any of the old abandoned mines or tunnels in the area, like the Hawk's Nest are breached. I mean, has anybody thought about that?"

"I can't speak to that," Dillon apologizes. He looks to the woman who announced him.

She stands up. "Yes, sir, it is possible that there could be some old mines that are capable of caving. The company would be required to do all in their power to avoid..."

"But you can't promise us nothin', can you?"

She looks stunned. "No, sir, I cannot."

The crowd begins to rumble again.

"What about if the blasting will send clouds a' dust into the air," yells a woman standing at the back row. She's got two little kids holding onto her thighs. "What's that dust called? The one that's real bad for us ta breathe?"

"Silica-laden dust," replies the announcer.

"Yeah, that one. What about that?"

"Yes, ma'am, it is very likely that some silica will be released during the blasting phase."

"This is wrong!" she yells, as she grabs a hold of her children like a mother trying to brace them for an accident.

Dillon walks down the aisle toward me. I can't help it that I'm relieved to be near him once again. As he sits down, I take in his scent. It makes me warm. When he's near, I'm home.

"I told you people!" yells the old woman who earlier had screamed that her father had been killed by a chemical. "And that's the one that killed him, silica. Chronic silicosis. You should'a seen him trying to breathe at the end. Worked so hard, he done come home covered in dust. It took him a year ta die. I was just a little girl back then. Makes me sick to my stomach."

I grasp a hold of Dillon's rigid arm and nuzzle it. His body is filled with tension. He's looking at the woman who's remembering about her father, but he puts his hand over mine as if to ask me not to move it away.

"Much shorter exposures at higher concentrations can result in a very deadly type of the disease called acute silicosis," Dillon says. "This can happen after a single heavy dose or brief exposures to very high concentration of silica dust," Dillon explains. "Children are especially susceptible to this type of exposure."

"It can kill?" asks the mom holding her children for dear life.

"Yes, ma'am," Dillon says.

The nice man with glasses on his nose who earlier had silenced the other man in the 'Ansted Coal' jacket stands up. "I think I speak on behalf of most of the people here tonight that the citizens of Ansted are opposed to the permit being issued for mountaintop coal mining. Can we put it to a vote?"

"Sir, this is not being voted on," says the announcer.

"Nevertheless, we're allowed to show our numbers in opposition, right?"

"Certainly, Reverend," she replies.

"Well, then all of us who oppose the permit please raise your hand."

I'm not surprised when almost every person in the room raises their hand. A photographer is taking pictures, the chirp of the flash like little bursts of lightening.

A tear falls down my cheek before I realize that I feel anything remotely close to the feelings that usually move me to tears. I raise my arm, too. Dillon's is already up. Donnie's is not.

"Thank you," says the woman. And in a placating tone she adds, "We will keep this in mind as we make our final decision." Her fake smile does not deceive me.

The crowd rumbles. It didn't work on them either. She waves to them and makes her way off the podium. Dillon stands up with me in tow.

"How are you?" he asks. *I want to look at my phone.*

"Fine," I say, looking up into his eyes. They look like uncertainty.

"I'd like to talk to Revered Morris before we go," he explains.

"Okay," I say as he grasps my hand in his, where it feels like it should be for the rest of my life.

Dillon shakes the man's hand. I knew he must have been a pastor. "Reverend Morris, I'd like you to meet Sadie Sparks, the author I was telling you about earlier."

"Oh, yes," he says, putting his hand out to shake mine. I smile and shake. I've really grown accustomed to this. I'm great at the meet and greet. "I hear you're interested in helping our cause," he says, kindly.

"Yes, sir. I am. I'd like to help as much as I can before I need to go back to California." Dillon tenses as if he's just remembered I would leave him again someday soon. "Have you heard of Hands Across the Sand?" I ask.

"Uh, no. I'm sorry. I haven't," he says. His eyebrows shoot up in the hopes that I've got some useful information.

"Well, this group met up all along the coast to protest off-shore drilling by grasping hands in unity. I mean, it didn't stop anything from happening but it was great at getting publicity."

"It didn't stop it though," he says, disappointed. He needs something real, not some show of opposition.

"No, you're right. But what just occurred to me is that we could get enough people to go up to the blast site and create a human barrier so that they couldn't detonate without actually killing someone. It might work," I explain.

His eyes light up. "Yes, yes. This might actually work."

Because I'm scared to death of Donnie, I've actually kept track of his whereabouts the entire time I've been talking, as if I'm plugged into him by an imaginary string. I notice that he's talking conspiratorially with the man who'd yelled *"Don't turn your lights on!"* to the woman with the father who died in the Hawk's Nest Tunnel Tragedy.

The man tries to hand Donnie a thick envelope from inside his jacket pocket. Donnie pushes it back and leans into the man's ear. It looks like he's in trouble. I don't think anyone else just noticed.

I knew it! He's involved in this. He's helping out the coal company. That man's trying to pay Donnie off.

"Sadie," Dillon says. I look at him and it's clear that I've missed something.

"I'm sorry, what did you say?"

He looks to his left where I'd been watching Donnie almost take a bribe and it looks like he realizes that I had been looking at his brother again. He shakes his head. *Please don't put this together. I've got this.*

"Reverend Morris was just asking if you would come to the meeting tomorrow night and tell the others about your idea."

"Of course. No problem at all." I nod at the Reverend and shake his hand before he excuses himself. I feel like I'm caught. I better quit watching Donnie or Dillon's going to figure this out.

"Are you ready to go?" he asks. His eyebrows are furrowed. He does not look pleased. A man as smart as he is must be figuring all of this out. My only hope is that he's in denial. People never want to realize the truth about their own family members.

"Yes, I'm exhausted."

He takes me by the arm as we walk by Donnie. I swear he cuts across his neck with his finger so slyly that only I would notice. I squint my eyes.

What he doesn't know is I'm the one holding the 'knife' this time.

Once in the car, it's clear that Dillon is brooding. He's not turning on the music like he usually does. Maybe he can't think of a song that asks, *'Is my brother your rapist?'* He's not talking to me. My phone feels like it's growing wings and needs to fly into my hand to be checked to see if I captured that conversation.

When I get back to my momma's house, I'm going to have to upload it to my computer and get it online somewhere so that it's safe and cannot be destroyed.

"What were you and Donnie talking about?" Dillon asks. Oh crap!

"Mostly about my Momma being sick. He asked about my book and wanted to know when I was going back to California." *Detour this conversation to me leaving instead?*

"When are you going back?"

Phew, it worked. "I'm going to help out with the mountain, but I'm going to have to go back at some point after Momma, you know."

"Still," he says, as if he needs time to understand.

"That's where my life is, Dillon."

"I'd just thought. I thought maybe, I don't know," he's stumbling over his big huge heart.

"I can come back to visit." *What would I do? Could I stay here if Donnie couldn't hurt me anymore?* I can write from anywhere. I would just have to go back and forth for meetings about the movie. I just can't fathom the idea of living here where Donnie will be able to stalk me, watch me, threaten me constantly. I don't think he'll ever just go away. But, the recording could be a game changer. There's just too much to think about.

"It's just, Sadie, I'm having trouble with the thought of dropping you off at your momma's house, let alone seeing you get on a plane for who knows how long."

"I know."

He shifts in his seat and puts his left arm resting on the doorframe, his fist up to his mouth.

"Can I stay with you tonight?" he asks.

"What?" I blurt.

"Please, I don't want to leave you alone. I have this uneasy feeling and I want to... I don't know. I mean, I won't try anything with you, Sadie. I promise."

"We cannot do this, Dillon."

"Sadie, would you tell me if something was wrong, if you weren't okay?"

No. "Yes," I lie. *I'm protecting you this way.*

"Something's wrong. I know it. You always told me everything when we were kids. All you have to do is say the words. I can help you." I hear his breath hitch in his throat. "Was he there?"

"No." I concentrate on looking like I mean it.

"You don't need to go stand by a cop all night to be safe. Let me help you."

Oh, he thinks I was standing near Donnie to be safe from someone else. He knows my rapist was there, but I was right. He's in denial. We're pulling the car up the driveway making mincemeat of all the tiny pebbles under our path.

"Will you stop this if I let you stay?"

"You won't tell me then?"

"I can't." *That's being as honest as I can be.*

His chin starts to tremble. His jaw is tight and his mouth in a thin line as he parks the car in front of the brown house that always wanted to be brighter.

"Then yes. I'll stop asking if you let me stay with you and protect you."

I won't lie, I've wondered most of my life what it would feel like to lie down in my childhood bed with this man. I'd imagined him there many times in secret thoughts that went nowhere.

Now, I guess I'm about to find out.

Chapter Fourteen

To Me, You Are

I'm relieved as I open the front door that Missy isn't waiting up for me. It feels like I have a shadow in the dark as we walk down the hallway toward my childhood room. I know I'm a grown woman, but this feels absolutely forbidden. *What in the heck am I doing?*

I turn on the light and there he stands in my room. He hasn't been in here since he was about twelve. Daddy hadn't let him come in here anymore after that. It wasn't proper. The room looks like it's too small for him, kind of like an ill-fitting shirt on a super model.

"What are you going to sleep in?" I ask.

"Um, is it okay if I sleep in just my boxers or would you rather I kept my shirt on, too?"

"You should keep your shirt on, I think." I nod my head. *Yep. That's a smart choice.*

"I'm going to go change in the bathroom," I say, grabbing my cotton nightgown from the chair I'd laid it on this morning at too early of an hour. This has been one of the longest days of my life.

I yawn as I walk down the short hallway. The bathroom light buzzes on, searing my corneas with its too bright threads behind the clear glass bulb.

I grab the phone out of my purse and swipe it on. The app is still up. My hands are shaking and the knot in my throat is back—big time. I'm fumbling the buttons on the shiny glass touch screen, touching too hard, or too soft, or in the wrong spot.

How do I know if it's got something in there? A few taps and then I see there's a recording. I push play. I hear whispering. A rustling sound. That must be when I pushed the mouthpiece out a bit. And I hear my voice calling Donnie a pig. There's Donnie's voice. Clear. As. Day. "You wanted me. Look at you. You're so turned on right now..." I shut it off.

I've done it! I hop around the bathroom like a child on a pogo stick, holding my breath so I don't squeal. I've got to get this somewhere permanent.

I push another button that says 'share'. I decide to text it to my assistant back in California. I tap the screen.

ME: Jenny, I need you to upload this recording to my blog but do not, I repeat, DO NOT make the post live unless you don't hear from me at least once per day by 2:00 pm Mountain time. I want this done tonight. DO NOT LISTEN TO IT. Text me back ASAP.

I take off the tan dress and decide to leave my bra on before I slip on a modest cotton nightgown. It's long enough to be decent. I pull the toothbrush out of my travel bag and squeeze some white TOMS of Maine on my recycled fiber brush. My phone buzzes. I almost knock it off the sink but grab it just in time.

JENNY: Understood. I will text when it's complete. R U OK?

ME: Yes. I am now. Thank you.

My toothbrush is shaking in my hand. What am I going to do with this recording? Do I tell him I've got it? I think that's the only way. If he knows, he'll have to leave me alone. If I don't text my assistant because he's done something to me, the blog goes live and all of my fans will be listening to my rapist admit to almost killing me, letting me drown, and threatening to kill Dillon and me.

My phone buzzes.

JENNY: Done. Did you want to add some copy?

ME: It should say: "This was recorded at the Ansted Middle School Auditorium in Ansted, West Virginia, on September 21st, 2012. The voices are those of Sadie Sparks and Donnie McGraw, Ansted's Chief of Police." That's it.

JENNY: Got it.

ME: Thank you.

I brush my hair out. *What am I going to do?* I scrub my face too hard with my beige face wash. I'm going to sleep in the same bed with the only man I've ever loved. The only man I haven't been able to keep my hands off for an entire day. I'm not ready for this. I'm just going to tell him he's being ridiculous and needs to go home. Besides, I'm safe in here.

What was that?

Outside the bathroom window, I just saw something move by the tree. Is it Donnie? He knows Dillon is in here with me. I turn off the light. Staring at that same spot for what seems like ages, I see nothing. *No. I'm just imagining things. There's no one out there. I'm just paranoid.*

I tiptoe toward my room but walk past the light shining on the floor from the bottom of the door and turn the lock on the front door. I walk to the kitchen and lock the back door. No sense in making it easy on him to get in if he is out there. Daddy had a gun, didn't he? I bet it's up in the closet of Momma's room.

Here goes nothing. I open the door to my room and find Dillon lying on the bed on top of the covers. He's wearing some snug, grey boxer briefs and a white sleeveless T-shirt.

Whoa

He is a man now. His arms and chest are so powerfully built—not bulky, just defined and full of vigor. Through the thin fabric of his shirt on his stomach I can see ripples of muscles tucked under the upside down V of his chest. I don't want to look below his waistband. I'm still too afraid. My mouth goes dry.

"Is that a wife beater?" I ask, remembering Jake calling it that yesterday.

He laughs, "Yeah, that's another name for it, I guess." His deep laugh makes my nerves fizzle away like bubbles in a lukewarm bath. He pats the unoccupied side of the bed. "Come here," he says. The nerves come right back.

I drop my dress on the chair and plug my phone into the charger on the desk.

That's when I notice on his left bicep is a huge tattoo that stretches all the way down, almost to his elbow. Part flower, part print. My name is on the top in dark black, cursive ink. Below it is a flower that has always grown wild in our yard each year. It's a 'great laurel,' as Momma always called them, a long-petaled, pink-tipped flower with slight green accents. It has long tendrils that reach out to find a bee for pollination. It's quite beautiful and makes me realize that it must remind him of me. Below the great laurel is a poem or a verse. It says,

Place me like a seal over your heart,
like a seal on your arm;
Many waters cannot quench love;
rivers cannot sweep it away.

"It's pretty," I say, rubbing my left arm and giving him a slight smile.

"It's nothing like the original," he says, unfaltering. I feel like swooning. *How does he do this to me?*

"What does it mean?" I ask.

"It means, it means that I belong to you," he says, staring into my eyes. I look at the corner of the room to escape the overwhelming sincerity in his eyes. My heart beats like a little scared bunny.

"The poem is kind of gloomy."

"It's from the Bible," he says. "Do you remember it?"

As I'm trying to remember the verse, he pats the bed again. I rub the annoying lump in my throat, and turn off the room light. The moon casts a blue hue over everything. There are little shadows flitting around coming from the wind blowing through the trees outside my room. My heartbeat staggers, then it feels as though it cannot stay in my body as fast as it is beating.

I cross my wrists in front of my body and look back to the corner of the room. He's going to have to help me. I can't go to him right now. I feel stuck to the ground.

"I think we need to talk about the rules again," I admonish and peek at him through my lashes.

"Sadie, you have nothing to worry about."

I raise an eyebrow. How can he be so sure? "After all that's happened today," I say under my breath.

"I want you, more than you know. I've never wanted anything more in my life than to show you how I feel about you. That's not what I'm saying. But I want to wait to make love to you until we're married," he says, resolute.

"Who says I'm ever getting married?"

"Well, if you're not, then I guess I'm going to be celibate the rest of my life," he jokes as he swings his legs over the side of the bed and leans his forearms on his knees.

"I doubt it," I pout and cross my arms across my chest. I look away. *Ms. Robbins is probably ready to help him out in that department.*

"I'm not going to mess this up like I did last time, Sadie," he says, sitting upright.

"Like last time?"

"When I kissed you, touched you. You were too young. It was an accident, but you ran off because of me."

"Dillon," I try.

"And, if I understand this right, you've never been with a man," he says, cautiously and I think for a moment.

"Technically..." I shake my head no.

"And what I want," he says, cutting me off, "what I need, is for your first real experience to be done right. I want it to be pure and real, just like you—like us."

"I'm hardly a virgin, Dillon. You know that only so well."

"To me, you are." It's like the wind just got knocked out of me. I put my head down and bite my thumbnail so he can't see the ugly cry face. I turn and walk toward the corner of the room. I hear the bed squeak as he gets up and walks over to stand behind me. "Sadie?"

I shake my head no.

"What happened to you is not the same thing as what's going to happen between us, darlin'." His voice is soft like warm butter.

That hole in my chest is throbbing. I want him to fill it up. But I'm scared as hell. If he touches me I might crumble into dust.

"I believe you," I say, through my knotted throat.

I feel his warmth as he moves closer to me. I shakily reach behind and find his arm, pull on his tender strong hand and wrap it
around my stomach. His other arm moves my hair away from my
left shoulder before it meets with the first. He leans in and moves
down to kiss me gently on my neck.

"I will never let you get hurt again," he whispers into my ear. Oh,
that's it. I can't control the profound guttural cry that comes up
from the deepest part of my spirit, the most wounded part. The part
where maybe a bit of the old Sadie has still lived all these years. He
holds me as I lean back into him. He takes the tremors coming from
my body, absorbs them like shocks.

Holding onto his hand, I turn around to face him. I take his hand
and place it over my heart just at the top of my breast. He closes his
eyes, his lips purse together in an expression that looks like both pain
and pleasure.

God, I love this man. Before I know I'm going to say it, I do, "I
want you to make love to me right now."

He shudders, closes his eyes and tilts his head up to the ceiling.
He shakes his head from side to side, softly as if he's thinking of the
right thing to do. He looks down, his jaw squared and strained and
leans into me. My heart staggers and I gasp slightly.

This is it!

He wraps me up in his arms, picks me up off the floor so we're
eye to eye. He moves his left arm under my knees so that he's
holding me like his bride over the threshold. I wrap my arms around
his neck as he kisses me softly. It's a pure kiss—enduring, worship-
ing, cherishing. Gingerly, he places me on the bed as if I'm a fine
piece of silk. He pulls away, standing at the edge of the bed and
looks down at me as if he's seeing me for the first time.

"You're more beautiful than I ever imagined you'd be all grown
up," he whispers, leans down to me and runs his long thin finger
along my jaw line before he lies down along my left side. My body

starts to quiver beside him as I turn to my side and wrap my arm around his waist pulling him toward me. He feels so right.

"Oh, what I could do to you right now," he says, putting his arms on either side of my face. I feel as though I'm being cradled by him. The feeling of his body touching the full length of mine is intoxicating. He cannot hide the fact that he wants me, too. *A man's body gives everything away*, I think, as I push up against his developing arousal. I'm aching for him to touch back. It hurts for him not to.

Shutting his eyes, he pulls away from me slightly, his face pained. "It's very difficult to say no to you, baby." His warm breath heats my cheek. "But now's not the time. Do you understand why?"

No. Yes.

He opens his eyes. "I've always imagined our first time being after taking off your white wedding gown in our room in our big white house." I smile, remembering his promise to buy me that house. He smiles back, "I've seen it that way since we were kids. You deserve that, Sadie—we do," he says, looking into my eyes. His face is half in the light, half in the dark, but he's all good.

He's right. I only said that because I just want him to make me feel better, take the other memory—the bad one—and replace it with him; but that's not how it really works. I'm not ready. He knows me better than I know myself.

This should happen when we're both in a clear state of mind and I know nothing right now except that I love him and I always have. I don't know about marriage, about staying here. I don't know what's going to happen tomorrow, or two weeks from now. So, now's not the time. He's teaching me, again. I don't think it'll ever get old. I nod my head yes and he smiles, amorously.

"I can't believe you're here feeling so perfect," he says, as he pushes his body even more snuggly into mine, "wanting me back," he says, putting his right leg over top of mine, as his eyes move around my face and back to my gaze. He grasps my chin, runs his nose the full length of mine, and takes my lips between his, graceful-ly, gently, asking for nothing. Just showing how he feels for me. "I want it to be perfect for you," he whispers up to my lips, tickling them.

He has incredible self-control not to just seize what I was willing to give. It, literally, takes my breath away for a moment. He kisses my forehead and wipes the tears from my cheeks with his thumb.

He pulls the covers over us and draws me up so that my back is molded into his chest. Our legs cross over one another's. His arms cradle me and our hands become one over my heart. "Sleep, baby," he says, as he breathes me in.

And I do.

Chapter Fifteen

Between Awake and Asleep

I'm warm and wrapped up tight with the quilt and Dillon's arms. I want to feel content, but something feels *off* in the room. It's still dark out when my eyes flicker open. The room is illuminated by the slight glow of the moon; tree shadows dance about as my eyes begin to focus.

This has happened to me so many times. It's as if being asleep and being awake overlap for a brief moment and my dream manifests itself into the air. Sometimes it will be a gigantic spider posturing above me or walking along the wall; more often, it will be a butterfly, a large one that flits around the very top of my canopy bed at home.

Very rarely, I will see what looks like a man. Not his features or his clothes—just his shape leering from the corner of the room. I don't jump, ever, anymore because I know what this is. Dr. Amy has explained it to me so many times. It happens when I'm stressed and sleep deprived. *Like now*, I think to console myself.

It used to happen all the time after…and it used to dump me right out of my bed and push me, full of tremors and fright, into Aunt Lotty's in the middle of the night. It's called Hypnagogic Hallucination and it will be over in a minute. I blink.

It's still there.

I blink again, and a quake runs through my nervous system. There is a black figure in the corner of the room farthest from the door. This one's not going away like they usually do. I close my eyes as tight as they will go and pinch Dillon's fleshy arm between my thumb and forefinger. He jerks his arm away and bolts suddenly upright.

It all happens so fast. As the shape in the corner darts toward my side of the bed, I scream from the deepest part of my psyche and charge backwards slamming my skull into the headboard. The pain is nothing compared to the fear. A monstrous fear that comes from the past slamming into the present all at once.

He got in.

Dillon puts his arm over me and pulls me behind him on the bed.

"Run!" Dillon shouts, as he darts up and pushes Donnie, slamming his back into the other corner of the room. But Donnie shoves back and Dillon has to step backward with his right leg to stabilize himself. Donnie tramples into the light from the window and the two men wrestle to get the upper hand. I realize then that he's wearing a dark facemask and midnight-stalker clothes.

Dillon swings first, striking Donnie in the nose, it crunches and his head snaps back.

When Donnie's head comes back to center, he thrusts his fist into Dillon's gut once so hard that it sounds like thunder clapping in the sky and then punches him in the eye hard enough that even I see stars.

Dillon moans in pain and then Donnie takes advantage by holding his head in place so he can beat him over and over in the face. The sound of Dillon being punched, an empty sound like a watermelon falling to the floor, makes me cringe and roll up into a ball.

"Stop!" I yell, helplessly, frantic. This *is all my fault. He's going to kill him.* I never should have come here. I can't call Donnie's name or else he'll kill us now for sure. *How can I distract him?*

I bolt up to my feet on the bed as Dillon staggers and falls to one knee. Donnie looks at me wild eyed and evil as he walks around and purposefully kicks Dillon in the back, knocking him face down on the floor. Dillon rocks back and forth as if his mind says to get up but his body won't respond.

Donnie moves away from Dillon and stands wide-legged at the edge of the bed. His eyes stab through mine in the night like bullets.

My eyes flit back and forth between the two brothers. One who would do anything to protect me, and the other who has hurt me more than should be humanly possible.

He says nothing. I say nothing as I stand here vulnerably, shaking so hard the bed feels like an earthquake.

"Just do it!" I taunt him. "Everyone will know the truth," I whisper, in a low warning. "I have proof," I state, full of rage and fright. Dillon gets to his knees, finds his balance and reaches out, getting between Donnie and me.

Sounding like a siren, the baby starts to cry from upstairs. Donnie's knees bend and his arms go up in shock. It's as if he hadn't realized there were others in the house with us.

Getting a little reckless?

"Sadie!" Dillon shouts, as he scurries up, in front of the bed, blocking me from his brother like a human shield.

Donnie walks past him, slowly, methodically as if he's not sure he's really going to leave us alive. He passes through the doorframe like a phantom. We both jump as we hear the front door slam into the wall next to it as it's opened so fast and with such force.

Dillon is breathing fiercely as he bellows, "We have to call 911!"

Yeah, like that's going to help!

Because sometimes when I'm scared it looks like I'm angry, I push away from him and stomp up the stairs.

Missy, holding little Joe, wide-mouthed and loud, opens the door before I reach it.

"What's going on down there?" Missy says, with squinting eyes.

"He's here!" is all I can manage, as I push her out of the way, run past Momma's bed and pull on the closet door handle. "Where's Daddy's gun?" I say, my voice audibly shaky. Missy turns on the light as Dillon bursts into the room.

"Dillon? What are you doing here!" Missy cries, shocked most likely by the fact that Dillon is in his underwear.

"Someone was in the house," Dillon says. I'm pulling down boxes in the closet, searching. Frantic to find what I need—Where's the gun? Daddy's gun? *He will not hurt me again.*

I hear Dillon pick up the phone on Momma's nightstand and tap the buttons.

"We've had a break-in…Yes, that's the correct address. It was a man…all black, yes…black mask. Tall…muscular build. No…okay, yes…No, I have to go. Just get here fast," he says, before walking into the closet with me. I stop to take in what's happened to his face. His nose is bleeding and the soft skin under his left eye is turning a light purple.

The baby is still crying and Missy is humming a lullaby. I rub my knotty throat.

"Momma, just go back ta sleep. Everything's fine," Missy says, as little Joe starts to lower his cry to a whine.

"Sadie." His voice is shaky. "What are you looking for?"

"Daddy's gun—the hand gun he taught me with," I assert, as I pull on a box and another one falls above it. Dillon has to jump in front to keep it from hitting me on the forehead. He grabs it with both hands and puts it on the floor as I look down at my feet. "I need the gun!" I declare.

I'm shaking so hard that my teeth begin to chatter. "Baby. You're safe now. He's gone," he says, as he pulls me into his chest and wraps his arms around me. He feels jittery, warm. His skin is soft, but moist with that quick-sweat that rises on the skin during times of fear. The hairs on his arm prickle the top of mine as he consoles me. His heart is beating like the sound of the railway as he runs the tips of his fingers up and down my trembling back. I want to let go. Let him take over for me. Give up. But I can't. I won't.

"Did he touch you?" he asks, as he pulls me away from him for an inspection.

"No, I just banged my head, that's all. You should go get some ice for your face, though," I say, as I pick up a towel from the shelf and wipe his bloody nose with it. The under part of his eye is a deep grey and puffed up now, and a bruise on his jaw is coloring in front of me as I watch. Gently, he starts to check my head for a bump. When he touches it, I wince and his hand stops.

"Who is he, Sadie?" he asks, cautiously, but furious. "You know who he is." This is no longer a question for him.

I want to say no. "Yes," I say, as I nod my head slowly.

"Please, tell me," he says, with urgency. "I need to know so I can help you."

I can't tell him. Donnie could have killed us both in our sleep. *Why didn't he?* How long was he there, watching us?

Dillon's jaw is swelling up now under the purple bruise and his eye looks like raw meat—all red and veiny. I knew Dillon would be no match for Donnie's strength. I have to take care of this myself. I have proof now—proof that he can't destroy and there's no way he's going to risk losing everything once he knows what the stakes are. Right?

"I can't tell you," I say, unwavering.

"Why not!" he yells.

"Because he said he'd rather I was dead than with you. He said he'd kill you if I didn't stay away from you."

"That's why you need to tell me, Sadie," he asserts.

"I can't. Please, stop asking me to."

"Stop protecting this dirt bag," he says, like he wants to shoot venom into the neck of a faceless man he hates.

"I'm not protecting him. I'm protecting you!"

"How? By shutting me out? By keeping the secret?"

"You wouldn't be able to take it. If I told you, you'd never be able to help me. You'd go after him and he'd kill you. It's that simple."

He's stumped. He stands there like a mute as if he's trying to decide if he could help me if he knew who it was.

"If that's what you need, for me to help you. I promise. I won't go after him. I just need to know so I can protect you." He's begging now. He sounds as dangerous as a river too high for its banks.

"I think you really mean it, but everything will change when you find out," I say, as I look at the wooden floor. *It's your brother!* I want to scream. But he couldn't take it if I did.

"I know him then," he says, as if he's trying to make that real to himself. I look at him impassively. I can't let my face tell him my secret this time.

He looks at me with rage behind his eyes. His whole body is shaking with adrenaline. Out of nowhere, he bites his bottom lip and swings his fist, striking the wall to the left of me. Stunned, I jump to the side and cower away from him as he cradles his hurt hand, his mouth in a pained O shape.

"Oh, God! I'm so sorry," he says, as he tries to hold me. I push him away. "I feel so helpless," he says, in barely a whisper as he grasps his hand. "I just want to be able to make you safe. I couldn't last time," he cries, as he walks backward. Pain is written in the creases on his forehead. He leans his head against the corner of the closet, slides his back down the wall like a burden too heavy to carry anymore.

"He's right, Sadie. Telling us who this is. It'll protect you," says Missy in a hushed tone, trying not to wake up the baby tucked up to her breast.

"I just want to find Daddy's gun. Can anyone help me for Christ's sake?"

"The Lord's name," Momma rasps from her bed loud enough for me to hear.

I get up, walk past Dillon still leaning into the corner and stand on the side of Momma's bed. "I'm sorry, Momma. It won't happen again." I pick up her weightless broken-bird arm and stroke her fingers.

"I know," she stops to take a breath, "where it is," she says. I swallow so hard my throat aches.

"Where?"

"What happened, baby?" she asks.

"The man who raped me, he came here tonight. He was in my room when I woke up and he...," I want to tell her that he hit Dillon but I'm scared that she'll be mad that he was sleeping in my room. I'm still the pastor's daughter, after all.

"It's in the dresser, honey," she says, pointing her boney finger toward the highboy dresser underneath the 'Sadie's Mountain' painting. "Top drawer," she rasps.

As if in a trance, I pad my way across the wooden floor and pull on the handle. My hands are fishing around until I feel it encased in leather nestled between soft nightgowns. Cold steel—Power. Safety in one small package. This will keep me safe. It will be my armor. *He will never touch me again.*

I sit on the too soft couch in Missy's bright blue robe and watch as Dillon talks to the two officers who came to write down stuff in little notebooks. This is futile. They cannot help me. It's their boss who wants to kill me and bury me in his front yard like a hidden monument. They take a picture of the handle-sized dent on the wall opposite the door. They scuttle into my room and stare at the floor in the corner of the room where I said 'The Man' was standing when I opened my eyes.

"We're going to have to ask y'all to keep out of this room tonight. We're gonna need ta' bring the fingerprinting guy from Fayetteville to check the front door and the bedroom for prints."

"Okay," he acknowledges and looks at me with a troubled expression. It makes me sad and empty to see him so worried. To know that all he wants is to make me safe and I can't give that to him.

Part of me just wants to get on a plane right now. But the thing is, I've been running from that man for ten years of my life. Even when I was on the other side of the continent, he caught me in my dreams, and showed up at times in everything I did. The way I needed to feel safe. The way I needed everything to be clean. The reason why I can't have a real relationship with a man. Why I have to control everything in my life. The reason why I have no real friends. I don't even have a pet. I just live this empty existence filled with nothing but trying to accomplish more and more in my career.

It's how I've filled the hole in my chest. But unless I face him, I'm doomed to go back to a life I've just realized I don't want anymore. I know that now. I can't walk away from here again. Here, at home, with my people and on top of the dirt that has been home to my ancestors, I can be a real person. I can live a full life with this man who would do anything for me to love him back. There's nothing that can take me away from here again. Not even *Donnie*.

"We're just gonna wrap the front door knob so we don't wipe away any of the evidence. This room will have the yella' tape across so no one can go in there 'til it's cleared, understood?"

Dillon nods his head yes. "Where's my brother?" He asks. I wince.

"I'm not sure, sir," says the deputy who looks a little like Barney Fife, slightly more muscular, but an underachiever at best.

"Is he on duty?"

"Not that I know of sir?"

No, because he's a real shadow who steals women's virtue in his spare time.

"I'm going to call him."

I don't even move a muscle. He's not going to get a hold of Donnie tonight. I'm sure of it. His nose is probably broken. *How's he going to explain that?*

I just want to go to sleep. I'm not letting go of this gun either. I stare at the light grey metal—watch it sparkle in the light from the lamp on the side table. I remember, Daddy taught me about it when he showed me how to use it.

It's a Ruger Old Army.45 caliber. Daddy got it in 1976 when it was brand new in honor of our bicentennial. He loved it because of the swirled engravings and the random deep ridges in the sepia colored handle. As I run my fingers over the handle, it feels like it must be some type of animal bone cut into the shape of a handle and drilled in place. Daddy said it was mammoth tusks. I wonder if that's even possible. It's probably worth a lot of money—but it's priceless to me, for other reasons.

It's loaded now. Dillon did it for me, while I examined the process like a dog watching someone fill its bowl. I drooled over the sleek gold bullets as he slid them in one by one—six in all. I can almost imagine the bullets finding their target right now and it feels like retribution. I like the feeling of settling the score. He deserves it.

All he has to do is leave me alone and these bullets will stay in their chambers. But if he won't, I'll do what I have to do to survive.

Dillon grabs his jacket off the chair, pulls his phone out and taps before putting it to his ear. "Renae? Where's Donnie? No, they say they don't know either... Well, have him call me. We had a break-in over at the Sparks' house... No, everyone's okay. Thank you so much. Sorry to call so late... Okay! Tomorrow... Sounds great. I really appreciate it. See you then."

He puts his phone on the bed and stands in the doorway looking at me like a lost puppy dog.

"Renae, Donnie's wife, invited us over for lunch tomorrow," he says.

I nod my head yes, as if I'm being nonchalant. My head swims for a moment as if I'm spinning down the drain, but when it stops, I realize, *this is perfect.* I'm going to let him know, just like he informed me in the shed, next time there will be consequences for behavior like that. He has to let me go. He will have no choice. There, in his house, I will declare my own freedom and there's nothing he can do to stop me.

As Dillon walks effortlessly toward me, he sits down and turns his legs into a lap on the couch perfect for me to cuddle up on. He puts his arm over the top of the back of the couch and leans toward me, drawn to me.

"I need to get you some ice," I say, concerned.

Hesitantly, I put down the gun that I've been holding like a pacifier between my two cupped hands.

"I've got it," Missy says, wielding an icepack covered with a light green kitchen towel.

I take it from her and pull my legs up onto the couch under me like a spring. I don't even know where to put the ice first. I settle on his eye because it looks worse than any eye I've ever seen before.

With my other hand, I trace the bruise on his chin and lean in to place soft angel kisses on the darkest purple spot. He winces.

"We can't stay here on the couch," he says. "I'd like to take you home."

"Home?"

"To my house," he says, cautiously but there's a bit of enthusiasm in his voice. "We can sleep there. I've got good locks," he says.

For the first time, I look at the clock. It's 2:30 am.

"What about Momma and Missy?"

"Your brothers are coming right now," he says.

My eyes feel weighted. "I'm exhausted," I say, with a yawn so sizeable it hurts my jaw.

Just then, Seth and Jake wander into the living room, bewildered and brandishing shotguns. 'Barney Fife' is putting the finishing touches on the plastic on the front door. It's funny to me that the cops don't even flinch about all of us holding guns. It's just normal around here.

"Whoa, you guys aren't messing around? Where were you?" I say, shocked by the large weapons in their hands.

"We been stayin' nights at Missy's while Dale's gone and you're here," Jake says.

"You guys okay?" Seth asks.

"Yeah. We're okay," Dillon says.

"It don't look okay, man," Jake replies, pointing to his face and widening his eyebrows.

"I would take worse," he says, "for her." He looks at me with the one eye not covered by the light green kitchen towel.

"You guys taking off?"

"If you all don't mind. We can't sleep in there," he says, pointing at the door crossed off with yellow tape. It's almost funny to me that no one's wondering what Dillon is even doing here in the middle of the night.

"No, it's good. We've got this," Jake says earnestly, holding the barrel of the gun at the ground.

"Are you ready?" Dillon asks, standing up and reaching his hand down toward me. I put my palm in his and stand up next to him like a woman about to dance with her sweetheart.

I wonder if he really did buy me a big white house with a big kitchen and lots of rooms for all our babies. I guess I'm going to find out.

Chapter Sixteen

A Big White House

I've got my long barreled handgun in one hand and the one small bag I brought with me from California in the other. Before I make it to the front porch, Dillon takes my bag so he can hold my hand as we walk toward his Prius. I wonder if Donnie is watching us as we walk out of the house. I feel defiant as I hold Dillon's hand. It's likely that he is, since he'd watched me all the time, for years, without me knowing. I can't believe he told me that today. As a matter of fact, I can't believe a lot of what happened today.

It's so odd. Even though it feels like my plane landed months ago, I only stepped foot onto West Virginia territory two days ago. Thursday was my flight and it's only 3:00 a.m. on Saturday morning. Two days ago, if someone had told me I would be on my way to Dillon's house in the middle of the night I would have called them a liar. But here I am in my pajamas and wrapped up in Missy's bright blue robe, going to sleep in his bed with him, I've kissed him with a clear conscience, I've asked him to make love to me and he turned me down. So much has come about in these two days.

As he opens the trunk to stow my one small bag away for me, I realize it's not that irrational that two days could change the trajectory of my life when, in reality, twenty minutes in that shed altered my entire existence. I was on one track and then at a moment's notice, I wasn't any longer. I wasn't even the same person anymore.

As he opens the car door for me, I wonder about the house Dillon bought. Here I am, envisioning my future—a dreamlike future that now includes Dillon and a big white house, a big kitchen, and a lot of rooms that we're going to fill with our babies. It's great in theory. But, am I capable of such a normal life?

I remember his speech up on the mountain about what he wants from me. He'd spewed his ideal life into the air around us. I'd swatted it away as if I was unworthy of it, but one of the things I'd caught was that he had bought 'us' a house. Then, when he refused me in my room, he said that he'd always imagined taking off my white wedding gown in 'our' room.

As he turns on the engine that doesn't really turn on, I gaze up at his face, now marred by violence and a brother's fixation. He's swollen and bruised. His eye looks red and veiny. Seeing him like this is a reality check. Going to Dillon's house has me bopping around in la-la land as if Donnie hadn't just broken into my house and beaten his brother nearly to death.

If Donnie hadn't been scared off by the rest of my family he would have probably killed Dillon and then tried to violate me once again—take what he thinks is owed to him—or worse. This awareness is a rush of lucidity that takes me down quite a few notches on the happiness belt. I squeeze my gun.

I gaze up at Dillon who looks deep in thought as we glide onto Highway 60. I wish I could crawl in there, deep inside his mind and read his thoughts. Truth be told, he's probably wishing the same thing—much more than I am, actually.

I don't know what to say to make him feel better. He's so unaware of all that's going on inside my mind. The plans I'm making to let go, and truly be his in every way. But that hinges on my evidence and Donnie's reaction to it. I will use it, if I have to—that I know. He'll lose everything, his job, his wife, his children, if he doesn't let me go. Maybe I shouldn't even give him a chance to decide.

What if I just make the post live? No. I'm not ready to do that yet. To make public the most horrid event of my life, to tell everyone the secrets held deep within me for all these years. It would be like taking off my well-honed veneer and revealing to everyone the scarred little girl inside me.

"What proof do you have?" Dillon asks, out of nowhere.

"What?"

"In your room. You told him to *do* it because everyone would know it's him."

Oh crap!

"What proof do you have?" he asks again, impassive, serious. The last thing on my mind when I said that was whether or not Dillon heard me. I was frantic to distract Donnie so he wouldn't kill him, but he heard every word. I'm spinning through every lie I can tell right now.

The wheel lands on, "I was bluffing," I try, and then look out the window so he can't tell I'm lying.

"Well, it worked. I believed you, too," he says, almost as if he doesn't believe me. When I check him out again, he's looking at the road. He's holding the steering wheel too tight. He has the right to be perturbed over my not telling him—but I can't. If I did, if I just let him in here for half a minute, if I opened my mind and let him climb in, he'd be scratching to get out, begging for mercy. *It's better this way.* I feel guilty, but he really doesn't need to know. After tomorrow's lunch, I will be free—then we can really be together.

We've driven from Brandon Street down Highway 60 toward town. I wonder where he lives? Hesitation hangs in the air between us—like tension when answering difficult questions in an interview, but this is an interview with my future house. This is silly. I'm being silly, and I'm usually so indifferent to the workings of life. Well, aside from my career, or my antiques. *Is this the new me?*

When we turn onto Page Street, he slows down and takes the little driveway up the knoll to the Page-Vawter house, an old abandoned house that used to fascinate me when I was younger. I always wondered what it looked like inside. It was big enough to be considered a mansion. We'd peeked in through the dust on the tall windows at the oak floors covered in a thin veil of West Virginia grit that had settled there year by empty year. I remember there were so many fireplaces covered in pretty tiles that I'd lost count.

As his headlights shine upon the house, I realize it isn't rickety anymore and it's white!

"Dillon?" I question him as he pulls up to one of the most famous houses in Ansted.

"Yes, Sadie?" he says, suddenly buoyant—his voice hopping around like my mood.

"Is this your house?"

He stares at me through the darkness in the car. He turns off the engine and nods his head slowly to show me he really means it.

"How? What? Did you fix it up yourself?"

"I've done some of it myself. Some of it I've paid to get done."

I have to close my mouth on purpose when I realize it's wide open. I look at the house and back at him. *He kept his promise.* It makes my heart pound realizing that he'd never given up on me. My chin trembles so I put my hand to my mouth.

"Would you like to come in?" he says, seductively smooth.

The only thing I can do is nod. This is like the ultimate antique. Covertly, this house is what I've never had the courage to admit I always wanted—like a little seed of hope that I'd never watered. In fact, my house in California is a newer version of this house—L shaped and two storied with the gabled kitchen and a wraparound veranda. It has only a fraction of the charm, and none of the history—like a generic copy.

Dillon, having opened my door, is standing next to me, holding his hand out. I look down at the handgun and move it to my left hand so I can take Dillon's offer to have his support getting up—as shocked as I am, I need all the help I can get.

My black house slippers pit and pat along the rock-dotted path up to the front porch. I can feel the little solid mounds digging into the soles of my feet. We creak up the stairs, my hand in Dillon's like knotted wood, just like old times. He unlocks one of the double doors and lets it glide open of its own free will. As I cross over the threshold with his hand pressed into the small of my back, I find myself just where I'm supposed to be. I exhale loudly. I just realized I'd been holding my breath.

"Welcome home," Dillon says, like a foghorn welcoming me on to shore; and when I look at him he's smoldering again.

"Home," I say, as if I need to be reminded what the word means.

"What do you think?" he asks.

Inside, the house is just as it always was through the glass, except more real. It smells of polished woods, and newer paint. The wainscoting is cleaner with a new matte patina. It sounds empty, because it is. Even our breath bounces around, echoing like invisible boomerangs trying to find a soft spot to rest—and that makes me sad. This house is just waiting for a family to fill it up.

"You know I love this house. Why is it empty?" I ask, as I'm imagining all of my antiques in the places they were born to set down in for the rest of my life. Being here brings relief to my system, like a puzzle has been solved.

"I haven't got around to the decorating part. That's more your forte, right?"

What to say? What to say? He's very clear about his intentions. I can't tell him how I feel. If something goes wrong tomorrow at lunch, it'd break his heart.

"I can't believe you're here," he says. And I believe him. He looks confounded.

"Here is where I'm supposed to be, I think." I say it because I have to. It just tumbles out.

Now his bruised jaw is the one gaping open. "What did you just say?" he asks. I shrug my shoulders. "Sadie, what are you saying?" he sounds like he's on edge, his voice cracking.

"I…"

"Darlin' please. Say you'll stay," he says, grasping my hand to his chest. "I don't ever want to think of you leaving this place. This…"

"This is where I belong. Is that what you were going to say?"

"Yes." He nods, never taking his eyes away from mine. Try as I might, I can't wipe the smile off my face. He takes the gun from my fingers wrapped around it, and places it on the intricately engraved fireplace mantel. "It's okay, you're safe here. I'll set the alarm."

If I wasn't so enthralled with Dillon, I'd be inspecting the hand carved wooden mantel and ceramic tile. I want to promise him I'll stay, but I don't want to lead him on. Yes, I've decided but tomorrow is another day. I have to follow through with telling Donnie I have his voice recorded first.

"Can we look around?" I ask. He swallows hard and looks away, his jaw tensed. He puts his fist to his mouth and takes a deep breath. That wasn't the answer he wanted.

"Of course," he says, overly formal as he walks away, sets the alarm and then takes my hand in his, softly. *Live wires.* God, I hate hurting him. "This is the formal living room," he says, his voice straining to stay straight.

"I thought so," I say, trying to deflect with humor.

"All the floors are the original oak, as well as the oak panels and the wainscoting." He's still too serious.

"They are beautiful," I say, as I run the tips of my fingers over the panels, letting my nails find the divots between the wood. "How big is this house?"

"Fifty-eight hundred square feet."

"That's twenty-five hundred more than my house in California," I say, my eyes wide enough that they start to feel dry and I have to remind myself to blink.

"There's seventeen rooms in all. It has seven bedrooms," he says, and he squeezes my hand almost imperceptibly. "Plus, there's a butler's pantry over by the kitchen."

"Wasn't the kitchen added later?"

"Yeah, in the twenties."

"I bet it's lovely."

"I'm not done with it yet," he says, shyly. "I'm using a small kitchen that was put in when the house was a duplex."

"Can I see it?"

"The new kitchen? There's no power in that room. Can I show you in the morning? I'm sure you're exhausted."

"Sure," I pout, sticking out my bottom lip.

"Upstairs, the master has a separate dressing room. Do you want to see?"

"Sure," I say, as I start to get nervous again. The master must be his room.

As we walk along the bottom floor toward the stairs, I remember how puzzled I'd always been about the fireplaces. "How many fireplaces are there, Dillon?"

"Eleven," he says, quickly. "They all have hand-carved wooden mantels. Most are in different styles. I don't know a lot about 'em but I'm sure you can tell me."

I do a quick inventory. A formal living room, humongous dining room. Crystal chandeliers, oak floors, walnut window facings. The stairs are beautiful and look to be hand carved. I run my hand along the railing as I climb them. It feels as soft as a daisy petal under my fingertip.

At the end of the hall, passing by many other closed doors, Dillon leads me into the bedroom. *Our bedroom*, I think, and smile. Normally, I'd want to put on the brakes. I would have let my anxiety take over, but today, I'm a new girl—a woman now, or at least that's how he makes me feel. I'm not afraid. I just want him to hold me again. I won't be able to calm down until he does. He's like my panacea—my cure all.

Once inside, I smell him—his distinctive scent, the one that reminds me of childhood, happiness, warmth, and yes, of love. He's all over this room. This must be where he spends the most time. There is an intricately carved, hand painted bed in the middle of the room—our bed. It's a canopy bed with a square frame. There are no fabrics hanging from it but it doesn't look bare.

"It's beautiful," I say, walking over to the bed and running my fingers over the intricate details.

"Yes, it is," he says, his voice carnal and heavy. When I look up, he's looking at me, not the bed.

"Is it original to the house?" I say, and swallow hard. I feel like a fine delicacy in his sight.

"Yes, it was Captain Page's bed. I had it painted white to make it feel more like it's mine," he says, serious again. Good to know he's not a purist with his antiques. I love mine painted, too.

I can't look away from him. As I watch, the serious look on his face turns back into the smolder. I step forward and grasp his other hand in mine. We must look like a bride and groom standing next to the altar. Me in my long robe, he in his dark pants and shirt.

"Do not arouse or awaken love until it so desires," he says. *But I do desire.* I blink and shut my eyes. Where do I know those words? When I open them, he looks like he's in pain. Someone could be burning his feet with coals or slicing his heart open with a paring knife. That's how much pain I see on his face.

"What is that quote from?" I ask, bewildered.

"The Song of Songs in the Bible." He sounds like living water on a rainy day.

"Oh, yes. The Song of Songs is about..."

"It follows King Solomon's marital relationship from courtship through consummation." I have to shake my head. That's not what I was taught.

"I thought it was an allegory for the relationship between God and Christ."

"No, darlin' it's about making love for the first time," he says, staring into my eyes, my rosebud is growing, pushing its way up into my belly. I try to squeeze my thighs together to either make it stop or not make it stop. I can't decide.

"That's what your tattoo says. It's from the Song of Songs," I say, finally realizing where I know the verse I read on his arm. He nods his head yes, and swallows hard.

I reach up to his face, and he leans into my touch, even though it hurts him when he does. There's nowhere to touch that isn't bruised. He leans into me. Pressing his body to mine. And he starts to speak, mesmerizing me.

"My beloved spoke and said to me,
'Arise, my darling,
my beautiful one, come with me.
See! The winter is past;
the rains are over and gone.
Flowers appear on the earth;

the season of singing has come,
the cooing of doves
is heard in our land.'"

He's quoting the Song of Songs again. Speaking them to me as if I were the woman—the wife in the verse. Does he mean that the worst is over? Does he mean that the flowers are the happy life we deserve to experience together? And the singing. It is time to sing again.

And then I remember the line that fits our relationship. I'd heard it often enough that parts had been embedded deep in my memory. I'm glad I haven't forgotten because it means I can reciprocate.

"My beloved is mine and I am his;
he browses among the lilies.
Until the day breaks
and the shadows flee," I say.

His eyebrows shoot up and he pulls me to him, scooping me into his arms, allowing our bodies to touch. From this movement, I know how much he wants me, too. A man's body never lies.

"You remember."

"Yes, of course. Daddy taught me. He said it wasn't for the novices."

"Or maybe it is," he responds, seductively.

"What better way to get rid of shadows that come in the night..." I say, breathy, looking at him through my lashes. My tummy clenches uncontrollably now, and I push my body back into his so that every place that can touch him, does—as if we were made by the Creator just to fit together. Without taking my eyes off his, I pull on the end of the tie around the robe, let it fall, like shedding petals from a flower, to the floor, "...than to browse among the lilies all night long?" I am the lilies. My body is. It all makes sense now. He looks confused. He puts his hand up to his forehead.

He closes his eyes. "But this isn't going to be enough for me, Sadie," he says, running the tips of his shaky fingers up the small of my back, causing me to catch my breath and close my eyes. "Once we give ourselves to each other, I'll never be able to let you go," he says, as I open my eyes to see his pained expression. "If you left me again, after this, I…I couldn't take it," he says, taking his hand from his forehead and running his finger along my jawline. A chill runs through my whole body.

Just tell him the truth, I say to myself. I don't want to hurt him anymore. Touch me, my body is saying. It hurts for him not to. It's as if deep in my belly, I'm blooming, spreading out, and throbbing. I need him to quench it. Fill it up. I'm shaking now, and so is he. I'm gripping his arm so tight my fingers hurt.

"I want more," he admits. *Yes, more. More. Everything more.* Everything that he wants, I want. I swallow so hard I hear it and so does he.

"I don't want to be let go of," I say, because I have to, my eyes darting back and forth between his. "I want to stay. I never want to leave you again," I say.

"Then why do you have to?" he asks.

"Why do I? It's fear. That's all," I explain.

"All I know, Sadie, is that I've loved you all your life. Nothing will ever change that. I bought this house for you, in the hopes that you'd come here and we'd make this our home, fill it up with babies."

"That's what I realize I've always wanted, Dillon."

"You do?" he says, smiling.

"I want more, too, Dillon. I do. I want everything you want. I promise you, I'll never leave you again." I mean it, too. I won't leave, no matter what Donnie does tomorrow. This is my life. This is where I'm meant to be. His eyes shut and his head moves back abruptly as if I've just hit him with something he wasn't ready for.

"You'll stay? You'll marry me?" he asks.

"Please, one thing at a time," I caution him before he takes me up in his arms and swings me around. The feeling of being weightless, free of burdens and fear for a moment takes my breath away. I hear my own giggle floating around, trying to keep up with me. He stops, holding me around the waist in midair so we are eye to eye.

"That, I can work with, my darlin'," he says, before he takes my lips between his and moves his hand down, passing over my bottom, and landing on my thigh. We feel like electricity together. Live wires, again, everywhere. He sets me on the edge of our bed, and pulls up the hem of my white nightgown, slowly so that his thumb gently grazes up the length of my thigh. *This is close to his dream,* I think in consolation. It is a white gown, after all, and this is our room. My throat is dry, and I feel dizzy. I have to hold onto the ropey muscles in his arm for support.

"How beautiful you are, my darling!

Oh, how beautiful!

Your eyes are doves," he says, quoting the Bible once again.

"How handsome you are, my beloved!

Oh, how charming!

And our bed is verdant," I respond, before I'm speechless and so is he.

Chapter Seventeen

I Am The Lily

He plays me like a stringed instrument—picking softly and strumming, cultivating a reaction under his skillful touch. His long thin fingers know the right song to play over my skin to have me quavering like one of his dulcimer strings. While he sits next to me on our bed, I draw his shirt over his broad shoulders, and knot my fingers under his t-shirt, pulling it over his head, baring the tattoo of a lily over his heart. I knew he had two of them.

Place me like a seal over your heart, like a seal on your arm;

Oh, it all makes sense. The tattoos' placement comes from the Song of Songs. I am the lily; I am the 'great laurel'. I run my fingers over the ink mark, it feels smooth, and not raised as I thought it would. His heart beats through his skin, bonding us even more. My lip trembles and then I smile.

"You are my flower," he says, before smiling back. He pulls my nightgown over my head, letting me feel brazen under his blistering stare.

"You're so perfect, so beautiful," he says, through hitched breaths. I feel him running his nose up the full length of my neck, stopping just there behind my ear. "Your scent. Do you know what you do to me?" he says, into my ear. I feel a shiver that runs down my spine down to my core. It aches and grows. As we lie back together, he moves his right hand under my head. His other hand grasps my waist. I feel cherished, cradled in his arms.

His lips are on my mouth, grazing over my chin, soothing my neck, sinking into the rise and fall of my breasts like little mounds coming up to meet him. He's moving, wet and soft, achingly slow, down the center of my stomach as he unstraps my bra, wet from his mouth having just been there, and frees me. I am almost naked, but I'm not embarrassed. I want him to look at me—and he does. He drinks me in, every inch, like he's thirsty for me.

His left hand moves up my stomach until his thumb is just under my breast. I close my eyes as he's scooping me up so that I fit perfectly in his hand. *Don't stop*, I beg him silently by pushing back against him as his fingers clasp and his mouth makes peaks over my skin—my back bowing, my knees coming up like fleshy arches in the dim light.

Who knew I'd be so excitable? So natural at this. It's him. Our history together mingles with this, now, making it so pure, so right. A moan escapes from the back of my throat. It startles me. My hands are in his hair, pulling his mouth to mine, daring him to keep going. I need him to touch me. It hurts when he doesn't.

"It hurts," I announce, and he stops as if a bucket of water was poured on him.

Oh, don't stop.

"I'm hurting you?" he asks, pained, startled. I shake my head no.

"No, my belly aches right here," I show him, putting my hand over my lower tummy.

"Oh, darlin'," he says, with a chuckle. "That's natural. That's just your body reacting to me touching you like this."

"Make it stop. It hurts me," I say, in serious pain. He closes his eyes, and when he opens them again, I see something like devotion in his Tahoe blue eyes.

"I have to do this first," he says, into my mouth. "I have to get you ready for me."

His words alone are like fuel to my yearning—I feel frantic. Desperate for him. I'm begging him with my eyes, touching his chest, his back. Kissing him with a passion I've never know existed until now.

He pulls away slightly, never taking his eyes from mine, he takes off my pale blue panties, so slowly. I can still feel the path his fingers took down the full length of my right leg. Before I know it, he's running his hand up the inside of my left thigh. I can't help but jump backward as he nearly reaches the apex of my thighs. It's a gut reaction.

"Do you want me to stop?" he asks softly as if not to scare me, just to find out what I need. This makes me feel safe, like I'm in control, although I can barely control my own breathing as I bite my lip so hard I taste metal in my mouth. I want him to touch me. I want to experience what it feels like to be loved by this man, in every way. But, this area of my body has, until right this moment, only known pain.

"Darlin'," he says, looking deep into my eyes as I rest on his right arm. He kisses me slowly and releases my lip from between my clenched teeth. "We don't have to do anything until you're ready," he says, reassuringly—and I know he means it. He's halted his hand, but not moved it.

I close my eyes, and relax my body, purposefully, by taking a deep cleansing breath. I expressly remind myself that what I feel now is the opposite of pain. He would never hurt me. Although they are brothers, they are contrary to one another. What his brother took, Dillon will give back to me in his own way, and right now. "You're going to have to tell me when you're ready," he says, swallowing hard.

It seems like we lie here on the precipice for ages. When I don't feel like I'm going to react to the diseased molecules swimming on the surface of my perception, I say yes with my eyes and nod my head almost imperceptibly. If he'd blinked too long, he would have missed me giving him my consent.

I exhale, locking eyes with him as he glides smoothly through the petals of my flower. I feel it from the soles of my feet to the top of my head. Our bond is strengthened, stronger than before, and unable to be broken. I am his and he is mine. I push into his hand, squeeze my legs around his arm.

I am his instrument. He plays me and I sing in breathy tunes. I can't keep still. I need him to quench this ache, make the rosebud bloom and grow before it can close again like flowers in the night. My eyes plead with his. *I need you.*

"Please," I say, as that's all I can force my mouth to complete. He pushes off the bed, away from me. At first, I think he's changed his mind. But slowly, he unbuttons his pants. Pulling them down over his hips, he frees what had been pushed down by weight of the denim. I look at him sideways as I wonder about the mechanics of it and if I can accommodate him. He's a monument to the art of manhood. *I had no idea.*

Then I realize, as he looks at me so vulnerably trying to read my expression, that we fit together in every other way. The way our hands fit together—our fingers entwined like knotted wood, mine in his; how his hip rests just above mine when he holds me, and I fit perfectly under his ribs when we walk arm in arm. This should be no different. I wiggle under his gaze. I'm not afraid. I'm hearing the Song of Songs in my head. This verse makes so much sense now. The moment when the wife is introduced to sensual pleasure:

> *Like an apple tree among the trees of the forest*
> *is my beloved among the young men.*
> *I delight to sit in his shade,*
> *and his fruit is sweet to my taste.*

*Let him lead me to the banquet hall,
and let his banner over me be love.'*

These verses finally make sense. The couple is starving for love. The physical relationship feeds it—feeds them and makes them stronger. I want to be nourished. We will become stronger together.

"Let my beloved come into his garden and taste its choice fruits," I say, ending the verse I'd been thinking out loud. The look on his face, so serious, so amorous makes me feel like bubbles are popping under my skin, my eyebrows furrowed in longing.

He is drawn to me, and I to him like two atoms pulled into marriage with one another. He takes my lips between his. This is a new kiss, asking for something, coaxing my heart to connect with his on some level I cannot even fathom yet. My form comes up to meet him as he breathes out and tenderly finds his place within my body, just like my memories of him have always been inside my mind all these years.

At first, the pain echoes through me with a feeling like ripping paper. But he moves inside me so slowly you'd think I am an heirloom of thin glass that already has a hairline crack. He takes my pain, filters it into his mouth as I exhale it. Before I know it, I'm singing in a breathy tune.

Despite how fragile I am to him, we slowly begin to sing together—a duet of movement and breath, kisses that pitter-patter along mouths and necks. His scent and mine mix together in the air around us like a perfume that never existed until right this moment. I am overcome. I will never leave him. He is mine.

"I'm yours," I say, into his mouth as he stops, inhales and exhales heavy and deep, looking at me like his most prized possession. He cries out, sounding like a wolf howling in a low holler and drives himself inside me with a new potency—as if there is nothing separating us anymore. As if we are free.

My stinging tears mix with our perspiration, our scents dancing, his back wet under my fingers, our bodies powerfully gliding together in a slick covering. It's building inside. My skin feels hot. It's pain and pleasure in the same moment. We move together as one entity, I'm filled, and quenched, and bloom wider than I'd ever expected.

"Arise, come, my darling; my beautiful one, come with me," he says through clenched teeth, looking into my stinging eyes. He holds me, breaths frantic in my ear, as we shudder and quake together. I clutch him to my body with all four limbs, like he is the tree during a windstorm, and I am holding on for dear life.

I'm on fire, both inside and out. I push my face into his chest to hide the stinging cry that has turned into the loud, ugly cry. Suddenly, he's tenderly kissing my face, kissing my squeezed-shut eyes, my ruddy cheeks, my chin. He cradles my face between his long, thin fingers.

"Did I hurt you, baby?" I can't answer him. "Are you hurt?" He's getting frantic now. He pulls away from me and I wince from the shock of being separated so quickly. I almost want to push him away, but I force myself not to punish him for my inability to handle too much at once.

It's easier to push away than to hold on. It always has been. It's easier to feel angry than vulnerable—and that's how I feel now. Completely stripped of my veneer. My body has never known such tenderness, such urgency, such release, but this has drawn up what was really never healed in me like breaking open a glass case and spilling the remains to the floor.

"I'm okay," I chirp, through the spasms of my crying. "I…" I cover my eyes with my hand like a child who thinks they're invisible when only their head is under the blanket.

"I know, baby. Just let it out," he says. *Let it out?* I think as I refuse to pick up my broken pieces from the floor. I need to deal with this. He's right. *Let it go! Stop holding on to all of this. I don't need to do this alone anymore.*

I lean into his chest like a brace and he holds me while I grieve. I grieve my loss in a way that I was never able to when I was numb and empty. The loss feels so immense that I can't see the top of it from my perspective on the ground. I mourn in heaving tears, and acknowledge the old me hiding behind all of it as if she's just been waiting for me to let her out of the prison he put her in.

In fact, I know he did not kill her. It was me who let her go so I could move on—like cutting off a diseased limb before it spreads to the rest of the body. I'm ready now to bring her out and examine her wounds. I'm willing to call her 'me' again.

I acknowledge that her fears are my fears, let go of the guilt, and say goodbye to my empty life—really take my time until I'm nearly empty of all of that, for now. He holds me until my breaths are even and clear, until my limbs feel like loose rubber bands and my eyes, like steel weights. In my chest, I feel a white light. I embrace it, even if it is just for this moment.

"You're so brave, darlin'," he croons. I feel nothing but peace in my bones. "Sleep now, baby," he whispers as he pulls me under his arm, my head resting on his chest. I can't help it when sleep comes like a refuge in the safety of love's cocoon.

As my eyes flutter from shut to open, I'm greeted by the morning sun dancing in waves through the trees outside Dillon's, I mean, our room. I don't want to move because then we will have to get up—deal with the life that falls on me like a boulder from the sky. My mother is dying, Donnie wants to murder me and keep me enslaved by his sickness, I can't tell Dillon what's going on and he's pressing for the truth, and a coal company is going to blow up the mountain that my home town is nestled into—a town that I've decided I'm not going to leave.

On the other hand, I have this, right now. I'm in bed with my best friend, the only man I've ever loved and who loves me more than a fish loves water; and I've just agreed to stay here with him, in this house that has nothing but potential—kind of like Dillon and me.

Memories of last night come at me in waves just like the sunlight. I'm warmed by the pictures in my mind. My skin prickles and my stomach tingles. Physically, we are a perfect match. We'd always been emotionally perfect for one another. He never pushed me too hard, but always helped me be the best me. He's funny. Kind. Sensitive, but strong. He's perfect—too perfect for me, I think.

I smile wider than my face. *I want to do that again.*

"You do?" Dillon says, in my ear through a raspy, morning voice.

"Did I say that out loud?" I question him, as I yawn and stretch my body out like I'm reaching for both ends of the bed. I'm sore—but in a good way like after doing yoga or running in the park.

"Yes," he says, his left arm bent under his ear and his right hand resting on my stomach. We took no precautions last night. His hand there makes me feel like my body is shared with someone. I wonder if I could be?

"I'd love to take you up on that," he says, kissing my cheek. "We do have quite a few surfaces in said house to make love upon." I giggle, remembering his speech up on the mountain. I love it when he talks like that, super smart like the Ph.D. that he is. "I didn't want to wake you, but it's actually almost noon and we're late for lunch at Donnie and Renae's house."

And there's that boulder, falling right on my chest. I can do this. I have the upper hand this time. I'm ready to reclaim my life. One thing I know for sure. Things will never be the same again. And I'm okay with that.

Chapter Eighteen

Splinters

I have only a sheet covering my body; a comfy white sheet under a deep green duvet that's only covering our feet. Everything is soft, including Dillon's arm as his hand rests on my stomach. I don't want to get up yet. I know I have to go to lunch at Donnie's house today, but I want to talk first. I thought it was such a cliché that women want to talk after making love in movies. But that's exactly what I need right now.

"How are you feeling?" I ask. In the morning light, his face looks as bad as the punches sounded. He's swollen under his eye and on his jaw, his eye looks even worse now.

"I should be asking you," he responds. "Are you okay?" he asks, looking at me like he's done something wrong.

"I'm fine. Better than fine, actually. That was…"

"I know," he says, when I can't find a word to describe the wonder that took over my body last night.

"Is it like that all the time?" I ask, feeling a bit inadequate, and inexperienced. Then I realize I'm probably not the only woman who's been in this bed with him.

"No, darlin', what we have is very different. Special, you know? What we did last night, I've never done before. The emotional part, how much I love you, was even more profound for me than what my body felt. Other than our first *real* kiss, nothing from my past can compare."

I'm looking at him from under my lashes. "For me, too, obviously."

"I'm glad you waited for me," he says, as he nuzzles his long finger along my cheek. My heart starts to beat recklessly, and my cheek tingles under his rousing touch.

"Me, too," I say, but the truth is, I never really had a chance. My body said no to everyone else.

"Are you really staying here with me?"

"I meant everything I said last night. And I need to say something else."

"Okay," he says, looking a bit nervous as he moves his hand over the round part of my hip. I love it when he touches me. It makes me feel like I'm his.

"Thank you," I say, swallowing hard, my mouth dry, as I sit up in the bed and he follows.

"For what?" he questions, as he pulls me toward him. My legs are criss-crossed, and his, bent and open on either side of me. I realize he's put some grey boxers on. He must have been up for a while watching me sleep. He smells amazing. Like him, only magnified and mixed with me.

"For never giving up on me, Dillon. For doing this for me—for us," I say, waving my hand at the room inside the house of my dreams. "It's completely overwhelming to think that all these years…" My words are stuck in my head. I can't get them to come out the way they're lined up in my mind. He's watching me intently.

"No, I thank you, Sadie. For coming home, and for loving me back. I can't even believe it. All these years, I hoped, but now…," he says, grasping my hands.

"Have you ever," I clear my throat, "brought anyone else here?"

He stops and blinks a few times, as if my question surprises him. "No, darlin' you're the only woman I've ever brought to our bed. That's how it always felt to me. When I saw it, I knew it was yours—just like me." He looks so earnest. There's no way he's being dishonest. But I still feel territorial over him—resentful of any other woman he's been with. "Are you jealous?" he asks.

"No," I say. But I am. I want to ask him how many women he's been with. But what if I don't like the answer?

"Yes, you are," he says, tickling me under my ribs. I giggle and jerk away from him. When I do, he looks down on the bed where I was just lying.

"What's wrong?" I say, looking down, too. There, under where I'd been sleeping, in the spot where we made love in our bed for the first time, is a quarter sized spot of the deepest crimson, almost in the shape of a heart. *It's blood.* I look up at him, confused. I didn't think that could happen again.

"How is this possible?" I ask.

"Did I hurt you?" he asks, nervously.

"A little, but I feel fine," I say, puzzled.

"Well, this means I was right. To me you were, and I'm the only one," he says, in awe. It seems like his words aren't coming out the way they're lined up in his mind either.

He leans toward me and kisses me so ardently that I start to feel dizzy. I kiss him back, because I love him and because I want to feel this now before the world is turned upside down in the next hour of my life.

"You ready to shower with me, baby?" he asks, with an intense expression—like he's going to share something with me. I've never done anything so intimate, with the exception of last night.

I get up, embarrassed to be naked in the morning light. He smiles and moves my arm away from my breasts, taking me in. "Please, don't hide from me. I've waited all my life for this," he says, taking a moment to look at my naked body. I know there will be a time when this doesn't make me nervous, but my cheeks feel hot and the back of my neck feels damp. He grasps my other hand and walks backward with me into the bathroom attached to the room. "Do you know how beautiful you are?"

"I smell of you," I say.

"And I of you," he says, as he steps onto the cool tile floor. "I love it." He smiles, and I giggle. "What a wonderful sound," he says. "Your giggle reminds me of being a kid. Back when things were simple."

"Me, too," I say, and then look around.

The bathroom looks completely remodeled, but in an antique style. There's a claw foot tub, but larger than a normal one, gorgeous ceramic tile in a light green hue. Just the one I'd pick if given my choice. *He's really read my blogs.*

He turns on the shower and strips down. I wonder, as I blush all over, whether I'll always be dumbfounded when I see him nude. He's breathtaking—his muscles tight and ropey. His skin is flawless and I giggle thinking, if there is a God, he's been generous with him in every way.

"What's so funny?" he asks as we step into the modern shower under the stream of steaming water together.

"I was just thinking that God was kind to you." I blush, my eyes darting down for a brief second. He's not embarrassed. He's very secure in his nakedness. I'm sure any man who looks like him would be.

"I'm glad to hear you believe in Him again," he says, smiling and nudges me backward until water drenches me like mini-waterfalls over my eyes and the peak of my nose. He takes care of me, washes my hair, his long thin fingers massaging my scalp. He lathers lavender scented soap and rubs my whole body with it, taking care to even wash me in my most delicate area. I try not to let my body get too anticipatory. We do have to go.

I bite my thumbnail to stop the thumping in my heart and try not to push back into his soapy fingers. I close my eyes as he rubs my stomach and moves his hands along my lower back. I open them when he stops washing me. He looks lost, his arms around my waist.

"What's wrong?" I ask.

"This just seems so surreal," he says.

"Like everything is as it should be," I say, kissing his chest, before I move around so I'm behind him and reciprocate. He winces when I wash the foot sized bruise marring his back. I want to take his bruises away. Erase them. It's my fault. *No, nothing Donnie does is my fault. I know that now.* I just need a reminder.

I wash his hair, which feels soft between my fingers, his skin warm and flawless, charged under my touch. When I reach around to his chest, my arms under his, and move down toward his stomach with soapy fingers, I find him wanting more as he turns to face me.

This is so intimate and fills my chest with too much steaming air to breath normally. I wrap my hands around his neck as he presses my back against the now warm tile, pinning me ardently with his hips.

He kisses me carefully, as if he's holding back, and pulls his mouth away, then presses his forehead lightly against mine. How easy it will be to be his wife, to live my life with him. This is so perfect, so right, I think into his eyes—with one red and broken. His wounds make me sad, then livid and defensive. No one will hurt us again.

"Next time," he promises, with his eyes shut and his lips curved upward. It feels like an invisible current flows around us in the steam. He kisses me lightly on the cheek, as if he were kissing my lips again, he'd be lost. He turns off the water.

"I'm not on the pill," I blurt, as the water drips and pats on the tile shower floor.

"I figured as much," he says, smiling candidly. "We do have all of those other bedrooms," he reminds me. As I try to fathom the idea, he rubs me down with a sweet scented, fluffy white towel. When I'm dry, I rub his hair with a towel wrapped around my hands as he leans down to make it easier for me. I'm wondering if deep in my belly a tiny new life is growing molecule by molecule—sprouting up out of what used to be ruins but now feels like fertile ground.

I don't know if I'm prepared for that.

We get ready together, quite aware that we are new to this dance around the room. He reassures me with kind touches, as we pass by one another, him leaving the sink, me on my way to my one small bag. He gifts me loving smiles from the bathroom mirror as he shaves and I dress in my fitted dark jeans, a dark blue button up shirt, my suede boots, and my grey scarf. The one I'd been wearing the day I arrived. *Was that really only three days ago?*

With damp hair falling in tendrils just over his eyebrows, he pulls on some black boxer briefs, faded jeans that fit on his hips just so, and a white pull-over, cotton long sleeved shirt.

As I apply some eye shadow and a bit of blush, he leans into the deep sepia colored linen cabinet and watches me with a sly grin. "It's so weird to see you doing normal stuff," he says.

"Well, I am a real person. Maybe you put me on too high of a pedestal."

"Maybe I did," he admits. "But I love watching you."

I don't have time to dry my hair so I brush it into a ponytail. "You look stunning," he says, shaking his head as if he's amazed. I grab my small purse and sling it over my shoulder. Where am I going to keep the gun? I should have brought a bigger purse. I should be okay. I'm armed with something even better. Proof.

In the car, he turns on the radio. "I think you know that I've been playing you songs that remind me of you," he says, while tapping the screen with his long thin fingers. "I can play this for you now because we're almost there."

"Almost?"

"Yes." Oh, he means he wants to marry me.

"Adele again," I fake a smirk, as *'One and Only'* pops up on the little screen. He grins at my teasing.

A lovely piano begins to fill the car and as she starts to sing, I think that this song is about him having doubts about me. I bet he did for a while. Then, it's clear. He wants to be my one and only. He wants me to forget my past and choose him. He's right. Had he played this for me, even yesterday, I would have burst into tears and felt guilty. Now, with an almost clear conscience, I hold his hand and rub the tip of my finger over the little scrapes on his knuckles. I wonder if he got them from fighting or from punching the wall in Momma's closet.

"Were you nervous last night?" I ask, thinking of the line in the song about having imagined being with the one you love so many times that you wonder why you're even nervous.

"Oh, God, yes," he says. "I wanted it to be perfect for you. I was scared I hurt you."

"It was perfect. You are perfect, just how you are. But I'm not, Dillon."

"Sadie!"

"I think you should stop putting me on that pedestal. I'm just a regular, flawed person, you know."

"I'll try," he says, staring at the road. "But, to me you are everything."

I'm going to disappoint him. I know it.

We are almost to my Momma's house, but we're going next door. I have those boomerangs again in my stomach, like the ones I felt on the plane three days ago. I feel like I'm going to be sick. I hold onto the door handle. I think I could rip it off in one fell swoop.

"Don't be nervous, baby," he says, as we pull up to his childhood home. A deep brown stained house, two storied and cottage-like. From where we are, I can see the top of the roof on the shed. The setting for the most horrific thing that's ever happened to me. I want to throw things at it. As I get out of the car, I'm actually measuring up rocks that would do the job. "Everything will be better once we talk to Donnie," he says, reading the change in my mood, taking my hand.

Yeah it will. I don't want him to catch me looking at the shed. I'd already mentioned it up on the mountain the first time we saw each other again.

"Speaking of that, Dillon," I say, trying to stop the shaking in my voice. "I really don't want to hurt your feelings, but I'd like to talk to him by myself."

He pulls away from me, but I don't let go of his hand even though mine is shaking. He's facing away from me, running his right hand through his still damp hair.

"Are you going to tell him, though?" he looks at me with frustration written in the creases in his forehead.

"Yes." *Yes, I am.* I'm going to tell him he's never even going to look at me sideways again or I'm making that post live.

"I just wish you trusted me enough," he says.

"I trust you more than you know. But, not this. Please, I need to take care of this myself."

"Okay," he says, biting his bottom lip.

A woman comes out of the front door. The top story is the main floor in this house, so there are about ten or twelve steps to climb to reach her. As we get to the third step, I remember how the porch wraps all the way around the house. When I was ten, I accidentally dropped Dillon's black lab puppy from the railing. He was okay, but I felt a lot like I do now. Worried, guilty, wishing I was anywhere but here.

"Sadie, this is Renae," Dillon says. I shake her hand and smile. I'm still great at the meet and greet. She's a small woman, petite, with long dark hair parted in the middle with two barrettes in her hair fastened just at the top of each ear. She pulls up the dark jeans that are too big for her, and fixes a button on the checker-box-patterned shirt with colors washed-out from years of wear. She crosses the faded black sweater over her stomach and folds up the sleeves.

For some reason, I want to adopt her and take her home with me. She gives off an aura of uncertainty. Like a dog that gets kicked every day and will take any small amount of love tossed her way. And there's something in her eyes that reminds me of mine when I look in the mirror. How my eyes look dead. I feel like I'm looking at my true self in the mirror.

The little boy clasping her thigh puts his hands up to Dillon who picks him up and kisses him on the cheek. "Diddon," says the baby. I think Dillon said he was two years old.

"Come on in," says Renae, who seems a little nervous. Maybe that's just her normal demeanor. I don't want to, but I can imagine what it would be like to be her. I know it in every fiber of my being; she is an abused wife. Of course she is.

"I made us some chicken soup," she says. As Dillon starts to say something on my behalf, I look him in the eye and I shake my head. My lips are tight. I'll eat anything she gives me. I won't be able to stand hurting her feelings.

"That sounds perfect," I say, and fight back the nervous tears I feel for her that want to come out like fountains.

"When's Donnie supposed to be home?" Dillon asks, pulling out the chair for me at the dark wood table.

"Any minute now," she says.

I look at the table. It pulls on a string tied to a memory in my brain. This is the same one we used to do our homework on together. He taught me fractions at this table. I feel like one, too. Not quite a whole. My chin trembles.

"Sadie Jane," yelps a voice from the past that I know so well. Dillon's mom, Dot, pulls me out of the chair and into her arms. "You look so purty, honey," she says, playing with my hair. *That's it.* I start to cry and she holds me to her too large chest. "What's a' matter?" she asks.

"I've just missed out on so much while I've been gone," I say, looking at the grey in her hair, realizing the skin on her face makes her look tired in her older age.

"Well, yer home now, and you don't have to go nowhere, do ya?" she says, with a gleam in her eyes, her mouth folding up in a kind expression.

"No, I don't," I say as Renae hands me a tissue. *God, she's sweet.*

"Are you gonna finally marry this poor boy, put 'im out a' his misery and give me some grandyoungins?" she says, with a chuckle. "Lord knows, he's been a' waitin' on ya. Cain't no body tell him nothin'," she says. That reminds me, when is my period due? I think next week but I'll need to check my calendar. How does that pregnancy thing work?

"What happened to yer face?" Dot asks Dillon.

"I had to fight off the guy," Dillon explains.

"Lordy, son," she says to Dillon. "He'd fight off a whole heap 'a men fer ya," she says to me.

When I look at Dillon, he's beaming, glowing happiness from his pores. I want to go to him. I want him to hold me. I want to promise my life to him. I do want to marry him. But I have to do this first.

Another little boy comes out from under the table. He's cute, about eight years old and he's holding some kind of plastic superhero in his hand. "Daddy's home!" he announces, and my heart stops for a whole two beats before it starts up again.

I hear the front door open, and his boots tromping through the entryway before he walks into the kitchen wearing his uniform, with a gun on his belt. His nose is bandaged, and he looks at me with a surprised contempt I haven't seen before. This is worse than I thought.

"What are you doing here?" he questions Dillon.

"I'm sorry," Renae says. She's cowering over by the refrigerator. "I tried to tell you this mornin' but you was in such a hurry to get out a' here."

"We had a break-in at the Sparks' house last night, Donnie."

"I know that," Donnie says. *Yeah, I'm sure he does.* He looks shaken and starts to sit down at the head of the table. Before he can make it all the way down, Renae is placing a hot bowl of soup under his nose. He doesn't even say thank you. He's got her trained well.

"Why didn't you call me back last night? And what happened to your nose?" Dillon asks, raising his voice.

"My two boys look like they been beat," says Dot.

Yeah, by each other.

"I was on a call. Old Man Wilson was drunk again, beating on his wife. He got me pretty good," he says, touching his bandaged nose. If I hadn't been there last night I would have believed his lie, too. Plus, Old Man Wilson has been beating his wife since we were kids. It's a likely story.

"So, what are you doing about this?" Dillon asks.

"Let me eat my food, kid," he says, taking a big spoonful into his mouth. I wish I could melt into the wall. But I have a job to do here.

"Why don't y'all serve yourselves," Renae invites. I start to get up but Dillon leans over to me, saying, "I'll get it for you, baby." As he pulls away from me, I see Donnie's expression. His eyes are too wide; his top lip is twitching. He's squeezing the handle of his spoon so tight, I bet he's losing circulation in his fingers.

"Thank you, love," I announce to Dillon as I glare at Donnie and clench my jaw so tight it hurts. I lean back in the chair like a boss, and cross my ankle over my knee as if to say, *I'm not scared of you.* He gets my vibe and spoons a too large portion of the thick soup in his mouth. Some drips down his chin and, never taking his shaking eyes away from mine, wipes it with the sleeve of his dark blue shirt.

"How's yer Momma?" Renae chirps from the kitchen. She's filling little bowls of soup for the kids.

"She's doing as well as possible," I say, shrugging my shoulders. "But she's very sick."

"How long are ya stayin', honey?" Dot asks, as Dillon places the hot soup in front of me on the table.

"Thank you," I say to Dillon. "I'm not leaving, Dot. Even after the wake," I say, looking down, trying to push away the empty feeling of not having my momma alive. "Dillon's asked me to move into the Page-Vawter house with him." I refuse to look at Donnie. I feel anger emanating from his spot at the table. My breathing has taken a new pace. I'm shaking so I don't want to pick up my spoon.

"Oh, honey!" Dot says. "I'm so glad. This boy's been a' pining for ya."

Donnie shifts in his seat, but I refuse to look at him. Dillon runs his hand along my thigh under the table. It tickles, and I smile at him, taking my hand and placing it on his. He wraps his hand around the curve of my inner thigh.

"I'm going to have my stuff sent over in a week or two." Donnie drops his spoon on the table. I wince, and so does Renae, as the sound echoes through my bones like a cold wind.

"You didn't tell me that!" Dillon says, beaming from ear to ear.

"Isn't that what you want?" I whisper.

"Of course," he says, grasping my thigh. I look down at the thick soup. I haven't had meat in almost ten years. My stomach feels as empty as an air bubble so I find a nice sized carrot and spoon that into my mouth. It tastes like chicken, but I'm not going to say a thing to Renae. I can't bear to hurt her feelings. She's got the two boys eating their soup, and finally sits down silently, her back hunched over and takes a bite.

"I want some more," Donnie says, hastily pushing his bowl toward her on the table. She jumps up and fills his bowl as fast as she can. I glare at Donnie. I hate him. Hate, in fact, is not strong enough of a word to match the feelings I have for him.

As I sit here, chewing the carrots and potatoes that taste like chicken feathers floating in a strong breeze, I try to think of another word for hate. Even words like abhorrence and disgust, don't fully comprise my revulsion of him. There's not a single synonym that seems strong enough for how much I loathe this man. I want him to die a painful, slow death. I can just see my daddy's bullets piercing through the evil flesh that he pressed up against me over ten years ago. I can imagine the confused look on his face when he realizes I've killed him.

"Sadie?" My name sounds like it's being said in a tunnel. I shake my head. *Who said that?* Dillon touches my arm. "Are you okay?"

"I'm fine," I say, confused.

"Donnie's ready to talk to you," he says, pressing his lips together. I look around and everyone is done eating. The two boys aren't even at the table anymore. Dot is helping Renae at the kitchen sink. *How long have I been fantasizing about retribution?*

"Let's go out to the porch," Donnie bellows.

"Okay," I say, as my heart falls to my stomach. I stand up like a spring, the chair protesting against the wood under my feet. I catch my balance and bend down to kiss Dillon. *This is for you, too*, I think, as I allow my legs to take me somewhere private with the man who tried to kill me last night.

Outside, the crisp air ruffles my hair. From here I can see the rickety shed with its peaked roof. It looks smaller than I remember. It sits there like a disgrace. How opposite my experience with Dillon last night was in comparison to what happened to me in there. I can imagine what it would feel like to rip the wood apart with my bare hands. My compulsion feels so real, I can almost feel the splinters prickling my hands.

As I lean up against the railing, the same one I'd accidentally tipped Dillon's dog, Mitty, off when I was a kid, I think it sure is a long way down. I'm surprised he lived through it. As the back door shuts behind me, I spin around and start to talk before he can. I have the upper hand this time.

"What the hell was that last night?"

"What? You think you can bring *him* home with you and nothin's gonna happen?" he says, taking too many steps toward me.

"How long were you watching us?"

"Long enough to know he ain't no man," he says, moving even closer to me. I hold my breath. His natural scent has always been a deterrent—plus, it reminds me of the past, the shed, and what he did to me. I bristle as he leans up against the railing, boxing me in. His proximity makes me feel miniscule, like a mouse in a trap.

I force myself to speak. "He's more man than you'll ever be. He doesn't need a knife to sleep with me."

"That's all he knows how 'ta do, sleep," he says, with a deep mocking laugh.

"He didn't have to cut my throat to make me his," I say, defiantly, my voice deep.

"Watch yer mouth, bitch."

The tone in his voice turns a switch in me. I stand taller, moving my elbows out to make a reasonable space between us. "Let me make something very clear," I declare, heaving words at him as though they are toxic. "What happened last night is never going to happen again. Do you understand?" I say, slowly, methodically. *Damn that felt good.*

"Listen up," he says, coming even closer to me, making himself taller, more angular. "I'll say it slower this time so ya' understand what I mean." I lean back and cross my arms. "You ain't allowed to see him no more. You definitely ain't movin' in with *him*, neither."

"What if I don't care what you say?"

"If you don't do as yer told, next time you won't be so lucky," he says, putting his hand on his gun holster and smiling to cover up the demon hiding behind his teeth.

"That's just it. There won't be a next time, Donnie. Things have changed and I think you should know just how much." I reach into my purse, pull the phone out and hold it between my hands like a relic of my faith. "Before you even think about trying to take my phone, just know that you're going to want me to have it. Without communication from me to someone back home in California, the happy little life you have here is over."

He swallows hard and takes a step back. Finally, he looks scared. This feels amazing.

"Before I share my proof, just know that what I have here is already completely safe. I've recreated it so that everyone in the world will be able to hear it in a matter of minutes."

"What the hell are you talking about?" he says, scraping at his stubbly chin with his fingernails. He looks completely confounded.

"I think it's better to just let you hear." I push the play button. His voice reverberates in the air around us like a landslide.

"Dillon can't stop me, Sadie. Besides, that wadn't the deal…I ain't sharin' you with him. I won't, ever again. Do you have any idea the things I done to men during this war? I could take care of it so he's in extreme pain for the last moments a' his life and nobody's gonna ever find his body. Places nobody goes to up in the mountain. Perfect place to put somebody you don't want around— somebody who'd be gettin' in the way."

"So, you'd kill your own brother?"

"In a heartbeat. I told you, I ain't sharin' you."

I push stop. His nostrils flare, his jaw clenches, and he stands there like he's a bomb ready to explode. He grunts and paces, pushes his fist into his palm like he's smashing my face instead. I need to remind myself to breath. I exhale and brace myself with the railing, push my back into it until it hurts.

Aunt Lotty had a boyfriend for a while who was a loan officer. He told me once that when you propose a deal to someone you state the expectations and terms and then stop talking. The first one to speak is the loser. I've stated my deal and I'm not talking first.

I stand here for minutes in complete silence as he paces back and forth like a wild lion who knows the taste of blood, knows what it feels like to hunt, but can't anymore because it's newly locked behind a chain link fence. I'm sure he's trying to think of a way to kill me right now. Maybe, just maybe, he realizes he lost. He can't hurt me or he'll be ruined. He can't even piss me off because I'll post the recording and he'll lose everything. He'll go to prison. He did this all to himself—dug the hole and now he has to lie in it.

"So what yer sayin'," he says. *Ha! He spoke first.* "Is you don't want nothin' to keep that recording private 'cept for me agreeing to cancel our original agreement," he says, as if I might be recording him again.

"That's what I'm saying."

"And you'll promise not ta make the recording public, then?" he asks, cautiously.

I nod my head, yes.

"Can I get that in writing?" I scrunch my face. What a weird thing to ask for.

"What? You want your lawyer to draw up the papers? I think having my word is enough."

His mouth goes into a thin line, his jaw is tensed and he crosses his arms across his chest.

"Let me add, if I ever find out that you've hurt Renae or the kids, that recording goes live."

"What?"

"Do you think I didn't notice the way you treat your wife?"

"She's fine. Ain't nothin' happened to her."

"Just like I was fine?" I taunt. "Some people just can't be tamed," I state, nonchalantly. "Just shouldn't be allowed out in the real world. If you prove that you can't control yourself, I'll make sure you never get out of jail. On that recording, you just admitted to stalking me, raping me, letting me drown. Then you threatened to kill me and your own brother. Just think what they'll do to a cop in prison. I'm doing you a favor right now, 'cause I relish the thought of you finally knowing what it felt like for me in that shed," I say, pointing at the wooden hell that sits there in the grass at the edge of the property like an abomination.

I force myself to stare into his shaky eyes that look like little black dots enveloped in a bright white casing. "We have a deal," he says through his clenched jaw. He looks like he just ate poison and wishes I was the one who was sick.

"If anything happens to my phone or to me, that recording goes live by default," I say. "Just remember that." He shakes his head yes, pacing and watching me intently.

"What are you going to tell Dillon?" I ask, still leaning my back into the railing for support.

"Just that I can't tell him who attacked…"

"Raped, Donnie. Who raped me," I shout, but under my breath so no one can hear us inside the house. I'm leaning forward, pointing my finger.

"Right, who raped you and broke in the house last night." He's speaking in little frantic spurts of words, like a person who just got caught on ice too thin to hold him up any longer.

"All right. Why don't you tell him you got rid of the guy? How about that? I'll even let you take the credit." My heart is beating so fast I think I can hear it like a drummer's beat all around us.

"Sounds fair," his voice says, but his eyes are saying something more ominous.

"Fair? None of this has been fair to me," I growl.

He glares at me, frozen in the spot where he's stopped pacing.

"I think I'm a merciful, generous person, Donnie, for not just posting this recording right now."

"Do it and I'll come after you. I'll have nothing left to lose." I swallow hard enough that I hear it and so does he.

I have to force the words out. I don't even care that they're shaky. "I hope that felt good, 'cause that was the last time in your life that you will ever threaten me again." His lips quiver and the left side pulls upward in a scowl before he puts his fist to his mouth as if it's taking everything in him not to pounce on me like prey he's stalked all night long. "This is over," I say, as I walk past him, open the door, slam it shut, and stand in the living room like I've just gone fourteen rounds with my toughest opponent, ending it with a knock out. In a way I have. It scares me when my phone buzzes in my hand like it's possessed.

It's Missy. "Hello."

"Sadie? You need to come home."

"What's wrong?"

"The hospice worker just left, and Momma's taken a turn fer the worse."

"What do you mean?"

"They just went over the stages with me and Momma has most 'a the stuff that people get right before they die."

"Is she still talking?"

"A little. If you want to hear her voice again, I'd get over here right now."

"Okay, I'll be right there." I press the end button on the screen and when I turn around Dillon is standing in the room with me.

"I need to go."

"Okay, Sadie. Let's go together," he says, reaching his hand out to me. I grasp hold of him and bury my face in his temperate chest.

"How am I going to say goodbye to my Momma, Dillon?"

"I don't know, darlin' but you'll do the right thing. I know it."

I hope I do. I sure hope I do.

Chapter Nineteen

For My Momma

We walk hand-in-hand toward my house from his. The path was well-worn when we were kids but now it's barely visible other than to us who'd traveled it so often and for so long. I even remember Dillon's Dad telling me I'd ruined the grass seeds he'd planted. He said he had to measure my footprints and add enough grass seed to make up for the ones I'd smashed too deep into the dirt to grow strong and sturdy.

How true it is, being smashed down by feet or by circumstances does really take its toll. How did I grow and bloom after I'd been pressed down so violently? If I hadn't left here, what would have become of me? Would I have been absorbed into the mountain soil just like those seeds, never to have sprouted into anything at all?

Dillon's daddy passed away when Dillon was sixteen, just two years before I left. He was a stoic and pensive man with dark hair and deep set black eyes. He mumbled rather than spoke directly. That's probably why I remember so well the exchange about the grass. He barked at me, and I nodded and twisted my ankles back and forth on either edge of the soles of my feet. It must have meant a lot to him, the grass. He was a lot more particular about his yard than my Daddy was.

Thinking back, I guess that's why I'd never even batted an eye-lash about Donnie being so quiet and brooding all those years. It seemed normal for the men in their family to behave that way. Not Dillon, of course. He was, and still is, the essence of kindness. His face is most used to being set in a smile. *That's his nature*, I think, looking up at the now grown man—so loving, so perfect.

Once this is all over, we will have our chance to create a life conducive to those natural smiles. *Will it ever be over, the Donnie part that is?* I know I'll always have to watch my back. Donnie is like a dormant volcano still bubbling under the surface. To ignore him will be like moving into the ruins of Pompeii and pretending Mount Vesuvius doesn't exist. I will never be able to relax fully, ever.

We walk past the horse stables and the square horse fence. Monty neighs and scratches the dirt bringing me out of my reverie. I walk by, not having the time to stop and pat his muzzle.

As we walk up the steps to the porch, Dillon squeezes my hand reassuringly. I turn the doorknob not knowing what will become of me once Momma is gone.

No one is in the living room or the kitchen. We creak up the stairs while I'm thinking of a way to bargain with God. I want to get back the time I lost with my momma. I scowl as I blame Donnie for taking this from me, too. All those years, gone, just like an old dried leaf blowing away in the wind.

As we stand in the doorway, looking at Missy, the boys, and the two kids gathering around Momma's bed, I really grasp the fact that ten years have gone by. Ten Christmases, ten birthdays, ten Mother's Days. I've missed her voice and the gentle thump of her heart when she hugs me. I've missed her laugh, the one that comes from the stomach. I've missed her homemade birthday cakes with the almond flavored frosting, and the way she cooks the eggs just right with the perfect amount of salt and pepper. I've missed everything—all of it. It makes that hole in my chest come back again—the one that Dillon got rid of last night. And that lump in my throat is back—bigger than ever. I try to swallow it down. I should know better; that never works.

I don't want to walk into the room yet. Once I do, it will be real. My momma is going to die and there's nothing that can change that. My hip buzzes and I jump. Dillon moves me away from the door into the hallway.

"Do you want to get that?" he coaxes.

"Oh, okay," I say. I feel like I'm in a movie or I'm suddenly living someone else's life. *It's Jenny.*

"Hello," I whisper.

"Sadie, is everything okay?"

"Yes, why?"

"Well, it's 2:10 Mountain time and you haven't texted me about the recording going live on the blog. You said I should…"

"Oh! Yes. Everything is okay for today. You can leave it as is."

"Great. I'm glad to hear it. Is there anything I can do for you?"

"Actually, could you transcribe the recording I sent you?"

"Transcribe it?"

"Yes."

"Well, you said not to listen to it." I turn around and look at Dillon. He's leaning against the wall in the hallway looking at the floor nonchalantly.

"I'm trusting you with this very important project. Of course, remember that you've signed a confidentiality agreement."

"Oh, yes. Of course."

"Can you email it to me by this evening and add it to the blog, but don't make it live?"

"Sounds good."

"Tomorrow I'll text you on time and thank you for checking in with me."

"No problem, Sadie."

"Thank you," I say, turning off the phone from the clear screen. As I turn around to look at Dillon he seems puzzled.

"Is everything okay?" he asks.

"Yes, I just have her working on a project for me." He nods his head, and purses his full lips.

"You can tell me anything. You know that," he says. I know he's not prying. He just wants me to know.

"Thank you," I say, looking down.

"Are you ready?" he says, as he walks with me inside the room that smells of medicine. Momma is surrounded, but Missy grabs my hand and pulls me into the circle. I'm petrified to touch her, but I reach out and take her broken bird-wing hand in mine. It feels cold like a piece of fruit taken out of the refrigerator.

"Why's she so cold?" I ask, shocked.

"That's one 'a the things they told me about this mornin'," Missy says. "It happens when her vital organs are ready to shut down. Somethin' about her blood not flowin' to the extremities."

"Oh," is all I can say. I'm preoccupied by Momma's breathing. It's so fast and shallow that it makes me want to deepen mine. It tugs on a memory, the time when I couldn't breathe when I'd fallen into the moss patch in the dark. I don't want to revisit that memory. I can't or I'll fall to pieces like that glass container I'd mentally left on the floor last night. I thought after I took my life back from Donnie that I'd feel empowered. But losing my momma is going to be one of the hardest things I've ever faced. Now that I'm not easily numbed, I'm really going to experience this. Without my normal coping mechanisms, will I be strong enough to deal with this monumental, ever permanent, loss?

"Sadie?" Momma rasps.

"Yes, Momma," I say, rubbing the tip of my finger over her hand.

"Did ya' do it, baby?"

"What, Momma?"

"Save Sadie's Mountain?" she asks. It takes so much energy for her to force the words out that it makes me hurt for her. My fingers cringe. I have this enormous need to let her feel relief. I feel guilty that I want her to stay when it hurts her so.

"I promised, Momma. I will save our mountain. I will," I say. I can feel Missy's disbelief as she breathes out unusually loud as she stands to my right. But I don't care.

"The meetin'?" Momma questions.

"Yes, Momma. There's one more tonight." Missy pulls back and she walks out of the bedroom and stomps down the hall.

"You have tago," she rasps.

"I will, I promise," I say, putting my head on her chest lightly. She feels fragile, and hollow. Her hand moves up and she touches my hair. How many times has she touched my hair? Ten years less than she should have. Tears sting their way down to Momma's white night gown. I don't think I'm strong enough to make sense of this. To add this to my mental filing cabinet. If I grasp onto her she cannot leave me. I feel so selfish because I know she's holding on for us. Not for her.

I climb up into the bed and lie down on top of the covers. I would never do something so impudent but I've lost all sense of propriety. Right now, I want my Momma. She puts her arm over me as I mold myself to her. I begin to shake like when I'm cold on the inside.

"Sadie Jane! You get out'a that bed!" Missy shrieks from the doorway.

"No," Momma says, and presses her hollow bones onto my back. I close my eyes. I'm stuck in a dichotomy. I want her to stay. I want those ten years back. But I crave relief for her. I want her pain to stop. But I'm not ready to let her go. I bury my head in the pillow next her. I'm so heavy and weighted. My eyes weighted as my limbs start to feel light and my breathing gets slower and louder in my ear. It soothes me. Momma soothes me and I fall to sleep.

"Dillon?" I ask, as my body begins to tingle and my head feels as though it's coming out of a fog.

"Yes, Sadie," his deep, calm voice says, from somewhere in the room. I move around and find him sitting patiently, in the chair tucked into the corner of the room.

"What time is it?"

"It's about 4:30," he says.

"What time is the meeting tonight?"

"Sadie. We don't have to go to that."

"But I've promised," I whisper.

"Of course, baby," he says, soothingly. "Then I should feed you and get you over there in the next hour or so." I nod my head and lean up to kiss Momma lightly on the cheek. Her breathing is slower, too slow. I take her in. I memorize the way she looks, the way she feels—alive. I force her as she is now into the deepest part of my brain where the memory cannot leave me. So that I can pull it out when I need to when she's not here anymore.

I slide off the bed and Dillon takes me in his arms. "It was beautiful to watch you sleep so peacefully. You needed that."

"I've got to do this for her."

"Baby, you don't have to worry about the mountain right now."

"But that's all she's asking for from me. I left her. This is the least I can do."

"Okay, darlin'. Calm down. Whatever you need. I'm here for you."

"I'm not really hungry," I say, looking at the menu at Gino's Restaurant, a chain restaurant I never thought I'd see again. It's cozy in the booth, like a warm memory. I'd only been here once before. It was a new restaurant ten years ago. Back then, there were only a few names written on the walls. They let their customers write all over the place. Now everything's covered in layers of customer graffiti.

"Do you like banana peppers?"

"I don't know."

"Well, their vegetarian pizza has them."

"I can't eat." He purses his full lips and stands up, marches over to the counter and places our order. He's so gorgeous standing there. *He's mad at me?* When he comes back my stomach starts to hurt. I can't deal with him being angry with me in addition to everything else.

"Are you angry with me?" I ask, as he sets down our two drinks.

"I'm not. I just want you to eat."

"Is that it?" I ask, taking a sip of the lemony drink.

"I'm worried about you."

"Because of my Momma?"

"Yes. I mean, you've really surprised me. The way you've handled the break-in. How brave you've been with me. I'm confounded, really. But I'm worried about what will happen when your momma passes on."

"I'm worried about that, too," I say, looking into his eyes. His eye looks a bit better. "Normally, I just get numb when I'm overwhelmed. I avoid a lot of issues, triggers, that way. But since I've been here with you, I'm actually feeling things. I don't think my coping mechanism will work this time and I'll have to find a new way. It makes me nervous, too."

"I'm going to be with you every step of the way."

"I'm not going to push you away this time. Things have changed." *Yeah, I scared Donnie away for a while.*

"I know they have," he says, his eyes twinkling under the chandelier lamp. He looks at me lovingly.

"My momma told me something the other day that's been bothering me."

"What?"

"That she had miscarriages."

"It's a common problem here," he says.

"Why?"

"The elevated levels of toxins in the water supply. West Virginia ranks second in coal production. We have higher rates of birth defects than the rest of the country. It's very likely that the coal plant that was here did some damages to our water supply back in the forties and fifties."

"Where did you go to college?"

"The University of West Virginia."

"Oh, I thought you went away."

"They gave me a full scholarship all the way up to my Doctorate in Biochemistry and Molecular Biology. Plus I wanted to stay close. In case you came back."

"How were you so...?"

"Sure? I've always known, Sadie."

"I just don't think I'm worthy of all this."

"I'm not worthy of you, baby. I let you get hurt. I couldn't help you."

"What happened to me is neither of our faults. Stop blaming yourself." *There's only one person to blame*, I think.

He looks far off in thought, pained as if he's reliving how he found me in the creek. I'm thinking about what he said about my Momma's miscarriages. "Let me ask you about the water supply. So, does that mean my momma is sick because of the coal plant that was here?"

"It would be hard to prove, but I'd say it's a likely cause," he says, rubbing his bruised chin with his long thin fingers. I'm trying to make sense of that as the waiter brings our deep-dish pizza and sets it on the red and white checkered tablecloth. The scent of the bread and the sauce, the cheese and the veggies reminds my stomach that it's empty. All day, I've only eaten a few carrots and potatoes from the chicken soup.

Dillon pulls on a piece of steaming pizza with cheese stretching out until it's set on the white plate and hands it to me. I take the first bite, even though it burns my tongue. It tastes so good, the crust flaky, the cheese salty, the veggies perfectly cooked, and the spices blooming in my mouth, that I don't look up again until the whole piece is gone. When I do, he's smiling, holding a nibbled piece of crust between his long fingers.

"Do you want some more?"

"I'm really full."

"Okay, baby. Let's go then."

"Can we write our names on the wall?" He smiles and picks up the white pen they leave just for that reason.

'Dillon loves Sadie,' he writes. "Are you ready to go?" he asks. I nod. "I don't want to keep them waiting on you," he says, smiling. We walk out, hand-in-hand, my tummy full, and my head swimming with all this new information. My momma is sick because of coal. She's dying too soon because of coal. I'm on a mission. This won't stop until a change happens. A shift. My ability to write and Dillon's science background makes for a perfect match.

"Let's do this," I say, getting into the car.

I'm greeted by so many Christians inside the Episcopal church on Taylor Road. Luckily, we didn't have to come to my Daddy's old church, Ansted Baptist. Its red carpet and sun-like circular window above the platform would remind me of the guilt I had all my life when I did something wrong.

"We're so glad you came," says Reverend Morris. "Please, have a seat, you two." The group has made a chair-circle and have drawings and charts up on a board in the meeting room. They really look like they know their stuff.

"We're expectin' the EPA to grant the permit to the coal company most likely on Monday or Tuesday of next week," he says to the circle.

"So soon?" says another man, grey haired and with a calming voice.

"Yes, Bob. But we're real lucky to have Miss Sadie Sparks here this evening 'cause she has an idea for an action we would be able ta use against 'em when they do grant the permit."

"Yes. Thank you for inviting me. I'm not sure if you all know, but my momma is on her death bed and all she's asking of me is to save Gauley Mountain."

"I'm sorry, Sadie. I didn't know," Reverend Morris says. "We'll be praying for her. I'll have her put on the prayer chain this evenin'."

"Thank you," I say, swallowing hard. "I really need to get back to her, but my idea is to do the Hands Across the Sand idea except call it Hands Across the Mountain. In this case, we will go up to the blast site and grasp hands in unity. The coal company will not be able to detonate without hurting one of us, so they won't do it. It will cause the media to take notice. I'll write a press release, send it to all of my media contacts, and post it on my blog, too. We will end up getting a lot of people to support our cause publicly. Hopefully, we'll get some of the major networks. My hope is that this movement will be enough opposition that they will decide to withdraw on their own."

"Do you think it will work?" says a woman introduced to me as Nina.

"As long as we have enough people to go up in shifts over an extended period of time, then yes."

"Would people actually get hurt up there?" asks a woman with a light grey bubble cut.

"No, hopefully not. They won't be able to detonate with us up there," I say.

"We have to organize this but I'm sure we'll have enough people," Reverend Morris says.

"I think this is an excellent idea," Dillon says, taking my hand in his. *Live wires!* It makes me blush. "My only concern," he says, "is that the coal company will block us from being able to go up the road."

"In that case, we'd have to go on foot or on horseback. If that does happen, we should be ready for Plan B," I say.

Nina is writing and the others, including Reverend Morris, are nodding and discussing enthusiastically.

I look at Dillon and he knows I'm anxious to leave. "We'd really better get going," he says, standing up and I follow.

"Thank you so much for coming out this evening, Sadie. I really think this is going to work," Reverend Morris says.

"It has to," I say, shaking his hand. It has to.

As Dillon's tires pummel the rocks up to Momma's house, there are no less than eight cars parked along the drive.

"Dillon?" I question.

"Sadie, if there'd been a change, Missy would have called. That's Pastor Cole's car," Dillon says, pointing to a silver Pontiac.

"Who?"

"He took over the church when your Daddy passed on."

"Okay," I say, nodding to make it right in my head. I've got to go in and speak to the people I know from the past. The people who know what happened to me. The people whose judgment I've been running from for years. I have no choice but to deal with this, with them. I hold onto the door handle with a shaky hand.

"I'm right here, darlin'," Dillon says, in the dark.

"This is a private matter. I don't want them here."

"It might be what your momma wants, okay? Can you do this for her?"

"For her," I say, to make sense of it. It's been all about me for so long. I haven't had to think about others until now.

"Are you ready?" I nod as he kisses the top of my hand. I open the car door and that's when I hear them. They've always been so showy in their praying, especially when speaking in tongues, the language they believe speaks right to God. Their prayers echo around rebounding in waves off the leaves of the trees. It makes my head ache and my chest burn with anxiety.

This is not about me. This is for Momma, I think as we open the door and face death, face their response to it. They are calling to God with their songs, with their foreign sounding made-up words. Dillon holds my hand as we go up the stairs. I've got to say goodbye to my momma.

Chapter Twenty

A Fiery Peace

As we walk into the house, the prayers become even louder, momentarily stunning me. Then I see Elise and little Joe tucked under some covers on the couch, and a tall stocky man standing in the kitchen. He's drinking some water when he sees us and walks into the living room.

"Dillon, long time, no see," he says, with his arm reaching out to shake Dillon's hand.

"Dale, it's great to see you," he responds as his arm shakes up and down.

"Who's this pretty lady?" he asks, looking at me.

"This is your sister-in-law, Sadie."

"Sadie," he says. "It's nice to meet you. I'm Dale, Missy's husband."

I reach my shaky hand out to meet his. I look him in the eye, briefly and he looks concerned. "Hi, Dale."

"I'm sorry 'bout your momma," he says, bowing his head a bit and looking down. The sounds coming from the stairs are rushed and heavy; the foreign words are bouncing around like a ball thrown too hard in a square room. My stomach is churning around and around. I regret eating that pizza, even though it was so good.

"I can't do this," I state, as if it's a fact we all know to be true.

"Anything I can do?" Dale asks Dillon.

"She's having a hard time dealing with all the visitors," Dillon explains.

"Heck, we can just ask 'em to go on home. It's late," Dale decides.

Upstairs, I hear a man's voice saying, "Lord, we pray for healing. In Jesus' name, Lord. Heal this woman, let her get up and walk, Lord!" His words make me sour and bitter. I feel a ball of fury, of anger, of resentment growing in my gut. How dare he demand healing? He should be praying for her to feel peace, not asking for what isn't even possible.

I start walking toward the stairs as if in a trance. Dillon comes up next to me, holds my hand, and heads up the stairs with me. It makes me dizzy so I stop midway up the staircase. I close my eyes and breathe. I listen to the sounds of the prayers. They sound like childhood—both good and bad.

Their songs pull on a string attached to a memory in my brain. The echoes of memories, of melodies, voices bouncing off the walls in church are all coming back to me. I remember how Momma's off-key voice comforted me as Daddy stood up behind the podium looking handsome in his grey suit. Missy was to one side of me. Momma to the other. I remember the scent of the church, like Sunday bests, watered-down coffee, wooden pews rubbed with oil. I remember the hue of the red carpet. The way my shoes sunk into it just enough not to click as I walked down the aisle.

I remember how all of us singing together felt like being wrapped in a warm blanket. How it touched my heart. I remember the way Momma looked from below, as I was so little, while she raised her arms to the Lord, her fingers reaching gently like a dancer's would. Her arms swaying. Her face at peace. That's how I want her to feel now. If they do that for her, if these prayers make her feel good, then I'm glad they're here—I have to be, for her.

As I walk down the hallway, my breathing has quickened so much that my limbs are tingling. My heart thumps. My scalp prickles and my face feels puffy and hot. The voices are loud, but I tell myself that they are soothing, even though my body says to run away, to hide in a corner. They are just people after all. They are people I know. They are people who once loved me.

I look up at Dillon just before we make it to the entrance of Momma's room. He looks worried. His eyebrows are furrowed. His mouth in a thin line. His jaw is clenched. He squeezes my hand and I force myself to smile. Not a fake smile. A real one meant just for him. I look back at the open doorway and walk in. Momma looks pale. Her mouth is open as if her jaw is not strong enough to keep it closed anymore. Her eyelids are slightly open. She's completely still.

Dillon lets go of my hand as I walk past everyone, tuning out all of the singing. It's as if Momma and I are alone. I stand by her bed; tilt my head sideways so I can look at her straight on. I pick up her hand. She feels so cold, but I can hear her slight breaths, breaths that sound like she's gargling marbles, so I know I'm not too late.

"Momma," I say. She stirs and squeezes my hand, her mouth closes and her eyes open and find mine. "I want you to know how much I love you, to thank you for being there for me all of my life. For loving me no matter what." She smiles ever so slightly. "There's so much that's honorable about you, right down to the core-good. Anything that's good in me, it came from you. From everything you taught me. And I just want to thank you for letting me go even though it broke your heart. You are so selfless. I'm so sorry that I left you. I really, really am. But I want you to know that I will protect the mountain. I'm staying here with Dillon. I've decided to move here and take my life back."

She nods her head. Her voice is gone. I know she cannot answer me. It pricks a hole in my chest. I will never hear Momma's voice again. I grit my teeth, my legs collapse and I put my head down on the bed. I hear them praying again. For a while I'd tuned them out, but now I hear them singing. Some are praying. Some are speaking in tongues. The room is spinning although I'm completely still. I feel the bile start to rise in my throat. I need to run but my legs feel about as sturdy as water.

"Dillon," I say. I feel him picking me up in his arms like a weightless flower. "I'm going to throw up," I say, putting my hand over my stomach.

He walks me toward the bathroom, setting me on my knees in front of the white porcelain. Everything comes up. My pain, my fear. It's emptied out of me until I feel as though I could float away.

"Do you need a doctor?" he asks. I realize he's holding my ponytail back for me.

"No, Dillon. Please. Don't embarrass me. I just need to sit here a minute to catch my breath." My knees are pressing into a pink bathroom rug. I remember this bathroom rug, actually. She's had it a long time. I lean into Dillon's chest as he reaches up, grabbing a washcloth from the towel rack. I hear the water run. I close my eyes as he washes my face with the warm cloth that smells like Momma's soap.

I realize that my chest is sweaty and my eyes feel like they are bulging out even though my eyelids are closed. He wets the cloth again and unties my scarf. He runs the warmth soothingly along the back of my neck. My whole body aches. I wish I were numb. But I don't want to slip into that hollow reality. I want to be here for Momma.

"I need to go back," I say. My throat is so sore.

"Are you ready?" he asks.

"I need some mouthwash."

"Let me look," he says, as I hear him rummaging through the cabinet under the sink. I keep my eyes shut. The light hurts my brain. It feels like knives piercing into the soft tissues behind my eyes. He hands me a little cup and I swish, and he stands me up next to the sink so I can spit. I splash my face with water. When I open my eyes, I'm shocked by what I see in the mirror. This is not the 'me' I'm used to. This woman has been through it. What stands out the most are the deep-set eyes with gloomy circles around them the color of night. My skin actually looks to be olive green. And without my scarf, I can see the scars on my neck. Three of them. Two short, one long. I lean down to pick up my scarf. As I'm tying it around my neck…

"Momma!" Missy yelps from the deepest part of her soul. My eyes dart to Dillon and he looks panicked. His eyes are too wide. I don't want to go. I'm stuck for a moment. I know my Momma is gone, but my legs turn into springs beneath me. They run of their own free will.

Verta Lee, our church secretary, is wringing her hands in the doorway. "She's gone," she says, her eyes watering as I run past her. Missy is holding Momma's hands but I can't look at her yet. I'm too scared.

The familiar people in the room are defeated. Their last minute pleas to God did not work. I'm no longer angry with them. All of their intentions came from a good place in their hearts. I know that. I feel their sadness. The room is enveloped in it. As I walk toward the bed, I catch a strong scent of some flower that never existed before—very strong, pungent, but sweet and soothing.

I don't know what tells me this, but somewhere in my depth, I know this scent is Momma's spirit, freed from the body that betrayed her and wasn't strong enough to hold her any longer. It feels as though her spirit is joyful, free. I'm glad for her. Sad for me, for Missy, for the boys, who I realize have been here all along. But I'm happy for her. I take in her jubilant scent; make it a part of me. I hold it in. I feel Dillon standing behind me. He touches my arm, and

I reach back inviting him to come with me as I say goodbye to the shell that used to be my momma.

I touch Missy's back. She's shivering. I still haven't looked at Momma. "Do you smell it?" she asks me.

"Yes," I say.

"We all do, dear," says Verta Lee. I look at her and nod my head. Missy stands up and grabs me. Her knees buckle under her and I struggle to hold up her slight frame. She's always been so solid, so resilient. "This ain't fair," she says, into my neck. Her body is full of tremors. I hold her and let her grieve. "It ain't right!" she yells. It's so true. We knew she was leaving, but knowing it and actually having it happen are two different things.

"Thank you for all you did for Momma," I say. She squeezes me tighter; her cries are coming up from her gut. I still smell the flowers. I breathe them in. "You did such a good job," I say. I don't have tears. I'm solemn. This doesn't feel real.

Behind her, Dale comes up and rubs her back. He's got his head down, and when he lifts it, I see that he's wiping his eyes with a white handkerchief. Her legs must take form again because I feel her lessen her grip on my shoulders. She kisses me on the cheek.

"I've got to get out of here," she says, turning around and letting Dale take her out of the room. That's when I notice Jake and Seth are rubbing their eyes as they stand on the other side of the bed. They are both looking at her. They look quietly resigned but there seems to be despondency in their eyes. They aren't as angry as Missy.

I close my eyes. "Dillon," I whisper. I hear crying, some soft, some loud and sniffley. I feel him come up behind me. His body is warm, and radiates kindness. "I can't look at her," I say. "What does she look like?"

"She looks peaceful," he says, into my left ear, as he wraps his arms around my waist. "Her mouth is open. Her eyelids, too. But she looks calm. She's not in pain anymore, baby." Slowly, I open my eyes. I force them to look down at her. I gasp slightly because she is definitely no longer living. It shocks me, even though I knew it. She looks empty, like a doll on a shelf. There's no other way to describe it. Her eyes look grey, vacant. Her spirit no longer rages behind them.

My hand is reaching out of its own free will. I see my fingers in her hair, pushing the thin strands away from her face. I'm surprised when her face is still warm. I thought death was cold, but I'm mistaken. Her skin is soft under my fingertips, like a peach just off the vine. I have to open my mouth to breathe. I need more air than my nose alone can provide.

I pick up her lifeless hand. It's cold, pliable. I place her hand over her stomach. I look at the boys, and Seth reaches over, picks up Momma's other hand placing in on top of the first. Jake reaches up and closes her eyes with the tips of his thumb and forefinger. I look at Momma sideways.

This was the vessel she walked the earth with, but I know her spirit is free. She feels no more pain, or sadness. No regret. It pains me to see her this way. The reality of it feels like a cold wind rushing through my veins, but this isn't about me. This is Momma's passage—her journey to heaven. What a privilege it is to be here, to have said goodbye, to know that I can keep Momma alive in me, in my actions, in my promises.

That's when I think of the scripture, "Precious in the sight of the Lord is the death of his saints," I say out loud, causing Momma's church friends to begin crying out. One of them starts singing *Amazing Grace*. More voices join in. Their voices are rising, and rising. But I'm no longer afraid of their sentiments. They are soothing to me, too. They remind me of innocence, of times when everything was as it seemed right on the surface.

"Is that Psalms 116?" Dillon asks. His arms are still wrapped around me. I lean into him for support and nod. The scent is gone now. Her spirit has dissipated, gone to where she's always known she was meant to go, to her Heavenly Father.

I can hear her telling me about heaven with its pearly gates. How up there, you don't look old. You look the way you did when you were at your happiest. I can see her that way, too. She's wearing her Sunday best—a pretty flowery dress that came to her knees. It has buttons up the front that look like little pearls. Her eyes are a greyish blue with life in them again. Her long dark hair falls in curls down over her shoulders. I can smell her favorite perfume that came out of a little bottle that she used to dab just behind her ears. And if I concentrate, I can hear her voice singing with them. Her voice, off-key but pure and vigorous, reaching the notes, rising above it all. That's where she is. Where she has to be.

When I look up, Missy is standing in the doorway. I don't think she can come back in. She looks frozen, rigid. Her eyes are red and her cheeks are wet. She's waiting for the song to end.

"I called Restlawn. They're on their way ta come'n get Momma," she says in a monotone. Oh, yes, Restlawn Memory Gardens. That's where I sent the gaudy flowers when Daddy passed on. I know it's wrong, but I don't want anyone to touch her. If I stay here, I'm going to panic when they take her away.

"Dillon, can we go now?" I ask, squeezing his hand.

"Yes, baby," he says, and I turn to face him. I bury my wet face into his chest. "Thank you," I say. He says nothing. He quietly takes my hand as we walk away. I turn one last time to look at her. The boys are still standing there. From this angle, she just looks asleep. She looks beautiful, actually. No more pain in her face. Just peace.

As we walk down the stairs, I don't feel like I thought I would. I'm not numb, I'm not cracked and fragile. Maybe it's just not real to me yet. I'm not going to question it. I'm grateful for this. I was able to say goodbye to my momma—and it didn't break me. This must be the new me.

Chapter Twenty-One

Don't Slip Away

"She was warm," I say, after we'd sat in silence all the way down Brandon Street, his hand on mine over the center console.

"I'm sorry, Sadie, what do you mean?" he asks.

"She was warm, her face was, when I touched her," I say, as I stare at the bright yellow line down the center of the road as it dots past us on the left side.

"Oh, yes. Baby, she'll be warm for a little while. She'd just stopped breathing."

"Just stopped," I repeat. How do I make sense of that? Momma doesn't breathe anymore. Her body is empty, her eyes were dead. I close my eyes. I try to remember them when she was alive. I can't. I just keep seeing her eyelids as slits. Her vacant stare as she looked out from them in death.

"Dillon, who comes to pick up my momma's body?" I ask, as the car suddenly feels very tiny and lacking of air. I push my hand into the car door to try to make it bigger in here.

Dillon pauses for a moment. "Well, in the area, Wallace and Wallace is the usual funeral home that people use."

"Uh-huh. So, is it an ambulance that comes or a hearse?"

"A hearse, I believe. Darlin', are you okay?"

Am I? "I don't know," I say.

"Do you need me to do anything for you?"

"I just want to know what's going to happen to her."

"Okay. I can call and find out."

"No. No. That's okay." Then it hits me. The image of the boys standing by the bed with Momma. Two orphans. "The boys!" I shout.

"What about them?" he questions, nervously.

"I didn't hug them, Dillon. I just walked away and left them in there by themselves. They're alone with Momma's body!"

"No, darlin' there were all those other people there. They aren't alone."

"I'm so selfish. What's wrong with me? I left them when they needed me. I promised Jake. No, I promised Seth I'd be a better sister."

"You will, baby. Don't worry, okay?" I can't breathe. My gasps are shallow and my heart is beating in my ear like a pounding fist. My stomach feels as if there is something sharp inside it. It's ripping its way out–pulling me in two.

"Dillon. Pull over, please." I realize, he's already stopping the car on the side of the road.

"Do you want to go back?"

"No! I'll see them taking her away. I can't." I'm writhing in pain. My legs won't stay still. My hands are numb and tingly.

"Do you want me to take you to the hospital?" Everything is spinning around me. The inside of the car feels like the inside of a drain. I take off my seat belt, put my head between my knees. He must get out his phone. "Hello. I need to bring in Sadie Sparks. Her mother has just passed away and she's having a severe panic attack."

I don't want to go. They're going to medicate me. Why am I hurting this bad? Where's Numb Girl? "No!" I squeal.

"Sadie, what can I do?"

"I don't know? I've never had one this bad before," I say, looking up at him from my knees. I bolt upright. My stomach feels like knives are crawling around my insides. The hole in my chest is constricted like it wants to strangle me. It throbs, aches like it's hungry and devouring the rest of me. My neck feels tight like the fabric in my scarf is stretching against the seams. I rip it open, watch it crash against the inside of the windshield. But I don't feel any relief. I'm on the edge of the seat pushing my palms into the dashboard.

"What can she do?" he says, into the phone. "Okay, thank you," he says. "I'll call you back."

I feel his hand on my back. "Baby," he says, as soft as a warm blanket. "What you need to do is concentrate on your breathing. Can you do that for me?" I look up at him. His eyes look wide again, too wide.

I want to do what he says. I close my eyes and tune into the frequency of my inhalations. They sound shallow and frantic. Rushed like a song being fast-forwarded on a CD player.

"Good," he says. "Breathe through your nose, okay? It'll help you slow it down."

When I open my eyes, he's right in front of me. He's pulled me toward him so that we're facing each other. He has one arm around me pressing lightly on my back. With his other hand, he pulls my palm up to his chest. I feel this upper body moving up as he inhales deliberately through his nose and then down as he exhales from his mouth. "Do you feel my breathing? Pace yourself to me, darlin'."

"Okay."

"Just slow it down," he says, gently, methodically. He rests his forehead against mine so I can feel his breath on my face. I am taking deep painful gasps. This is better than the shallow ones. My hands don't feel numb anymore. My legs relax again. The knives in my stomach are stilling, not all at once though. More like one at a time. I feel his breath. I make mine like his. Quiet. Slow. "You're doing a great job," he says, into my mouth.

I crawl over the console and sit in his lap. I wrap my arms around his neck, my knees push into my chin. My feet rest on the center console. I press my right ear against his chest and listen to his heart beating. It soothes me. Maybe this is what it sounds like in the womb. I feel limp. My limbs are heavy. My breath swims in my ear making me feel like sleep would be the best thing in the world right now.

"I'm so proud of you, Sadie," he says. I feel him start the engine. My left hip is pressing against the steering wheel. But I don't want to move. I kiss his neck, thankfully. Run the tip of my finger along the curve of his ear. He's protected me again—helped me.

"I love you," I whisper, as I feel the car hum upon the black asphalt.

"And I love you, darlin'," he says. The hole in my chest is warmed. It no longer aches or throbs. It's full and tamed. My eyes feel unbearably heavy. I give in to it. Sleep comes like an island in the middle of an angry ocean. Dillon pulled me ashore. Saved my life.

"I will be your wife," I say, into the echoing dream that pulls on me like a heavy weight.

I know I'm being carried. I feel the cold night air as it pierces through my shirt and blows my hair around like a windmill. The stride of his long legs rocks me as I'm draped over his arms. I feel weightless, cherished. I nuzzle his collarbone with my nose. He smells divine.

We are inside, with the scents of the polished wood floors, the fresh paint. His footsteps echo through the house and up the stairs.

He's not even winded. *He is so fit*, I think. So opposite from Momma's body. Empty and dead.

I want to open my eyes, but I can't. I must just be exhausted. I do not want to be numb again. I will myself *not to become numb*.

I'm on the bed. I don't want to open my eyes. I let him pull my boots off one by one. He unbuttons my pants and pulls the zipper. I feel his fingers on my hips pulling the denim down me like peeling the skin of a banana. "I can do it," I say, groggily.

"Let me?" he asks.

"Yes."

I feel his hands moving down as he untangles the buttons from my shirt. As I open my eyes, I focus on him in the dark. I force myself not to think about Momma. They must have taken her by now. I cannot slip away. I have a life to live. Promises to keep. A memory to keep alive.

"Will you take a bath with me?" I ask him. I hear his sharp intake of breath.

"Is that what you'd like?" he asks, earnestly.

"I need to feel things right now, Dillon. I'm afraid of going numb again," I say, as I sit upright, move my right hand into the soft waves of his hay colored hair.

"Did you mean it?" he asks as our mouths are so close I can almost feel his lips on mine.

"What?"

"While you were sleeping, you were talking again."

"What did I say?" I ask, as he pulls the white long sleeved shirt up over his stomach and then his arm moves up over his shoulder, pulling the shirt up over his head.

"That you will be my wife," he says, fast, as if it couldn't be real.

"Yes, Dillon. That's what I want," I say, looking at his wavy hair in the dim light.

He kisses me softly, purposefully. His kiss feels like it's coming through a screen. As if I'm slipping away. The numbness is right on my perception like I'm standing on a precipice between darkness and dawn. "I'm going to do this right, Sadie."

"What do you mean?"

"I'm going to talk to your brothers first. Then, when you're not expecting it, I'm going to ask you properly."

"You don't need to do that. I've already said yes," I say. I'm dizzy. I put my hand up to my forehead.

"It's important to me," he says. "I've imagined it a certain way. Please."

"Of course," I say. "It sounds perfect." *It does. Too perfect for me.* He leans in, rubs his nose against mine. I feel lethargic. As if I'm on pause.

"I'll be right back. I'm going to start the water in the tub."

I watch him stride toward the bathroom. The muscles in his back tense as he walks. He's nothing short of beautiful. I hear the water turn on and I jump. On edge, my heart begins to race.

Numb or jumpy. Which one will win?

As he walks back into the room, I notice how his pants hang from his hips just so. I'm slumped over. But the line of his hips as they meet his abdomen and disappear into his pants makes me sit upright. He reaches his hand down to me. "Come," he says, devoted. Controlled.

I stand up. "I'm afraid, Dillon."

"Why?"

"I think I'm going to slip away, go numb."

"Love, this is different. You're just tired, drained. I won't let you leave me again."

I smell lavender from the tub as I feel my feet pad their way toward the cold tile, my hand in his like a baby's. My limbs feel heavy as he unstraps my bra, freeing me. I'm not embarrassed this time. There's nothing left in me to be.

The dim light of the candles he's lit flicker in my eyes. I feel like a tree swaying in the dark forest standing here. He pulls down my panties as I rest my hands on his shoulders for support. It reminds me how different I'd felt last night when he'd done this. Like his fingers were on fire as he touched me, igniting me. Now I feel too heavy to respond to the trace of his fingertips.

He undoes the buttons on his pants and lets them fall. He slips off the boxer briefs and steps into the too large tub. The candles flicker over his muscles. Over his nakedness. He's perfect inside and out. My heart should quicken, but there's nothing in me to pump the blood faster.

Holding his hand, I step in and we sink down together. He puts his long legs on either side of me and I press my back lightly into his now wet and bubbly chest. As the warmth from the water steams my face, I'm almost not capable of staying awake.

He wets my hair, the warm water falling over my face in streams. He massages my scalp with shampoo that awakens my senses slightly. He rubs me with soap, and then moves around so that he's in front of me. He rubs my feet, massaging each and every toe. It makes me smile. The way he takes care of me, like I'm delicate and his.

"Let's go to bed, darlin'. It's nearly eleven." I nod my head. He helps me up and then out. It's cold. I know I'm alive because of my goose bumps as he rubs me down with a white fluffy towel. Then he ties it around his waist. I watch as water trickles over his chest. It reminds me of tears. It reminds me of grief. I shiver.

He grabs Missy's bright blue robe and lets my arms sink into them before he ties it neatly around my waist. He sets me on a chair in the bathroom, brushes through my hair softly. He rummages around under the sink and then walks over to my bag to look. My eyes open and then close. Open and then close.

"I'm going to dry your hair," he says. I don't respond before the hot air begins to take my hair from stiff and cold to warm and pliant as it falls down my back in tepid strands.

"Come sit on the couch over here so I can change the sheets." I shuffle over to the couch and drop down into the fluffy down cushions and watch him in a daze as he replaces the sheets. I stare at the white pile in a rumpled heap and wonder what he'll do with the little heart we'd slept over last night.

I want to keep it, I think as he flaps the top sheet in the air. I'd like to help, but I don't think I have the strength to stand on my own.

He helps me to the bed. Takes off my robe and slips a white T-shirt over my warm hair. I fall backward onto the bed as he slips on some baggy boxers. I like the other kind. The tighter ones.

He slides onto my right side and we fuse together like we are one. We are one, aren't we? "Don't let me slip away, Dillon. I'm scared."

"I won't, baby. Sleep now. I'll take you to get pancakes tomorrow," he promises. It's funny to me how a promise of food, sweet syrupy food, makes me feel something kind of like life flow through my veins.

He runs the tips of his fingers along the curve of my back. "You're mine," he whispers in my ear. This is the second time anyone has said this to me. My eyes shoot open. For a moment I wonder where I am. No. I'm in our bed. I'm safe. It's Dillon.

Donnie is scared somewhere. Worried I'll hit the switch and ruin his life.

"Yours," I say, with a clear conscience. *Yours.* There's nowhere else I'd rather be.

Chapter Twenty-Two

Wake Up!

It's been a recurring dream. Nightmare, really. It's the kind of dream that I remember the next day with a furrowed brow. The kind that can force me to pry my eyelids open to escape from it in the dead of night. Then, when I finally get to sleep again, it starts right where I left off, as if I'd put it on pause and said, okay. Start.

It's always the same. Well, it starts the same, but over the years the ending has begun to get worse and worse.

I'm in the backyard of Aunt Lotty's California ranch style house. I'm digging up the clay dirt and mixing it with the earthy goodness from the mountain to make a thick fertile plant bed. I add the flowers and pack them in. It's so real I can feel the dirt pushing up under my fingernails. I feel so proud of my flowers. Like they are life—thriving, and blooming. Like I'm worthy of such beauty.

As I sit here, feeling the warmth of the clay earth under the sun's reaching tendrils, each flower shrivels and curls up into itself. But I don't give up. I will not succumb to the failure that threatens to consume. I try it over and over. Adding the flowers, watching them die.

There has to be something wrong with the dirt. So I begin ripping up the dead flowers. I can feel my hands in the earth looking like cringing claws as I dig deeper. Searching for what lies beneath. What's killing my flowers, my chance at happiness?

That's when I find the bone. I pick it up and know. *This is a human bone.* Someone has been buried under my flowerbed, tainting it. Poisoning everything that will ever grow above it. Guilt takes over then. I feel guilty even though I did not kill this person. I did not bury them or hide them there.

The guilt comes because I bury them again and tell no one they are there. The crime is not mine, but it feels like it is. I take ownership of the crime. The heaviness of the guilt. The death of the flowers. It weighs on me until I cannot go on. I want to tear my eyes open at this point. It's a lucid dream. I know I'm sleeping and I want out.

Over the years, I begin to find more than one human bone in the dirt upon unearthing it. I find a full skeleton, and bury it again. Tell no one. Live with the guilt. Live with the dead flowers. Soon, I'm not only unearthing the bones but then I'm moving them to another location. Digging up another spot, and burying them again. Telling no one. The guilt festers. Still the flowers do not grow. They wilt and die.

Tonight's dream starts out the same as all the others. Except this time, I am planting lilies. Sometimes I wonder why I keep trying. I lie in wait; I know they will die. When they do, I'm forced to dig up the dirt. Pull it up in heaping piles of musty deadness. I can feel the soil in my hair, under my nails. That's when I grasp hold of the cloth. It's moist and cold, marinated in muck. The compulsion to see who's buried here has me by the throat. I feel the stiff body under my fingertips. I swipe the dirt from the face.

The body is me. The old me. She's wearing the pretty little flower-dotted dress. The brown boots that used to be Missy's but she'd given to me when my feet grew into them. Her hair is long, and thin. Messy and windblown.

She takes a deep breath into her chest, comes to life. I hold out my hand and she takes it. I help her up and we stand here examining each other. I touch her neck. A neck that's not yet been sliced open by a fishy knife. I take up the hem of the dress. It's white. Pristine, as all of the filth she'd been covered in has disappeared. I push the fabric between my thumb and forefinger. It feels like innocence, not yet tainted.

I take her hand in mine. I'm asking her to come inside. I wave inward. *"Come with me,"* I call to her. She shakes her head no. She's saying something but it's as if she's behind a glass wall and I cannot hear her. She's getting angry. Her words are coming out of a yelling mouth, all wide and frantic. Then she points and her eyes grow wide. She's pointing behind me.

I bristle.

When I turn around I'm in the shed again. Donnie is blocking the door. When I look to my right, I see the old me. She's negotiating with him. But he's looking at me. He's not interested in the girl in the little flower-dotted dress. He wants the woman. The one covered in guilty dirt.

I kick at the walls inside the shed and one of the slats breaks away from the frame. I push my way through but I can feel his grasp as he holds tight on my legs. He always catches me in my dreams. It never fails.

I'm pulling but I cannot go anywhere. I feel too heavy. I'm leaving her again. I'm leaving her alone with him in the shed. He's going to kill her again.

Wake up!

Wake up!

As my eyes open, I can hardly catch my breath. Dillon's arm is over me. He's still asleep. I rub my eyes and slide out of bed. I need some water.

I walk softly out of his room and into the empty house that's just waiting for a family to grow up in it. I walk through the dining room, listening as my steps echo around in waves. I find the kitchen. The old one he's remodeling. It's huge. I can just imagine how beautiful it'll be once we build it back up. I want a country sink and a big island in the middle. White cabinets. Reclaimed wood. Butcher block counters.

I find the other kitchen. The small one he's been using in lieu of the magnificent one that doesn't exist yet. It's simple. I wonder what we could do with it once the other one is finished.

All of these thoughts are merely a distraction. The truth is, this dream proves what I already know. Donnie still has a hold on me. Recording or not, I'm going to live my life in fear as long as he's free. My inaction is allowing him to hurt me. To hurt Renae. *I have to tell.*

I realize that my asking Jenny to transcribe the recording was a way for me to test the waters. I can tell her, or rather let her find out, because she's not allowed to tell anyone. Her judgment won't hurt me. She's far away. But she's the only other person in the world who knows who did this to me.

There's one person I want to talk to. Renae.

As I sit behind a huge stack of pancakes slathered in fluffy white butter and doused with syrup, I'm preoccupied with how to tell Renae what happened to me. How will I ask her if she's being abused? The guilt is killing me. Her abuse is, in essence, my fault. I cannot let it go on. Not in good conscience.

"Please, darlin' take a bite," Dillon coaxes.

I cut into the thick stack and stick it in my mouth allowing the syrup to drizzle down my chin. He leans across and wipes my face.

"You didn't have to do that," I say, frowning. "I can wipe my own face."

"I'm sorry," he says, and then looks out the window tucked into the wall at Tudor's Biscuit World, the restaurant we always visited after church on Sundays.

I should apologize. But I don't. I'm so edgy. I feel so many things at once. Momma is gone, dead. It's my fault Renae is being abused. Until I deal with this, my flowers won't grow. I feel like a flower that's ready to wither and die.

I watch as Dillon doesn't eat his 'Big Tater' breakfast. It looks like too much food slathered in too much gravy. He's just watching the cars as they drive by. He's anywhere but here. I knew it. He'd get sick of me soon enough.

"I've got to call Aunt Lotty!" I state, as it dawns on me.

"Sure. After breakfast, okay," he says, off-hand.

"You don't have to stay, Dillon. I can see you've had enough of me."

"Sadie, I wasn't expecting you to snap at me," he says.

"I just wanted to wipe my own face."

"No. You're right. I'm smothering you," he says. "I'm going to take you to your momma's house and then I'm going to go to work for a few hours."

I want to say I'm sorry. I've hurt him and he's been nothing but good to me. He's still got bruises on his face because of me. He's helped me through my momma's death. He's dealt with me being completely neurotic for days. *He needs a break.*

"I'm sorry, Dillon." He doesn't say anything. He's on the verge of tears as he takes a sip of his coffee.

As we crunch up the driveway, I can't help feeling anxious about him leaving me. I know it's wrong, but I don't want him to go.

"I'm so sorry, Dillon," I say, as he stops the car in front of the now Momma-less house. "I'm a jerk."

"Sadie, please, don't take this personally. I really do need to go to work. It'll just be a few hours."

"But I hurt your feelings. Just admit it."

"Yes. You did. But I'm also emotionally and physically exhausted. I'm not angry with you. I promise."

"You'll be back for lunch then?"

"I'm going to get my laptop and pick up a few things so I can work from home."

I lean in to kiss him. He defrosts a bit when our lips touch. "Thank you," I say, looking into his eyes before I jump out and prepare to deal with a house laden with death. A house full of memories that will tug at me from every angle. On the bright side, I'm not numb. I hadn't even realized that until this moment. *Dr. Amy would be so proud of me,* I think as I climb the steps.

Missy is sitting on the couch. The boys are in the kitchen. Dale is playing with the kids on the floor. They all look my way as I walk in the door.

"We need to get you some more clothes," Missy says.

"I'm going to have my assistant send me some," I say. *I need to text her on time today.* I've worn these jeans three times now. "This is a different shirt, though," I say, grasping the deep green collar of my shirt and sticking out my bottom lip. She always knows how to put me in my place. "Has anyone called Aunt Lotty?"

"No," Missy says. "I thought you'd want to tell her." I nod. She's right. It should come from me. Aunt Lotty is Daddy's sister. She had been very close to my momma, though. When Daddy died, she came back. I'm sure she's going to want to come back this time, too.

"When's the wake so I can invite her?"

"It's Thursday. We're havin' the viewing in the mornin', the burial at noon, and then the wake'll be all evenin'," she says.

Aunt Lotty cries through the whole conversation. Once again. Knowing someone is dying is completely different than having it happen for real. She agrees through sniffles and tears to come to town for the burial and the wake.

I spend the rest of the morning trying to be busy. I can't really think about Momma without crying. I help Missy pick out a dress to bury her in. It's a white dress covered in pretty flowers and has little pearl-like buttons all the way up the front. It's the one I'd imagined her in. *I knew she had a dress like this.*

I find it nearly impossible to be in her closet. It smells of her and makes me feel lonely. It makes my chest feel tight like it's about to break open. The medicine smell is still in the bedroom but hasn't infiltrated the closet. I find myself on the floor examining her shoes.

There's a pair near the back wall that I remember well. They were her everyday shoes. She cleaned the house in them, went to the store in them, made dinner in them. I stare at the soles and examine the way she wore them down. Each sole is worn differently. She favored her right leg. I realize these shoes represent life. A life lived well, so I smile.

I stand up and lean into the clothes with my arms outstretched as if I'm hugging them. I try to pretend she's here with me. I grab some jewelry to put with her in the casket and close up the closet like a tomb. I can't bear the thought of losing the scent in here. It's a scent that won't exist in this world again. I need to contain it.

Around noon, I wonder where my gun is. Oh, yes. It's on the mantel in the living room at Dillon's house. I want to go talk to Renae but not without my gun. I swallow some food. I don't care what it is. I think some kind of potato. At noon, I text Jenny. She follows back with some weird code that I'm sure means she's scared to death that I'm still here with my rapist running free. I ask her to send me some clothes.

I help Missy plan the funeral. I make calls to invite people. They all seem surprised to hear from me. I apologize to the boys for leaving them last night. They pretend like they don't care. I make a mental note to stop being so selfish and integrate them into my life.

As the day wears on, I wonder if Dillon is coming back at all. I want to call him, but I don't even have his number. There hasn't been a need to call him until now. This is what scares me about being in love. How vulnerable it makes me feel. How much I need him now. When I hear his tires crumble up the driveway, I actually run out the front door. My stomach coils up and I wait for him to come to me so I can hold him, so he can hold me.

"What shed was it, Sadie?" he asks, urgently. His hands are grasping me just at the top of my arms.

Stunned, I stand here, my palms facing up. He remembers me saying that up on the mountain. I shake my head no, trying to back away from him. He's scaring me. The intensity of his grasp, the wild look in his eyes. He's pieced something together. What he knows, I'm unsure. But he's one step closer at least.

"It was my shed, wasn't it?" I can't move. Then he takes off. He's running toward his momma's house. *What's he doing? Is he going to the shed?*

For seconds, I can't will myself to move. But I have to know what he's doing. I take off after him. Feel the shock of my legs as they run along the wild path between our houses. Hear him throwing things around inside of the shed. The door is wide open as I approach apprehensively as if the shed itself is what hurt me, not the man who met me inside. Changed my fate forever. The man I know I have to tell on.

I close my eyes. Take one deep breath before I take a step toward the entrance. There are ghosts inside this place. Someone died in here. This is true. Maybe if I can calm her spirit, she'll stop haunting me in my dreams. Maybe my flowers will bloom again.

But when I see him inside, I know something has changed. I see them in his hands. Light pink, stiff with old blood. My light pink panties. The ones he'd seen when he kissed me for the first time.

"Where were those?" I cry.

"Wrapped in this cloth and tucked into this spot right here," he says, pointing to a spot in the corner. "These are yours," he decides. Part of me wants to break to pieces. But I'm worried about Dillon. I'm not ready for him to know. "This is where you were. I was running around looking for you. And this is where you were. Right here. Right on my property."

I can't respond. I want to take the panties. Hide them. Bury them. Bury someone else's crime.

"I came here. Called to you," he says.

"He had a knife. It was up to my throat. He'd already cut me. When we heard you, he threatened to kill me, then kill you."

"Oh, God!" he says. The look on his face will never leave me. I want to crawl away. Hide. I fall to my knees. Bury my head in my lap.

When I look up, I see the gas can. It's in a haze that I watch Dillon douse this shed in the sharp scented liquid. I want to yell *stop*. But no words come. Nothing seems to make sense.

I see the flames. Feel the strong arms taking me away from them. But I have to watch. It really is hell. Flames lick upward like tongues as I take it in, watch it become an inferno. I smile at the crackling sound of the boards being robbed of their hold on me. My own personal hell. *It's gone!*

Chapter Twenty-Three

The Link

The hell mouth. That's what the shed reminds me of. The place where sinners' bodies are devoured, consumed. But not this one. I can imagine the spirit rising above the flames. The spirit of me at fourteen. The one that wanders around in that shed in her dreams pleading for her life, for her virtue, for the last ten and a half years. She doesn't have to do that anymore.

For her, this feels like justice. I realize I'm on the ground when the wet grass leaks through the fabric of my jeans. I look around for the first time as the flames consume both the shed and my senses.

"Dillon!" I scream, and then cough. I can't see him through the smoke. He's pulled me all the way toward the property line where the trees grow untamed and rough. That's when I hear him. He's behind me in the trees. He's pulling branches. Throwing things from the ground into the leaves and needles. I stand up, walk toward him.

"Dillon," I say, reaching out to touch his back ever so carefully. I see my hand shaking uncontrollably as it makes contact with his white shirt.

He flips around, wild-eyed, nostrils flared, his mouth in a knotted scowl. His hands are in fists. His arms and neck look like they might burst. He's breathing so heavily it makes mine quicken, too. He starts pacing.

He's angry with me. That's what this feels like.

He's blaming me for not yelling for him when he called my name.

The guilt comes back to me again, and I turn away from him. I feel so ashamed of myself. So dirty. So unworthy.

Just like Daddy blamed me. Just like Donnie blamed me. *Not Dillon, too.*

That's when I see them. The pink panties are lying on the grass near the shed. He must have dropped them in his ferocity to destroy it. They're going to burn up.

It's evidence. DNA, both mine and Donnie's. I've got to get them. I run as fast as I can toward the shed. Then they are in my hands. They feel like a combination of softness and death. Blood and silk. I feel like a lucky thief as Dillon pulls me up and away from the flames.

"What are you doing?" he screams. "Trying to get yourself killed?" I shake my head no. I hide the panties in my hands and clasp them to my chest as he pulls me toward him. He's shaking, breathing fast and quick in my ear. "I'm...I'm so...," he tries to say, between the rumble of adrenaline and the quick breaths.

"It's not my fault!" I scream, and pull away from him. "How can you blame me for what he did to me?" I'm pointing at his house. I put my hand down quickly.

"No," he says. His eyes are wide again like under the windowsill. He's reaching out to me. "Baby, no. Not. Your. Fault!" he pants. "Mine. I let you get hurt. Me." He's pointing at his chest. Pounds his breast with is fist.

I'm petrified as he comes toward me. He must know I'm scared because he forces his fists to become hands again. Taking a cleansing breath he comes toward me—warily this time like I'm a wounded animal. "I'm sorry," he croons. "I'm sorry, baby," he says, wrapping his arms around me and rubbing my back. He smells like gasoline, smoke, and evergreen trees.

I look up at the house. Dot and Renae are on the wrap-around porch. Dot's holding a phone up to her ear. I look at the driveway. Donnie's white cruiser isn't parked there. He must be out on his shift. I slide the panties into the right front pocket of my jeans.

"It's my fault," he says, taking my face between his two shivering hands. Pain is right on the surface of his face. "I was right here as you were. And he was. With the knife." He shakes his head back and forth. His eyes, vacant.

"Dillon," I try to reason with him.

"Tell me who he is!" he cries.

"No. Look at what you've done. You're so reckless. You just burned down this shed. The kids are inside. Your mom." I'm pointing at them. He looks up and sees his family on the porch peering out into the darkness as the shed falls onto itself. Fire and smoke bloom, overtaking the hell mouth.

It makes me smile for a moment. *It's really gone.* But then I look to Dillon. The pain visible in the wrinkles on his forehead. The bruises on his face. The black eye. He's running himself into the ground.

"You won't be able to control yourself when you find out," I say. Not in anger. Just in truth.

He pinches the little V that forms between his eyes. Shakes his head no. "I can't live like this. Not knowing who. Worrying he'll come back. Thinking about the years we lost.—No, were stolen from us. Seeing all the pain you're in every day."

"I know, Dillon. I'm going to make you a promise," I say, as his eyebrows shoot up. "After my momma's wake, I'm going to tell you who it was. I'll tell you everything. But I can't do it now. There're things I need to take care of before then. Do you understand?"

"What are you going to do? Is it dangerous?"

"I can't tell you," I say, thinking of the evidence in my pocket. "It's not dangerous."

"Sadie!"

"No, Dillon. You won't be able to help me if you know. Look what you've done," I say, staring into the flames. I've got to get this tested. I've got to build up the evidence before he can get to me. It has to be a surprise attack. Dillon would try and give them to Donnie thinking that he could get them tested for us.

Dillon probably thinks that the panties just fell there inside the shed and were never found until now. But I remember. Donnie put them in his pocket after he raped me. He'd touched them with his hands drenched in my blood, probably his own semen, too. He kept them in the shed like a prize. Like a trophy. He probably thought no one would ever find them. But I have them now.

We're sitting inside Dillon's childhood home with the lights from the fire truck waving around through the window. Renae and Dot wouldn't take no for an answer. They stuck a mug of hot tea in my hand and covered me in a blanket. Dillon stands. Then sits. Rubs his hands together and then stands again. He begins to pace.

"Luckily it didn't spread to the grass or nothin' else," says Dot. "What happened, son?"

"I did it. I burned it down, Momma. That was where..." His breath hitches. He must have a lump there, too. He's rubbing his throat. Puts his hands on his head.

"Where, what, son?" she asks, nervously.

"Sadie was..." He can't finish his thought, pushes his fist into the palm of his hand. His chest looks tight. His white shirt is dotted black from the smoke outside. Dot looks at me puzzled. I realize I'm rubbing my teal scarf right above my scars so I stop. She must understand then what her one good son can't verbalize, because she puts her head down and covers her eyes with her hand.

It's where I was raped by your evil son! I want to scream. It takes her a while, but she gets up and sits next to me. She puts her hand on my back and covers her mouth with her other hand. Renae comes out from the hallway with the baby on her hip. There's a new look on her face. Kind of like when you accidentally catch yourself in the mirror in a store and weren't expecting it. That's how she looks.

The door slams open.

I bristle, hold the cup tight like I wish it were a gun.

His boots stomp into the living room. When he sees me, there's a realization in his eyes that shows he knows he'd better be careful. Is he caught? That's what he wants to know. "What happened?" he asks, looking at Dillon. He looks like he's on that ice again. The kind that's too thin to hold him up any longer.

"When was the last time you were in that shed, Donnie?"

"Why?"

"'Cause, whoever raped Sadie stashed 'em in there all these years. They were stuck behind the feed in a crevice between the floor and the wall slats."

"I don't know what yer talkin' about, boy," Donnie bellows.

Dillon paces again. He's not going to tell Donnie what he found. *Is he accusing him? Trying to catch him?*

"Look, Sadie's told me as much as she knows. As far as I can tell, the guy's skipped town," Donnie says.

"What about the fingerprints at the Spark's house?" Dillon asks.

"Came back with nothin'," Donnie says.

"Sadie, do you know what happened to the… To what I found?"

"I didn't see them again. You must have dropped them in the fire," I say. *I hate lying to him.*

Why is he hiding this from Donnie? *I think he knows.* I think he's just waiting for the proof. Denial is a hard state of mind, a tall thick wall to break down. But it has to come down to reveal the truth walled in behind it.

I get up, tossing the blanket on the couch and make my way toward the restroom. I remember where it is. After I wash my hands and open the door, Renae is standing in the hallway. The baby is asleep on her shoulder. She's wearing a long beige robe. "I need ta talk to you, Sadie," she says, in a dark whisper. But then the harsh boots begin to stomp toward the hallway and she retreats into a bedroom across from me into the shadows.

I bristle again and try to stand my ground as he ushers me back into the dark bathroom. "What did you tell him?" he asks. His bear paw around my wrist feels like worms crawling under my skin. He closes the door. We are alone in the bathroom. Another closed space. I start to make some guttural sound I don't recognize.

"Don't scream. I ain't gonna hurt you." I can't breathe. I'm stuck to the ground. *He's not going to do anything. He's not going to do anything.*

"I didn't tell him. He figured it out," I say, unforgiving and swift.

"What does he know?" he asks as he comes closer. I think he's leaning down, smelling my hair but it's completely dark and I can't see. I'm helpless in this moment. I don't know what he's doing, so near me in the dark.

As I press my back into the wall, I can only hear his breathing—the sound reminds me of a deep pummeling rhythm. I can only smell his scent, the very one that I'd never liked, that reminds me of pain, of a knife blade pinching. I can only feel the vibrations of his body being far, far too close to me. I feel the bile rise in my throat, but the fear keeps everything down.

"He doesn't know anything. He found the panties. But he threw them down and they probably burned up," I say, quickly. *Get this over with.* "Let go of me right now or I swear to God…," I say, like a little dog trying to bark deep.

He lets go of my wrist. But I know by his scent, by his vibrations that he's too close, pinning me with his proximity. I move to the left toward the door handle and run straight into his arm. He's pinning me in place with his arms like a cage. Our breaths are loud; they echo together in the stiff air like ghosts.

"Why did you keep them?" I taunt.

"When I touch 'em, I feel you again. Smell you," he says, taking a deep breath of me.

"You're disgusting."

"Nothin' you do will ever break tha link we have, Sadie," he says into my ear. I press that side of my face into the wall. I didn't know his face was so close to mine. "You might keep me away, but you won't break it," he whispers into my other ear. I push his chest away from me. It feels like guilt. Like bodies under the dirt.

"Maybe not," I challenge, "unless you are dead," I snap. Pulling open the door like a saving grace, I run back out to the living room. Dillon is standing next to the window. He's looking out to where the shed must still be smoldering. I run out the front door leaving it wide open. I have to run, I need to get somewhere safe.

I find a path that we used to take from his house. I know where I'm going to go. The cave. The one that Dillon used to take me to that had the remains of some animal in it. That's where I'm headed. I'm pushing through the branches. Listening to my breaths. Seeing them puff out of me under the lamp light of the moon. I turn and run toward the cliff. The cave is just right under the lip of it. I find it covered by overgrowth. I don't care. I just want to be safe. Alone.

I rip away the foliage. Duck under the lip and cast myself onto the ground. I roll into a fetal ball. I'm rocking back and forth. *Break his link with me. I'll break more than his link with me.* I'm going to expose him and when he comes after me, I'm going to kill him. I will do what I have to do to survive. If that's the only way to be free.

"Sadie," I hear Dillon calling me. I don't want to talk to him. "Sadie!" He sounds frantic. I remember him sounding like this before. It's like a flashback. Everything is a flashback tonight. I can't believe I let Donnie get so close to me again. He touched me. He was savoring me in that bathroom. He's never going to let me go.

"Sadie, darlin'. Please!" I don't want to scare him. He's been through enough.

"Dillon," I say, but not loud enough. "Dillon!" I shout and stick my head out of the cave. He's past me on the trail and he turns around. I go back into the cave and sit down. I hear him walking toward me. I keep my head down. My heart beats through my chest. What am I going to say?

"Sadie, don't do this to me again," he says, hastily sitting down in front of me. Grasping my face between his long thin fingers. "The last time you ran off…" he starts.

"I know, Dillon. I'm sorry."

"You asked me to tell you," he says. "In the restaurant."

"Tell me. It's okay," I say, as he puts his legs on either side of me.

"After I touched you, you ran. But I didn't go after you at first. I was really pissed off at myself because I'd always promised to treat you right. I spoiled it. I felt so guilty. I didn't even realize until I did it. I was euphoric after kissing you. And you were letting me look at your panties," he says, with a slight grit to his teeth. He's remembering them bloody just as I am. I can feel them pushing up against my hip through the pocket in my jeans. "I just reached down and swatted the mosquitoes. It didn't feel wrong until I saw the look on your face."

"I remember. I felt like we'd gone too far. I felt guilty."

"I couldn't see where you ran to. But I had this knot in my throat. Like I knew something was off. I can't explain it. When I kept calling you, I was sure you'd come out. Smack me on the chest and pout. I could say I was sorry and then you probably wouldn't have let me kiss you again for a long time," he says, with a slight giggle. "I would take that scenario in a minute if I could."

"It's weird, isn't it?" I say. "How there's this whole other life we could have lived if I hadn't been raped."

"That's exactly how I see it, Sadie. Like the life I wanted with you was robbed from us."

"I know. But we can make it right. I'm here now. I'm not going to leave you again. I can't." He looks down, rubs his chin.

"I went to the shed. I thought I'd heard something in there. But it was locked so I left. I went down to the creek, but you weren't there. I checked this cave even. I was looking for it right now. But I couldn't find it," he says. "When I came back, the shed door was wide open. That's what I was thinking about today. You said 'the shed' up on the mountain. I just couldn't bring myself to believe that it was my shed. The one me and Donnie built with our dad," he says, shaking his head.

"When I found you, baby," he says, and puts his fist up to his mouth. He takes my face again in his hands, lightly, lovingly. "You were," he stops to take a breath. "You were floating face down, bumped up against a log. I ran into the water. Pulled you out. You were so cold." His eyes change. They look vacant. Numb. "You were dead."

"What did you do?"

"I did CPR. I learned it at school the year before. I worked on you for probably three minutes before you took a breath. I died a thousand deaths in those three minutes."

"Three minutes," I say. *I had no idea.*

"And then your daddy whipping you. All the blood in the house. I didn't see all the blood out in the dark. You were covered, I was covered in it."

"Where did you go when Momma made you leave?"

"I slept on your front porch," he says. "I couldn't leave you. Your momma found me out there in the morning. Told me you were okay, to go get cleaned up. She hugged me while I cried. It wasn't the manliest thing I ever did," he says, with one of those laughs used to mask the sound of tears stuck in the throat.

"I'm sorry, Dillon," I say, running my fingers along his wet cheek. I guess I hadn't realized how much pain Dillon experienced over this. The guilt he feels is just like mine. "Please, don't feel guilty. You saved my life."

"I wasn't quick enough. If I'd 'a ran after you right away."

"You can't think that way. It happened. There's nothing that's going to change it. There's no reason to go back to that day over and over. The past will never change, Dillon."

"The past will never change," he says. It seems like a light bulb moment for him.

"All we have is the future," I say. "Just give me time to sort this out. But you can't fly off the handle like that again. I need you to be calm if you're going to help me. Okay?"

"I've never been that angry in my life, Sadie. It's like the past caught up with me and exploded *inside my body*." Inside my body. That reminds me.

"Do you want a baby, Dillon?"

"What?"

"I just have this weird feeling like I'm going to have one. I haven't taken a test or anything. It's only been a few days but I feel like my body is shared with someone."

He blinks a few times, leans forward and kisses me then. It's that kiss where he's asking for something again, and I want to give it to him. That's when I remember the verse in the Song of Songs.

I pull away from him and say,

"My dove in the clefts of the rock,
in the hiding places on the mountainside,
show me your face,
let me hear your voice;

for your voice is sweet,
and your face is lovely."

I don't wipe his tears. I let them fall down on me like love—absorb them into my skin, into my soul. "Promise you'll never leave me," he says, his voice and face so earnest, so true.

"Never," I say, and he pulls me toward him by my hips as I wrap my arms around him and kiss him, slowly, purposefully to show him I mean it. Here in the spot where we used to giggle and play rock, paper, scissors, Dillon and I are going to make love for the second time.

We stand up and undress each other. There's an intensity between us as we do. His eyes never leave mine. We have a shared past. A shared future. It's chilly out as he lays our clothes on the rocks. But I'm so connected to him that I feel heat coming up through my pores. He sits down and eases me into his lap so that I'm resting on his thighs and open to him.

He readies me with is hands, the tips of his fingers, his mouth until I'm begging him for more. He fills me up, slowly, deliberately, as I offer him my bare neck to tease with his warm lips. With every movement, he fills my spirit with a radiant heat.

"Look at me, baby. Please," he says, tilting my chin down to his gaze. My lips tremble as he looks right into the deepest part of me, the most wounded part, and loves me anyway.

He holds my back with both hands so that our chests are pressed together. I'm looking into his blue eyes as the light from the moon flickers around inside our cave. He kisses me, our tongues dancing, whispers sweet nothings in my ear, and rocks with me slowly until I know I'm going over the edge with him. My body is shared with someone. I wouldn't have it any other way.

Chapter Twenty-Four

The Overlook

A s we walk along the old path, my hand entwined in his, we are careful to avoid the smoldering shed that neither of us wants to deal with right now. I'm thinking about what we've just done. *Who does a thing like that?* But for us, it was so easy. It's like we are in our own world, just he and I. A world where rosebuds bloom into beautiful flowers, not withering and dying like in my dream. The outside world is where sheds burn down, where shadows come to life and hurt people. Inside our room, in the cave, we are an unattainable force of nature.

I wish it could just be the two of us. That it could be simple. That there could be no secrets between the two of us. That's my goal: to be free and able to have the life with Dillon that we both deserve.

Once again, we've used no protection. It's nearer to when my period's due, so it's likely that we could have a baby. I want to smack myself on the forehead. *What am I doing?* Bringing another life into this tragic situation. It's definitely not the smartest move I've ever made. But, that makes me resentful because Dillon and I should be parents. We should have all of those things just like normal people.

Donnie has taken so much from me. Not this, too. I will have babies to fill up that house. I don't want to wait. I want it all—now. I won't let Donnie take another thing from me.

As my mind travels back to the cave, blood pumps through my veins like medicine for the faint of heart. I can still feel him. Everywhere he's touched is tingling. When we share ourselves with each other like that, there's nothing that can disturb the peace we feel in our hearts. It's perfect. Untainted.

Thinking of hearts has me remembering the little one embedded into the white pile of sheets on the floor in our room. How odd it is that both brothers made me bleed. But the experiences cannot be more different. I'm in possession of evidence of the first. This could be just the thing I need to catch him so we can be free.

That's when it hits me. I know where I'm going to hide the evidence. The letters Dillon wrote to me before I moved to California are hidden under a board in my old bedroom closet. Tomorrow I'll have to figure out who I can trust to take the panties to so that they can be tested. For now, they are going in that old cigar box just nestled under the wood plank.

"I'm just going to run inside for a minute and say goodbye to Missy and the boys. Will you wait for me a minute?" I ask, just outside of my childhood home.

"Sure," he says, visibly puzzled that I don't want him to come in.

I run up the steps and into my old room. I'm moving old boxes of my clothes out of the way so I can get to the board that pulls up in the back left corner of the closet floor. I stick my fingernail under the plank and wiggle it free. Inside is the brown metal cigar box. I pull off the lid and stare at the love notes from Dillon wrapped in a green ribbon that he wrote to me while I was disoriented and shattered. It was the only way he could communicate with me. So, he did it often.

I pull the panties out of my pocket and look at them in the light. Panties an innocent girl wore right up until the end. They are a light pink satin with deep stains the color of ripe beets. Hard spots that have congealed and dried up like a dead rose petal—sort of like the dead flowers from my dreams. The right side is cut by his knife. The left side is ripped and jagged.

It makes me wince. I can feel his knife pulling against the fabric. The warm trickle of blood down my leg right after. I can feel the cold blade pinching across my neck. Feel my neck weeping warm blood down the front of my dress. I wrap them up inside themselves and place them in the box.

After I've secured them under the plank, I scoot out of the closet only to find Dillon standing behind me. I jump like a kid just caught stealing money out of their daddy's wallet.

"What are you doing?" he asks, his voice soft but confused. Oh, crap!

"I was looking for some clothes," I try. *I feel so guilty.*

"Why'd you ask me to wait outside?"

"I thought I'd just be a minute," I say.

"I wish you'd just tell me, baby. Aren't you tired of hiding everything from me?" he asks, disappointedly, as he walks away. I shuffle behind him. I say nothing as I wave goodbye to the boys, Missy, Dale, and the kids. I'm sure they want to know what happened to the shed. I'll just tell them tomorrow.

We are silent all the way home. I reach for his hand. He feels stiff when I bring his hand to my lap.

"After the wake, you'll tell me everything?" he asks, unsure.

"Yes." *Oh, God!* I did promise him that.

"What if you don't have everything sorted out by then?"

"Well, that all depends on your ability to control yourself."

"I'll work on that, if you'll work on trusting me with the truth."

"Deal," I say. I feel him relax in that moment. He feels like him again—not a stiff ball of resentment.

After we take a bath in the too large tub, he sings me to sleep. Soft cooing lullabies I can imagine him singing to our child—children even—in a life I am working toward deserving. He's worth it, and I want to believe I am, too.

It's Monday morning and I'm scarfing down homemade biscuits in Dillon's interim kitchen when his phone buzzes in his pocket.

"Dr. McGraw," he says. "Yes…from home for a few days…oh…I see …alright…I'll be right in."

"I have to go into work for a bit," he says.

"It's okay. I'm sure Missy needs some help over at Momma's."

I grab my Daddy's gun off the beautiful hand carved mantel in the living room before I follow him out to the car.

On our way to Momma's house, I'm wondering how I'm going to accomplish the move from California to here. I need to get my desk set up soon so I can finish the new novel I've been working on. I've got an editor who likes to set mini deadlines for me and one's approaching in a week or so.

All of this feels futile unless Donnie is out of the picture. His words keep ringing in my ears, *"Nothin' you do will ever break tha link we have, Sadie."* It makes me shiver, and a helix of turmoil forms in my gut. I want to chop at that link, but it will just grow back—fuse itself together again. He's right. It is there, thick as steel. I realize I'm scowling so I make an effort to unscrew my face.

That's when I remember, *Renae*. She heard everything he said to me last night. In fact, I think she was about to say something to me when Donnie came stomping down the hallway. I've got to talk to her. *That's two people who know what happened to me now:* Jenny and Renae.

"I'll come and get you in a few hours," Dillon says. He's gifting me with that I'm-yours smile. "I have a project I'd like to work on for your momma's funeral," he says, as he crumbles pebbles on my childhood driveway.

"I've got to take that car back," I say, nodding toward the black Buick LeSabre I'd rented last Thursday. "I'd like to get my car sent over from California."

"Music to my ears," he says. His eyes gleam as he leans forward and kisses me before I run up the stairs.

When I walk into the house, the kids are in the living room playing. Missy puts one hand on her hip and glares at me while she stirs something on the stove. "Sadie Jane," she says. "What in heaven's name did Dillon do to that shed?"

"It's nice to see you, too, Missy," I say, as I walk through the living room and lay the gun up on the countertop, high above where little hands can reach.

"Well?"

"If you must know, Dillon burned it down because he figured out that that's where I was raped. Happy now?"

She drops the spoon into the pot and steps back, places her hand over her stomach as if she needs to stabilize herself against a blow to the gut.

"That's where it happened, Sadie?" she asks, as her face scrunches up, and an elephant-sized tear charges down her cheek. I had no idea my rape affected her at all. But then again, she had to live with me for months after it happened. Then, I left her, too. Just like I left Momma.

I nod my head yes, and sit down at the table. "I saw you real quick, before I ran off," she says, as she slips into the chair next to me. "I was hiding in our room when Dillon brought you in the house. I heard everything, but I was too scared to come out. So much blood, I thought you was dead. And then, the screaming. The sound you was makin', shrieks really. I couldn't handle it."

"I remember when I woke up one time, I was in the bed, but you weren't there."

"I slept upstairs with the boys that night," she says, looking down. "I'm sorry, Sadie."

"It's okay," I say. That's all I can think to say. Without warning, she swoops me into a bear hug, Missy style.

That's when my phone buzzes in my purse slung across my shoulder. I smile at her to let her know I'm not angry as I take out my phone. "Give me a minute?" I ask.

"Sure," she says, standing up and walking back to the stove. I don't recognize the number but it's local.

"Hello?"

"Sadie Sparks?" asks a man's voice in a thick West Virginia accent.

"Yes." *Who is it?*

"Sadie, this is Officer Lee Howard. I was there the night'a the break-in at your momma's house."

"Yes, I remember you," I say, confused. *The man who reminded me of Barney Fife.* "What can I do for you?" I ask, trying to keep my voice straight.

"Well, to put it bluntly, I have questions about the break-in. But I don't wanna meet you at the station. We need ta talk in private."

"Why?" I ask.

"Can I ask you somethin'?" We wait for a minute in the silence. "Do you know who did it?"

"Yes," I blurt and then hold my breath.

"Why didn't you just tell us, then?"

"Because it wouldn't have done any good."

"Is this break-in related ta' another incident, ma'am?"

I swallow hard. Close my eyes. *What does he know? Did Donnie tell him to call?* "Why are you asking me this?"

"'Cause I take ma' job serious, ma'am. No matter who did this. You deserve justice."

"I'm sorry, but I don't trust you. Your motives."

"I got a call today, ma'am. A real important lady, someone I trust and wouldn't'a lied to me. She thinks something happened to ya a long time ago. I need to talk to you. But not at the station."

Renae? Did she call him? I walk out to the porch. Stare in the direction of her and Donnie's house. "Where would you like to meet?" I ask.

"The Overlook at Hawk Nest State Park. Do you know where that is?"

"Yes." I do remember. A scenic place, with a cobblestone wall overlooking the bridge and the river. It sure is a long way down over that wall. But I have a gun. He will, too. It may be misplaced, but I have a feeling I can trust him. "What time?" I hear my voice say.

"Half an hour," he answers.

The next thing I know, I'm pulling the panties out of the cigar box, shoving them in a plastic sandwich bag and into my purse. I run up to Momma's closet. Grab a purse that's big enough to hold my gun. Run back down the stairs. Shove my little bag and the gun into the thin leather.

I don't tell Missy where I'm going. I just grab the keys to the LaSabre and I'm on my way. My heart is beating hard against my chest. When's Dillon supposed to be back? He'll want to know where I am. I've got to text Jenny on time today. It's 11:25. Good thing I'm meeting with him now so I can threaten him with the recording, too. If he's working for Donnie, to protect him, then he'll already know about part of my evidence.

Before I know it, my car is sitting in the lot near the park office. Just a short walk through a scenic pathway and I'm in front of the steep overlook. I realize I've not even checked the place out. I walk up to a rough barked tree and camouflage myself behind it so I'll see him first. I check my phone. It's 11:42. He should be here any minute.

That's when I see him. He's dressed in his deep blue uniform, wearing the straight wide-brimmed hat. The gun on his hip shines in the light coming through the trees. I don't see anyone with him but I stand here pressing my palms into the tough hide of the tree for a full minute before I step out. Grasping momma's purse close to my side, I walk toward him and then stop.

"Miss Sparks," he says. I nod to him, and walk again, slowly, as if he's a bomb that could blow up any moment.

"Will you walk with me?" he asks.

"No. I want to stay out in the open."

He nods. "All right." The way he's got his hands up to calm me is a reminder of Dillon. Somehow, I know to trust him a little bit.

"Will you sit down with me?" he asks, motioning to a bench nearby. That sounds good, actually, since it's farther away from the steep overlook. Away from the sharp spiked wall.

I sit down first. Then he sits and turns to face me. His eyes, a light blue color, remind me of the sky. I feel bad for thinking he was an underachiever, at best.

"What exactly do you know?" I ask as the breeze quickens, getting up under my skin. My voice sounds high-pitched, shaky.

"What I know, Miss Sparks, ain't much. But I think a lot 'a things. That's why I'm here talkin' to you."

"What do you *think* happened, then?"

"I *think*, ten years ago, you was raped in that shed on Chief McGraw's property. I *think*, Friday night, the same man who raped you, who cut your throat, came back and broke into your momma's house to kill you."

It's like the wind got knocked out of me. My chest is so tight, I can't breathe. "How do you know about my throat?" I ask, touching my teal scarf.

"I saw it the night'a the break-in."

"Very observant. Who do you think did it then?" If he doesn't know, then I can't tell him. It's his boss, after all.

"That's what I was hopin' you could clear up for me."

"I can't tell you. If you say his name, I'll nod. But I can't say it. I never have. Not out loud."

He shifts in his seat, so I squeeze my purse. I can feel the outline of the gun through the thin leather.

He reaches back to his belt and I freeze, hold my breath. When his hands come back into view, he's holding a black leather case that flips up to reveal a pen and pad. I take a deep breath as his pen whispers on the page. He scratches something off and then turns it to face me.

There it is. Plain as day.

Chief Donnie McGraw

Such a simple thing. Black ink traced along the surface of white paper. But, how it means so much more. I feel a rumble of emotions run through my nervous system. Fear. Relief. Fear again. I nod. My cheeks are wet. I wipe them with my sleeve.

"He's the same size as what Dillon described. None 'a us could get a hold'a him that night. When he came in the next day, his nose was broke. I didn't believe his story about Old Man Wilson. I checked up on it and Chief McGraw hadn't been there at all that night. No paperwork on it at'all. I took an oath. I don't care who it is. Even if it is him. You deserve justice."

For a second, I want to run away. I can almost hear the click of the soles of my boots along the cobblestone path. But then I blurt, "I have evidence."

"What? What kind?"

"A recording and…" *should I tell him?*

"What kind of recording?" My shaky hands take the phone out of the little bag inside Momma's leather purse. I open the app. Press play.

As Donnie's murderous words play in the air around us, Officer Howard places his thumb and forefinger on his chin. He's listening, but not reacting. When it's over he asks, "When did you record this?"

"At the EDA meeting on Friday night."

"The night he broke in." I realize I'm biting my lip far too hard but I can't stop. I need Dillon to kiss me so I can release it. I check the time. It's 12:14.

"This is good evidence, Sadie. If I was on the jury I'd convict right then and there, but there's always the chance that his lawyers might get it throw'd out on the grounds that it weren't obtained legally."

"Is there a statute of limitations on rape?"

"No, ma'am. In fact, 'cause he threatened you, cut your throat, and 'cause he's what, eight years older than you? How old was you back then?"

"Fourteen."

"Yep, then since he's at least four years older than you, he'd get no less than thirty years to life in prison. Maybe more since he admitted to lettin' you drown."

"I have something else," I say. I sound like a mouse softly scurrying toward restitution.

He looks at me intently. I don't want to give this up, but I am ninety-eight percent sure that he's on my side. Three people know now: Jenny, Renae, and him.

"I'll give it to you as long as you promise me one thing."

"What's that?"

"That you won't tell any of this to Dillon."

"Sadie, I can't tell him nothin' even if I wanted to. It's confidential. But we'll need his testimony. And you're right. He ain't too stable minded the way he went and burned down that shed. Damned shame. Prolly had some evidence in there."

"There was."

"What?" That's when I wonder. What if Donnie just sent him to talk to me so he'd know what my evidence is. Maybe he sent him to take it from me under the ruse of catching him.

I stand up. "I...I need to think about this."

"Miss Sparks," he says, his one hand out to show he means me no harm.

"I need to talk to someone first. Then I'll tell you."

"When?"

"Tomorrow. Same place. Noon," I say, before the soles of my boots are, indeed, clicking along the cobblestone path.

I need to talk to Renae. As I pull into her driveway, I notice there is no patrol car parked here. I'm relieved a bit, but I still hold tight to my gun through the thin leather purse as I climb the stairs toward her front door.

When I knock I realize I've pounded quite loud. As the door swings open, I see myself, my dead eyes looking at me as if in a mirror. She has that look on her face again. The one where she looks like she accidentally sees herself in a mirror at the store. Surprised recognition.

"Come in," she says, her shoulders curved over like a candy cane.

"Where's Dot?"

"At the church."

I walk in but I can't sit. I pace and she watches. "Last night. Did you hear?"

"Yes," she nods.

"Has he…" I stop to swallow the fear caught in my throat. "Has he done that to you, too?"

She bites her lip and with her head held low, she nods ever so slightly.

"Did you call Officer Howard?"

When she looks up, I see a gleam in her eye. "Yes," she says.

I sigh long and heavy, as if I'd been holding onto the same breath for the last hour of my life. I reach my hand out to hers. At first she winces when I touch her, so I pull away. She's just like me.

"You know you can trust him?"

"I wouldn't 'a called him if I didn't," she says, meek and quiet.

"You're very brave," I say.

"Or just tired," she says, leaning her back against the wall. "I want him gone," she says. "I hate him more than I ever hated anyone in my whole entire life."

"Me, too."

"He'll get real time for what he done to you."

"We can hope, right?"

"I ain't goin' to testify though," she whispers.

"I know."

"You'd better skedaddle. He's gonna be home in about half an hour." I smile at her. She smiles back.

I walk out the front door and when I turn around to look at her again, there's something in her eyes I don't recognize. Is it power over her own life that puts that gleam in her eye? Just a small piece of my brain whispers to me, *maybe she's on his side. Setting you up.*

Which side do I listen to? I've until tomorrow at noon to decide which part of my brain to believe. The right side or the wrong side.

Chapter Twenty-Five

Pearls, Pearls, Pearls

I have so much to think about as I sit here on my childhood bed staring at the ripped and torn panties I've stuffed into a plastic sandwich bag. They are the only evidence that proves what happened to me is real. I'm terrified to risk giving them away and losing my chance at justice. I stand up and walk toward the mirror set up on top of the long dresser against the wall. I pull off the grey Schiaparelli scarf and force myself to look at my scars.

I loathe them so much that I usually avoid looking at them directly. There are three in all. Two smaller ones and one longer where Donnie sliced across my throat as I tried to fight back. Raised and annealed, uneven, pink, and slightly glossy. They are worthy of being covered up.

Is this the link between us? I shake my head no. Our link goes so much deeper than that. Our link is a virus he implanted somewhere deep in my brain. It was a combination of his actions and his words mixed with my fear that caused it to embed so deep within my psyche that I don't think it'll ever be removed. The virus is part of me now, like how an oyster turns an impurity into a pearl layer by layer. It's the only way to allow the imperfection to stay so near. The antiques, the scarves, the career. Pearls, pearls, pearls.

Dr. Amy picks away at this virus here and there. Parts have healed a bit. Some parts have grown back together. Some parts have strengthened me as a person—made me who I am today. But other parts have been my downfall in so many hidden ways that I've dealt with on my own. All I want is to be free. It feels a bit like being a prisoner, but it's my own mind that locks me in.

This is what I'm fighting for. To be able to let go of the fear. I've chosen to stay here and that means he can't. I keep thinking about Renae. I wonder if he raped her before they got married. Or if it's something he did later, because he's so sick he has to rape women to get off.

I think about all the signs that prove she's been abused. Her eyes, how they look dead, the way she brought him his bowl of soup before he'd even sat all the way down in the chair, how she tried to talk to me after the fire, how she winced when I touched her hand. It's clear, the right part of my brain to trust is the one that has Renae in it. Does that mean I should trust Officer Howard?

I think about Donnie. Even before he raped me, I used to bristle when he was near. Something in my body told me he was danger. I didn't get that feeling about Officer Howard. And Renae, she trusts him. I think my best chance is to meet up with him and ask how long it will take to test the evidence. How long until Donnie will be in custody?

Maybe I can just text him. I have his number in my phone. So I do it before I can trick myself out of it.

Me: *How long until DNA evidence would be confirmed if I gave it to you tomorrow?*

I get the cigar box out of the closet and stare at the letters wrapped in the green ribbon. I pull out the one on top and open it. I recognize his handwriting immediately. It opens so many memories

in my brain. Happy memories. Him showing me how to do fractions. Him editing my essays. Him making little cards for me.
Writing me notes. And of course, this letter itself, which had always
caused me to think of him every time circumstances caused me to
look at the moon. It's thick—about three pages. I begin to read:

Dear Sadie,

It's been so long since I seen you. I miss you. The other
day I went down to the creek to go fishing and I was
remembering how you always made me stick the pink
fish eggs on the hook for you. I remember the look on
your face when you watched me do it and I was laughing all by myself on the shore. I left you flowers again. I
put them on your windowsill. I hope you liked them.
They made me think of you.

Did you like the fish? I know trout is your favorite.
Your momma says your appetite has been coming back
a little. I haven't been swimming in a long while. It's not
the same without you. Last summer you kind of turned
out to be a pretty good swimmer. Remember when we
went down to the river? You swam for a long while and
kept up with me real good.

I remember how proud of yourself you were. You
looked so pretty that day. You got a little bit of sun and
your hair was wet and you had on your yellow swimsuit.
I was thinking how we was going to bring our kids there
and teach them how to swim too someday.

I ain't given up on that you know. I never will. I've
loved you all your life. I'm leaving real soon in about a
few weeks for college. I don't want to. Not like this
when I can't say goodbye to you proper. It makes my
stomach hurt when I think about it.

Until I can see you again I want you to know that every time you look up at the moon I'm looking at it too. It's the one thing we'll both be able to see no matter where we are. It's important for me to tell you that because to me the way we feel about each other doesn't happen for everyone. You are a part of me and I am yours forever. Nothing will ever change that. Not for me. I just wish things were different. I wish that every day.

I miss so many things about you. Everything here makes me think of you. I miss hearing you talk. Walking to the creek reminds me of your stories. And the color of your eyes. They remind me of the trees here in Ansted. The way you flip your hair when you walk. It reminds me of the wind. I miss your giggle under our tree. I can't go there no more. I miss hearing you sing. I can't play music no more neither. Not without you. It's just not the same. And the flowers. The flowers remind me of you. "You are my flower that's blooming in the mountain for me." That's our song. Don't forget. Promise me you won't.

Someday we'll be together again. That's the only thing that gives me hope. I love you Sadie.

Yours forever,
Dillon

When I look up, he's standing in the doorway of my room. He's grasping a blooming handful of wildflowers. *He got his wish.* I put my hand to my mouth and begin to cry. It's the ugly cry this time.

"Baby?" he says, as he comes to me and kneels down to hand the flowers to me. "What's a' matter?"

"I was just reading this letter," I say, holding it out to him. He takes it and looks at me like a lost puppy dog as he tilts his head to the side.

"You kept them?"

I nod my head yes. "They're all right here," I say, motioning to the stack of letters held together with the green ribbon. He hands me the flowers and I hand him the letters. He sits down next to me on the bed. *Crap! The panties!* I think as I look to my right and see them sitting on the bed just out of his sight.

As he unfolds the letter I was reading, I grab hold of the panties and try to think of how I can hide them without jumping up and running out of the room. When I can't think of what to do, I push them under my left thigh and watch his pained expression as he reads.

"This was the last one you got," he says, wiping his eyes.

"Yes."

"I brought you another one a few days later. Your momma told me you'd left the day before. It was like she'd put her hand right through my chest and ripped my heart out."

"I'm so sorry, Dillon," I say, taking his hands in mine.

"You don't have to say that."

"I just mean that I know. I'm realizing, I mean, as we've been together again that, well, just how hard this has been on you."

"I feel like I finally have you, but I could lose you again if this guy isn't caught. I'm scared of losing you."

"You won't."

"I brought you the flowers for the other night. To thank you for…" he stops. Rubs his chin. "For giving me the opportunity to show you how I feel for you."

"Do you mean in the cave?"

"When you asked if I wanted a baby, it's like something just clicked in my head. It was just you and me again in our secret place.

This time you're telling me you think you want a baby. That maybe we've already made one together. I just... Do you know how much I want to believe this can happen for us?"

"It's not the smartest thing I've ever done. It's very reckless. But I don't care. I just want you and our life together. I want to have children running around in the house you bought for us."

"Me, too," he says, as he grasps me by my hips. It's so intimate the way he touches me. He takes his chin between his thumb and forefinger and nods his head as if he's hearing little feet pit and pat along the hardwood floor of our house. "Won't you join me for dinner?" he says, standing and gallantly putting his hand out to me.

"Where?"

"Can't you smell it? Missy's made a real nice dinner. Spaghetti. She even made a sauce for you without meat." I giggle at how eighteenth century English he looks as he stands with his hand out and his feet pointed out just so. "Ah. That sound. I've missed your giggle."

"And I've missed yours," I say, as I slyly grab the panties as I stand up. "I'm just going to wash my hands and I'll be right there." He takes me in his arms. When will I ever stop feeling those *live wires* when he touches me?

I hope never, I think as he kisses my forehead and walks toward the living room while I walk to the bathroom.

Under the too bright naked bulb, I hide the panties in a box of Q-tips under the sink, wash my hands, and make my way out to the kitchen. Missy set the table but I realize Dale's spot is empty. "Where's Dale?" I ask.

"He took an overnight run. He just wanted to make sure he'd be back in time for Momma's service an' all."

"Can I help you with anything?"

"It's all done now," she says, and then smiles slow and weak. "We need to talk about the house, Sadie."

"Oh, okay," I say, as Dillon pulls my chair out for me. I kiss him slowly before I let him walk around and sit down across from me.

"You two," she admonishes but grins ever so slightly.

"Let's say grace," she says, bowing her head. "Dear Heavenly Father, we pray in Jesus' name. Thank you for all 'a your blessings and for the food you've provided for us to eat this evenin'. Thank you for helping Momma to pass on so peacefully, Lord. Please help Daddy to get home safely from his job. In Jesus' name, Amen."

When she said, *"Daddy,"* it threw me off. But then I realize, she meant little Joe and Elise's daddy.

"So, Momma left the house to both 'a us," Missy says, shoving the twirled pasta on the fork into her mouth. "And there's the boys we need to think of," she says, nodding to Seth and Jake.

"I think we should stay here," Jake says.

"But you're only thirteen. Seth's only fifteen. Y'all ain't livin' here by yourselves," Missy declares.

"What about the horses?" Seth says.

"That's what I'm goin' ta tell ya," she says. "Dale 'n I've been talkin'. We think we should rent out our place since we don't have no animals and move into this house with you two."

"Oh," says, Jake. He looks down, then at Seth. "What do you think?" he asks his brother.

"That's a good idea. That way we don't gotta move or sell the horses."

"I just wanted to ask Sadie. What do you think?" Missy asks.

"I love that idea," I say, finally tasting the pasta. No one is eating. They're all looking at me. "What?"

"Well, what's goin' on with you? Are you stayin?" Jake asks.

I look at Dillon. He smiles so huge it's as if he's one big smile. "She's agreed to stay here. To move into the Page-Vawter house with me."

"Are y'all getting' married?" Missy asks, disapprovingly.

"I've agreed to marry Dillon," I say. "But he wants to ask me in a special way when I'm not expecting it." Missy smiles. It's the kind of smile that comes naturally and you can't fake.

"I wanted to ask you boys, and you, Missy, if you'll approve of me and Sadie getting married?"

"Well, heck yeah!" Missy says. "We can't have y'all livin' in sin."

"I think it's good," says Jake. He's smiling but he's trying to hide it. I think back to what he said to me on Thursday about the saddle. How he'd told me about Dillon's tattoo.

"What about you, Seth?" I ask.

He looks emotional. I can't decide if he's angry or happy. "So, you're not goin' back to California?"

"No," I say, shaking my head.

"Then, I think it's good," he says, looking at me and grinning slightly. He reminds me of that little boy who used to sit at this table in a high chair and make a mess like little Joe is doing now. He's big now, but his smile is still the same. It warms my heart how much he wants me to stay.

"Thank you," I say. He nods and then looks away. There's been too much emotion for him for one week I'm sure.

And just like that, I have a family again. A future. A new life. I feel peaceful for the first time since Dillon and I made love on our gorgeous canopy bed in the house of my dreams.

And then Missy says, "So, where did you run off to today?" My heart drops down into my stomach as my eyes dart up to Dillon who looks puzzled.

"To run an errand."

"Well, you had me scared. You get a phone call and run off like that. We don't need no more problems 'round here. Got enough as it is." I glare at Missy, who doesn't seem to notice my annoyance at her big huge mouth as she takes a bite of red coated noodles.

When I look at Dillon, his eyes are big again like under the windowsill. What's he going to do? He knows I had plans to settle things. That I couldn't tell him what they were. But, I'm sure it's excruciatingly painful to be shut out like this. To be lied to by me again.

I put my head down. What am I going to tell him?

Once we're in the car I realize he's not going to ask me where I was. But the tension between us, if visible, would be thick as cream. I think now's the time to ask him, to see if he will believe Renae has been abused by his brother. To see how he reacts. It's almost like a test. If he gets defensive, it will show me how he might react to finding out what his brother is really capable of. Also, it might soften the blow when he finds out because he'll already know his brother is capable of such evil doings.

"I saw Renae today," I say, and look up at him through my lashes.

"Is that who called you?" he asks, his voice shaky.

"No."

"Why'd you go over there?"

"I think Renae…" I stop to take a breath, brace myself on the car door handle. "Renae's being abused by Donnie." *Oh, god. That felt good to say out loud.*

"What? Why do you think that?"

"Because she told me." I wait. I stare at him to see if his face changes. He looks impassive as he stares at the road. He puts his fist up to his mouth.

"I mean, Donnie's just like our dad. He's kind of a jerk to her sometimes, but," he stops, waits. "Our dad, he hit my mom, too."

"In front of you?"

"Yes, in front of both of us. Donnie used to stop him, when he got older. That's why I'm surprised she would tell you that," he says, with pain written in the creases of his forehead.

"So, you believe me? You believe Renae."

He bites his bottom lip. Never taking his eyes off the road. "I want to, but it doesn't make sense. He's a cop—the Chief of Police, for Christ's sake!"

"I know, but…" I try.

"He didn't tolerate it in the house once he was old enough to stop it. Why would he do the same thing to his own wife?" he says, confused.

"She has no reason to lie," I say, crossing my arms. "She trusted me enough to tell, and I believe her." When he turns to look at me, his face is defensive. Angry. Hurt. "It takes a lot for a victim to tell," I state, because I know so well.

"I don't think you've ever really known my brother, Sadie," he decides.

Oh really?

"What if there are things *you* don't know about him?" I ask.

"He was always there for me, for Momma. He protected us. Dad, he used to get violent, you know, with us boys. Donnie, he used to take it so I didn't have to. He's a good man. He's served his country, his town. I know he's kinda an asshole sometimes. But… To hit his wife. I don't know why she would… It just doesn't make sense."

"Never mind," I say. It hurts deep in my gut. He doesn't believe her. He doesn't believe me. How could he be so blind?

"Just let me think about this. I need to think about what you're saying. I'm not saying you're lying, or she's lying. I just need to process this. Okay?"

My phone buzzes in the cloth purse strung over my shoulder. It's a welcome distraction.

Lee Howard: *You don't have to worry about that. I will expedite thru State Crime Lab due to recent actions causing a serious threat to the victim. I just need you to turn over evidence and make statement. I will take care of everything from there. Shouldn't be more than a few days.*

As I read those last seven words, somewhere deep in my brain I felt a small piece of the link between Donnie and me being snapped, detached from me for good. This is happening. But how is Dillon going to feel when he finds out? Is he going to believe me? I feel for him. Really, I do.

To find out that someone you love is completely different from what you've always thought. To see under the façade when there's a monster underneath. It would be devastating. I've been wrong to protect Dillon from the truth. His brother is no hero, and he needs to know. Everyone does.

I just hope he can handle it when the time comes. That he'll still love me when he knows the truth. I look up at his perfect profile as he drives. That is one of my worst fears. I'd thought it in the shed ten years ago, and it scared me enough to try and fight back. The largest scar on my neck is from that moment. I touch it through the scarf and swallow. The reality hits me so hard again right now that my stomach hurts and I feel a cold sweat forming on the back of my neck and my upper lip.

Dillon might not love me when he learns the truth. I shake my head and look out the window. I can't even process that. I've been running from this long enough. I have to do this for me, for Renae. I have to. I can't turn back now.

Chapter Twenty-Six

What Justice Will Feel Like

Sitting at the table in Dillon's interim kitchen eating the eggs he's made, I realize I'm starving—and tired. Oh my goodness. We haven't slept a wink. In fact, I'm hoping I can take a nap. My muscles are sore. My body is singing with overuse—but in a good way.

"What are you smiling at?" he asks.

"I didn't realize I was," I say, looking up at him through my lashes.

"You are," he says, as he takes a bite. "You're beaming."

"You didn't lie," I say, "when you said every surface in the house, you really meant it."

He just tilts his head down and smiles a mischievous grin, reaching across the table to touch my hand. His touch, even now, even after we've enjoyed each other for hours, ignites me again.

"No, I need to eat," I say, with a giggle as I take my hand away from his in an exaggerated gesture. "You're insatiable, Dr. McGraw."

He nods and sits back in his chair. The muscles on his chest flex, his stomach ripples. "I'll never get my fill," he says, making my stomach clench and my heart quicken. I take a bite. I need sustenance.

There's no part of my body that he hasn't explored, memorized with his hands, his tongue, his lips. I can still feel him. Everywhere he's touched is tingling.

My brain is filled with images, memories of last night and this morning. The way his hands cupped under me as he pressed my back into the warmed tiles in the shower. How the steam billowed up all around us mirroring the way it felt deep inside my skin. I just wanted to feel him again, before he finds out the truth. To block the world out for a night. So it was only him and it was only me.

The feeling as I arched my back, lifted up to meet him from the wooden floor in our room. The sensation of the smooth, cool wall in the hallway as I leaned into it while he lifted my thighs to his in the dim light.

It all started in the tub after we came home last night when our bodies began to speak to each other on their own frequency. I was looking at him, my chin immersed in bubbles as he took my hand in his and brought me to him, easing our need to be one after our argument in the car. Then we moved out to the couch in our room. Oh, and the stairs. The stairs were fun.

I blush when I think of the look in his eyes, like pure devotion. The sound of his breath in my ear, how it felt like a song created just for me. The scent of his skin, the taste of his chest, his neck. The feeling of the light-colored hairs on his chest as they tickled me. How his body trembled in sync with mine. How it strengthened us. How he and I were always meant to be together. I know him now. And he knows me, in every way.

We did not bother with using protection. I'm sure that on that first night, after he'd serenaded me with the Song of Songs, he'd planted his seed deep within me. How selfish of me to want his child to develop inside me—to sprout up out of what used to be a wasteland, but now feels like fertile ground. It's a need—a desire as early as the beginning of time.

As I take the last bite of the warm yellow eggs, I look up and see that he's watching me. He doesn't need to say anything. I know just by the glow of his skin, the upturn of his mouth, the gleam in his eye. He looks how I feel. Loved. Cherished. Connected on some level that never existed before right this moment. I push away the doubt. This kind of love—it lasts. It withstands. It has to.

I let my eyes speak to him and he rises to find my lips from across the table. He opens the white shirt of his I'd thrown on and grasps me by the softest part of my hips. His hands move up into my hair as his lips and mine co-mingle, coaxing each other. Tingles everywhere.

"The table," he says, as he takes our plates and sets them on the counter behind him. I nod in agreement as he comes around and lifts me, setting me on the casual lightwood oak. My hair reaches the table second, as he places the soft pad of my right foot on his chest so that he can run first his finger, then his lips up the inside of my leg, slowly, methodically, to drive me crazy with anticipation.

The loud bell of the telephone ringing makes me jump.

He looks at me puzzled. "Your land line?" I ask.

"That's weird," he says. "No one ever calls me on this phone. Don't move," he says, smiling and all sparkle-eyed as he trots over to the phone hanging on the wall in the kitchen.

"Hello… This is he…Oh, I see…both of us…where?…"

I sit up on my elbows. He looks formal—un-relaxed. His chest looks tight. "Can I have the address, please?"

Then I bolt upright. *What's going on?*

"That's about an hour trip…one o'clock will work…thank you." As he hangs up the phone he turns to me. He looks perplexed. "That was the State Police. They want us both to come down for interviews. It looks like they found something in your room and have some questions for us."

"What?"

"We have to go, Sadie. Maybe they've caught him."

"I…" *What is going on? Did Officer Howard do this?* "Okay," I say. It's as if I've jumped on a roller coaster and someone pushed start before I had my seatbelt on. "I need to go to the bathroom first," I say.

"You can come shower with me," he says, nervously.

"Start the water and I'll be right there," I say, smiling that smile I give my fans when they ask for autographs.

I've got to call Officer Howard. I'm sure by that look on his face, he knows my fake smiles from my real ones. As he walks away I feel like I'm standing on a cliff. I don't know if I have the courage to take the leap. I have no clue what's on the other side, or if Dillon will still love me when I'm there.

Please just let this be okay.

I climb the stairs. I can hear Dillon starting the water as I walk into the bedroom. I throw on Missy's robe, grab my cloth purse and walk down the stairs again to find the bathroom down here. This bathroom still needs remodeling. It's not my favorite to go in. As I shut the door and find the number in my phone, my heart is racing. The phone rings in my ear in little short spurts.

"Hello," he says. "Lee Howard."

"Officer Howard. This is Sadie Sparks."

"What can I do for ya, Miss Sparks?"

"Why did the State Police call and want Dillon and me to come in for an interview?"

"Did they call you?" he asks.

"Yeah. They called Dillon's land line."

"Okay. I should explain," he says. "The guy from Fayetteville found a hair when he done the fingerprinting. We sent it to the State Lab. It came back as the chief's over the weekend. We'd thought Dillon brought it in with him. Or the Chief'd been in the house socially 'till I got the call I told you about."

"Renae."

"I can't say, ma'am. Yesterday, I called 'em with my suspicions. Talked to Sergeant Daniels about the call I done got and what you said. Guess they're ready to proceed."

"Why are they taking over?"

"They police the police, Miss Sparks."

"I just don't think I'm ready. Tomorrow's my momma's funeral."

"I know the timing ain't right, but we're on your side. Just think what justice'll feel like."

What justice will feel like. What does justice feel like? Maybe a little like having wings.

Our car ride is filled with music, some thoughtful questioning by Dillon, and some vague answers by me. It takes us nearly an hour to make it to South Charleston. I've taken to shaking like when I'm cold on the inside. I keep seeing a strand of hair trembling around in my peripheral vision. It's annoying and soothing at the same time.

My cloth purse feels meaningful as it's pushing up against my hip filled with my phone and my panties covered in blood, DNA, and someone else's sin.

He's had a hold of my hand for nearly the entire hour, but has said nothing about how it's been shaking in his. "Are you ready?" he asks, as he turns the key to kill the engine.

I nod my head yes as I feel a wave of nausea hit me like a bucket of water. I force myself to take a deep breath. "Let's get this over with," I say, as I shove open the light door harder than I need to and dash out walking toward the brick building contrasted only by the metal letters spelling out West Virginia State Police. For a minute I think it just might say *what justice will feel like.*

Dillon opens one of the glass double doors for me. As we enter it smells of fake wood, coffee, and crisp apparel. All the troopers are wearing deep hunter green uniforms. It's busy inside. Before anyone speaks to us, Dillon says, "Sergeant Daniels, please."

The young trooper behind the counter nods and disappears into a hallway. My legs want to walk or move. They do not want to be still. I look up at Dillon. His jaw is clenched. He's crossing his arms across his chest. He's in his jeans. The light colored ones that hang on his hips just so. A crisp white shirt. He turns to me and his eyes soften around the edges.

He reaches down and takes my hand in his. I watch him as he looks at my hand for a moment, then his eyes slowly move up to mine. It's like his eyes are speaking to me. He looks nervous, but hopeful. *That's how I feel, too.*

"Sadie Sparks," says a voice from behind the counter. A tall thin man in a hunter green uniform, probably in his late forties, with light brown eyes walks out from behind the counter and shakes my hand. His grip is firm and trustworthy. "Dillon McGraw," he says, taking Dillon's hand into a firm shake. "We're going to do the interviews separately, if you don't mind," he says, unwavering. "I'll be meeting with you, Miss Sparks, and Trooper Norman will be meeting with you, Mr. McGraw," he says.

"Doctor," I say, before I realize I was going to say it.

"I'm sorry?" he asks, as Dillon nervously moves his weight from one foot to the other.

"It's fine," Dillon says, looking at me apologetically.

"Dr. McGraw," I say, quickly and look down.

"Thank you. Dr. McGraw," he corrects himself. I look up at Dillon as if to tell him I'm sorry.

He leans down to me and says, "This is what we've been waiting for. This is a good thing. Just tell them everything, baby. Okay?"

"I will. I promise." He kisses me softly at first and then as he's pulling away, he leans into me, urgently kissing me once more. This kiss is a promise. A pact, and I accept. I let go of his hand one finger at a time, turn and follow the deep green suit down the hallway. I turn once as Dillon is introduced to a short, stocky man who's wearing a straight wide-brimmed hat indoors.

I have a bad feeling about this.

As we walk down the hall I say, "Dillon doesn't know who did this to me," to the officer who nods in acknowledgment and motions to the third door from left.

He opens the door and I step in. It's cold in here. Too cold. I realize I left my blazer in the car. I shiver once—deep and heavy like a dog shaking off after a dip in the creek and practically fling myself into the stiff looking chair tucked under the Formica table with the metal legs. I hate pressed wood with plastic veneers. It's like something pretending to be pretty, hiding the ugly, but doing a very bad job at it—maybe it reminds me of me.

I wonder where Dillon is. For some reason I need to know that before we start. "Where's Dillon?" I ask as he takes the seat opposite from me.

"He's in the room next door," he says, honestly, evenly. "Is there anything I can get for you? A pop? Water?"

Although my mouth feels like the Sahara Desert, I shake my head no and rub my arms so that friction will ease the goose bumps popping up to protest the chilly air. "Would you like a coat?"

"Yes," I say. My mouth almost won't open to let the words out as my jaw is clenched and I'm shivering in waves and spurts. I rub the lump in my throat through my teal scarf.

He disappears and I search for lint that may be hiding on the top part of my only pair of jeans. When he returns, he's holding a hunter green trooper coat. I sink my arms into it and turn to face him. At least the outside of me will be warm.

"Miss Sparks, thank you fer coming in. While we're in here, I'd like ya ta call me Herman."

"Herman," I say, to try it out.

"First 'a all, we're bein' recorded in here. See the camera mounted up in the corner there?" he says, pointing to the glass eye bearing down on us. "I know this is hard on ya, so I'd like to tell you, honestly, that I'm investigatin' more than just the break-in at your momma's house on last Friday night. I have reason ta believe that incident is related to a' unreported rape that took place ten years ago. Is that correct?"

I nod my head, yes. My face feels like a statue's—cold, numb.

"Do you know the man who broke in, Miss Sparks?"

"Sadie, please." *Deflect.*

"Sadie." I nod my head yes. "Who was it, Sadie?" he asks, his voice warm like sitting by the fire on a cold winter's night.

I want to say it. I open my mouth, my aching jaw almost feels as though it's creaking over from silent to the truth. Now that my mouth is open, I have to get the words to come out. I've never said it. Not out loud.

My heart quickens as I'm about to say it.

"Donnie McGraw," escapes from the dry open cave of my mouth. I wince. It's like I've expelled a demon into the air around us. I'd swear it's heaving itself around into the walls of the room. He nods his head to acknowledge my admission.

"Thank you, Sadie," he says, as he leans in and steeples his hands on the table. "Now, were you raped ten years ago in Ansted, West Virginia?"

I nod my head, "Yes. But Dillon doesn't know it was his brother. Please, he can't find out."

"The trooper'll wait for him to say who he thinks the suspect is."

"Okay."

"Thank you. Now, I need you ta' tell me what you remember."

"I have evidence," I blurt.

"What do you have?"

"A recording and…" I stop and pull the cloth purse from my shoulder. "Here," I say, setting it on the table between us.

"I have your permission ta look in your property?"

"Yes."

He opens it and takes out my phone, then the plastic baggie holding my pink panties. He sets them down one next to the other. What a simple act, but how it means so much more. How it's one more step toward *what justice will feel like*.

"There's a recording on the phone with him admitting what he did, threatening me and Dillon. The panties were mine. He cut them and then ripped them off me in the shed after he'd cut my throat. Dillon found them in the shed the other day before he burned it down. I picked them up. Are you going to take them to the crime lab?" Once I can talk, I really do. It's like a dam broke open.

"Yes, I am," he says, in his warm fire voice. "I'm gonna step out and get the evidence bags. Be right back," he says.

As the door shuts behind him, I hear raised voices coming from somewhere in the building. I can't make out what they're saying. I put the sleeves of the jacket up to my cold nose. It smells like my daddy's cologne—both good and bad at the same time.

When he comes back in, he looks slightly rattled. "Is everything okay? Did they tell him something?" I ask.

"No need to worry, Sadie," he answers. I watch as he pulls on the latex gloves one at time. He opens a paper pad, lays it down flat, rips apart the locked baggie and takes the panties out, setting them on the paper so that they are open and flat. It makes me squirm. For some reason, they remind me of a butterfly pinned into one of those glass boxes.

He pulls out a camera, takes a picture, flips them and clicks again. "It's good that you gave these to me directly. It's better in court if it don't change hands too much before it gets to the Crime Lab."

"Yes, I see."

"They're in good shape. Where were they when you found 'em?"

"Dillon said they were in the corner of the shed between the floor boards and the wall slat."

"Could be a problem. DNA is harder ta read after it's been exposed to the elements like that."

No. I know they have something embedded in them to save me. They have to.

"I have something else." I slide open the lock on my phone, click the app and press play. Donnie's words bounce around from wall to wall as if the spirit of what he did to me hides behind every word.

"I'm gonna need ta take this phone, Sadie," he says.

"Take it? I need it. Can't I just send you the recording from the phone?"

"I'm sorry, but our technicians are gonna need to validate when it was recorded, and that it was recorded from this device."

"I have to text my assistant by two o'clock or she's going to make the post live. I mean publish this recording on my blog," I say.

"Did you threaten him with that?"

"Yes. To keep him away," I say through a shaky voice.

"So, the post ain't gonna go live unless your assistant gets a text from you each day?" he asks, sitting back in the chair behind my evidence out in the open for the first time. No longer in the dark. No longer a secret.

"Sadie, you should have her delete it."

"No!" I shout. *Why am I shouting?* I take my voice down a few notes, "I'm sorry, but if he does something to me, that's my only proof of who did it."

"Well, text her now. Tomorrow you'll need to make otha' arrangements. But I don't recommend using this as a weapon."

"I'm not deleting it," I say under my breath. I open the messenger app. Crap it's 1:49. I was almost late. I text Jenny and hand over my phone. *One more step.*

"The evidence you've given me should be enough probable cause to get an arrest warrant in the next few days. But I need a statement from you. Are you ready to do this?"

Am I ready? Can I handle this? I'm shaky, really shaky, but the lump in my throat is gone. I can breathe. I can do this. I deserve this. I imagine flowers blooming in my dreams.

"Yes," I say, and nod my head.

"Let's start at the beginning," he says, in his warm fire voice. "Do you remember the date of the attack?"

"It was in May. Mid May of 2002," I say. Just then, I hear a voice. A voice I know. Dillon's voice, screaming, "Who's your suspect?"

"Dillon," I say, jumping up out of my seat. "Did they tell him?" I scream, and back myself into the corner of the too small room.

"Sadie," Sergeant Herman Daniels says, with his hands up to calm me down. I jump as there's a loud booming thump against the wall opposite from me, too fast and way too hard.

"What happened?" I cry. "Oh, God! He knows, doesn't he? They told him?"

"Just wait here. I'm going to go find out what's going on," he says, as he disappears through the door.

I force myself to walk toward the wall that I share with Dillon. I put my hand on it, then the side of my face, my ear. "It's okay, baby," I croon. I want to hold him. I wanted to be there when he found out so I could help him through it. I'm sure he's known for a long time somewhere deep in the back of his mind. But just like momma dying, knowing and having it happen are two different things.

I listen to the muffled voices through the wall. Feel the pain he's enduring in this moment. The ultimate kind of betrayal he's feeling for the first time. The aching reality. And then it hits me again. *Dillon's not going to want me after what his brother's going to do to me.* The thought I had when I was in the shed, immobilized by a fishy knife and an evil brother's disgusting intentions.

We may not be able to move on from this. It may just be too close to home for him. It may be the thing that pushes him away for good. I thrust myself away from the wall.

I want to leave. I want to get on a plane right now. The guilt. The dirty feeling covering me, he's going to see me like that for the first time. He knows what his brother did to me. How disgusting I am. He's too good for me. Always has been.

It's fine. I don't care if he doesn't love me anymore. My imaginary wall back in place soothes me, protects me.

Is this what justice feels like?

Chapter Twenty-Seven

Like The River, They Say

I feel like I'm in a tunnel as I trip over my own foot, stabilize myself, and then walk stiffly back to the chair, tucking my legs under the Formica table. I feel very blank—cut off from my feelings. Safe. Numb.

Dillon knows, I think. But I have no feelings about that. It's as if all of that just happened to someone else that I don't know. A woman who was normal for a brief moment in time, but she's gone and been replaced by Numb Girl. Regular Sadie will replace Numb Girl in time—just like before.

I'm silently making plans, because that's what I do. I'm going back to Momma's house tonight. I'll just pick up my one small bag from his house, ask Missy to come pick me up. Tomorrow's the funeral. I need to call Jenny. She needs to book me a flight back to my house in California. There, it is orderly, clean, sterile. Lonely. No, there's nothing wrong with solitude. My stomach hurts, but I ignore it.

Sergeant Daniels comes back through the door. His brow is sweaty. He takes out a handkerchief and wipes it before sitting down across from me.

"How is he?" I ask, calmly. I sound like a robot.

"Honestly, Sadie, he ain't takin' it too well. Seems he'd had some inklings, but he wadn't expectin' us to confirm that we suspect his own brother. He's angry, but he ain't hurt. He threw a chair. That's the sound you heard. We're a' talkin' to him 'bout how he needs to calm himself down or else he's gonna mess up our investigation. He goes after his brother and we got us a whole other mess a' problems."

"No, we don't want that," I say, staring at the fake knot in the plastic Formica table. I want to scratch it down clear to the pressed wood.

"How'd ya keep the secret for so long?"

"My daddy blamed me. My dress was too short. They sent me away after about four months. I haven't been back since." Facts. I can do facts.

"Are you alright?" he asks. He genuinely looks concerned.

"I'm ready to make my statement," I say. It's all business from here. He asks me, and I tell. I have no feelings about it. I could be reading him a cereal box for all I care. They are just details after all.

He writes everything down, excuses himself for about ten minutes. When he returns he's holding a typed version of my story. He asks me to read it. How surreal it seems. It feels hazy in this room, completely dreamlike that I've just shared my deepest darkest secret with someone, let alone a police officer. My secret is transformed into words, typed up, spit out with deep dark ink on white paper. If I felt anything, I'm sure it would be relief. Fear, too. Normal Sadie, she feels a lot of fear.

"Is everything there true to the best 'a your knowledge?"

"Yes," I say.

"Then, please sign here," he says, handing me a grey pen. It's see-through so I can see the tube of black ink waiting to prove I was here. I was raped. I was ruined.

"Is he angry with me?" I ask as I hand him the pen and stare at my signature smeared across the black line.

"Sadie, this ain't your fault," he says. I look up at him. His light brown eyes scream sympathy. I don't need sympathy. I just want to go home. Tomorrow, after the funeral, I will. No sense in waiting.

"Can you just make sure he wants me to ride home with him?" I request, as if it's completely normal that we should part ways at the State Police office. "I can contact my sister to come pick me up."

"Okay. I'll check," he says, puzzled and disappears again. I hear voices from the room next door. My heart skips a beat, but goes right back to normal as I stare at a stain in the paint on the wall. An ink stain, I believe. It's been wiped from the sterile grey wall, but where it was will never be the same unless they paint over it. Even then, it will be underneath, just covered up—kind of like my smiles.

I hear the click of the doorknob and I jump when I see Dillon standing in the doorway. He's got red eyes, and creases in his forehead. He is a raging river of emotions squeezed into one perfect body. He hates me. It's absolutely clear. He stands far away from me. The look on his face is that of abhorrence.

"I can call Missy if you want," I say, as if this happens every day.

He stands there, puts his hand to his forehead. See, I told him. The girl he loved. That girl died that day. He just realized it right now. "I don't want you going back to your Momma's house," he says, through gritted teeth. "Not 'till he's arrested."

"It's not up to you," I state. "I just need to collect my things from your house. I'll call for a ride from there."

"What are you talking about?" he asks. His eyes are shaking. His blue eyes have morphed into a deep dark grey.

This discussion is going nowhere. I stand up, peacefully walk toward the door and wait a safe distance away so he can either move or open it. His hand turns the knob and the door opens. He lets me go first. He follows like a stranger behind me on a crowded street. I feel a pang of emptiness in that hole in my chest. But if I ignore it long enough it will go away.

"Sadie!" he yells, protectively. I walk back toward the hallway. Both officers are speaking zealously to Dillon, who looks like an angry ocean in mid-storm. They must be reminding him not to go challenging Donnie to a fight. I walk closer. Sergeant Daniels says, "The best way to protect her is to control yourself. Let us take care'a him."

"I know. I will," Dillon says, through gritted teeth before they both pat him overly hard on his already heavy back. I can't read his expression as he walks slowly toward me. We walk silently toward the car.

I face the window on the drive home. When I glance up at him, he looks stern. Taciturn. He looks like someone I don't recognize. I look back out the window at the blurry trees, the deep set clouds that cover the blue sky that must be up there somewhere.

Random songs play on his iPod, but when Adele comes on sing-ing about 'Turning Tables,' I have to bite my thumbnail until I leave bumpy teeth marks in the pad of my thumb. I feel dizzy. I lay my head back onto the headrest. Close my eyes to let sleep soothe the tired that creeps up swift and easy.

The sound of falling water rushes through that moment between sleep and awake. I smell the water, hear it rushing along. I smell the pine oil in the trees as it makes contact with my senses as I open my eyes. I stretch my neck and realize I'm alone in the car. I'm covered with a blanket. *Dillon must have covered me.*

The windows are both cracked down. The doors are locked. *How long have I been sleeping?* It's dark out already.

We're parked along the river in front of the Kanawha Falls. I know this place well. The sad brick buildings that seem to hover above the water just at the edge of the falls look so alone. Although they are together, they feel solitary, especially the one on the end. There's no pretty façade for it to hide behind. It reminds me of how I feel.

Out in the distance in the dim light, Dillon is standing at the edge of the water next to a stump that used to be a tree. I can see the silhouette of his fine features as he stands there. The wind is churning his hair around like how my stomach feels.

I touch my tummy. Maybe I'll have a piece of him to take with me. If so, not all is lost. Maybe he or she will look like him, that way ten years from now I won't find that I've missed the color of his eyes, or the feel of his hair, or his laugh, or his smiles—all of the different ones. It's a gloomy condolence, but it will have to do.

I watch him in the distance. Distant.

It's okay, I tell myself. I look down at the center console. There's a white bag with little grease spots leaching through. I look inside and find a sandwich made with thick bread. The scent of the bread, the cheese, the lettuce, and the tomatoes makes my stomach rumble in anticipation.

I open it to check. No meat. It must be for me. There's a drink, too. I stick my straw into it and before I take a breath, I've downed half the liquid in the paper cup. Famished, I eat in big bites until the sandwich is nothing but a few crumbs in the sagging arch of the white paper.

With a heavy tummy I fumble around with the seat until it reclines. I close my eyes and listen to the sound of the rushing water. It's strange how something in such turmoil, this water upheaved and in constant movement, is also so peace inducing in me. I let it rage for a moment and feel the ease on my heart. I pull the blanket up to my chin and then the next thing I know Dillon is helping me walk up the stairs of his house.

"I need to go to Momma's house," I protest.

"I already stopped by there," he says. "I got your box."

"What box?"

"The one with all your clothes," he says. He sounds puzzled or frustrated. I can't tell which.

Once inside his room, I feel like I don't belong, so I stop as he walks in and closes the bathroom door. I'm so tired. I have no phone to check the time. There's no clock in here. He uses his phone as his alarm clock. I shuffle toward the couch. I could sleep here for the night. My last night here.

He comes out of the bathroom and walks right by me. I take off my boots, but don't feel comfortable changing into my nightgown out in the open. I change in the bathroom and when I come out he's set a box on the floor near the couch. Those must be the clothes Jenny sent from my house. He's not here, though. Maybe he wants to sleep downstairs somewhere. Still, I lie down on the couch, pull the soft blanket from the back over my legs, my arms. He should have the bed.

My dreams are filled with music, sad, melodious, and soulful. When I open my eyes Dillon is sitting cross-legged on the bed. He's wearing no shirt or pants—just his boxer briefs. On his lap is the dulcimer, and he's singing a song I've never heard before. It's about a river, about peace—finding peace. About heaven.

I close my eyes again, but the song plays over and over, like a day that never ends. When I wake up in the light of day, Dillon is still in the same spot. His eyes are red, there are deep circles under them. His face is unreadable, but it's clear he's been watching me sleep.

"Why did you sleep on the couch?" he asks.

"So you could have the bed," I say, as if there could be no other reason. He shakes his head, moves the dulcimer off his lap, and looks out the window.

"What time is it?"

"Time to get ready for your momma's funeral," he says, his jaw clenched, his eyes anywhere but here. His voice is raspy from no sleep, and probably from yelling at the police yesterday.

How has the reality of the funeral eluded me? Just too much going on, I guess. Aunt Lotty will be here today. That's good. It will be nice to see her.

"I'm going to take a shower," I say, walking to the bathroom and shutting the door behind me. As I do, I watch Dillon through the slight crack of the door. He's still looking out the window. It will be easier for him once I'm gone. He can go back to his girlfriend, Miss Robbins—Claire, I mean. Only this time, he won't have the ghost of perfect-me-who-doesn't-exist hovering over his happiness. Now he knows why things between us would have never worked. It was a good thing that we met again. Knowing him helped me face my fears. Helped me realize I might be capable of more than the life I'd boxed myself into.

While Dillon is showering, I peruse the outfits Jenny's dutifully placed in garment bags. Missy must have packed some of my clothes in here from the closet in my old room, too. There's the faded jeans. The jean shorts. A few t-shirts and the boots. The ones I was wearing that fateful day, and the day I met Dillon again on the mountain.

I choose the flowy black silk dress, and the grey cardigan. I put on the dark tights, the dress, the heels, and the black silk scarf. I apply some minimal make-up and wait for Dillon downstairs.

I'm sipping coffee as he comes into the interim kitchen. He looks so distinguished, and handsome in a black suit that fits perfectly—like it was made just for him—a white shirt, and a black tie. Some men would look stiff, but he looks like a model in a magazine, like casual sophistication. His hair is slightly damp. Although he won't look me straight in the eye, I can see they still look red, deep set. He's holding his dulcimer case. I don't question why.

"Are you ready?" he asks, looking impassively at me, at my dress and heels. I nod my head. My stomach feels as empty as an air bubble. It rumbles, but I don't want to eat. "He's going to be there," he says, his jaw tight, his eyes skittish.

"I know."

"I don't want him anywhere near you," he says, puffing his chest out.

"He's not going to do anything unless he thinks you know. Unless he suspects something."

"How do you know?" he asks; his hands are fists.

"Because he's afraid of some evidence I have. He's scared I'll…" I look at him sideways. *Shouldn't I just tell him the truth?* He knows now—he knows how ruined I am. How much mud covers me in my dreams. He can probably see me that way now.

It's too late to take it back—too late for a lot of things. It's not like I can play the recording for him anyway. They took my phone. "He's scared I'll publish a recording on my blog of him threatening me." I don't think it's a good idea to tell Dillon he threatened him, too.

"Holy crap? You threatened him? You recorded him and then you threatened him?" He says, putting his hands on his hips.

"Yes." He starts pacing. His chest is tight. The muscles in his neck are strained.

"When?" he asks. He looks so full of angst it could spill over onto the floor like glass marbles.

"The night of the presentation."

"That's why you were standing by him?" His eyes are looking far off into the past. "You were staring at him all night. That's why you were so scared when he caught us kissing. You tried to catch him that night."

There's nothing to say, so I just look at the floor. When I look back up, in his eyes I see questions. It's the first time he hasn't looked just plain angry since yesterday. "How did you...?" he starts to say, and then he turns from me, walks toward the doorway and stands there with his fist up to his mouth. He coughs loudly—a nervous cough to hide the feelings festering deep in his gut.

How I did what? How did I keep the secret? How did I stomach it? How did I endure being near Donnie again? *I did it for you—to protect you.* I did it for me, so I could be free, but I wouldn't have done any of this had I not run into Dillon on the mountain. I think all these things as I look at his back. For a moment I feel abandoned, but then I tuck it away so I can just deal with the day, deal with leaving here tomorrow.

"I want you to keep the gun with you at all times," he says, business-like.

"Okay," I say, remembering that I'd put the gun upstairs inside Momma's old purse.

"Did you eat?" he asks. I shake my head no. "You need to eat," he says, frustrated.

I just shrug my shoulders and walk away. I'll be gone soon, out of his hair.

Up in his room, inside the box Jenny sent me, I remember a larger vintage Coach bag that has a long strap. I yank the bag out and arm myself, sling the bag over my shoulder. When I come back down to the kitchen he's poured me a bowl of cereal. *Still so kind,* I think as I crunch flat brown flakes of something. He looks off in any other direction—deep in thought.

"Please, just don't do anything. It's my momma's funeral."

"I don't want him to even look at you," he says, standing up and taking his bowl to the sink. When he turns to face me, he's scowling.

"Maybe you should just stay home," I say. Not in anger, just in truth. I don't think he's going to last two seconds in the same room with his rapist brother.

"How can you say that to me?" he says, walking toward me. He looks so disappointed in me. He stops a safe distance away, tilts his head to the side and looks at me with a furrowed brow. "Sadie?" he says, his voice like a raging river.

I step backward. I don't want him to come too close. If he touches me I won't be able to take it. "We need to go," I say, taking another step back.

"Sadie?" he says, again. For a moment, it's as if I'm looking at the Dillon I know. The one who taught me to swim and ride my bike. The one who held me while I cried. The one who made love to me inside our cave. It tugs on the emptiness that envelops me. But I wrap it back around me like a safety net.

"You won't have to worry about this for too much longer," I say, under my breath, and walk all the way to the car alone. *Alone.*

Chapter Twenty-Eight

Does This Feel The Same?

I'm standing by the car, my back facing the house when I hear his slow footsteps coming toward me. I purse my lips together and close my eyes. I hear him walk around to the driver's side and the locks pop up. I climb into the car and try to steady the beating of my heart.

He puts something in the trunk—his dulcimer I think—shakes the car as he closes the trunk, and folds himself in next to me. I can feel him looking at me, but I don't look back. Looking at him will just make it harder for me to leave tomorrow. In between us, I feel a thick barrier. I've placed it there to save my heart the trouble of trying to reconnect with his. That's over now. I force my mind to move on to other things. I haven't even talked to Jenny yet. I need to call before 2:00.

"Did you bring your phone?" I ask.

"I did. Do you need it?"

"I need to text my assistant or…"

"Or?"

"The recording goes live on my blog," I say, matter-of-factly. He nods his head up and down. Pieces are coming together. All of my plotting, all of his suspicions are finding their way into a pattern he must have imagined a different way. Now he knows almost everything. Now that everything is ruined.

I'm sick of thinking about Donnie. Worrying about him. "Don't they have enough to arrest him on the break-in?"

"The hair. Yes. They could arrest him for the break-in. I asked that. I asked when I found out," he says, his breath hitches in his throat.

"Why don't they then?" I ask, my voice flat.

"He'd get bail. He'd be out right away. Out and pissed off. If they find his DNA on the panties you saved from the fire, they'll be able to keep him. He won't get bail, they said. Since he threatened you. Since he broke in, no judge would give him bail on the other, more serious, charges."

"I'm slipping up. I should have thought of that," I say. It's true. I'm not thinking straight. I'm in a fog where logic bends like water over the falls. "He told me if I published the recording, he'd come after me. He'd have nothing left to lose."

"When did you threaten him with that?"

"At lunch after he broke in."

"I should have recognized all the signs," he says, through gritted teeth, as he squeezes the steering wheel until his knuckles turn white.

"Truth is, we always think it's the strangers we have to worry about," my voice is tired, emotionless. "In school, the videos about 'Stranger Danger'." My voice picks up in anger, "Where's the videos that tell kids what to do when it's someone they know who's abused them, or still is?"

"I'm sorry, Sadie. I'm sorry I didn't believe my instincts. I didn't believe you in the car when you were trying to tell me about Renae," he says. He's still holding the steering wheel too tight as he turns into the drive up the knoll dotted with death stones here at Restlawn Memory Gardens.

I want to feel something as he apologizes to me, but that barrier between us keeps me safe and numb. I lean into the car door instead.

"There's nothing you could have done differently," I say as the car stops and I shuffle out and stare at all the graves until I'm cross-eyed and they all start overlapping. *My daddy is out there somewhere.*

I jump when he pops the trunk and takes out his dulcimer case. As his jacket lifts up to put the trunk down, I see a flash of leather and a sparkle of silver. *He's carrying a concealed gun.*

"You're not going to use that, are you?"

"I'm going to sing a song for your momma's funeral," he says. "Remember, I told you I was working on a project for her?"

"No, I mean the gun," I say, as I can feel Daddy's bicentennial piece slap against my thigh as we walk.

"Only if I need to," he says, walking stiffly along the path toward the entrance of the chapel. "I don't want to get caught off guard."

Me neither.

Inside the chapel with the taupe carpet, the wall of flowers and placards, the chairs lined up, where the air is warm and stuffy, is a picture of Momma as I remember her. It brings up another beloved memory.

It was the day before my birthday. She was making me a birthday cake—my seventh birthday, if I remember right. I wanted the kind of cake that looks like a Barbie doll, where the dress is the cake. I can still see her standing next to the table with bowls full of icing in different shades like pink, green, and blue. "Bowls," a one syllable word that Momma made into a two-syllable word.

"Hand me that there bow-el," I can hear her say, in her chirpy sing-songy way. It makes me smile. When I look up, Aunt Lotty is standing in front of me. Her hair is stylishly grey, cut in an a-line and sleek. She's wearing a black suit-dress over her shapely frame and she's propped up on high heels. She smells like White Diamonds—

her favorite perfume. She grabs me and hugs me tight. Tight enough to make me feel something like emotion.

"Honey, you look tired. You okay?" she asks. "No, that wasn't right of me to say," she says, as she pets my head in that way she used to when I would get numb in front of her. "You can look however you want. It's your momma's funeral," she says, as she wipes her nose with a fluffy white tissue.

That's when I see the casket near the far wall. It's open with momma's head propped slightly on a pillow. The rituals of death long passed down to us have almost all been replaced by modern society. We didn't stop the clocks, or cover the mirrors like our ancestors did—full of suspicions about more death on the way.

A pregnant woman isn't supposed to see the corpse. It's supposed to mark her baby. I never understood that one. Mark it with what? A birthmark? Anything my momma could mark this baby with, the one I'm sure is growing molecule by molecule as I stand here, would be good. My momma was nothing but good.

"Do you want to see her?" Aunt Lotty asks.

I nod my head yes, square my shoulders, stick my chin out, and force my feet to take me forward. This is supposed to be good for the person grieving, a way to say goodbye to the vessel that housed the spirit of the loved-one. It's supposed to be closure. All of this, the chandelier lighting, the soft colors, the make-up on her skin, the way they've made her eyes stay shut, and closed her jaw so unnaturally, are all ways to help us say goodbye; to mask death with an unnatural beauty. To make her look like her broken bird wings grew feathers and took her away.

I don't need this. I've already said goodbye. I've taken the essence of her spirit into my lungs as it dissipated like the scent of some flower that didn't exist.

This is what Missy needs, I think. She needs to have all the memories of Momma looking sick replaced by this angel lying in a white fluffy casket.

"Where's Missy?" I ask.

"She's makin' the final arrangements," Aunt Lotty says, in her slight accent.

"Did she see Momma?" I ask.

"She did, honey. She had them fix her nails a bit, too. Had them polish them up with that pink there. It's a pretty pink."

"Momma did like that polish," I say. *Yes. This is for Missy,* I think.

"Who's that handsome young man you came with?" Aunt Lotty asks. I turn around and find Dillon standing guard at the entrance to the chapel. I really need to talk to him about how he's acting. Donnie's going to read his body language in a heartbeat.

"That's Dillon," I say. "Remember, I told you about him? He was my best friend growing up."

"He's watching you like'a hawk," she says.

"Is he?" I say. How odd. I've felt invisible since yesterday when he found out.

When my eyes find his from across the lines of chairs, I see him again as if for the first time. Maybe it's not anger. Maybe it's fear in his eyes. Betrayal. *Betrayed by me?* That's what I see.

My stomach starts to hurt and that hole in my chest begins to envelope me like a vise. My brain is banging into my skull. I put my hand on momma's casket to help me stay up. My legs are bowing. *Am I losing it?* I blink, feel the strong arms lifting me.

"Darlin'," he whispers. "Baby, sit on down right here," he says, helping me into a stiff flower covered couch in the front row.

"She's having a panic attack," Aunt Lotty says, as she sits down, pulls my vintage Coach bag from my shoulder, and starts to fan me with a flyer printed with Momma's picture.

"Am I?" I question, as Dillon pulls me into his chest. He doesn't let me pull away. He smells so good, like his momma's homemade soap. I feel him tense up as the room spins around and lands on Donnie and Renae, dressed in black, and standing in the doorway of the chapel. The shock of it knocks me cold. Adrenaline powers through my system.

I cannot fall apart. Not now.

I turn my back on Donnie and look at Dillon. His eyes are full of a petrifying rage as he stares down the man who raped me—his own brother—for the first time knowing who he really is. His whole body is rock hard, filled with wrath and a need for vengeance. He's shaking in rumbling spurts, and holding me tight around my waist.

I need to help him. "Dillon," I say, in a soft whisper and put my hand up to his scruffy chin. "Look at me, please." His jaw is tensed, making it look angular, unfamiliar. He's broken into a sweat on his forehead. "Dillon." His eyes dart down to mine. "Please, turn away from him," I say. "The way you're looking at him. He's going to know."

"I thought I could do this. But I…" He's shaking his head, closes his eyes.

"Just remember what they said. Let them take care of him. Take me to see my Daddy's grave. Please?" I ask.

We've got to get out of this room that feels like it's closing in on us. When I look away, Donnie and Renae are standing next to Momma's casket. I grab Dillon's hand, and start walking toward the door just as Dot comes in dressed in a long black dress. She's got both boys with her. The little one's on her hip. I turn around and look for Aunt Lotty. I mouth the words, "We'll be right back," and she nods.

"How are ya, little girl?" Dot asks, taking me in her one free arm.

"I really need to get out of here. Dillon's taking me to see my daddy's grave."

"Oh, honey. Don't you let me keep ya then," she says, and kisses me on the cheek. She kisses Dillon, whose brow is creased and sweaty and we make our way toward the entrance. I push the door open and take a deep breath of the clean mountain air.

"I need to use your phone," I say. "You don't have to take me. I was just trying to get you out of there."

"Have you ever been to his grave?" Dillon asks, as we walk out onto the wet grass. I have to walk on my tiptoes or my spiked heels dig into the dirt.

"No."

"It's under that white tent out there," he says, pointing to the spot where Momma will rest next to Daddy for all eternity. "Come on," he says, putting his hand out to me as we walk.

"Dillon, you don't have to do this. Not anymore."

His hand is still extended toward me, threatening to burst through the numb wall I've built for protection.

"What time is it?" I ask, stopping.

He pulls his phone out of the pocket in his jacket. "It's 11:45. What time do you have to call her?"

"I'm supposed to call by 2:00. Since I don't know what he's going to do today, I'm going to wait until closer to 2:00. Can you help me keep track of the time?" He nods his head in agreement. "So, Dillon. I've decided to go home tomorrow." He steps back, his face long and drawn in shock. That's not what I was expecting.

"To get your stuff?"

"I mean, now that you know who, I don't expect things to stay the same. How could they?" I say, my palms facing up. "You don't owe me anything. It can be a clean break."

"Dammit, Sadie," he says, glaring at me. "Don't do this to me," he says, walking away and swinging his fist in the air like he's punching an imaginary enemy between us. "Not again!" he says, turning around. He looks so vulnerable. So hurt. He looks like *my*

Dillon. His words push their way through my wall. They sting and soothe at the same time. *Does he mean he still loves me?* How is this even possible?

"Dillon, I…"

"Sadie!" yells Aunt Lotty from the entrance to the parlor. "They're starting." I look at Dillon. He's holding his stomach. His brows are furrowed. His glaring eyes make me squirm. I bite my thumbnail and kick at a pebble in the grass.

"Let's talk about this later," he says, running his hand through his hair and wiping an angry tear from his cheek.

It hurts to see him this way, so I look away. He comes closer but gives me space. Keeps my personal bubble in place. "This isn't your fault. It's his," he says, pointing at the chapel gritting his teeth, his eyes squinting in fury. "I've got to get through this today knowing that it's my own brother who raped you, who stole all these years from us, who broke in and fought me in the middle of the night. But I don't want to have to worry that you're leaving me on top of everything else. Just tell me you'll stay." His hands are fists. The pain is written in the creases of his perspiring forehead.

"Dillon," I say. If he wants me to stay, maybe it's me who can't face him now. "But you know you'll never be able to look at me the same way you used to."

He bites his lip and grabs my hand. "I think that's something you need to work on. Not me!" he says, and squeezes my hand so tight it hurts. "Let's go."

He starts walking so fast I almost can't keep up. My heels are sticking in the dirt and he's pulling my arm. When we get to the door, he pulls me past the bushes, around the corner, and pushes my back into the wall of flowers and marble placards with names engraved in them.

He's breathing heavy, and though we are saying nothing, our bodies are speaking on that frequency that calls unlike atoms one by one together into marriage. He puts his arms on either side of me and pins me with his hips.

With his right hand on my hip, he moves the other up to tilt my chin to meet him. "Close your eyes," he says, evenly but resolute. I do as he asks, and when his lips meet mine, I find them to be so, so soft, and as warm as a blanket in the hot sun.

He tilts his head to the side and takes my top lip between his forcing my mouth open. When our tongues touch, it's like live wires everywhere. I put my hands in his hair and kiss him back—kiss him like we are alone in this world and together we create all the meaning that exists in it. My stomach clenches when I push back into the arousal growing between his hips. He forces himself away. Both arms on either side of me are pressed into the marble wall.

"Does that feel the same?" he asks, ardently, frantic. "Look at me. Look at the way I look at you," he begs, and takes my hands in his. His eyes, full of familiar devotion, are darting back and forth between mine. Calling for me to believe him. I nod my head, and try to take a breath.

"I've loved you all your life, that won't stop for nothin'," he says, wiping my tears with the tips of his fingers and then taking my hand and placing it over his heart, letting me feel how frantic it beats—for me.

"You've said that to me before," I say, winded, remembering his words to me as I lay slung over his arms, just fresh out of the river.

"I meant it then, and I mean it now," he says, through hitched breaths. "Tell me you don't love me anymore and I'll let you go. But if you can't, I'll fight for you, Sadie. I'll follow you back to California if I have to."

It's agonizing as my numb wall melts in a pool around my feet. The knot in my throat is back, I'm shaking like when I'm cold on the inside, but now I know we can face this together. *He knows, and he loves me anyway.*

"I do love you, Dillon."

"And I love you, Sadie," he says, and kisses me again, soft and slow. Deliberate and controlled.

I hear heels clicking along the sidewalk and he pulls away from me. His eyes have softened around the edges, his lips are wet, and he smiles that I'm-yours smile. He does look at me the same way he used to. I feel like I'm blushing from deep within my core.

"What in heaven's name are you two doin'?" Missy admonishes, her hands on her hips.

"Dillon's helping me face the day," I say, as we walk toward her, our hands entwined like knotted wood. She crosses her arms, and taps the tip of her black pump on the sidewalk, looking at me with her mouth in a twisted grimace.

"Come 'ere," she says, pulling me into a big hug, Missy style. "It's time. Pastor Cole is waitin' on us," she says, and all three of us walk back silently to the entrance of the chapel.

Inside, the room is full of familiar faces. I'm so bad with names, but I remember almost everyone. A lot of them are from church. There's extended family, too. Some people have traveled a long way to get here, even from other states.

My fear causes a symptom; I'm locked into Donnie like there's an imaginary cord plugging me into his emotions, into his every move to make sure he's not going to snap. The link between us is still thick as steel. As I walk past him and Renae, Dot and the boys, I check his expression as he glances up at us.

His black eyes lock with mine as he lays his arm across the back of the chair and crosses his ankle over his knee authoritatively. The black slide on his head is combed perfectly. His nose is still bruised, but un-bandaged. He's suited up. His chest is tight, his jaw squared and tensed.

In the two flowered chairs in the front row are my brothers looking handsome in black shirts and pants. I lean down and hug them both before Dillon and I sit down at the end of the flowered couch in the front row next to Aunt Lotty. Missy sits down on the other side of Dillon next to Dale and the kids. Elise and little Joe jump onto their parent's laps.

Pastor Cole begins to talk, "Let's open in prayer," he says, bowing his head and all of us follow suit. "Lord, we're here today to honor the life of Leda Jean O'Dell Sparks. Leda Jean was wife to Eugene Sparks for 32 years, Lord. She was mother to Missy Harper, Sadie Sparks, Seth Sparks, and Jake Sparks. She was also grandma to Elise and Joseph Harper. Lord, bless this service, ease the achin' hearts of this family here Lord Jesus, in Your name. Amen."

The crowd responds with, "Amen."

I hear sniffles behind me. But right now I have no tears. I'm too full of fright and nerves to feel sorrow for Momma's service.

"From the Psalm, 121," Pastor Cole says, *"I will lift up mine eyes unto the hills, from whence cometh my help. My help cometh from the Lord, which made heaven and earth. He will not suffer thy foot to be moved: he that keepeth thee will not slumber..."* I feel dizzy. The air feels too thick. Dillon puts his arm over my shoulder.

"Behold, he that keepeth Israel shall neither slumber nor sleep. The Lord is thy keeper: the Lord is thy shade upon thy right hand..."

Just over Dillon's protective arm, I can see Donnie in a fuzzy unfocused haze. I look to his left and Renae is hunched over. The weight of his arm is too heavy for her wounded frame. On her collarbone, I see a new purple and red bruise. That's what that has to be. He's hurt her. Gone back on his word.

"The sun shall not smite thee by day, nor the moon by night. The Lord shall preserve thee from all evil: he shall preserve thy soul."

Renae locks eyes with me. I look at the bruise and she pulls her too large dress back up to cover it. When she looks back to me, I know it.

Donnie hurt her because of me.

I mouth the words, "Does he know?" and my eyes dart around. No one's looking at us. She puts her small hand up to her forehead, and nods almost imperceptibly.

"The Lord shall preserve thy going out and thy coming in from this time forth, and even for evermore."

No, I think. *What does he know?* Does he know he's a suspect? How did he find out? Did he threaten her? Did she break under the pressure?

"...and we have a song in honor of Leda by Dr. Dillon McGraw,"

"Dillon," I whisper.

"It's okay," he says. "I'll be right up here," he says, standing up and walking over to the blue chair next to Momma's casket. I grab Aunt Lotty's hand as he picks up his dulcimer and puts a neck harness on so he can play his harmonica, too.

I need to talk to Officer Howard. I look around to see if he's here. I don't even know his number. I'm stuck in a room with a psychopath, and he knows I've told on him.

What's he going to do?

I think as my eyes dart back and forth between both brothers. One who would do anything to protect me, and the other who gains the utmost pleasure from my pain. Everyone I love is in this room.

What am I going to do?

Chapter Twenty-Nine

Full Of Lessons

I can feel the unyielding piece of metal that lies in wait under this soft vintage Coach fabric. I push the bag up to my thigh and try to will my knowledge into everyone else in this room. I want them to run or attack. If we all pounce at once, he would be overpowered and I would be free.

"This is an old gospel hymn written by Reverend Charles Albert Tindley," Dillon says, his voice unwavering and steady as he strums the dulcimer on his lap. "It's called, *What Are They Doing in Heaven Today'*."

With long deft fingers, he starts strumming an unhurried melody on steel strings that feels like warm wind crossing over bare skin. Soon, he hums into the harmonica from the neck strap. He halts, but keeps strumming, looks right at my momma's body, at me, and back to her. His eyes shut, I'm sure to close out his brother's presence for a moment.

"I'm thinking of friends whom I used to know..." he begins to sing, but I can't keep up with the words although he's singing them painstakingly clear and full of sentiment. Immediately, the crowd begins to sniffle and cry. Aunt Lotty squeezes my hand.

"Sin and sorrow have all gone away. Peace is found like a river they say. But what are they doin' there now?" he sings, in his perfect pitch, his deep

and light baritone. His words hit me like a moment of deja vu. It's like a life lesson that I keep failing to apply.

This is a day to celebrate my Momma's life. To be here, to be present for my brothers, my sister, my renewed family. She's at peace now just like I felt for those brief moments by the river while Dillon stood by the stump and watched the falls.

Donnie is ruining it, and I'm letting him.

I force myself to unplug emotionally from Donnie. If he's going to go berserk, I'll pull out my gun. But I refuse to sit here like a victim over and over, allowing him to ruin my momma's funeral just like he's tainted so many other things in my life. His diseased molecules imbedded so deep within me stained so many chances for happiness, for being fully present in my own life.

The string I feel now comes from my heart and not my fear. It is attached to Dillon, plugged into the man who knows everything there is to know, and yet he stands by me. He's singing this song— for me, so that I'll feel peace like a river. I finally need a tissue. Aunt Lotty hands it to me.

Dillon's song breaks and he begins to hum into his harmonica again, methodically, so that it reaches deep within me and pulls on my memories of Momma.

As I look at her I remember her little baby kisses. Her hugs, the way she was just the right amount of soft. Her hair when it was the color of a crow's feather. Her scent—the one before the medicine— was like almonds and applesauce.

She was always my rock. Which brings to mind the scripture she loved, Luke 6:48. She taught me to recite it. It's a metaphor for what I'm trying to do now—build my life on solid ground. It went, *'He is like a man which built a house, and digged deep, and laid the foundation on a rock: and when the flood arose, the stream beat vehemently upon that house, and could not shake it: for it was founded upon a rock.'*

And so, I am built on a rock. I'm on that rock while my two brothers, Dillon, and Dale carry my momma's casket out onto the lawn and under the tent. I am on that rock as tissues are soaked, and Renae cowers under Donnie's grasp.

I am solid, but present, tearful for all the right reasons as I tighten my grasp on Dillon's hand and lean onto his steady arm while Pastor Cole delivers a message from first Corinthians, *"Death is swallowed up in victory. Where, O death is your victory? Where, O death is your sting?" The sting of death is sin, and the power of sin is the law. But thanks be to God who gives us the victory through our Lord Jesus Christ."*

I am built on solid rock as she is lowered into the ground, as the dirt is thrown on her casket, and Missy can't stand on her wobbly legs and has to be held up by Dale. I am built on that rock right up until the people start hugging me and I look up and Donnie is leaning down, grabbing my hand tightly and in a portentous whisper says, "You look beautiful today."

Inadvertently, I try to step back to escape, but I trip as my heel digs into the earth and I fall forward. He catches me by my arms—I feel trapped, restrained. I push away against his dense chest. It all happens so fast. Dillon is there in a blink of an eye, and the two of them are standing chest to chest with me behind Dillon's back, his arm touching me protectively.

The energy between them could light a small town. They say nothing. It's all in the body language. Dillon looks taller, more angular, authoritative, protective. Donnie looks like he's on that ice again, the one that's not thick enough to hold him up any longer. But then his eyes change as I watch them over Dillon's shoulder. It's as if that ice cracks and he knows he's been caught. His brother is not going to let him near me, and he's livid.

Maybe he doesn't *know* anything yet. Maybe he just suspects like Dillon did. Thinking something and *knowing* it are two different things. I look at Renae, but her head is bowed like a prayer. Dot is watching, but doesn't step in.

Donnie takes a step back, runs his hand through the black slide on his head, sucks his teeth in that way he does when he's making a point, and turns around walking away into the death stones like a bad dream. He turns and whistles for his wife like a dog. She follows behind him with Dot and the boys.

I take a breath. I didn't realize I'd been holding my chest so tight.

"What was that?" I ask Dillon. "He has to know you think he did it."

"What did he say to you? I was talking to your brothers," he says, pacing. "Then I look and he's leaning over you."

"He said…" Dillon stops pacing and nods. He's breathing heavy as if he'd forgotten to take a breath. "He said I looked beautiful today."

If anger had a face, it would be Dillon's right now. Aunt Lotty walks up to us apprehensively. "What's going on?" she asks.

"Can I tell you later?"

"Sure, honey. I need your help in the kitchen at home. I've got to get this casserole in the oven before everybody gets there."

"Sure. Sure. Dillon let's go, please." He's watching the path Donnie took to leave as if the ghost of him still lingers there.

"Can I have your phone?" I ask when I realize I'm almost late calling Jenny on our drive toward my momma's house.

He hands it to me, and I rack my brain for her number. She's in my contacts so I've never had to dial her directly. It takes me four tries to reach her.

"Sadie?" Jenny says.

"Oh, thank goodness. I couldn't remember your number, Jenny. There's been a slight change. I don't have my phone anymore. It was confiscated by the state police as evidence. I'm calling you from my boyfriend, Dillon's phone."

"Boyfriend," she says, with a giggle.

"It's a long story."

"Did he get arrested?" she asks.

"Not yet, they're testing some evidence. It should just be a few days," I say, and look up at Dillon who's biting his lip. "So, listen, I need a new iPhone sent to my momma's house. Just have it over-nighted."

"Sure thing."

"Thank you, Jenny, for all your help."

"No problem," she says.

"Talk to you tomorrow," I say, before I go.

I look up at Dillon through my lashes. I bite my thumbnail to calm my heartbeat. It feels like an animal beating on the cage of bones it's housed in.

"Dillon, did you see the bruise on Renae's collarbone?"

"No," he says, squinting in confusion.

"I mouthed the words, 'does he know,' and she nodded yes."

"Well, we're just going to have to be extra careful the next few days 'till they arrest him. I don't think he's coming to the wake, so we don't have to worry right now. I know my momma will be there. Nobody could keep her away, but I don't think he'll let Renae come without him."

"Okay, we'll be careful."

Everybody I've ever known and many I've never met but have known me from afar are at my momma's house after the funeral. My momma's two brothers. My daddy's brother and two other sisters besides Aunt Lotty, who helps me make my favorite casserole.

She used to fix this for me all the time when I lived with her—it's comfort food made of potatoes with cream of mushroom soup, garlic, and onions. Almost everything else has meat in it, so I'm glad for this. There's just so much food, so much chatter, so many stories about Momma. It's a bit overwhelming—but I know all their hearts are in the right place.

As I check in with my brothers, I catch Dillon talking to Miss Robbins, Claire, I mean. Even though she looks disappointed when he hugs her, as she walks away she comes up and gives me a hug.

"I'm sorry for your loss," she says, but she doesn't look me in the eye. As she's walking out the door, I realize I'm hoping she finds someone—someone good who loves her back. Even though she hit me with a door, I'd hate for her to be lonely for long.

Dot arrives carrying food, just as Dillon said she would. Renae isn't with her.

"Where's Renae?" I ask her nonchalantly as we cut pieces of cake for the kids at the kitchen table.

"Well, truth be told, honey, Donnie said she cain't come 'cause he wadn't comin'."

"Is everything okay?" I ask. The concern is real, although she's not going to guess my real reasons.

"That boy's just got too much'a his daddy in 'im," she says, looking far off in thought. "Always wants his life to be like a game'a checkers that he's a' winnin'. 'Cept when the pieces don't do as he wants, he thinks forcin' things is the best way."

I stand here deciphering her message remembering that she was beaten by her husband, too. "Just too much like his daddy," she says, and hands little Joe a piece of chocolate cake.

I worry about Renae. What her night will be like makes my fingers cringe up. I've got to call Officer Howard and warn him about what Donnie might know. About the bruises. I'm looking for Dillon so I can use his phone when I hear something that catches my attention.

"They got the permit. We've got to go up there first thing in the mornin'."

I recognize the voice. The first time I'd heard it, he was demanding respect for the lady who was trying to get people to realize how bad mountaintop coal mining would be for Ansted. It's Reverend Morris. He's dressed in black. His glasses rest on his nose and he looks up from them to find me standing next to Dot.

"Reverend Morris," I say, sticking my hand out to meet him half way.

"Miss Sparks," he says. "I'm so sorry 'bout your momma."

"Oh, thank you. But, uh, what were you saying about going up there tomorrow morning?"

"I didn't wanna trouble you with it. Not here, now."

"What's going on?" I ask. "Dillon!" I say, waving him over.

Dillon excuses himself from the older woman he's talking to. I recognize her from church.

"Hello Reverend. Thank you for coming," he says, shaking his hand.

"I'm sorry. I didn't want to tell you all this right now," Reverend Morris says.

"What's going on?" Dillon asks.

"The permit was granted today. The coal company is going to start the demolition 'a the mountain tomorrow afternoon."

"I thought we had until next week," Dillon says, shaking his head, and putting his hand through his stubborn hair.

"What time do you need us there?" I ask.

"The earlier the better," the Reverend admits.

"Sadie," Dillon says, "this is not going to happen."

"But I promised my momma," I say, throwing my hands down in defiance. "That's all she wanted. That's the only thing she asked me to do for her and I'm going to do it."

"Sadie," Dillon says, grabbing my arm and taking me past the crowd and into my old room.

"My brother is going to be there—and after what happened today, he knows."

"No! He's not taking another thing from me," I say. "He's taken everything else. Not this. This is for my momma."

"No," he says. "You're staying home, Sadie. Any other day after he's in jail. Not tomorrow."

"Dillon. I'm going up on that mountain tomorrow. I'm doing this for her. It's your choice. You can either help me, or you can stay home."

"What a selfish, selfish thing to say," he whispers because it burns coming out. If he'd yelled it, it would have been aflame.

"But don't you see?" I say, wiping the tears away, the kind that come out in anger. "If I stay home, he's won. He raped me. He took everything from me that day. He's caught me in my dreams all these years. He's threatened me again and again. He wins every time I act out of fear over what he's done to me already."

I walk over to the bed. The flowers Dillon gave me days ago are still on the bed where I'd left them in my rush to hide the panties. I'd forgotten the beauty in life due to the fear. Another life lesson. Another piece of evidence about how I've lived my life in constant alarm. I pick them up, touch one of the petals and it crumbles to dust.

"If he is stupid enough to try and attack me up on that mountain in front of all those people, this thing is over for good and he's finally going to be behind bars."

"It's a risk I don't want to take, Sadie. If he does something to you again… I've got to keep you safe," he says, pushing my hair out of my face with the tip of his finger.

"But if he really knows he's caught, nothing will keep him away. It could be in our sleep tonight. It could be a surprise attack or a public one so he could go down in a gunfight. Who knows?" Dillon looks puzzled. He rubs his chin.

"But if I stay home, the control he has over me, I swear, it'll never go away. This is me taking my life back. Don't you see?" I say, holding the dead flowers, wishing they were alive.

"I understand," he says. "I do. But we both have to have our guns. We stay with the group the whole time," he says, holding my hand.

"Yes. And we need to tell Officer Howard what's going on so he can help us, too," I say.

"And the state police. We need to call them," he responds.

"There's going to be media there, police. It might be the safest place to be," I say, and he nods.

"So, we're going to do this?"

"We're going to do this together," he says, and pulls me into his chest. I have so much to do. I have to write the press release. I need to have Jenny start contacting the media; but for this moment, I just let Dillon hold me.

And as I look at the flowers, I realize, there's no place I'd rather be.

Chapter Thirty

Across The Mountain

I tap my toe on the wood floor in Momma's living room waiting for the right time to leave. We've got to make all of our preparations for Hands Across The Mountain tomorrow morning. There are still so many people here, family members and people from church, that leaving now would seem rude.

Dillon's been talking to my brothers about momma and about being more involved in their lives. He's exuding nervous energy though, and sometimes when he says something to them, it's too loud, but they don't seem to mind.

Aunt Lotty comes into the living room from the kitchen. I'm sure she's washed a whole heap of dishes. Her hands look pruney.

"What's goin' on, Sadie?" she asks me.

"Just a lot going on."

"Is it being around all these people?"

"No, Aunt Lotty. I found out earlier today that Gauley Mountain is going to be demolished tomorrow. Have you heard of mountain-top coal mining?"

"I have, yes. I read an article about it. Our Gauley? That's horrible," she says, her face scrunched up in protest as she sits down in the chair across from the couch.

"I really need to start writing my press release."

"Your what?"

"Well, Dillon and I are going to try and stop it."

"Well, honey, that's really nice of you to write something for them."

"No, I mean, I'm going up on the mountain tomorrow, too." The look on her face changes from oh-that's-nice to what-the-heck?

"This isn't like you at all, Sadie. You're usually so safe. So controlled. This sounds reckless."

"A lot has changed since I've been back," I say, looking over to Dillon, wishing I were holding his hand.

"Yes, I see. But this is dangerous, isn't it?"

"I just can't stand by and watch the mountain I grew up on raped and emptied," I say, louder than I'd expected. With Aunt Lotty, I've always felt comfortable enough to speak my mind. But now I've I caught Missy's attention. She stands there for a moment, and then walks over to us, crosses her arms and glowers down at me.

"Missy, don't start. I'm not going to change my mind," I say, flicking my eyes away from her and squaring my jaw. In the corner of my eye, I see her arms uncross, and it seems like she uncoils and relaxes. When I move my eyes up, she looks vulnerable. Sad.

"Missy?" I ask, confused.

"I just don't want you to get hurt, Sadie." *That's what this is about?*

"I won't. We'll be careful. I have daddy's gun."

"But now you're stayin' here. People ain't gonna like it if you take sides."

"Aren't you comin' back to California?" Aunt Lotty asks.

"No, I'm not. I know it's a shock, but I've decided to move here. Dillon bought us a house."

"You're movin' back here?" she asks, her eyebrows furrowed.

"I'm not getting run out of here this time. Plus, we're in love," I say. I feel the blush come across my cheeks in a warm wave.

"Sadie, that's great news," she says. "But isn't, I mean, the man who, you know… He's never been caught, has he?" she asks, in a soft concerned tone.

"Not yet."

"Yet?" Aunt Lotty says, her eyebrows shooting up.

"It should be just a few days."

"What are you talkin' 'bout, Sadie? You told? Who did you tell?" asks Missy, sitting down next to me.

"I told the state police," I say, to these two stunned women who look at me like I've just grown an extra arm.

"Does Dillon know?" Missy asks. I bite my thumbnail and nod my head yes.

"Oh my gosh," Aunt Lotty says, as a mist forms over her eyes. "In all the things you've done, I've always been so proud of you. But, this is just such a brave thing to do," she says. "Telling your secret, standing up against mountaintop coal mining, of all things," she says, looking at Dillon as he sits on a chair by the window with his ankle resting on his knee. "I guess I ought to thank him for the change in you," she says.

"I guess I ought to, too," I say.

She leans into me real close and whispers, "And he's real good lookin'," she says, grabbing her purse.

"Are you leavin'?" Missy asks, the shock of me telling my secret hasn't worn off.

"I am, honey," Aunt Lotty says. "I've got an early flight," she adds as she wraps Missy up in a hug. As she turns to me, she puts her hands on her hips. Before I know it, I'm in her familiar arms.

"You done good," she says into my ear as she squeezes me. "I love you, honey," she says. "You better come visit me. I know you have a real momma, but you're the closest thing I have to a child 'a my own."

"I love you, Aunt Lotty," I say, before she slips out and disappears into her car in the dark driveway.

When I turn to Missy, she says, "What can I do?"

"About what?"

"To help."

"Do you mean with the mountain?" She bites onto her bottom lip and squeaks out a half smile.

"That's what I'm sayin'. You'd better take advantage of me while I'm all soft-hearted and willin' to help."

I look at Dillon and Reverend Morris, who's been waiting patiently. "Well, we could use your table, a laptop, and the phone."

We stand up and she pulls me into a hug. She feels so small in my arms, like little bones wrapped in skin.

With that, we dive in. Hands Across the Mountain is in full swing.

As I spend too much time crafting, tweaking, and finalizing the perfect press release, Missy calls local media. I glow with pride. Missy, helping us. It's almost too much to take all at once.

Once I'm done with the press release, Jenny sends it to all of my media contacts and posts it on my blog.

I can't stop to think, to process this. It's all in a blur as I start getting calls on Momma's, now Missy and Dale's, phone to schedule interviews.

"Why don't you just agree to a press conference at 7:00 a.m.?" Dillon says.

"I can't believe the amount of press that's gonna be there," Reverend Morris says, holding the map.

"How many people are coming with us?" Dillon asks.

"We've lined up good numbers, about forty people," he says.

Together, atop the old wood table of my childhood, we go over the map again and again, checking for routes to take if we have to go up on horseback.

It's then that I find out, it's the back side of the mountain they are going to demolish—hollow out the center, make it look like the façade of a real mountain—one that's dead inside. And if they do, Rich Creek will be no longer. It makes my eyes sting—this kind of cry reserved only for people or things that I love the most.

I'm so caught up in my thoughts about the desecration of Gauley Mountain, about the death of Rich Creek, I don't even notice Reverend Morris leave.

Dillon's voice comes in through my jumbled mind as I'm going over and over what we have to do tomorrow.

"It's time to go, darlin'," he says.

My stomach is coiled up in knots when I shake my head and look up at him. "Oh, okay," I say and look at Missy.

She smiles at me. It's a forgiving smile. A proud smile. A sisterly smile.

I walk over and give her a hug. "Thank you," I say.

"You're welcome," she says, and looks at me with the kindest expression. "Be careful tomorrow, lil' girl."

"We will," I say, as Dillon and I make our way out to the car sitting in the dark. As we walk out, my hand in his, I wonder if Donnie might be watching us. Even though I doubt he'll do anything to us right now, I push daddy's gun into my hip to remind me I'm safe. There's still some of Momma's family in the house. He's not that reckless, is he?

I'm standing in the kitchen trying to remember what I walked in here for when I hear Dillon's footsteps searching for me.

"I'm in here," I say, as I realize I wanted a glass of water. I pick up the glass and turn on the faucet.

Well water tastes like childhood, I think as I take a sip. Through the underside of the glass, I see Dillon standing in the doorframe holding something. I put down the water and swallow hard.

"I want you to wear this," Dillon says, holding a gun harness like the one he had on during the funeral. "Do you know how to use it?"

"I've never worn one," I say, as I bite my thumbnail.

"Here, let me put it on you," he says, standing behind me while he straps it on under my left arm. I hold still as he adjusts the straps, taking the time to make sure it's on properly. It reminds me a bit of guardian angel wings strapped to my back. Like the kind I wore to a Halloween party when I was a kid—except this is no party. This is something real—something I might not be ready for.

"See, you just reach across like this," he says, moving my right arm across my chest and shoving my hand inside where the gun will be.

"Go get your Daddy's gun," he says, impassively.

I walk quickly up the stairs to find my purse. My eyes dart around until I find the vintage Coach sitting innocently on the fluffy couch. I reach my hand inside and find Daddy's cold gun lying in wait. As I stroke my fingers across the sepia colored handle, I wonder if I really have it in me to use it. It's been such a long, long time since Daddy showed me how to aim with one eye shut and pull the trigger.

When I come back to the kitchen, he's on the phone, "...but you'll be there," he says. "Okay, thank you, Officer Howard."

I walk over to the mirror in the dining room—an ornate mirror that must have come with the house. I hear Dillon talking to someone else. It must be the state police.

I run my fingertips along the engravings in the metal gun and catch my eyes looking back at me in the mirror. I usually avoid looking at them. They have always reminded me that I'm not right—that things are wrong deep inside. But as I stand here, my moss green eyes have taken on a foreign appearance. They don't look dead or empty. They look alive with worry, alive with a different kind of scared. I take the gun and place it in the holster, feel how it presses against the ribs on my left side until it hurts.

In front of no one but myself, I reach across my chest and pull out the gun, point it and know. I can do this. If he comes near me again, I'll do what I have to do to survive.

Something in my eyes looks different, that's for sure, I think as I look at them from behind the barrel of my Daddy's gun. Is this what Donnie will see just before he's dead? My lips curl at the thought of it. Of him being gone. Of this being over. It feels like poison in my blood. I need an antidote.

"Sadie?" Dillon says, in a curious tone.

I put the gun down and look at him. He's wringing his hands.

"What were you doing? Practicing?"

"Yeah," I say, putting the gun back in the holster and biting my thumbnail.

"Do you want to shoot it outside? I can take you out to the woods and let you try."

"No. I think it's like riding a bike. You never forget," I say. "What did Officer Howard say?"

"He agreed to be there and keep an eye out," he says. "But he does say that our rally is against the law and we can't block the coal company from using their permit."

"Or what?"

"Or they can arrest us." *I can't even think about that right now,* I think as I close my eyes and rub my temples.

"What about Sergeant Daniels from the state police?"

"He wasn't as forthcoming, but he said he doesn't think they'll be ready with an arrest warrant for a few more days—unless he does something to one of us in the meantime."

The look on his face, the concern written in the creases of his forehead, makes my head pound like a hammer against the skull. We've made up our minds. Donnie could do this anywhere at any time. It could be a surprise attack out in public or he could sneak in here at night. He's a cop so he could find us anywhere we went to hide. There's nothing we can do to change it.

This is for my momma, I tell myself. This is the only thing she asked of me. I know it's not my fault—leaving her—but I've got to fill myself with bravery. I've got to.

"Come with me," he says, impassively, resolute.

He takes my hand and walks me up the stairs, past all the rooms we've plans to fill with all our babies. I touch my tummy and wonder which room will be this one's. Even though I haven't taken a test, it's just something I know to be true, just like the sky is blue, or air is see-through. I am carrying Dillon's child. I have to be. It makes me smile.

Even just from the touch of his hands, I know that Dillon's charged with emotions. But it isn't until we lie down together in the king sized canopy bed of my dreams that I realize, as he shows me with his fervent kisses, his needy hands, his ardent drive to connect with me, just how scared he is to mess this up—to lose everything.

Still shaking from the tremors of release, he's hovering above me on his forearms. My blood pumps too fast through my veins as he looks so far into my eyes that I have no more secrets; I can tell him no more lies, "Everything will change tomorrow. Good or bad, it won't be the same," he says, through hitched breaths.

I feel his meaning so deep within my bones that I shiver. He kisses me again like he means it, like we are on a precipice together, and tucks me under his arm. I twirl my fingers through the light hair on his chest and worry about tomorrow.

It's still dark out as we sip coffee while standing in the kitchen. I'm dressed in my faded jeans, a black t-shirt, a coat that used to be Missy's, and the brown boots I wore that fateful day when my life changed forever. I wish I didn't have to wear them, but they're the only pair I have for running around in the West Virginia mountains. I feel uneasiness bubble up like boiling water. "What are we going to do if they block the road?" I say, the words forcing themselves up through my knotted throat.

"We're coming back for the horses," he says. "But we stay with the group. Let me see your gun," he says, and I lift my jacket to show him the harness and Daddy's gun tucked inside.

We walk out to the car, and strange thoughts start rolling around in my brain. I know I need to do this for Momma, but I wish we could just run, hide somewhere and never come out until this is over.

It's an anxiety ridden drive up the back of Gauley Mountain with our backs pressed into the seats. Dillon puts his hand on my knee and his shoulders look as though he's holding the weight of the world.

The road winds around like a board game. When we come around a corner to take the road toward the blast sight, the line of cars comes into view.

"Are you ready for this?" Dillon asks. When he turns to face me, I see dread in his eyes.

"It's going to be okay. Look at all the people here," I say, fake-shrugging my shoulders.

He hugs the curve and pulls over to the side of the road. He pulls out his phone and taps the screen.

"Reverend Morris?... Okay...Well, we'll come out and take a look..." He squints his eyes, looking a few cars up ahead.

He puts his phone down. "They blocked the road but there's a podium set up for the press conference. We'll head back to get the horses after that. Okay?"

"Sounds good," I say, swallowing hard. My body can hardly contain the nerves coming up like a mini earthquake. As I open the car door, the sounds of so many people knock me sideways. There's honking horns and people holding signs. There are media vans with their antennas high enough to meet with their mother ships in town.

"Wow," I say, as Dillon comes around to my side, protectively, and gives me his hand.

"There she is!" yells a man with a camera rushing toward us. "Are you Sadie Sparks, the author?"

"Yes." I'm barely able to respond before I'm surrounded. Dillon squeezes my hand.

"How do you feel about the turnout to your Hands Across the Mountain Rally?"

I stop and smile. It's the fake smile I reserve for my book signings and readings, for giving autographs. "I'm honored to be a part of this effort to stop the destruction of Gauley Mountain. I grew up here and this is an amazing town that doesn't deserve this. Blowing the top off this mountain would be doing a disservice to the community. We're a tourist town now and..."

"Don't turn your lights on, then!" yells a man with a sign that says, "*Coal Keeps the Lights On.*"

"I'm sorry, sir, but we're opposed to this specific method for getting coal. Why don't they come back and use the mines they left behind before they go blowing up a mountain as old as the beginning of time?"

Much of the crowd begins to surround us so I back myself into the tall dirt bank with trees sticking out of it like forks stuck in the mud.

"We don't need no outsiders comin' in here, no tree huggers takin' away our jobs!" yells another man holding a dark black *"Coal"* sign with white letters.

Dillon has his arm around my back. He's tense and full of angst. "Are you okay, Sadie?" he asks.

For a moment, I want to run, to hide under his arm like a baby bird. But this is my town, and these are my people. Out of the corner of my eye I see the white police cruiser that Donnie drives.

He gets out and stands near the crowd, moves his hand to his gun, and widens his stance, his face impassive. He's trying to intimidate me. For a brief moment it works. I put my head down, squeeze my eyes shut. I have to will myself to stand up against the rape of Appalachia.

It's not just momma wanting the mountain safe. In a way, what I've just realized is I want to protect Gauley Mountain like I wasn't able to protect myself from being used, emptied, and left to die. This is about momma, but this is also about me. About my family being safe, about my future children growing up on untainted land.

"I'm from Ansted," I yell, defiantly, taking a step forward and grasping Dillon's hand. I force myself to take Donnie out of my peripheral vision.

"Most of us are the descendants of coal miners who lived and breathed in these coal mines. How many of you believe that Appalachia can be saved?" I hear a rumble of applause. The group who I'd met at the church the night my momma died are holding signs that say, *"Save our Mountains."*

"The industry claims that rallies like this one are started by out-siders, by tree huggers. Well, that's just not true." Tears are forcing themselves down my cheeks and my fist is in the air before I even know it.

"None of us want the dust of coal pollution getting in our lungs or our children's lungs," I yell, and the people rumble, clap, and boo. "No one wants our beautiful rivers and creeks to disappear, to turn to slime. And no one wants to watch our mountains ripped to shreds, raped and emptied when there's other ways to keep the lights on!"

With that the crowd erupts upon us like hot lava. There are people crying, people up in each other's faces. I see hands becoming fists. Horns are honking when Reverend Morris' voice comes blossoming into the dimly lit scene like silken cloth. He speaks slowly, calmly, patting down the air with his hands.

"We are not here to fight with anyone," he says. "We only want to protect what's been given to us by the grace of God. For the Lord said in Numbers thirty-five verse thirty-four, *'Defile not therefore the land which ye shall inhabit, wherein I dwell: for I the Lord dwell among the children of Israel.'* Please, Lord," he starts to pray and the crowd begins to hush in waves of shushing and silence. "Bless this day in your name, Lord. Please send calming spirits to help us see eye to eye. We ask that you give us the resolve to continue to stay peaceful with our brothers and sisters who believe differently than we do. Thank you, Lord. Amen."

Someone begins the sing, *"Amazing Grace, how sweet the sound…"* and like putting ointment on a burn, collectively we all take a breath and begin to sing along. *"I once was lost, but now I'm found…"*

"Let's go get the horses," Dillon says, into my ear. But when we turn toward the car, Donnie is standing in our way.

"Leavin' so soon?" he laughs. His hand is still on that gun. I squeeze mine into my ribs to remind me I'm safe.

"Excuse us," I say, and grab Dillon's arm pulling him right past his brother.

"You can try, Sadie. But you ain't gonna break it," he says behind our backs, and I wince.

"Just ignore him," I say, when we get our fingers under the lip of the door handle. I stumble inside.

As Dillon folds himself inside the car next to me, he hands me his phone. "Call your brothers and have them saddle the horses for us," he says, curtly.

So, I do. And then I sit tight as we drive home in silence.

"What did that mean? You won't break it?"

How do I explain this to him? "He said it to me after the shed burned down," I say looking at my knotted fingers. "He said I might be able to keep him away, but I'll never break the link between us," I say, peering up from my lashes.

"Like, because of what he did, you two are linked?" he says, tightening his grasp on the steering wheel.

"Yes."

"You don't believe that, do you?" he asks, his voice steel-plated, confused.

"What he did changed everything for me."

"Yes, but…," Dillon tries.

"And he's right," I interrupt. "It's like a virus in my brain. It tainted my life up until I came back here and you forced me to deal with it. Every time I stand up for myself, every time I don't do what he says, I feel that link getting weaker."

He squeezes the steering wheel so tightly that his knuckles turn white. I know he's angry with Donnie, but it feels like my fault.

"I don't want him to be any part of you," he says, putting his fist to his mouth. "I wish I could erase him from the face of the earth."

"Him being gone won't change it."

"What do you mean?" he asks.

"I was all the way across the continent and he still caught me in my dreams."

"But when he's arrested, it'll change," he says, optimistically.

"I have to change. I have to learn to live my life. To not let him or what he did affect everything I do. Once I can make those changes, I'll be free."

He shakes his head to acknowledge he's processing what I've said. We crumble up Momma's driveway and hop out of the car. I see that my brothers have Monty and their brown horse saddled and ready to go.

"I'll do whatever it takes to help you get through this," he says, taking me into his shaky arms.

"Why do you always say the right thing?"

He smiles. It's the first time I've seen his smile in a long while. It warms me, sustains me.

"Just a sec," he says, with his finger up so he can deal with the vibrating phone in his hand. When I walk up to them, my brothers hug me one at a time. It surprises me, but in a good way. When I turn back, Dillon is pacing.

"So you guys are heading up there on your four wheelers? We're taking the horses up the back trail…meet us there…yep, the spot we agreed on last night by the clearing…Okay. See you in a bit."

I look Monty in the eye as I rub his muzzle. "Can't be nervous on a horse," I say and Jake chuckles.

"You'll do fine," he says.

"Thanks, Jerky Jake."

"Jerky Jake?" Seth asks.

"Yep. That's his new nickname."

"It'll work," Seth says, jabbing his brother in the ribs with his elbow.

I run my fingers through the black fur speckled with silver. "Be good to me, boy. I really need you," I whisper to my horse. He makes the blowing sound and neighs. I stick my foot in the stirrup and swing my other leg over. I take a moment to feel connected, to make it real.

As Dillon walks effortlessly toward us, he stops, tilts his head to one side, and blows his nervousness out in one breath.

"It's not too late to change your mind," he says.

"I have to do this," I say, looking down. When I look up Jake hands the reins into Dillon's outstretched hand.

"I know," he says. "Let me see your gun," he says, swinging his leg over. I show him again, the unyielding metal that protects me, and he clicks his heels into the horse's flank.

"I'll follow you," I say, as he takes off.

I wave to my brothers, click my tongue and nudge Monty with my heels just before we disappear under the dense canopy of the trees.

We are silent for the thirty-minute ride up the back side of Gauley Mountain. It's ironic that this place seems so peaceful, but if the coal company has their way, it'll be a warzone soon. All the trees, animals, native plants: gone, gone, gone.

I force myself to think about the mission. I need to let the media know where we are.

"Can I see your phone?" I ask.

"Here," he says, reaching it over to me from atop his horse.

I scroll through the recent calls and find Jenny's number. I hit send and listen to the buzz before she answers.

"Sadie?" she says.

"I need you to put out another press release."

"What should it say?" she asks.

"The road was blocked by the coal company and by the police. We're coming up on horseback. It's possible some really good reporter might make it up the mountain to cover this."

"Will do," she says. "What about the blog post?"

"Just hold onto it," I say. "If you don't hear from us in an hour, give us a call."

"Be careful," she says.

"Okay, thank you. Bye," I say, with nerves taking over my voice.

"I'm going to call Reverend Morris," Dillon says, so I give him back his phone.

He uses the speakerphone so he can hold the reins. The phone buzzes loudly before Reverend Morris' voice comes through as if he's yelling into a cone.

"Dillon!"

"Where are you guys?"

"We ran into a couple'a officers from Fayetteville waitin' for us coming up the trail," he says. "They sent us back down but we're looking at the map so we can take another trail," he says. "The coal company's suspended demolition while all these people are protesting, and some of us are up here and they don't know where we are."

"Alright Reverend. We'll be waiting for you. How many are still coming?" Dillon yells into the phone.

Far off, I hear the buzz and rumble of a four-wheeler coming up to my right but I can't see anyone. "Did you hear that?" I ask. This feels all wrong. I wish we could turn around, but it feels like it's too late.

"There's still 'bout ten of us," he says, out of our speaker.

"Did someone make it past the cops?" Dillon asks.

"Not that I know of."

"What were the cops riding? Motorcycles? Four-wheelers?"

"Four-wheelers," he responds out of the speaker.

The buzz and rumble sound of a four-wheeler is getting louder. Monty stops and flings his head up in fright. He's always hated loud noises. Dillon looks at me in a panic.

"Let's get off this trail," he says and he yanks the reins to the left. I duck under a branch as Monty follows Dillon's lead. He's doing such a good job. An old horse running uphill at this pace. I pat his neck.

"Sadie," he says, "we're up here alone. We don't have the group to protect us. I don't want you yanking that gun out on cops, but just keep it in mind. I have mine, too, remember."

I bristle.

It's right at that moment that I know I've made a mistake. A mistake that I can't take back, when a four-wheeler carrying Chief Donnie McGraw rumbles up out of the shadows of the forest.

It's so loud it spooks Monty. He bolts forward to get out of the way, when a loud bang shouts through the trees and leaves. Dillon's shirt puffs up, and I'm trying to figure out why as he grabs his chest. His eyes are wide like at the windowsill and I finally understand.

He's been shot.

I jump down off my horse, feel the shock as my ankles protest the jolt, and run toward him screaming his name.

"Dillon!"

It's a guttural scream. One that asks to go back in time and change everything. One that regrets. One that begs for mercy.

Before I reach him, I'm yanked backward by my hair. I feel an intense blow to my back. I fall forward and roll, kicking and punching as hard as I can, making contact with some part of Donnie's stone dense flesh.

My cheek stings as he swats me with the back of his hand so hard I taste metal in my mouth. I'm dizzy and out of breath as he yanks me up and flings me around so that I'm facing Dillon. He presses up against my back with his chest—just like before.

I want to run. But then I feel it. The cold end of his gun as it's pressed into my temple. "I'm sorry, Dillon," I say, closing my eyes. "This is all my fault."

"Let her go, Donnie!" Dillon yells into the chilly mountain air. My eyes open and face reality.

The look on Dillon's face at this moment will never leave me. He's off the horse, holding his chest as his blue sweatshirt is gathering a darker color around his left hand.

"Dillon!" I cry. At the end of his outstretched arm is his weapon pointed straight at me—wishing I wasn't in the way.

He squints his eyes, obviously in pain. His breathing is too fast, too shallow as blood comes out and moistens his lips a deep shade of crimson. "Dillon! Go get help," I say. My voice shakes. The knot in my throat is the size of a golf ball.

"I'm not leaving," he says, clear, resolute. He coughs, wicking blood to the surface of his lips that he wipes with his shoulder. The dark spot around his hand is widening, and my knees feel about as sturdy as water.

"Drop your gun, Dillon," Donnie says, in his booming cop voice. "I don't got no problem shootin' her right here, right now. Cept', I was plannin' on some alone time with 'er first. But, hey, I'm just livin' out the last moments 'a my life right now, too. Think I'm gonna let y'all send me to prison?"

"If you're caught, Donnie, why do you have to take her with you?" Dillon says, ignoring his demands, buying time. He keeps his gun up and takes a step backward. It doesn't look planned. He's stumbling, forcing himself to stay upright.

"Because she's mine!" Donnie screams through my eardrum. With his right hand, he starts running his bear paw up my ribs under my right arm. I squirm in aversion to his touch.

Think strategy, I tell myself. He doesn't know I have Daddy's gun strapped up under my other arm. I push it into my ribs until it hurts.

As his hand moves upward, I writhe in revulsion and he leans into my ear, whispers, "I'll shoot 'im again. This time it'll be in the head. Hold still."

I hold my breath. I'm helpless like a groped statue as he moves his hand up my coiled stomach. He stops just under my breast. I know what's coming, but there's nothing I can do to protect myself.

"You see this," he says, louder, directed at Dillon who's just as helpless as I am. I blow out a pained breath as he begins to knead at my breast. I cannot look at Dillon. I'm so ashamed as forceful tears stain their way down my face. It makes me sick to my stomach, but my fear keeps everything down.

"Keep your eyes open, boy," he says, as he squeezes at me so hard that I cry out.

"That's how she likes it," he says, as he lets go, and slowly moves his hand down my stomach, surely toward the apex of my thighs. "This is how I felt watchin' you with her, all these years!" he hollers.

"Donnie!" Dillon says; it's a demand to stop.

Just go numb, I think. *I can't do this again.*

"I told 'er she needs a real man," he says, rubbing up against me with the sick arousal he has growing between his hips.

"Stop, Donnie!" Dillon yells through the pain, through the panic. He stumbles again and nearly falls, but keeps his gun straight and takes a step forward.

"Just remember who was here first," Donnie says into my ear, relishing me as he starts to put his hand down the front of my pants. "And the last."

Those words again just like in the shed. The feeling of being pinioned, being forced, being used by him again, now, right in front of Dillon, fills me with a rumble of adrenaline.

I look at Dillon directly in his eyes; will my thoughts into his brain. I nod slightly to where my gun is under my left arm as if I'm asking him for permission. He nods his head yes. 'Do it,' his eyes say as he points his gun, steady.

But Donnie is nearly all the way down the front of my pants. I squeeze my thighs shut. I can't let this happen—not again. It's at this precise moment when I know it. I will not let him turn me into a numb victim again.

I will not let him push me into the sickness that is his world. My hand moves across my chest, under my arm—just like in front of the mirror.

I feel the handle of the gun, and with the boots still harboring the evidence of the last time he tried to take my life, I stomp down making contact with his foot, turn and knee him in his groin.

I was quick enough, I realize, as he cries out and bends at the waist, trying to ease the aching pain I've induced upon him for the first time in my life. I step back, widening my stance and cock the gun, my Daddy's gun. The one he taught me with and I know is as precise as a thin piece of thread.

"You'll never touch me again," I say, my arm steady as I point my weapon at the teeth he uses to mask the demon hiding behind them. "Drop the gun!" I demand.

"Bitch, I ain't droppin' my gun," he says, trying to straighten his back.

"Sadie," Dillon wheezes from behind me. "I've got this. Just call for help," he says, and coughs.

"Yeah, Dillon's got this, Sadie." Donnie laughs; it echoes all around us. "We're all gonna die today," his voice bounces around the trees like a demon. "It's just a matter 'a who I'm gonna shoot first."

How many times have I wished him dead? How many times have I visualized the look on his face as he realizes I've killed him? He's straightening his back, as his hand squeezes around his gun. Dillon needs help right now. And Donnie is just in the way.

I move my gun slightly to the left and close my left eye to take aim with the right one—just like Daddy taught me. Donnie sees it in my eyes. Just like I did in the mirror last night. These eyes are alive again. These eyes are proof that I'm a survivor. He straightens his back and begins to lift his arm.

I squeeze the trigger.

The vibration of the golden bullet sliding against the metal gun barrel reverberates through my arm, through the air like I've let lose my fears in that one crush of my finger against the curved metal trigger. Donnie's arm flings backward as the bullet rips through his forearm causing him to let go of his gun.

With my arm still outstretched, I walk toward him, relishing the stunned, terrified look on his face as he holds his arm. I kick his gun, slamming it into the trunk of a tree. As I stand here, my feet are firmly planted to the ground—the ground of my ancestors, the ground that he chased me from but I've reclaimed again.

I feel the crisp air as it passes by the skin on my face, my out-stretched hand. I hear the cooing of doves; Dillon's pained breaths from behind me. Everything is suddenly so very clear.

As Donnie's eyes line up in front of my gun, I know what I have to do. I have every reason to; no jury in the world would convict me for it.

But, I don't want him to die. Dying is too easy. He needs to pay for what he's done. He needs to be penned up like an animal. He needs to feel it—what he's lost, every day. He needs to rot.

"What are you waitin' for?" he asks. "Just do it!"

"Dillon, please call for help," I say, clearly, but resolute. That's when I hear him fall. It's a soft thud. An emptiness in the air where he should be standing. "Dillon?" I yell, frantically, never taking my eyes off Donnie.

"I'm okay," he says through pained breaths, but I don't believe him.

"Just put the gun down," says a breathless voice from the trees.

"Who's out there?" I yell, as Officer Howard comes out, pointing his gun.

"I've got this, Sadie," he says, winded but forcing his voice to seem calm. "I'm gonna handcuff him. Just put your gun down."

"Dillon needs help. Is someone coming to help us?" I ask. My voice echoes against the trees. I back up with the gun still pointed at my opponent who's on his knees, his head bowed and limp, his arms empty and powerless. He looks defeated. The ice finally broke under him, and with that, the link between us seems to fizzle away like dead leaves crumbled in my outstretched hand.

"We need a rescue chopper, now! Two shot. One in custody," he says, into his radio.

I hear the static laden response as Officer Howard pushes Donnie face-first onto the ground, pulls his arms behind his back, and clicks the metal handcuffs in place. "You have the right to remain silent…"

I tear myself away from this scene. A scene I thought I'd never see. Donnie in handcuffs.

"Dillon," I say, as I crawl over to the man I love. Put my right hand under his head and press the wound with my other hand, cradling him like he'd done to me the first time we were able to physically express our love for one another.

"Sadie," he says, and coughs. Gently, I wipe his mouth with my jacket sleeve.

"Dillon, baby. Look at me," I beg.

He opens his eyes and I stare into those Tahoe blues, try not to panic at the sight of blood wheezing out of his mouth in a fine mist. I hear the buzz of Dillon's phone. *It must be Jenny.* She's calling about the blog—but that can wait.

What can I do? How can I help him?

The verse from the Song of Songs that Dillon quoted to me, "the season of singing has come." That's when I remember the song. The one he taught me on his granddaddy's dulcimer. The one that I was singing when we ran into each other on this mountain. And I know if there's anything that can reach him now, it's that song.

"I'm going to sing to you, baby. Our song, but you have to promise to stay with me. They're coming for us with a helicopter. But you have to stay awake," I say, pressing my palm into his wound, trying to stop the outpouring of his life into my hand.

"I promise," he says, his breathing is short and unsteady. He's forcing a smile, trying to be strong—for me.

"You are my flower," I sing to my lover, my best friend.

"that's blooming in the mountain for me
You are my flower
that's blooming there for me
Hmmm…hmmmm…hmmmm."

As I'm finishing the first part of the song, I hear the chopping sound of the helicopter rotor as it comes to rescue us. Men rush toward us. They place him on an orange gurney as I hum the song to him. The one that he taught me a lifetime ago, back when life had grace and dignity.

"Hold my hand," I say, "Don't let go," as men load him into the helicopter and pull me in beside him.

"I won't let go," he says, as they cut his shirt from his chest, and examine the bloody hole left behind by a brother's sinful obsession. "Sing to me, darlin'" he asks, and so I do.

"The air is just as pure
The sunlight just as free
And nature seems to say

It's all for you and me
Hmmm…hmmmm…hmmmm."

My voice mixed with the whipping sound of the rotor is almost as soothing to me as it is to Dillon. I look down and see the man who took everything from me. He's handcuffed, defeated. He's small like a driver's license photo, and getting smaller as we climb upward, force strength into the wind, and leave him behind where he belongs.

I look at Dillon, and sing,

"You are my flower
that's blooming in the mountain for me
You are my flower
that's blooming there for me
Hmmmm…hmmmm….hmmmm…"

And as we fly away from the mountain, my hand in Dillon's like knotted wood, I wonder if this is what justice feels like? It *is* a little bit like having wings.

Epilogue

I'd heard it once at a wedding as the couple said their vows, but it's never made more sense to me than now. *"Love is friendship…caught fire,"* they said.

I can think back to when we were kids, our shoes slapping against this dirt path on our way to swim, or to try our luck at catching red tinged trout in Rich Creek. I can hear us giggling under our tree, the one that as I look up, still has the shabby rope tied to it, now threadbare, weathered and worn. My breath comes out in puffs. It's December now—white ice and snow covers everything in a fine lining of mostly see-through white.

What I know is that our friendship is the foundation for such a profound connection that my life has been forever altered by it—I wouldn't be the person I am had I not been blessed with him, with his essence of kindness.

"Dillon. Look," I say, pointing up. "It's still here. Your rope. The one you'd climbed up there to tie. You accidentally fell and I couldn't stop laughing. Remember?"

When I look behind me, he's not there. "Dillon?" I say. "Where are you?"

"Here," he says, and I start walking toward his voice, crackling ice and snow under my feet.

"Don't play with me. You make me nervous," I say.

"Ah, but I have a surprise for you," his voice says, and I follow as the wind blows my hair out from the warm hat around in gentle circles.

When I make it to the rock with the woman's face embedded into its façade, it feels like a moment of déjà vu—oddly familiar but a reminder that I'm right where I'm supposed to be.

"Dillon?" I say, looking around.

As he walks out from behind the rock, I watch as his boots stroke the ground on his way up to me. He's smiling that secret smile. The one when he's hiding something from me—something good.

As if in slow motion, he bends down on one knee and holds up his hand for me to place mine in his.

Oh my gosh! This is happening!

"Sadie Jane Sparks," his voice is soft, earnest, "you are my best friend, my love, my joy, my dream manifested. Will you be my wife?"

He's smiling the I'm-yours smile. I hold his hand for dear life. I want to memorize this moment—paint it in my mind with soft wet brushes.

I move his hand down to my tummy just now starting to pooch out in a small mound. "We say yes," I say, through the lump in my throat, and he leans forward, kisses me where our baby grows and stands up, effortlessly, and takes me in his arms for a kiss.

Out of the pocket of his jeans that hang on his hips just so, he finds a brown wooden case and pops it open to reveal a silver antique band with a single square diamond. I put my head down to hide the ugly cry face. "It's perfect," I say, as he slides the band up my finger where it will stay until the end of time.

"It's an Asscher cut," he says. I know it. He's going to teach me about it. As he holds my hand I listen to him explain the cut and the antique band, "It was hand etched, the diamond comes from Canada," he says, and I smile wider than my face.

I'm thinking about the week that I came back home, how he brought me back to life, forced me with his love to divulge my secret, and in return we are now free to live the life that we deserve. We've come so far, in so little time.

"It's a conflict free diamond," he says, leaning against the rock, holding my hand. We're gazing at the diamond. Watching it catch fire in the sunlight streaming in through the gaps in the leafless trees. "Most diamonds are mined using slave labor, so I had to search for a company that mines ethically," he says.

I mean, who knows this kind of stuff? I think. He always amazes me with his smarts.

I almost lost him that day up on Gauley Mountain. The doctors said Donnie must have been aiming for his heart, but since he was so far away he missed and hit Dillon in the lung instead.

They'd pushed tubes into his throat while we rode together into the air and I sang him our song. They had to inflate the part of his lung that collapsed from the impact of the bullet. The hours I spent in Plateau Medical Center after the helicopter delivered him were the worst—not knowing if I'd lost everything. If I would ever hear his voice again, or feel his touch, or get to tell him how he changed my life. I shook like a mini-earthquake until the doctor sauntered out and declared victory over the bullet.

"Diamonds are pushed up from the earth," he explains. "The rocks that carry them are raised from the mantle to the Earth's surface by these deep volcanic eruptions," he says, demonstrating the movement with his hands.

I had to wait for him to get out of surgery all alone. Missy couldn't come because Dale was gone. The boys were busy trying to get the horses off the mountain. Seems they'd run off because of the gun battle and the noise of the helicopter.

I called Dot and Renae, but I found out later, Donnie had tied up Renae and Dot and their eight-old, Conner. He'd locked them in the basement and put the baby in his crib before he left that day to confront Dillon and me up on Gauley Mountain. He hadn't planned on coming back.

He's pleaded not guilty by reason of mental disease or defect. He's not contesting that he was going to rape me again, do it in front of Dillon if he'd lived through the gunshot wound. Kill me, and then kill himself.

He's actually admitting to it, using that to show that he can't help himself. That he knew it was wrong but because of his illness, he wasn't able to control himself. I know it's going to be a taxing trial. But for now, I just try to heal from this. Dillon had to heal physically. We both have a long way to go to heal emotionally.

The whole thing was on the news—although I'll never watch it. The very thought makes me want to rip my hair out. The secret was out—in a very public way. This was sort of good for me because the ugliness was not mine to hide away, but also horrifying because now everyone knows what's under the façade. I can't pretend I'm normal anymore. I'm still getting used to that—when they look at me now, they know—everything.

After our last press release that afternoon, a reporter had found his way up there and recorded almost the whole incident. They went to breaking news with a live feed, and the authorities were alerted.

When I didn't answer Dillon's phone, Jenny saw the hit on my name online. She posted the blog and millions of people listened to him admit to raping me, heard him threaten to kill me and Dillon at the same time they watched him try to make good on his promises. It was a national story, but I do my best to avoid it.

Luckily, that day Officer Howard was nearby. He'd been following Donnie covertly, he said. He told me the whole story next to Dillon's hospital bed. He had heard the first shot, when Donnie shot Dillon, and was running toward us when I shot Donnie. I guess when Donnie's plan went awry, he thought I was going to kill him. But I know it, deep in the understanding of myself. If I'd shot him that day, I mean, shot to kill, the link between us would have stayed thick as steel.

What I did, letting him live, was like ripping a long-standing burden from my back. Taking control and making sure justice is done is going to allow me to move on with my life.

Renae, she's moving on, too. It's been three months and she's already signed up for nursing school. She starts in January, right after the New Year.

What I've learned since that day is, I have to forgive Donnie—not for him. I have to forgive him for me. Like Buddha says, holding onto all of that anger, it's like squeezing a hot coal and wishing he's getting burned, while the only person burning is me. So, I'm working on letting go of that hot coal. It's taking time.

I've started to bring my life here to Ansted. I've had most of my antiques sent here, and we've even started the design for the new kitchen. Our life is on track. Me and him together is perfect—that's the honest truth.

"It's so interesting," he says, "The magma for a volcano has to start way down at a depth where diamonds are created for them to make it all the way up to the earth's surface," Dillon says.

"Do you mean that all this beauty comes up from the pits of hell?" I say, and giggle.

"In a way, Sadie," he admits with a chuckle. "But I wanted you to have it because even though this diamond had such a traumatic journey getting to you, and even though it's not perfect, you know, all diamonds have flaws, it represents us and the life that I want to give you, to share with you."

"You mean that the best things in life come through persistence?"

"It reminds me that true beauty, inside and out, comes out of great struggles, and from being able to wait for the right moment to surface—just like you did," he says, taking me in his arms.

We didn't stop the mountaintop coal mining that day alone. Our group has had to stage more rallies and make more signs, and generally make a lot of noise about this. Dillon and I haven't been able to help as much because he was recovering—and that's taken a while—but we're committed to this—and to each other.

"Diamonds at a molecular level share a covalent bond," he says.

"What's that?" I ask, although I already know he's going to explain it to me.

"It's the chemical bond that involves the stable balance of positively charged and negatively charged forces between atoms when they share electrons," he says.

"What the heck does that mean?" I ask, as I wrap my arms around his waist and stare up into his Tahoe blues.

"It means that we're meant to be and I want to kiss you, my soon-to-be wife and mother of my child."

"Then you should," I tease.

He takes me in his arms, pulling me into his chest so close that I can almost feel his heart beating like the sound of the railway. We fit together, always have, like we were made by the Creator just for one another.

As he tilts my chin up, he says, softly but resolute, "Close your eyes," and I do. He takes my lips between his until I am lost in him. As he eases away from me, just inches from my face he says, "I love you, Sadie."

"And I love you," I say.

"The sun's about to set," he says, and I turn around to rest my back on his chest, his arms wrap around me and rest on my tummy. I'm stunned when I see the mountain from this perspective. The same one that my momma saw and captured in her Sadie's Mountain painting that now sits in a place of honor just above the fireplace mantel in our master bedroom.

The colors in real life are just like her painting: vibrant, only softly muted by the cold—greens and reds, yellows too. It makes me feel connected to her—to be here standing where she stood when she was carrying me while I'm carrying a child now, too. I smile and run the tips of my fingers along Dillon's hand.

As the dimming evening sun shines in my moss green eyes, and the wind blows on the strands of the tall wispy grass, it awakens another memory in my brain. A happy memory of a girl and a boy who used to play hide and seek in that grass, who will soon chase their child through that grass, and who will stay here and protect the heritage and the land that was given to them by the grace of God.

As I stand here, I know. There's no place I'd rather be, and there's no one else I'd rather share this with. This is a return to a time when life has grace and dignity, when life has meaning. And we are really free.

The End.

Preview:
Phoenix Rising: The Stage

This story is not a part of this Reclaiming Life Series. It's still angsty, though, but depicts a relationship between a hot alpha rock star and a 19-year old girl striving for stardom.

When Mia Phoenix ends up on Kolton Royce's team competing on the nation-wide show, The Stage, she's not sure if it's her he's protecting, her voice he's striving to control, or if it's his past that's keeping them apart.

Chapter One

Call Back

"Your name?" asks the woman from behind the Call Back check-in table for the new singing competition, The Stage.

"Phoenix. Mia Phoenix," I answer with my heart pounding against my chest wall.

"ID, please," she says, quickly, so I rummage through my bag. Nothing's in order since they made me dump everything out during their security check. I hand her my driver's license.

"Good name," she notes idly as she glances at the card. "We can work with that. You're nineteen?"

"Yes."

"So tell me, what's your story?" she asks impatiently, her foot tapping rapidly under the table.

"Story?" I ask, genuinely confused.

"Yeah, you know, like what have you had to overcome in your life? What kind of hardships are you dealing with? What drives you as an artist? We're looking for contestants who have a story—for the ratings."

"Tell 'em, Mia," my eager and ever-frustrating best friend Kaya pipes in. I shake my head no as she pulls on my sleeve.

"I just want to sing," I tell Kaya. "I'm not going to capitalize on what happened just for a chance on this show."

"Capitalize on what, Ms. Phoenix? Because we already know you can sing. This is the call back, and you wouldn't be standing here if you sucked. If you want a chance on the show, you should probably share with us what sets you apart from the others."

I glare at Kaya. This is all her fault, convincing me to come after the producer contacted me on YouTube, forcing me to take the bus all the way to The Conference Center in San Francisco, waiting here two hours past my call back time. All of this.

But the truth is, I know, deep down, I want this. There's no better way to boost my non-existent career than to get on one of these nation-wide competition shows. And, according to the posters all over the flippin' place, there's some big names signed on as coaches: Kolton Royce, resident rock god, Danny McKoy, country artist extraordinaire, Pulse, the R and B soul man, and Selma Ramirez, the sexy Latina with the voice and booty to die for.

Usually these shows are judged by seasoned, older stars. What's kind of cool about this competition is the artists aren't judges. They're the coaches of their own team of competitors. Plus the artists are on top of the billboard charts and iTunes now, not ten years ago. It seems like a fresh take on the whole singing competition thing, too, because they promise there are no silly contestants in chicken suits, and the way to get on a team is through a silhouette audition.

The auditions take place with the contestant on stage in the dark until two of the four coaches vote yes. Then the lights turn on and everyone can see what the singer looks like. Not that I look bad, but it forces them to just hear me before making up their minds. It's kind of liberating—and unique.

It might be my chance. And I don't have only myself to think about. There are two of us. Me and Riley. She needs more than I can give her as a struggling college student and part time singer, with a dwindling bank account from the insurance money that's not going to last long.

"There was a fire," I finally say. "Last year. My parents. They both died. I'm raising my nine-year old sister, Riley. Alone."

"Were you in the fire, too?" She asks, and for a second, I smell it, the sharp scent of smoke in my nostrils, like burned wood, furniture, lives turning to ashes. I see the window where my parent's bedroom was—flames reaching out like arms in the night. I can feel Riley's soot covered hand in mine as I pull her down into the grass in the front yard. I can feel the burns on my feet like they're raw and new—stinging from contact with the night-time dew clinging to the leaves of grass.

I nod my head yes.

"Holy shit!" she says. "Your last name is Phoenix. It's like the Phoenix rising from the ashes. Like, literally." And, just like that, I just sold my soul to the devil. One little piece, but that's how it works. I close my eyes and make a promise to myself. After this, you will not use your pain over their deaths to promote yourself—ever again.

But, I realize, in life we all use each other. They'll use me for ratings. I'll use them to get myself out of this mess of a life I've inherited. Humans use humans. It's just the way it is. I can see it now—the slippery slope of inevitability. They'll ask me to share pictures of my parents, of my sister. They'll try to make me cry before singing some tear inducing song and their ratings will go through the roof.

And I'll get votes. I'll get my voice on iTunes. I'll find a certain type of safety: financial security.

This is for Riley. I don't have the luxury of holding on to my dignity, or my values, when I'm running out of money. And, why waste this opportunity? They wrote to me, after all.

"Here's your artist pass," she says, handing me a badge. "Now, follow the green arrows down that hallway. You're going to sing again, this time on camera, and in front of a panel. She has to stay behind," she says, nodding to Kaya. I reach for her and she hugs me.

"You've got this, Mia," she whispers. "I'm sorry I made you tell. I'll take you to the Stinking Rose after this."

"No one'll be able to stand us on the bus ride home," I tell her softly, feeling a little teary-eyed.

"Who cares? It's worth the stinky garlic breath," she says, shrugging. I nod and push back my fears, turn, and walk down the hallway that leads to an open door. It's simple inside. A camera is pointed toward a folding director's chair that glows from strategically placed lights in front of a dark blue backdrop. The previous contestant is just finishing up her interview. She's crying. Shit!

"Your artist pass," says a young woman wearing jeans, a blue shirt, and a hat that says, 'The Stage'. She's listening to her headset and reading over my info. There's a table next to the camera with producers tucked behind laptops.

"Mia Phoenix," she says. "Have a seat."

We all have to make sacrifices, I think as a lady comes up to me with a make-up cart and begins applying foundation, and then some blush, mascara, and some light gloss.

"The camera will wash you out," she explains before pulling her cart back off to the sidelines.

I feel the camera lens boring into me. It feels hot in here. I feel my eye twitch. The lights burn into my skin. The laptop people don't talk to me, which makes me even more nervous. I start picking at my nail polish.

This is for Riley—for our future, I remind myself, and swallow down my nerves, force them to go away. Just like I've always done on stage. I purposefully bring out the Mia Phoenix who can't be fazed.

A lady with frizzy hair talks to me from behind the laptop. "Hi, Mia," she says. "How would you describe your style?"

"Kind of Lorde meets Adele," I say, and smile at her, knowing I'm really smiling at some executive who'll be watching this video. As long as I'm good on camera.

I give her my meek, shy smile, and run my fingers through my long black hair.

"Great. We'd like you to sing the song that best showcases your voice so we can share this with our executive producers."

That's fine. It's what I do best. As I sing all the way to the hook for Adele's Rolling in the Deep, she raises her hand.

"Do you have anything else?"

Shit. "Yeah," so I move right into Anna Kendrick's When I'm Gone. Singing actually calms me down; although, I know she's going to ask me about my parents, so I'm on edge. My palms are sweaty.

"That's enough," she says as I sing the last line. "So, Mia, can you tell us a little about your parents and the fire? You're raising your little sister alone. How much would it mean for you to win the first season of The Stage?"

Relief. I'm glad she's not asking for a play-by-play. So I decide to give it to them. I look at the camera and say with all sincerity:

"It was my parents' wish to see me sing on a real stage. When I'm up there, it'll be in honor of them. What I do, the singing, is for my sister Riley. I'd like to be able to give her the life my parents always wanted for her. She deserves some happiness after all that's happened to her—to us."

But what I hadn't planned on was how saying the words out loud, however true they were, would pinch my heart. Just then, my throat feels like it's closing up, and a real tear wells in my eye before falling down my cheek, followed by another on the other side.

I tilt my trembling chin down, but a sick little part of me knows: That was the money shot. And, with that, I hate myself a little more than I already did when I walked in here. In this moment, getting on that stage seems like the biggest thing that could ever happen to me. It can change our lives. I'll do whatever it takes. I won't give up. Not yet.

"Thank you, Mia," says the frizzy-hair lady. "Once the final decision has been made, you'll get a call about coming to the silhouette auditions."

"So it's not a no?"

"Definitely not. We just need to run you by the executive producers."

"Thank you," I say, feeling giddy, but also like I just sacrificed my first born. Kaya hugs me when I walk back out to the congregating tryouts, and their supporting friends and family, yet to find out their fate. "Well?"

"It's not a no," I say, smiling half-heartily.

"Are you okay?" she asks.

"I cried," I say. "Not on purpose."

"Of course, not on purpose," she says. "No one'll hear your story and think you're using it to get ahead."

"But aren't I?"

"No. Stop it. Now, let's go eat too much garlic. You deserve it."

We take the red trolley—because I've always wanted to, and walk up to the Stinking Rose, a restaurant Kaya's been to before. San Francisco is cool, no matter what time of year. Summer, too, like now. Ocean mist infuses the air making it crisp, cool.

They seat us in the first booth opposite the door. There's a mirror wall beside us that I keep catching Kaya looking at herself in. I dip the bread in, basically, a raw garlic dip and my mouth bursts with appreciation. It's so bad it's good. She and I decided to share a pasta dish—their food is pricey. And, when we leave, the crisp ocean breeze air hits my hot garlic mouth and makes it feel like I'm sucking on ice. Man that garlic is strong.

Those poor people on the bus with us on the way home didn't know what hit 'em. But all I can think about on our long drive back to Sacramento is, will they call me? Did I do enough to make it on the show?

It won't be long before I find out the news.

Available soon:

Phoenix Rising:The Stage

The Reclaiming Life Series:

Sadie Survived (Book Two, Dillon's story)—no release date

Almost Whole (Book Three, Renae's story)—no release date

ABOUT SHELBY REBECCA

 Originally from Wasilla, Alaska, I now live in Northern California in my first real house with my husband, John, daughter, Elise, our two mutts, and our fish, Jade. Sadie's Mountain is my first romance novel. I'd planned to write a follow-up novel to Sadie and Dillon's story called *Sadie Survived*. However, the emotional impact of this story forces me to take a break from this series. I've put *Sadie Survived* aside to write a few other stories, like *Phoenix Rising: The Stage*.

If you really want more Sadie and Dillon, I'd need to hear from you:

www.shelbyrebecca.com

Shelby Rebecca's Facebook Page
https://www.facebook.com/shelbyrrebecca

Sadie's Mountain Facebook Page
https://www.facebook.com/SadiesMountain

Twitter Page
https://twitter.com/shelbyrrebecca

Goodreads Page
http://www.goodreads.com/author/show/7161929.Shelby_Rebecca

If you enjoyed this book, don't forget to add your review to Amazon, Goodreads, or Barnes and Noble. When you do, be sure to email me at shelbyrebecca_author@yahoo.com and I'll send you a personal email to thank you.

Thank you for helping to support Indie authors by letting others know what you think. To help spread the word, you can loan this book and tell your friends! Take care and keep in touch.

ACKNOWLEDGMENTS

To Elise Adrianna. Thank you for putting up with Momma having her face in the computer screen too much. I'm sorry I've been so busy typing away this past year, but you always know how to make me laugh (no feet tickles, 'kay) and keep me humble. I love you more than a fish loves water. You are the reason I am the person I am today. You make me want to be better, to do more with my life—to make you proud. You teach me that life is about the journey, not the destination. You always help me take time to smell the flowers, listen to a story, giggle, sing songs, and have a picnic or drink some tea on the back patio. You're the fastest eight-year-old reader I know, the most creative writer, the cutest piano player, and the best little actor in the school play. Momma loves you, baby goose.

To my husband, John. Thank you for having my back, for loving me even when I'm grumpy and thinking about characters instead of listening to you. I know I don't say enough about all that you do for us. But I notice it and I'm thankful for everything. You're my rock. I'm glad I said, "Don't you even wanna kiss me?" all those years ago. I love you, Pook.

To my momma, Sherrie Brown. You've always supported me no matter what, but I share this book with you because you have been with me throughout the whole process. I'm sure many of the Biblical allusions come from the values you've instilled in me. I'll never forget when you came last Christmas and I tried out Chapter Twenty-Six on you. I watched you reading from the living room. Your eyes grew wide and you said "That was racy!" But then you were hitting the arrow button trying to read more, only I hadn't written any more yet. "I can't wait to read the rest, little girl," you said. Thank you, Momma. I know I can always talk to you about anything, and that keeps me sane.

Kimball Brown, thank you so much for your help in finding just the right scriptures for Sadie's momma's funeral. I'm glad that you've found a church, even though it's too far away.

To my brothers, Wayne Norton, Chris Davis, and Joe Davis, I love you guys, even though you've picked on me my whole life (and still do) you guys are still cool and always, always have my back. You are my home base, and always keep me humble. I love you guys. Pam, Nathan, and Coty Norton, Shaun and Tyler Davis, Tina Laboa, Alix Davis and Mae Mae, Craig and Kendall French, I can't ask for better a family. My only regret is that my dad and Mitch aren't here to see my dream come to fruition. Thanks for reminding me they'd be proud.

To my in-laws, Luisa Rodriguez, Joe Rodriguez, Leah Rodriguez, Genielle Rodriguez, and Ashley Reeves who read my book not just because they are related to me and they love me, I think they actually liked it! I'm proud to be in this family and thank all of the Rodriguez' from Texas, California, Alabama, and Arizona for your unconditional love and support; no matter where we've been, no matter how far away we go, we always love each other.

To my Aunt Sue Sue, aka Susan Jones. I want to thank you for reading faithfully every week, even reading re-writes and always being honest with me. I think writing this book brought us together in a new way. I know we have some similar experiences. I thank you for sharing those with me. I'll never forget our phone conversations during the six-months I was writing. Your thoughts and encouragement helped me finish this book. I love you.

To my cousins Melissa Banian, Calvin, Cori, and Wade Fox, thank you so much for supporting me, liking my statuses, asking about the progress toward publication. I feel a family reunion in our future. What do ya say to that?

To Aunt Truth Ashby Moulton, I think I got the writing bug from you—just like the chicken knick-knack collecting. Thank you for reading and for your encouragement. The times I've spent with you at your house will never leave me. There's no one in the world just like you. You're so unique Facebook doesn't even believe you're real. I love you more than words can say.

Donna McDonald and Carol McDonald, you two were the first women I shared my idea for the book with. You were there urging me on even before one sentence was written. Thank you for listening and for helping me with plot ideas. P.S. I won't bring so many baked potatoes to our next barbeque ;-)

Lindsay Lopez, thank you for all of your help on West Virginia. You spent endless amounts of time listening to me talk about Dillon and Sadie, helping me research facts to get just the right details. I value your opinions more than you know. Thank you so much. P.S. There's no one else I'd like to take a Los Banos detour with on the way to Disneyland—but we made it, eventually. *Wink*

Heather McCormick, like we always say, we've lived the same life, just in different bodies. Thank you for reading even when you had morning sickness. Your comments made me feel like I might have something here. Kiss little Ariana for me!

John Telles, I wanted to say thank you for reading as much as you did even though this is definitely not your preferred genre. There were many times when you came forward with much needed advice and I really do appreciate it.

Ladies, Janell Troy, Brenda Spears, Robin Wibbels, Nakia Davis, and Melissa PavlikAtencio, I've known you girlies for over half my life. You are some of the best friends a girl can ask for. The fact that you've not only kept in touch with me for all these years, but you read my book, too. I'm so lucky to have you all in my life. Now I owe you one.

To my bestie, Lakisha DeVone Cortinas, we've grown up together. We really have. Your spunk and creativity has shaped me as a writer. I bet you don't know that, but it's true. Thank you for being a part of this time in my life so we have another set of memories to add to the rest. Like, how many other besties even have their own language? We were using the word "Vanilla" long before *Fifty Shades of Grey* (And it has a whole different meaning to us). I'm so glad I got to hug you for almost a whole half an hour this summer. You are my Dale…right? Or are you Chip??? Love you, girl.

Some of my newer friends have been so supportive as well, Kat Brooks, and Amy Sue Fields, I mean. What can I say? The support you two have given is priceless. Kat, you have been so honest with me. I think the ending would be a lot different had you not been willing to tell me the truth. I am so grateful for that. And Amy, geez. I think you hold the record for reading it the fastest of all. Two hours. Yes, you read that right. She read the whole book, all 105,000 words, in two hours. Thank you both so much.

All the way out from Manassas, Virginia, Ray Madonna, you have been so supportive I just might have to drive out there next summer and visit you and the family. You've always been such a great friend and a heck of a drummer. Thanks, man!

I also want to thank my writer friends who have been so supportive and have helped me, by being beta readers, and giving me content advice, self-publishing advice, advice on copyrights and trademarks, book covers, editors, tattoo script, present tense versus past tense, you name it. You all are so selfless and have made this book so much better. Karen Mueller Bryson, Lea-Ellen Borg, Erin Walen, Dani Greer, S.E. Duncan, Sue Jerrems, Mia Ellames, and Tammara Webber, I owe you so much and I hope that I can help you all in the future, in some small way.

I must thank Fiction Press. There are some awesome beta readers over there that followed me, and tuned in every week. You gals give me hope that my book will reach others and make its mark in the world. So many of you contacted me and shared your stories. That's something I hadn't expected but truly appreciate.

There have been artists that have been so inspirational to me during this process. Michal Madison, your art moves me in a way that is life-changing. Thank you for the work you do to raise awareness about sexual abuse. If I had more money in the budget, your art would be on my cover, but you know that. Thank you for helping me believe my book will be healing for other survivors.

Lisa Lambert of Lj Photography, I have three of your photographs of landmarks from scenes in *Sadie's Mountain* hanging in my hallway. And even though I've never been to your neck of the woods, I feel like I go there a little bit every day. You have a way of capturing and sharing West Virginia that I've never seen in any other person's work. Thank you.

If you've read *Sadie's Mountain*, you know just how important songs from Adele were to the plot. I listened to the Adele station on Pandora while I wrote many times, and her words always seemed just right because they come from a real place. Your voice is my panacea—my cure all. Thank you.

Thank you to David Jacome from Peers Music for helping me secure the rights to use lyrics from "You Are My Flower" by M.P. Carter. I love that song and am glad I didn't have to part from it. It's so symbolic to this story and to what Sadie means to me. I hope I get to deal with you again because that means I've sold 10,000 copies.

I want to thank my editor Stephanie Lott. Without you there would be a lot more rosebuds and knotted wood in *Sadie's Mountain*. You taught me that there can be too much of a good thing. You bring out the best in my writing. Because of you I feel good putting my work out for the world to read.

My book cover designer, Kari Ayasha at Cover to Cover Designs is so amazing. She was able to help me re-design a more romantic cover and brought Sadie and Dillon's love into the light. Thank you.

I want to thank Ansted and Fayetteville County in West Virginia. So many supportive people out there have liked the Facebook page and supported me in my journey toward publication. I really want to make it out your way soon to see the beauty of your part of the country for myself.

Last, but not least, I want to thank the people who are out there raising awareness about mountaintop coal mining, especially the folks over at ilovemountains.org, Elizabeth Stephens, Bob Kincaid, and also Ashley Judd. I don't know Ashley Judd personally, but it was her dedication to the cause for ending MTR that led me to choose Ansted, West Virginia, and Gauley Mountain as the setting for Sadie's Mountain. There are so many men and women out there fighting the good fight every day, making changes, and stopping these real mountains from being raped and emptied when they don't have to be. In real life Gauley Mountain wasn't saved, but there are others out there that can be.

I thank all of you for your continued dedication, and I hope that my novel is a help in some small way to raise awareness and make changes to the laws that allow the complete devastation of some of the oldest mountains in the history of the world.

If you've gotten this far, it means you've read my book. So thank you for supporting me and please keep in touch.